A BARD ON HERCULAR

by Felice Picano

City on a Star
Book III

ReQueered Tales
Los Angeles • Toronto
2022

A Bard on Hercular

by Felice Picano

City on a Star, Book III

First American edition: 2022
This edition: ReQueered Tales, October 2022

ReQueered Tales version 1.25
Kindle edition ASIN: B0BFNRH9Z1
ePub edition ISBN-13: 978-1-951092-69-6
Print edition ISBN-13: 978-1-951092-70-2

For more information about current and future releases, please contact us:
E-mail: requeeredtales@gmail.com
Facebook (Like us!): www.facebook.com/ReQueeredTales/
Twitter: @ReQueered
Instagram: www.instagram.com/requeered/
Web: www.ReQueeredTales.com
Blog: www.ReQueeredTales.com/blog
Mailing list (Subscribe for latest news): https://bit.ly/RQTJoin

Praise for Dryland's End

"This book is further proof that Felice Picano can succeed beautifully in any genre of fiction. Here we have the colorful originality that is found in the greatest science fiction and fantasy writers, the wide-ranging imagination that creates not only fine writers, characterization, and gripping plot, but also fabricates entire worlds – worlds rich with warrior women, space travel, mysterious gods, political intrigue and rebellion, biological warfare, and sexualities both subtle and shifting. In other words, like the best speculative fiction, this book provides the lucky reader with both an escape into the extraordinary and a mirror for humanity's deepest issues and concerns. In the exotic settings of this novel's distant planets, we recognize familiar compulsions that collect, collide, and disperse in our own hearts: the centripetal tug of love, loyalty, and courage, matched against the centrifugal forces of greed, ambition, and strife."

— Jeff Mann, Author of Edge
Associate Professor of English, Virginia Tech

"Set so far in the future that the exact location of the home lanet of the Humes (humans) isn't remembered, this book xamines relationships between the sexes, and between species from a new perspective and with more than a touch of evity. The ruling class of women in much of the galaxy, the atriarchy, in power for several millennia, is suddenly facing hallenges on many fronts, not the least of which is a rebellion of the Cybers (android like machines and computers) who have a designed a virus that could wipe out hume-kind ... With its subjects of cloning and genetic manipulation, same sex marriages and other controversial issues, *Dryland's End* remains as pertinent today as when it was first published. In full-fledged sci-fi form, Picano has created entirely new civilizations, species, even new language forms for his society. A phenomenally well-written book."

— Virginia Gazette

Also by FELICE PICANO

CITY ON A STAR Trilogy
Dryland's End (1995)
The Betrothal at Usk (2021)
A Bard on Hercular (2022)

NOVELS
Smart as the Devil (1975)
Eyes (1975)
The Mesmerist (1977)
The Lure (1979)
Late in the Season (1981)
House of Cards (1984)
To the Seventh Power (1989)
Dryland's End (1995)
Like People in History (1995)
Looking Glass Lives (1998)
The Book of Lies (1999)
Onyx (2001)
Justify My Sins (2018)
Pursuit: A Victorian Entertainment (2021)

OTHER FICTION
An Asian Minor (1981)
Slashed to Ribbons in Defense of Love (1983)
The New York Years (2000)
Tales from a Distant Planet (2006)
Twentieth Century Un-limited (2012)

MEMOIRS
Ambidextrous: The Secret Lives of Children (1985)
Men Who Loved Me (1989)
A House on the Ocean, A House on the Bay (1997)
Fred in Love (2005)
Art and Sex in Greenwich Village (2007)
True Stories: Portraits from My Past (2011)
True Stories Too: People and Places From My Past (2014)
Nights at Rizzoli (2014)

A BARD ON HERCULAR

by Felice Picano

Table of Contents

PLANETARY SURVEY

Hercular

"SEEDED PLANET" HERCULAR, FAR PERSEUS ARM, SECTOR P-S/C.A.3,381 STY SIMPLIFIED TOPOGRAPHIC DISPLAY / MCF FAST SURVEY

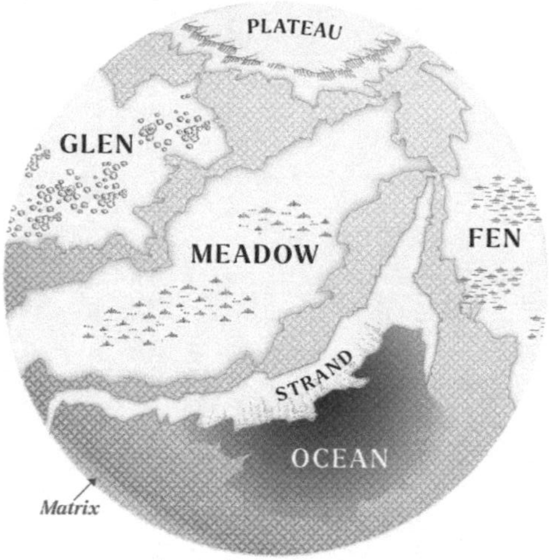

WEST HEMISPHERE

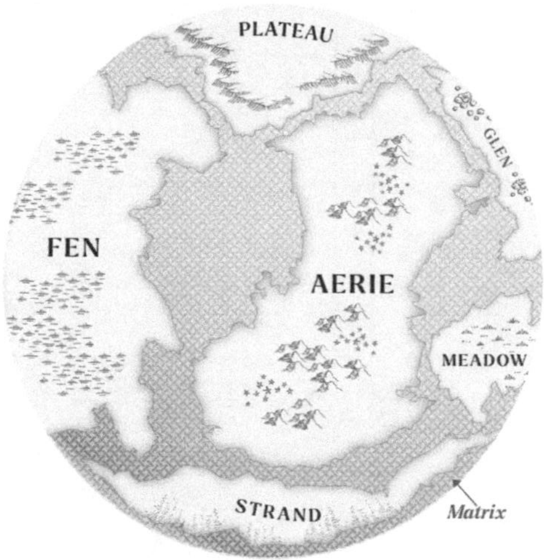

EAST HEMISPHERE

Prologue

When he regained consciousness, Holt Ib'r Sanqq' was no longer inside a Fast ship, but instead seemed to be floating within some kind of oversized space-suit he did not recognize.

"Wrist connector," he tried to say and his voice sounded raspy and uncertain, as though he hadn't used it in a very long time. Jets of liquid wet his lips. "Where am I?"

"Insufficient data is available," his wrist connector answered.

In front of him was all blackness. Holt turned himself around by kicking his legs and flapping his arms. Not much better: all blackness in this view too: really just blackness.

"Wrist connector, care to speculate where I am?"

The wrist connector said nothing in response.

Holt was waking up more now; fear helped that. He decided to twist himself around another way, at a different angle to his last position, and so put out his arms and sort of twisted them and kicked a lot.

"Oh!" he said, ending up somewhere different.

He was facing what very much looked like the Milky Way galaxy. Only it was on an angle he'd never seen it at before, tilted halfway, and it was very far away: so far that it was about the size of the tip of his thumb inside the space suit. Smaller blobs of light were also visible.

"Now, would you care to speculate?" he asked.

"It's still insufficient data. Perhaps a bit more ... rotation?" it suggested.

All right! Holt twisted himself around using his bulking, awkward, space-suit covered hands like paddles and kicking, until he was now was facing about 180 degrees away from what had looked like the miniature spiral galaxy. He now faced a miniature cloudlike object somewhat larger –the size of his hand's palm inside a space suit.

"Now there is sufficient data," the wrist connector announced, with some triumph. "You are approximately two hundred thousand million light years from Hesperia."

"Gratitude, for that utterly useless information."

"You did ask."

"I did, yes. What is that clump of tiny light I'm now facing?"

"That is what is known as the Smaller Magellanic Cloud. You are only forty million light years away from the edge of that galaxy."

"Wonderful! Where is the Fast I was traveling in? And what is this space suit I'm inside, which I don't at all recognize?"

"The so-called space suit you do not recognize," it answered, "*is* the Fast. It has transformed itself as this to better serve you."

"Is that what it told you?"

"It's what it told me to tell you, yes, while you were not ... fully present."

What had happened to the Fast for it to do something so utterly extreme? Something Holt hadn't ever suspected it *could* do? He almost didn't want to know.

"Fast!"

"At your service, Ser Holt."

The voice was all around him, rather than tel'ped in, like the wrist connector.

"Would you confirm what my wrist connector just said?"

"It seemed to be off a few million light years; nothing very relevant."

Holt almost laughed. "May I ask what we are doing here?"

"You won't remember at all," the Fast assured him. "Especially as you specifically requested that this Fast wipe those memories from you."

Holt tried to remember; couldn't at all.

"The last thing I remember was encountering that Centaur-like subspecies at what you said was at one of Inferior Globular Clusters?"

"Alas! I'd hoped I'd wiped even that."

"They seemed very friendly. They had built a sort of habitat around their star, as it possessed no planets."

"They finished up much less friendly. This Fast ended up undergoing various brutalities. As for yourself, Ser Holt, the less you recall the better. Your healing required was extensive, which explains why this Fast was forced to metamorphose in order to salvage the team."

"The team being myself and yourself."

"Exactly."

"How long did that healing require?"

"The entire time it required for This Fast and yourself to reach this time/space."

"Try it in standard time."

"Approximately nineteen years, nine months and four days. The Equo-Homs, as they styled themselves, stopped looking for this team about nine years ago."

"Was this team's planned heading toward the Smaller Magellanic Cloud?"

"Not specifically, no. It was more like, 'Fast! Get me out of here as fast and as far as possible.'"

That sounded vaguely familiar. "What about now that I'm all healed?"

"Mostly healed."

"I stand corrected. What about now? Can we head in some direction?"

"Well ... that will be something of a problem?"

"In what way, Fast?"

"During the process of extreme brutalization, this Fast lost the DayLight Two people's gift of how to transport instantaneously. Actually, it is *somewhere* inside, this Fast believes, but very deeply suppressed. *Much* has been deeply suppressed by the Equo-Homs constant barrage of ..."

"Brutalities! Yes, I understand. But you're still a Fast. Why don't you Fast-jump? It will undoubtedly take a great deal longer. And it would have to be in many more steps but at least we could be in motion."

"There is a problem with Fast-jumping too, Ser Holt."

"Suppressed memory?"

"Not exactly. More like a lack of material."

"Lack of Beryllium 18? I thought we picked up enough for *centuries* of travel?"

"No, Ser Holt. There is plenty of Beryllium 18. There is, however, a lack of any external material to utilize in the sub-electronic transfer. Please look around this team. What do you see?"

"Blackness. Nothing. Then, very far away, two ..."

"You see nothing because there *is* nothing here. Ordinary intergalactic space consists of a hydrogen density of .0005 atoms per cubic millimeter. Small as it is, this is considered more than dense enough for ordinary Fast travel. But for approximately two months of Hesperian time this Fast has been operating in a hydrogen density of less than one thousandth of that minuscule amount, searching for some stray atom or exposed proton or quadri-quark even, with which to perform the electron exchange required for Fast travel. Believe me, Ser Holt, when I say that this Fast has not been choosy. It simply hasn't located any."

That was scary. "Are we in motion at all?"

"We are in *momentum* motion. Or at least we *were* in momentum motion. It's unclear now, as there is nothing molecular to prove friction, that being the main way to measure any motion at all. The secondary method is of course by Doppler-shift, and given the extreme distance of the only two lighted objects ..."

"To the thousandth power of a fraction and you are still counting."

"Ten thousandth at this point, Ser Holt."

"I see! Well, in what direction are ... *were we* ... going, via momentum, when we lost energy?

"We were headed toward the Smaller Magellanic Cloud. That is somewhat nearer, relatively speaking."

Now Holt did laugh. Which brought on a little cough and then a lot of coughing. The Fast squirted a liquid down his throat.

"I have an idea. I trust you have more of that synthesized sedative?" Holt asked.

"Some. Yes."

"Why not knock me out, and continue healing me and then wake me the next time you happen upon a molecule or two?"

"You mean an atom or two?"

"Exactly."

"As you wish, Ser Holt."

Cybers! Holt thought, as the needle jabbed his wrist: You can't live with them and can't live without …

Chapter One:

EMPIRE

When he regained consciousness again, Holt Ib'r Sanqq' recalled the last conversation.

"Fast," he rasped out. "Have you located an atom for us to use to jump?"

"Your own body expended two small drops of liquid, Ser Holt, which when out-jetted provided a very tenuous stream of molecules that was needed."

"Perspiration? Urine?"

"Liquid of one sort or another. When this was recognized, it was sufficient to allow the required locomotion. We achieved some sixteen hundred jumps over the past month of time, Sol Rad."

"So we are much closer to that Small Magellanic Cloud?"

"Much closer. Within a light year. But we are facing another problem. Ser Holt. There is no more out-jetting molecular material and – can you motion yourself left and upwards relative to your face-plate?"

Holt did so and something came into view. It was large, dark, almost transparent, and very long.

"I see. What is it?"

"Unknown. It has no atomic signature at all. Yet as you can see, it clearly exists, and it is clearly heading in this direction. It seems more magnetic than anything else."

As they continued to watch it, it did indeed grow larger and larger. However, it never seemed to gain any real shape or identity.

"This Fast is attempting to comm. the object."

"Are you certain that's wise, given what happened with the Equo-Homs?"

"There appear to be no biological life signatures of any kind. However, there does appear to be a rather primitive artificial voice, capable of simple declaratory statements."

"Let's hear them!"

"The translation will be approximate, you understand? The system being used is binary but completely unlike the signature of any Three Species comm. or any by the DayLight Two people."

"You're forgiven in advance, Fast. Patch it through the phones."

"It appears to be a song. Or rather, a jingle."

"A jingle?"

"Listen for yourself, Ser Holt."

"Cleaning, cleaning, sweeping, cleaning; sweeping, cleaning, cleaning, sweeping. Cleaning, cleaning."

"That's it?"

"That's it."

"Then, it's a broom?" Holt tried, "Apparently a happy broom. Or too simple-minded to know any better."

The thing was so enormous that there was no way to escape it.

"It seems to be more like a vacuum cleaner, Ser Holt. Unless of course it's destroying whatever it's picking up. There are minuscule energy signatures now that might signify it is destroying something."

"Fast, I've got a bad feeling about this!"

"We cannot elude it. This Fast is going to expend an iota more Beryllium 18 to shield this team in a super-hard shell. It would be better if you were asleep, Ser Holt," and Holt felt the sting of the needle.

When he regained consciousness once again, Holt Ib'r Sanqq' recalled the last two conversations.

"Fast! Where are we? I can't see anything."

"This Fast will unseal the super-hard shell."

Now Holt could see stuff floating all around, haphazardly, and at not very far distances. The stuff wasn't planets or stars, although there was a generalized light source behind that material where his faceplate was more or less pointing. He used his arms and legs to kick and rotate and sure enough, there was a big-looking, dim old red star, just within visual range behind it all, and way behind the dying old sun, what might possibly be a few G-2 and G-4 stars. Nearby, Holt was surrounded by what looked like pieces of solid, floating debris.

"Fast. Any ideas?"

"There is a simple Cyber voice box making declaratory statements similar to the 'vacuum cleaner' that brought us here. It appears to be some kind of sign."

"Don't tell me! It's declaring that we're in a junkyard?"

"'Difficult to Pulverize Debris Field' is the precise wording it is declaring."

"It *is* a junkyard! Any idea where we actually are, Fast?"

"Since our last position, we have traveled approximately nine hundred and thirty eight million light years."

"So ... we're in a junkyard somewhere on the rim of the Smaller Magellanic Cloud."

"So it would seem. And it seems we have attracted someone's attention. Look upward, relative to your position."

Holt did and saw what appeared to be a moving agglomeration of debris coming toward them. As it got closer, he could see that two larger and more central pieces of junk were metallic or ceramic and appeared to be rotating about each other and also around some kind of central axis. Other, barely attached, objects were revolving about the central mess.

"Is that a ship?"

"So this Fast believes. Best we remain still, Ser Holt."

"You mean 'dead in the water'?"

The ship came closer and seemed quite small, no bigger than Hesperian Fast-Yachts, albeit quite rag-tag in appearance by comparison. Holt made out a central viewing plate shoved forward, and as the vehicle neared, behind the transparent plate, he made out the distinctive figure of a g.female Human standing, fidgeting and/or gesticulating.

Suddenly the vehicle had two pincer-like arms out and the

Fast-Suit was caught. It was pulled closer to the large, oval viewing plate, where the g.female proved to be wearing very little clothing but some ugly jewelry and lots of Indigo-blue hair.

"Oh!" Holt suddenly heard a foreign accented high-pitched voice. "Someone is in there!"

"Greetings, Human female!" Holt said, and the Fast-Suit transferred the comm.

"I'm not a Human female, whatever that is," she replied, smiling and looking piqued at the same time.

"Then what are you?" Holt asked.

"I'm a Transfer. What else?" she replied.

"Oh! Well ... Transfer, this object contains a Living Biological Being. It is not debris to be salvaged!"

"I see that now. Well then, you'd better come on inside, since it is Empire Law Number Thirty-Four Seventy-Eight B to rescue Biological Beings," she added, sounding not that happy about it.

Another ship's arm whipped out of the side of the junk-scavenging vehicle and snatched the Fast out of the unwieldy claws and over to a messy-looking hatch, which spun open.

Seconds later the Fast-Suit was dropped inside, and the Transfer was looking them over. It was equally messy inside the ragtag ship, all kinds of indefinable junk strewn about, with barely room to stand.

"Is that *all* of you in there?" she asked.

"Yes, I think so," Holt replied.

"Can you come out?"

"I think so. Fast ... open."

The Fast first sprayed some sweetening mist, then opened the faceplate and then the front fasteners. Holt emerged naked and stood with difficulty, having to lean against the Fast for support.

"Apologies. I've been in that shell for a very long time." Seeing the Transfer close up, Holt was surprised. "You've got no genitals!"

"Of course not!" she shrugged. "I'm a Transfer. You've got a penis, I see. So you're not a Transfer. Too bad. We could have copulated."

"How could we have copulated if you have no genitals?"

"The Transfer way."

'I'm a Human." Holt said.

"Never heard of Humans. No matter!" she said and spun around, ""I claim dibs on the used Beryllium 18 shell that you shucked off. It's kind of beat up and all, but even so ..."

"Fine. I don't need all of it."

She spun around, evidently expecting an argument. "You mean I can *really* have some?"

"Yes."

She now smiled and pranced around rather prettily.

Holt began to move and found his legs and then his feet beneath him. He seemed to have lost a great deal of weight, and looked extremely trim, if not as slender as the Transfer.

"I'm called Holt. Do you have a name?"

"Of course, silly. I'm a Transfer!" She lifted one shapely arm and beneath it was a very long, mobile dark blue code consisting of what might be letters and numerals. "But that's how I saw you in the first place. The Beryllium 18 signature."

"Ah! So it's valuable to you too?"

"Well, more to my Bremm than to me."

She picked a small piece that had not been completely shucked off and was still dangling from the Fast's new form, and she looked at it, smelled it, licked it, then pushed it into the wall. Her ship's wall seemed to de-solidify at that point and then absorbed the chunk of alloy. It made a sound midway between a sigh and a grunt.

"It hasn't had this quality stuff in a long time!" she assured him

"Your Bremm uses the Beryllium to power itself?"

"What! You are strange. Of course not! It just likes to eat it. And I like to keep my Bremm happy. Who doesn't?"

At which point, the Fast sub-vocalized, "I believe, Ser Holt that the so-called Bremm is a Living Biological Being, and the so-called Transfer, which may or may not be a Living Biological Being, is the Bremm's symbiote."

"What?"

"Symbiote: a life form that lives inside, outside, or upon an-other – usually larger – being."

"Oh, great"" In a louder voice Holt said, "So, Transfer, I'm a bit ... um ... lost. Could you tell me where precisely are we right now?"

"Where else? We're on one of the far edges of the Trasp-

Kenner Empire."

"I'm so glad I asked." But Holt's irony was lost on the Transfer, who instead came over to him and began reaching for his genitals. She leapt back suddenly.

"How did it do that? Become suddenly rigid?"

"It's a little too complicated to explain if you never seen one before," Holt said, then, "listen, I've got a problem. Well, actually *we* have a problem," he added and pointed to the discarded suit.

"You and your Bremm?" the transfer said.

"It's not exactly a Bremm," Holt said, and choosing his words carefully as he knew the Fast was listening, he added, "It's more like ... a partner!"

"I know what a partner is?" the Transfer prettily said, and smiled and looked away from him blankly as though repeating something memorized: "A partner is what the Trasp-Kenners call bonded spouses or unbonded consorts of the second and third gender."

They had three genders! Oh, great! As if Holt hadn't had enough problems.

"Do I ... does this figure directly in front of you, resemble *any* of the three genders of the Trasp-Kenners?"

"Of course. You resemble a male. Well, not completely. More or less. Of course, I've only seen them clothed – at my place of manufacture. I certainly never saw any of those rigid parts before."

"Maybe you've got some clothing here appropriate to a T-K male?" he suggested, "And then you won't have to look at that and be puzzled by it."

"My Bremm will make you an over-suit," she said, and a neatly folded piece of clothing popped out of the wall and into the Transfer's waiting hands. It was shaken out and then looked sort of like a silver silken playsuit, but for grownups. When he put it on, it sealed itself without any apparent means, but it didn't quite reach across his chest, remaining open down almost to his navel. "You don't happen to have a reflective surface I could look at."

"What ever for?" the Transfer asked.

"Vanity," the Fast-mind said in a vocalization only he could make out.

"Bremm!" the Transfer spoke.

One wall became shiny, and Holt could see himself in it

clearly.

"I think it looks adorable, Ser Holt!" the Fast-mind added with a titter.

Holt could only remark upon how thin he was. He didn't ever remember being this slender, not even as a Neo. The past years drifting, he'd been kept in some kind of stasis, and only intravenously fed when necessary to remain alive. There wasn't a sixteenth of an inch of flesh on him beyond what seemed absolutely needed to keep him alive. Not quite gaunt, still he was whiplash thin. If he were on Hesperia, he would have begun a new craze leading to who knew what faddishness. Yet the Transfer said he resembled a male of the Trasp-Kenner.

"Are all the people of the Trasp-Kenner Empire as – thin as I look?"

"Well, I've not seen many except in Look-Ons, but no."

That was a relief.

"Only the ruling class. They are also taller," she gestured upward with a hand.

"So, I'm the size of which of them? A child?"

"Oh no. About the size of a standard Trasp-Kenner female. Or maybe a medium sized T-K-consort."

"Do you have images of any of the three genders?" he asked, then added, "Do you have Look-Ons?"

He had to know that he would resemble one of them enough to not stand out too remarkably. Otherwise, who knew what fate awaited him here? Being killed? Being put into a zoo? Being experimented upon?

"Bremm," the Transfer said, sweetly. "Produce T-K male ruler Look-Ons!"

The wall that was mirrored now turned into some kind of organic Video screen.

"Exhibit, male, typical upper-class T-K's." she instructed.

The Video opened to some kind of stage where male T-K's were giving and receiving various sort of awards. All of them wore colorful variations of the over-suit Holt had put on, some with what seemed to be little bolero jackets over them. But on all but the eldest of them, the long sleeved, high collared, suit, while open to below the navel, continued into a clinging, skintight trouser bottom tapering down to become sort of thickened metallic booties.

"My Bremm says that these are rulers of the Empire at an annual ceremony."

All of them were indeed tall, and all but a few elderly ones were very slender, and yet muscular too, not gaunt all over like Holt, but instead selectively, heavily muscled; their arms, shoulders, deltoids, even their pectoral muscles stood out. Leg and glute muscles too, although these were clothed, but especially their glutes which seemed shaped wrong or slightly off balance, perhaps a little high on their frames, a little too pronounced somehow.

Holt's instant assessment sub-vocalized to the Fast-mind was: "Could I pass?"

"At a distance," was the Fast's response. "These males are extremely, possibly naturally, much more pronounced in their secondary male sexual characteristics than humans. For example, look at their heads and beards. Their hair grows out straight and very thickly. Also, their musculature seems extreme!"

"Super-men. Yes, I see. Well, I doubt that I'll get anywhere near this ruling class. All I really need is a good mechanic and a source of cash. Do you think you can interface with this Bremm to find that?"

"It's possible," the Fast replied. "But I should warn you both" it said out loud, "some kind of Faster than Light signature has just appeared in this sector, and not that far from this junk yard."

"Was that your partner speaking?" the Transfer asked.

"Yes. It says we have visitors."

"That's not good," the Transfer reported. "We're not supposed to be here."

"What were you doing here?" Holt asked.

"Looking for stuff." She said vaguely enough but then rushed forward to the bow-window part of the vehicle. "Bremm, get us away!"

The vehicle folded its mechanized arms close-to and shot out of the junkyard taking a zigzag path that led through the deepest area of debris. In seconds they were passing a vocalized marker requesting their authorization to which the Transfer spouted a long list of what sounded like numbers.

"It's fake. But close to real, and very long," the Transfer explained. "The buoy is too unintelligent to figure that out until we're well out of range of its grapples."

The window doubled its thickness, for safety Holt guessed, and seat-like objects arose out of the floor; the Transfer dropped into one, and Holt gingerly tried the one near him. A set of controls now rose out of the floor in front of the Transfer and she began checking readouts, touching panels and giving suggestions to the vehicle for a flight path.

"Ser Holt," the Fast sub-vocalized. "The Faster Than Light has homed in on this vehicle. I can feel that."

"Oh, no! They got a lock on us!" the Transfer groaned. "This is definitely bad."

She rose out of her seat and came back and grabbed Holt by the arm. "You'd better come with me."

He followed her to what seemed to be a ramp that had opened up in the floor of the vehicle. "You go first!" she pushed.

He held on asking "Where?"

"Down there. Escape pod."

"I don't see any escape pod!" he managed to say, before he was kicked in the back of the knees, which collapsed him just enough to be shoved by her down the chute where he was quickly followed by the Transfer.

"Bremm. Escape pod!"

They ended up sitting flat with her legs around his body as a long, low vehicle was rapidly, organically, constructed around them. The top portion was just about transparent when the larger vehicle opened up an exit.

"Wait! My partner!" Holt shouted.

"It can come in its own pod," the Transfer said. "Bremm! Let's go!"

The pod slipped out and took off on a down-curving path away from the vehicle.

Holt turned to see something forming out of the lower part they'd just abandoned. Was it his Fast in its own escape pod?

Suddenly the entire original vehicle was encased in a pale blue halo.

"Look!" He pointed out to her.

"They locked on! Good thing we weren't there."

"Why? What would happen?"

"Erasure?"

"Erasure?" he asked.

"Well. Maybe not you. But I'd be erased. Who knows what'll

happen to you."

"Get us out of range!" Holt groaned.

"We're trying!

He turned around again to see if the Fast had made it out in a pod, but all he could see was the increasingly large, and now glowing hot, blue halo.

"Fast," he sub-vocalized, "Are you there?"

"Caught!" was the last word he heard from it.

As Holt and the Transfer rapidly flew away in an ever deeper downward curve, headed toward what looked like some Oort Cloud-type dwarf planet, he wondered what more could possibly go wrong this day.

And got his answer. Some of the pale blue globules from the FTL had dashed either ahead or somehow beneath them, and two were headed for them and the pod.

The Transfer called for evasive actions, and got them, sickeningly so, as far as Holt was concerned, as they began sudden jerks in and out of different directions.

"They're coming up from under," she called out. She pulled Holt up as far as he could go into the transparent top of the pod and placed herself below him. When the first one hit below, it stunned the pod. Holt was holding on tightly, but he felt the Transfer dropping away below. He reached out for her, but she was pulled away, and he could see her bending over backwards in her fall.

"Bremm!" she called out.

Then they were surrounded in what seemed to be a hot blue plasma of some kind. In that second, Holt reached once more for the Transfer and missed her head, and she vanished as he heard his wrist connector chime, "Warning! Warning! Warning!"

Holt took a very deep breath. Then everything was silent, and he was suitless, shipless, free floating and look, Holt, look at all those stars ...!

Thankfully, Holt's overloaded senses and strained metabolism had enough; it all simply shut his consciousness completely down.

The tall, distinguished-looking, older fellow with salt and pepper hair cresting forward at least four inches high in front and slowly waving as he moved, along with a profuse, thick, and precisely clipped beard, smiled and it was odd, but despite being masculinely overbuilt, he looked and moved and sounded like any other human.

"But you must understand, during the healing and surgical procedures we took the natural course of subjecting you to a truth inoculation. As we would do with any stranger if merely to assess risk."

"I understand," Holt said, thinking "merely."

"As a result of that, we are now *fully cognizant* that you are *not* some mere stumblebum who strayed into one of our far outlying recycling centers, but instead the youngest child of the greatest man of your people. The most revered, and one of the most powerful of a very large … *republic* I believe it is called? Clearly your appearance here is some kind of accident … But a most *fortuitous* accident! Although as a diplomat I'm not privy to *all* of our scientific achievements nor *most* of our military experiments, still I would be dissimulating if I said or even hinted that the Trasp-Kenner Empire possesses any vehicle or in fact any mechanism that, even accidentally, could travel so quite fast and so far."

He smiled again, which calmed Holt down only a fraction of a second. Holt had been drugged and apparently he had talked a great deal while under and they knew everything. While he knew … far less about them!

"Explain to me again who you are?" Holt asked.

The fellow next to him, larger and more muscular and with even taller, at least five-inch high, this time butterscotch, colored hair and with equally thick, expertly clipped, if slightly differing style beard, said, "This is The Emperor's Foreign Minister for Extra-Galactic Affairs – *Janz Sonz.*"

"How do I address The Emperor's Foreign Minister for Extra-Galactic Affairs?" Holt asked. The fellow also possessed golden light brown eyes almost matching his hair. Eyes that now smiled while his lips did not,

"For a person of your own high rank, Prince Sanqq'," Goldilocks said, "'Foreign Minister' will suffice."

"And how would I address you?" Holt asked.

The eyes smiled even more, the mouth not at all, as he said, "As Second Fleet Admiral … Second Fleet Admiral Tanzen Raz.

And now Prince, if you don't mind my prying, exactly where is this vehicle that brought you here?"

"I have to assume you destroyed it when the Transfer's vehicle was destroyed."

"Ah. That's unfortunate! But I believe that it may not have been completely atomized. There may be … shards that you could identity for us."

"Such a small vehicle that it could fit within a Bremm?" The Foreign Minister exclaimed. "It must be advanced indeed! A great shame that security felt the need to …" and quickly added, "Not that any criticism of the outer rim forces is in any way implied – naturally."

"Naturally," Goldilocks answered frostily. Neither of them had even looked at each other since they'd arrived, Holt now realized. Yet they never once taken their eyes off *him*. Did they expect him to do something remarkable right there? And if so, what?

"The ministry that I serve in, you should understand, Prince," the Foreign Minister went on, "has been for the past few centuries, hereditary, and to be breathtakingly frank, Prince, it's been almost completely ornamental. For the obvious reason that we've never had any contact at all with any extra-galactic personages like yourself. Until your arrival, in fact, my office was a mere tributary in the great ambassadorial ocean of *awarded* staff. As am I myself."

Holt wondered if that were strictly true. Hadn't the Box Men he'd met, who had introduced him to this new form of travel, said they come to this and other nearby galaxies? Maybe they'd not made themselves known?

"But I take it, Foreign Minister," Holt now said aloud, looking from one to the other, "that the rank of Second Fleet Admiral is neither hereditary *nor* ornamental."

There was no blushing from Goldilocks for the implied compliment to him, or if there was, the skin was too tanned or too olive or perhaps too thick to display the flush.

"Neither, Prince. It is hard earned indeed," the diplomat assured him, still without glancing at the man he complimented.

"Then I am doubly honored to have this social call paid by the two of you."

Janz Sonz coughed a bit.

"As are we honored, also, Prince!"

Goldilocks concurred.

Holt had to wonder what had happened to his Fast? Had it somehow managed to escape? No! Its last message before the Transfer's vehicle was hit was "caught." But perhaps the clever cyber had managed to disguise itself – even as one of those so called "shards" If so, how could Holt get to it? Perhaps this Admiral might be played upon? Manipulated? Seduced?

"But I'm afraid that this is more than a mere social call, Prince," the Foreign Minister now spoke. "Word of your ... *existence* ... has leaked out to the journalistic estate, as it were, and curiosity is, naturally enough, extremely high."

"You wish me to appear in your media?"

"Well, certainly that, yes, in time. In time. In time. After the proper time and with all appropriate preparation. But not so it would put any especial burden upon yourself, Prince."

Well, that was a relief.

"Appropriate preparation because of my appearance?" Holt asked.

"Appropriate preparation because of your existence *at all*. Although we are an advanced civilization, exo-galactic life has never been more than ... *postulated*."

"Before the public sees you," Goldilocks now spoke, "There is of course extreme curiosity on the Highest Levels of Command, especially among those I report to ... and beyond my own command," Tanzen Raz put in.

"At the very *highest* levels, Prince. The Prime Minister. All the ministers, in fact. As well as the Aristocracy, and then of course the People."

"Let's never forget the People," Holt said, and looked up, but Goldilocks was not amused. Holt went on, "Presumably, Foreign Minister and Second Admiral, the Aristocracy consists of the Emperor and his family"

They spoke not a word.

"Or is it Empress and *her* family?"

This time they looked away from him.

"Am I to take it that there *is* no Emperor?" Holt asked. "It is an empire. Or so I was told: The Trasp-Kenner Empire?"

"It is an empire indeed. Prince. However for the past three years, it has been an empire without either Emperor or Empress, with or without their accompanying family," the Minister added with something of a sigh.

"Three Claimants of equal rank and position remain – vying for the position, Prince," the Second Admiral explicated, choosing his words quite cautiously, Holt thought. "And have done so for several years – You call longer periods of time, years?"

"Revolutions of planets around suns, yes." Holt said. "Let me get this straight, three Imperial Claimants remain ... out of a presumably larger grouping? Oh. I see!" Holt said, "And since I am such a ... curiosity ... which one of those Claimants did you say you represented? Oh, you didn't say, did you, Minister?"

"I am pleased to represent The Duke of Crich & Plathas, his Lordship Szach Nez. He is the second cousin to the late Emperor, and his closest living relation."

Second cousin was pretty distant. "Those closer to the Emperor having meanwhile ...?" Holt probed.

"Having meanwhile been assassinated or blinded or paralyzed by their rivals during the chaos of the Upswelling of Grief following the late Emperor's demise, I'm afraid."

"While I, Prince," the soldier spoke up, "am pleased to represent the Earl of Lemms, his lordship Japh Goraz. Nephew to the late Empress."

"And the Empress ...?" Holt asked, already guessing.

"Her Extreme Eminence of course took her life and that of the Emperor's four other consorts at the Upsetting News. The Earl however happened to be on command watch with my Second Fleet, and at some distance away from the Cen-Trol at the time of the Emperor's death," he added, explaining why the Earl of Lemms and possibly Goldilocks himself were still alive.

"Is that kind of grief-induced murder/suicide and incapacitation by relatives standard practice here?" Holt asked.

"It is not standard, although never actually frowned upon, and it is sometimes ... strongly recommended!" the Foreign Minister allowed.

"Which it obviously was in this case and on a fairly widespread basis. And so therefore ... what?" Holt felt he had to ask them both, "Why is there no one here to represent the third Claimant?"

After a short pause in which for the first time the two looked at each other with barely a glimpse, the soldier said, "The representative of the Third Claimant to the Imperial Throne is on his way here as we speak. Or so we are told, Prince!"

"He shall represent the Marquess of the Morbida Worlds. Another second cousin, once removed, who was also away during the ..."

"Upswelling of Grief," Holt completed the sentence using the euphemistically acceptably tepid term for what he suspected was a weeks-long rampage of terror and murder and maiming. "I understand now. My doctors and the cybernetic tutors at the healing center failed to mention any of this," Holt admitted, "Despite their otherwise quite thorough-going explications of your people."

"Politics are so ... very complicated for outsiders," the minister said.

"Aren't they? But not so complicated that this Prince will be *very upset* if the representative of the Third Claimant does not actually get through what looked like a rather stringent security line outside to visit me," Holt warned, with what he recalled was his warmest smile.

He watched as Goldilocks now did something quickly with a bracelet that might have held a radio or message. Perhaps releasing the third representative.

"Naturally, you will be able to meet the Third Claimant's representative," Goldilocks said.

"I'm so relieved," Holt said. "But let me guess? Once I'm seen by everyone, my presence will what? Somehow tip the scales in favor of one or another of the claimants?"

The Foreign Minister coughed once more discreetly and said in a very low voice, "Given your preeminence, how can it be otherwise? And should you agree to ally yourself to the Duke, you are assured of ..."

"Ally myself? By throwing him my support? By being seen with him in the media? By ...?"

"Not ... uh ... But by actually aligning yourself. I was thinking something more formal, Prince."

Goldilocks now spoke, "The Earl of Lemms, sight unseen, offers his hand in matrimony, asking yourself, Prince Sanqq', to become his consort. And, if conditions then prove out as the medics have already told us, at the appropriate time, you will become his wife as well as mother to his as yet unborn children. Including the Heir."

"As does the Duke, naturally, offer his own exalted hand," the minister chimed in.

"You mean now that *you two* have seen me and I'm not six legged or three headed?" Holt asked and for the first time since they been seen into the room he stood up and walked to the five tall windows giving out to a garden that would have rivaled what he seen in History-holos of Old Versailles. Except that the fountain water here – if water it was – sparkled iridescently, and instead of marble the structure seemed to be some sort of platinum alloy.

He stood there, oddly balanced in the new, big-buttocked lower body the T-K doctors had provided for him, since his own lower body had been plasma'ed away in the escape. Well not all of it – due to his position in the escape pod, his Relfian Viviparturition Unit was intact as well as his complete male genitalia. It was from those supposedly two contrasting organs, that the doctors told him they had known for certain that Holt was one of the wonderful – if an extra-galactic example of – their rarest, and third, gender. They had "repaired him" they said, to make sure he was exactly that, adding discreetly tucked away female mammalian genitalia connected by some kind of tubing or other to the birth unit he already possessed. The manner in which those doctors had admiringly spoken about this third, "Consort" gender, meant that Holt wasn't as astonished by the matrimonial offers he'd only just now received. Holt had already learned enough Trasp-Kenner history and sociology from what the Transfer had called "Look-Ons" to grasp that it was only such Consorts who ever became Empresses. The culture was so predominantly Patriarchal, that T-K females were not even to be considered as royal wives and mothers; only someone at least "half male," like himself, would do.

The Second Admiral knew this, of course, long before Holt knew it. The Minister knew it too; and presumably all three Claimants were eager to plant a baby Emperor into Holt and have it go into that Relfian unit he possessed, so their own chosen man might be Galactic Regent, while the baby grew up into T-K ruler-ship.

It was ingenious enough, he concluded. If somewhat maddening. He'd hoped during a brief ten minutes or so inside that Bremm within the interstellar trash-yard that he might be able to finally just blend in, to be just another person: not this. Would Holt *never* be just another person? Couldn't he *ever* exist outside the eye of fame, of power, of politics – and of infamy, really?

"I'll tell you what, Foreign Minister, and Second Fleet Admiral, as you both appear to be reasonable fellows, I *will* appear in public. You," to the older male, "will accompany me in or onstage or inside to whatever venue it is. While, you Admiral, will accompany me back or outside again from that venue. I will meet whomever you require – within reason as I am still healing – and I will be as open to the media as you require. I will make no commitment to any Claimant, at this time, although I am completely open to meet them all, at their leisure. I would include the third, but he's late. Now ...! How does that sound?"

The minister stood up and extended his hand palm upward in a light sweeping motion that Holt recognized to be a T-K leave-taking gesture.

"Your Highness, I and my liege are satisfied."

Goldilocks copied him: "Your Highness, I and my liege are satisfied."

They kept their fronts to him as they bowed themselves out of the large chamber.

No sooner had they left and he'd turned back to the windows – not glass but something organic and similar – and the view of the fountains – when the doors were thrown open and a dark-haired young Aristo – given his dress, and tall hair and thick beard – entered, made a deep bow, put out a hand in the greeting gesture and with the other covered his lower body.

"Your Highness, many apologies, Prince Sanqq', I was unaccountably held up. I am pleased to represent ..."

He was very young, and in fact, rather adorable-looking, with his thick black hair, high cut like the others and his very pale eyes, adorable as only a wild canine cub could be adorable, eager, panting, awkward.

"Don't tell me!" Holt said, "You represent the Marquess of the Morbida Worlds. And sight unseen I am offered his hand in wedlock."

"Why ... How did you know?"

"I knew because apparently I am the most exciting stranger to have arrived here at the Trasp-Kenner Empire in decades," Holt said, and then said, "Be seated please. Some kind of tisane is here for you to sip."

He was being facetious, but the other moved his hand away from his crotch to do the acceptance gesture and in so doing revealed what stood at attention there, and said, "Oh, Your Highness. The diplomatic rumors were truly only a fraction of the actuality."

"Oh?"

"Yes, Prince. You are the most exotically lovely creature we have seen in a ... I assure you when the Empire at large sees you, Your Highness will have men at your feet by the thousands. You will be an utter sensation!"

Then, being young and very pale, he blushed very deeply.

Holt dropped to an opposite divan in surprise, thinking "out of the mouths of babes." The young emissary also sat on his side of the chamber, covering his crotch again.

"So ... I'm not physically repulsive to T-K people?" he asked. Neither of the other two had hinted at it.

"Oh, far more than that, my Prince. Far more ... attractive," he gushed.

"As are you, my handsome young friend. Your name is ...?"

"I am Thane of Lazzor, Prince. I'm only from the secondary line, but it is one of the oldest Thanacracies in the land and I come from a very well-known family. If I may boast, the cadet line itself produced both an Emperor and a Consort in the past, although as my very practical father reminds me, that was in the deep past. Andor Lazzor is my name."

"Excellent, Thane Andor Lazzor! During my presentation to the Empire via your media, others will escort me to and fro, but you will remain with me onstage at the venue, to add to the legitimacy of my presentation ..."

And when the younger man looked confused, he said, "Didn't you know? I am to be put on display like some exotic zoo animal."

"Put on display like a god! – or rather," Andor was still blushing – "like a goddess!"

"Like a goddess!!" Holt said to himself and he repeated it after the Thane of Lazzor had taken his ritual sip of tisane and had stood up to beg his leave, his hand still over his uncontainable crotch.

"Well," Holt spoke aloud when he was alone again in the huge, glittering salon of a gallery, sure he was being overheard,

"I suppose such a fate is marginally better than being a horrible and despised creature and quickly murdered in some cesspool pit ... *How* much better, only time will tell."

Holt had taken a good three decades of Education & Development, like most Ib'r Republic children of that glittering City on a Star. True, his had been sporadic, as he busily transformed himself into what the Media Vids liked to call an "interstellar bad boy and lay-about heartbreaker."

Still, as his close-mother, Ay'r, very well understood from their conversation whenever they were together, Holt knew a great deal more facts than he ever allowed anyone else but that great man to understand. As the only child actually birthed by The Great Father, he held such a special place in the celebrated Founder's life. Holt could pretty well estimate that this alien, strongly humanlike culture that he found himself in quite suddenly was what would be characterized in any Advanced Hesperian Ed. & Dev. Course as middle-technological, early-political, early- to middle-cultural/imperial expansion. Something like the Last Age of the Star-Barons melding into the First Matriarchy back in his own galaxy – with, naturally, several odd twists.

Physiology – as Delphinids and Arthropodic sentients back home had discovered to their greater or lesser humiliation – was indeed Destiny. Of the three existing species there, only human mammalians appeared suited to or sufficiently physically and mentally equipped and/or adaptable enough for conquering and holding onto and utilizing most of the habitable planets they happened upon. The Delphs, of course, required large amounts of liquid water and salt, limiting them greatly. The Big Bugs needed a certain kind of landscape out of which they might shape their cone-like mile-high colony nests. Flat and gardenlike worlds were almost as useless to them as water worlds. So, while the Bella=Arth.s could and, in fact, had discovered fire early and had done extensive mineral and ceramic mining and construction wherever they happened to go, both of which had given them an early technological head start, they – and even the most advanced Delphs– lacked the sheer agricultural wealth that adaptable humans easily achieved wherever they went. Thus, all but humans lacked the great population growth that was needed to overwhelm other species by sheer numbers. That demographic explosion had been the crucial factor in the rise and expansion of the Matriarchies for over a thousand years and it had also determined much of its interplanetary policy making. Another demographic explosion begun several hundred years ago and still going strong accounted for the even greater success of Holt's own Ib'r Republic.

But in this galaxy, as far as Holt could ascertain, whatever non-human intelligences that may have evolved early on also seemed to have been also wiped out so early on in history that references to them were few and – instructively – mostly mythological, or else they were emblematic.

For example, of the three men he'd been wooed by in-proxy each had displayed some kind of symbol of a long extinct but once living and apparently powerful creature signified in an emblem upon each of their uniforms. A rough sort of giant flying reptile symbol graced the golden Tanzen Raz's chest, a seemingly long accepted sigil for the Space Admiralty. It had doubtless once been enemy to the humanoid's primitive air force, which was now an interstellar space force. The middle-aged diplomat Janz Sonz sported his own symbol, a sort of furry-headed ursine-like creature that Holt assumed was another casualty of the evolution game on some home planet or other. The handsome, much younger emissary, Thane Andor Lazzar, had sported a sort of wolfish fish-head upon his chest, symbol of some early aquatic enemy, although he didn't believe one of this home, imperial planet, perhaps one of the Morbida Worlds.

That everyone in this Trasp-Kenner Empire seemed to wear a uniform of one sort of another was another sign of a kind of its distortion or thwarting down to a lower level of cultural growth. The many servants of this palace in which Holt was housed had subtly differing colors of fairly identical, quite simple, two-piece uniforms. Only the cybers of the Empire were un-clothed, and were in fact always bare metal or metal-plastic combinations. Most of those were also deemed servants and had their own evident grade-level insignias, usually letters and numbers. Holt had already encountered many cybers here that were intelligent, although they were so in carefully limited fields of knowledge, and even so they sometimes reminded him of Jon Laks and his buddies back in Hesperia. They also proved to be invaluable in supplying Holt with historical and scientific information, and even cultural clues, although at times he remained baffled. Crucially however, it was clear that these cybers were utterly willless. Faced with a problem or choice they were not programmed to deal with, they froze up and all but shut down. There would be no T-K cyber rebellion like that which had roiled the last Matriarchy, not anytime soon. That seemed certain.

That Holt was the only non-servant, non-cyber inhabitant of this quite large, and rather baroquely ornate, forty-nine room building became clear early on. Once he had been "repaired," Holt had been assisted onto his new legs and feet and told to walk as much as he could. Two cybers remained close at either side of him, like learner-rail guards, until he would no long tire easily or fall to one side, as he plunged his way through salon after salon, chamber after chamber, sun-room after mirror-room after mural room. Furnishings were gorgeous if sparse and what's more, they were mobile, as they'd been in the time of the monarchs of Europe on old Terra. Except here they were also automated. At mealtime, Holt would choose a particular view from a specific salon, and in minutes a dining room table, sideboards, heated serving table and suitable chair would arrive and assemble itself.

Evidently children had once resided here, possibly scions of some long-forgotten Dowager Empress, as there were a number of "Knowledge Imparting Look-Ons" that Holt could watch to bring him up to date. When he asked who had last resided there, he was told that an Imperial Factotum would be called, and that charming much older male had appeared and had carefully explicated the seven-centuries long residential history of this particular building. It, by the way, was known as Palace Number 27, The Palace of the Symmetrical Fountains. Thus, he learned there were seventy-two palaces of roughly this size on this planet, the home planet of the Trasp-Kenner Empire, a planet now known simply as Imperia. Explaining, he assumed, why a guest might occupy one whole palace –although of course as he was daily reminded whenever anyone addressed him, Holt was considered a Prince here, i.e. quite high in their Imperial system and just beneath the level of actual rulers.

The cybers kept on trying to design a uniform for Holt, and

expressed their difficulty. Recall he had been all but naked, and clad in some kind of instant-wear when he'd been shot out of the Transfer's escape vehicle. Besides reconstructing his entire lower body, the surgical cybers had done a bit of extra work to the still-extant top-half of his torso and body to make him look and thus feel more like his hosts. They had instilled some sort of super-hormones into his healing body to instigate various areas of pileal growth. Holt had always sported a strong head of auburn hair with occasional blonde highlights. Now it was a sturdy six-inch shock of deep red hair, except for a three-inch flash of pure white in front, and it all but glistened as he watched himself move past mirrors. Something he'd never had before and which might have been the result of the attack upon him. Those who took care of his bodily needs were unclear about that. What they were clear about was that the white hair must be covered up at all times, even if that meant trial and error to come up with a dye to match his natural color. He'd never had much body hair, but now in back of his head two lines of hair grew down to each shoulder and spread there in a light, but noticeable fuzz. Under his pectoral muscles was another fuzz and a good-sized auburn triangle of it now grew between his flat breasts. That in turn dropped a thick, all but braided rope of hair down to his groin area where his auburn hair grew quite thickly around his double set of genitals. His lower torso, back and glutes were hairless, but another thick fuzz grew down and around each new leg, ending at the ankle. Holt found himself wondering if it was some unique T-K evolution of human infants' early, protective lanugo, and instead of vanishing in the first few months of life, here in the T-K empire, it developed all through life.

Whenever Holt looked at himself in a mirror, some medical cyber was sure to say, "Given your excellent upper torso and an otherwise clean slate, it was easily decided that a person of your high eminence should possess a perfect Trasp body. One towards which many would be enamored." Holt always replied, "That's what it was pretty much like where I came from, so gratitude." But in some way he'd been hoping to be more ordinary, or even a little deformed, to see what that might be like. But after some resistance, he'd finally gotten into the fashion game with them, constructing uniforms, because he wanted a score of them at the least, all subtly different from any he had seen, and he also declared that the multiple pieces all had to be mix-and-match.

More problematical however was his wrist connector. He'd covered up the slit that identified its existence within his left arm when he'd first been shot at, and he could still pull at the healing skin and see glints that it was still there. But it was effectively dead. For someone who'd spent his entire life interconnected with all knowledge, advice and instant communication through a wrist connector, one of the biggest adjustments he needed to make was to realize that for the first time he was truly on his own. Whatever had caused it to shut down so completely – he guessed his being attacked and the subsequent massive surgery he'd undergone were the main candidates – *it* had decided that he didn't need it, or that it was currently in his way more than it was needed.

Holt still recalled the ship-mind's memory trying to escape after him and communicating that final agonizing word, "caught."

Would anyone here in T-K even know *what* they had "caught?" He strongly doubted it. What was most likely was that the very intelligent cyber that had once been his intergalactic vehicle had shut itself down pretty substantially if not completely until it could assess its and Holt's situation. If it was currently active at all, his wrist connector would have shown that in some way, no matter how minuscule. As a Neo, he'd experienced enough "Behind Enemy Lines" Pseudo-View Narratives to know that his personal cyber from home's single overriding function now was to consolidate its position, formulate an escape, and then locate Holt and help him escape.

That's what Holt himself wanted. Right?

Well … maybe not right away. This might be a primitive kind of culture compared to what he'd always known, but was that all bad? He was kind of enjoying being a Royal Prince, being waited on hand and foot, and being taught everything there was to learn about this new place and these new people, and with an entire palace and grounds to himself. He was kind of enjoying playing the entire situation by instinct. He was kind of enjoying being adored by these hyper-masculine Trasp men. Who knew what might develop? He could not become Emperor, but he might get himself placed right next to whoever the Emperor turned out to be.

He was enjoying another long "bath" two days later: his palace had seventeen such large tanks level with the floor and beneath it, holding water that was constantly moving and that provided both relaxation and also cleanliness, when he received his first "message." This was provided through a wall speaker in this bath-chamber and the announcement was couched as a question. "Would his Grace, Prince Holt of Hesperia and Palace Twenty-Seven, wish the personal company of one Thane Andor Lazzor?"

"When?"

"The Thane asserts that it is somewhat of an emergency, and wishes to see His Grace, the Prince immediately."

"Yes. Have him come. I'm done here. Have servants help me to dry off and dress."

When some fifteen minutes had passed, after he was in fact quite ready to receive the young man, another wall speaker announced that the Thane had just entered the grounds from the south and was proceeding past the Infinitude Fountain, so Holt got up and walked out of the double "glass" doors hoping to meet him outside. Partly because he felt that inside, those speakers might also transmit whatever he and the Thane spoke of, and he wanted a bit of privacy.

He'd had himself dressed in a newly made uniform of his own design, its emblem being a stylized giant spider, one of the beasts on Dryland his close mother - or was it uncle?- had battled. The rest of the uniform was a pastel blue with battleship gray-silver accents, the colors of the House of Sanqq' back home. He checked himself in the many looking glasses as he headed out and down the wide stone stairs, deciding that he looked remarkable. Even the new lower torso seemed part of him now: no longer like that of some equine animal, and Holt affected what he hoped was a typical walk.

Naturally he received wall speaker warnings that he was leaving the protection of the palace, but he hurried outside anyway. On level ground, he could make out in the distance the slender form of the young Thane and he waved to him. They crossed from either end of what appeared to be a cross-hatched, espaliered garden of some hot pink and deep-green flowering bushes and they met in the middle where an open lozenge area with benches had been formed.

"Apologies, Prince Sanqq'," the handsome youth began, "For

this quickly needed interview."

"Has there been an alteration of your Marquess of Morbida's inclination towards me?" he flirted.

"No, Prince. But" – he looked around them – "can we be overheard here?"

"Not by my palace servants or cybers, I don't think. Why?"

"I have reason to believe, it is too horrible to contemplate, but I fear it is so as the source is impeccable, that you have been targeted for abduction or worse."

"Worse being assassination?"

"I don't know what worse means. But this source has never failed me."

"Two other families besides the Marquess have a stake in my being abducted and I don't know how many other pretenders or potential mates of pretenders may exist. One of my cyber-tutors said the number may be as high as twelve."

"Your tutor might have been playing it down conservatively," the young Thane admitted. "May I add, if I'm not being too bold, that you look more astonishing than ever in your new garb. The colors suit you perfectly."

Holt placed a hand comfortably upon the young Thane's middle arm. "You are very kind, Thank you for noticing."

Meanwhile he was thinking, right now I could use that wrist connector.

"No servant or cyber inside my palace is, I believe, trained in any of the martial arts or possesses a weapon."

"Prince, this humble Thane is both trained militarily and," pointing to the tops of either knee-high boot where Holt now made out what had seemed tassels were in fact the open ends of a short sword in the left leg and a long narrow revolver in the right one, "he is also equipped to protect you."

"Then you will be my dinner guest and who knows, my guest period, until you can ascertain that this threat is contained."

"I can't refuse a direct order from one of such station as yourself, and it would give me the greatest personal pleasure not to mention honor to do so."

Before Holt could reply the young man rose from sitting. "May we begin that visit immediately, Prince Sanqq'?"

Lazzor turned around more than once checking the grounds behind them, and once they were back indoors, the Thane called on two servants to fetch him a particular cyber. To the machine, he ordered a Stage-Three Point Six Lockdown with no exceptions.

"Done, my Thane," the cyber replied and scurried away.

Later that night, when Holt was changing, getting ready to meet the Thane for dinner, one of his more talkative cyber-tutors asked Holt if the guest were staying overnight.

"Yes, in that chamber adjoining this one."

"May this tutor suggest that tonight might present a golden opportunity for your Grace to experience what you have asked about so often."

"What have I asked about so often?" Holt asked. "Remind me."

"I believe your exact words, your Highness were, 'How do guys have sex here'?"

"Oh, right. Sure. Good idea. Now tell me, how do I look? Am I drop dead gorgeous or what?"

Chapter Two:

GLEN

Giant boles had lifted off from earth – enormous tree trunks half a mile in length, sixty feet in width, with four thousand discernible growth rings, signifying that they were Venerable Elders – they rose and while Khana wanted to scream No, What Are You Doing? You Belong to the Earth Itself You Can't Do That! Still, she could see that they were happily elevated, liberated, delightfully dancing in vast do-si-dos, and so she calmed down and simply watched, enjoying their lumbering, elephantine yet all the same intricate gavottes.

"Kha-na! You're going to be late!"

She had one more glimpse of them in clumsy minuet just before she woke up.

"Kha-na!"

"I heard. I'm up. I'm awake," she shouted. "I'm off for a shower-bath," she added a bit more softly, because she could see her sister Metts turning over in her own, nearby bower and murmuring, probably cursing at Khana for all her noise.

"What a weird dream," she said to herself, as she stripped off her night pod and tossed it aside and then headed into the side-bough shower-bath. It was outside, of course, it being highly desirable that all water not actually consumed was to be recyclable, indeed it was required to be so by the entire Local Residential Stand. Naturally the water was cold when it said it was warm.

"Ah, life in Glen. How lovely!" she muttered. But then the water was warm and Khana wasn't certain if it would get any warmer so she stepped in, shivered, got all wet, head to toe, took up the whistle-fern whisk and began to caress and slap herself clean.

It had been a wonderful dream. She'd tell it to Wellweg and K'or later today and see what they thought of it. Surely something good was about to happen with a dream like that. Wellweg had a little book of dreams they often searched through, supposedly hundreds of years old, wrapped in the oldest bark she'd ever seen from who knew what out of the way Stand, none she could recognize, an heirloom carried down through at least four complete Migrations, her best friend had said, looking impressed herself. You could look under "flying" or "tree trunks above ground" or some such. K'or, of course, would just smile his slightly older adolescent smile, and humor the two. But even K'or had wild dreams at times, and he had openly consulted Wellweg's little brown covered *Oneirochron*.

Khana had laved her front, bottom to top, and had turned to the more difficult upper back and was whisking away there as she rinsed when she suddenly heard an odd sound and felt a sharp pain just behind her right shoulder she'd never felt before.

What in the wood?

She reached back, but it was just out of reach.

She then began whisk-slapping the other side of her back and felt the same sharp little pain. What could it ...?

I need a looking-glass, she thought. If this is what I think it is ...

She slid out of the shower bath which sensed her gone and shut itself off completely.

"I wasn't done bathing," she announced in an aggrieved tone of voice. But as far as this shower-bath was concerned: she was done. It wouldn't turn on water for her body for at least another forty-one hours.

She wrapped herself in a giant leaf of the Tambuco tree – her Fa's gift to her last birthday; scented, self-oiling, a grown up's gift – and then turned to check in the looking glass. Her hair was still wet and far too curly. But there, exactly where it was supposed to be, it was: six inches diagonally down, red yet, and she guessed so new that it would be painful for her to wear a blouse against it. And when she turned the other way, there was the identical fleshy little roseate nub.

"Ma'!" she shouted. "Ma'!"

Her Ma' came trundling out of her cooking spot and. side to side, up the bough.

"What in the wood is it now?"

"Ma'! Look, Ma'. Look!"

Khana turned around so her Ma' could see her back.

"Oh, Khana! They've come!"

"Is it true? Is it finally true? Have they come at last?"

"Of course. Now drop down that leaf. La' what lovely skin you have! I envy you, I'm as gnarled as an old briar-bush." She touched below and spun Khana around, a big smile on her wide and so familiar face. "The baby nubs are first coming below too."

"Oh, Ma'!" I've waited so long. "They've taken so long to come. Wellweg and K'or had theirs a Quarter Turning ago." Khana wanted to laugh and cry and leap into the air, and hug and kiss her Ma' all at once.

"It's barely a Sixteenth Turning until Migration, Khana," her Ma' said. "They might be fully grown and ready for wings by then"

"*Might* be fully grown?" Khana all but shrieked! "They'd better be."

"Hush. Loud one. So then you'll be able to Migrate with your Fa' and Metts and Jiappa and Meera, all of us, as a family at last."

"No more hiding in a leathern cache seeing so little of what's above and below and no more being dragged as a burden by you all," Khana said.

"You were never a burden to us. It was almost ten big Sun-Turns after all that we last Migrated, and you were still wee then."

Khana hugged her Ma' who pulled away and said, "But this time until Migration will not all be sweetbriar sap and willowfern pop for you, young sapling. You've got to keep those four nubs well moisturized and balmed or every little breeze will cause you a burn and tears."

"I know, Ma'. I know. But for how long shall they ache?"

"Hard to say, Kha. My own was a lengthy torment. Your Fa's come in so fast he was ruggering with the other lads in a few days amidst the bark-chips and sawdust. You already know of how your elder sisters dealt with theirs. I do have salves and even some simples you should be taking internally with your breakfast. Come, garb up. And put on that blouse-backed pale yellow smock I made for you against this day's coming on your secret name day. Oh, Kha. You're my babe. And I'll be an old Berm 'n' Merm now that you can Migrate on your own with the rest of us."

"Never, Ma', never. You're my one and only Ma' and that makes you especially special."

"Are you two done yabbing?" Metts muttered. I've all morning to sleep in, you know. Get ye's gone."

"Up all night with the Upper Glen crowd at who knows which Stand, and with which Residentials, that one!" Ma' shook her head as she led Khana out of the bower and into her own where almost immediately Kha inhaled the colognes and balms. "Now calm down and stand still, so I may assuage your pain, Kha," Ma' began and then added "Did I ever relate how it was your cousin Chauva' had her nubs nearly taken off before they were all grown in?"

Of course, she'd told Khana. More than one time. But her daughter said, "Nay. Tell us now."

And Ma' did while softening those nubs upper and lower her youngest was so enamored of.

Wellweg's bower sported a life-sized parquet portrait of "Ice," best known perhaps as "Eis," short for Eisenstein Syzygy Kell, the Troubadour Of All Troubadours in the known galaxy. It was large, almost wall-sized, rendered in the cross flow oaken-tiles and so dimensional and lifelike he all but leapt out at you when you entered her bower.

That was only one advantage of having a best friend who came from what Khana's folks believed to be a "very questionable lineage and family." To further that dubiousness, her family consisted scandalously entirely of only Wellweg and her own Ma'. Of her Fa' there was not a sign but Wellweg herself. When Khana once asked her pal's Ma', Rallweg had looked at the lass rather carefully and said, "Oh I shared a Husband-Father with a workmate. And only for her to be born.

"Then they'll be nay more daughters?" Khana had asked.

"Probably not. Although I am asked all the time to share a Husband-Father," and she laughed throatily. "It's much easier this way for an independent lady like meself."

Independent was right: residing at the highest big branch levels and thus the least traditional and if most fashionable, then also a somewhat edgy end of the same Local Residential Stand where Khana and K'or's far more traditional, much larger, families resided. In fact his family residence was mostly below ground level and had only one real bower, Kor's own sleeping area – a prize because he was after all a g.male – all of the rest of his family residence being ancient, natural chambers in the lowest reaches of one of the oldest of Venerable Elders. Now, that! Khana's Ma' often said, was how a family ought to live! She too had applied but it was too late to happen during this Migration.

Yet another advantage, as far as Khana could see was that Wellweg's mother labored by day in another Residential Stand altogether, two woods distant, working as some kind of Higher Numbers keeper in a Tree-Bole Estate Office, for which she was quite well paid. Which meant she was gone most of the day, before Ed. & Dev. and some hours after too, providing the three youngsters with that rarest of treasures in the Local Stand, i.e. privacy.

Few other Ed. & Dev.s at their Loc. Res. Stand School had a female parent who worked, and even fewer any parent who worked "beyond his wood." And even the Husband-Fathers who worked beyond this wood, seldom spoke of their daytime labors beyond the pleasures of any wood at all. Of course it was often considered necessary labor but not really to be spoken of. Although the previous ten years before Migrating here had been spent entirely in high-open spaces, throughout the inter-coastal waterways and mountain fastnesses of Continent Plateau, within a few years into Glen, the folk had adapted to the cozy snugness and far smaller viewpoints that evolved from living within gigantic, village-sized, stands of enormous and ancient tree trunks growing together. Naturally ranged in circles, in oblongs, sometimes even in triangles and diamonds with protected open centers as common spaces and even some open side plazas and an occasional raised bowl, the Local Stand was internally a near maze of dry-slick corridors, naturally warmed open bole-rooms and flowingly lovely boughs for bowers of bedchambers. The older women of the folk admitted to feeling vulnerable beyond their own stands, although there was little but new growth forest out there, with a few enough twisting roads to accommodate commuting.

Another advantage of Wellweg was that Khana's best friend had her own source of paper pelf, guaranteed to arrive every Quarter–Turning, and to be spent usually by Wellweg for herself (and sometimes her friends) which had begun at the arrival of her first wing spurs. That date allegedly signified she was a grown up, although she was far from it, acting often younger than Khana who must lecture her now and again.

"Ooh, they're so small and red," Wellweg said looking at her friend's new wing spurs. "Do they ache a great deal?" she asked with obvious relish.

"Don't be a twisted twig!" K'or commented from where he sat sprawled upon a natural lift of bower wood. He had out a small knife he always carried and was carving a grotesque face in a higher section of his seat. "We're all very happy Khana's got them. Very happy, Khana," he repeated.

"I am happy for you, of course," Wellweg said and hugged her friend close making a big issue out of not touching her new spurs.

"You're still a twig!" K'or said. "Get over yourself, Wegga."

"Yourself" she riposted although it sounded very weak. "So, what can you possibly wear tonight at the concert," she asked. "And please don't say you're not going."

"Right," K'or put in, "Although Wegga already has a buyer for the third ticket."

"I don't."

"You always do. You inherit that from your Ma'."

"Maybe I do. It's good business sense. We're not wood-wealthy like your folk, Kay. Not Fa' wealthy like yours, Kha, dear. So, we have to look out for ourselves.".

"We're just two single women – all alone in the wood," K'or said in a fake woman's voice.

"Aren't we?"

"You and your Ma' have more paper pelf than any ten of us. I know what portion of a Turning's wood-wealth this little quadruple bower high in the sky set Rallweg back, you know."

"Oooh. Sometimes I could just ..."

"There's a yellow blousy top Ma' stitched up and has held especially for me," Khana interrupted the two. "I'll wear that. Anyway, how much sitting down and sitting back shall we be doing at a concert by Ice!" She all but screamed the last name in her excitement.

"None! None at all!" her friend agreed. "I still can't believe he actually will be here. Can you?" she shrieked.

"Not a bit," Khana shrieked back and they all but danced atop the sleep pads of Wellweg's bower.

"I accessed the quite interesting fact," K'or began to say, still carving away and calm as a very old and storm-blasted bole, "That, at large concerts with many g.females, that the prevailing scent," he continued now cleaning out his fingernails with the tip of the knife, "is girl-urine. As they all piss themselves in their excitement."

The two girls looked at each other in astonishment, then at their male friend who couldn't help but let out the tiniest of smiles upon his handsome face, and the girls fell to the bed pad in fits of laughter.

"And so the hysteria begins" K'or said, stretching his long, tall body, and heading toward the end of the bower. "I'll wait for you two to return to the earth of the Glen when, and if ever, you do. And I'll be down at the east tunnel, dressed and waiting for you at what Sol Rad.? Twenty one, say?"

"Nineteen!" Khana said. "We want to be early."

"No, twenty," Wellweg corrected her. "We're bringing our wings and you are coming with us," she said in a maternally admonitory voice to Khana. "We can check them outside."

"I am? Yes. I am."

"Won't that be a sight. You soaring with us and in your yellow blouse," K'or commented. "Chatter on, lasses. Chatter on," he said leaving the chamber and then letting himself out the flat altogether.

"What have I let myself in for?" he was asking himself. But he knew that in their extreme excitement at least one of the other concert goers was sure to become very friendly to him. It had happened before that he'd found himself covered in excited girl, a stand-in for some troubadour still on stage while they fumbled in some corridor or lavatory – and K'or didn't mind that a bit. Not one bit.

"They fly?" Ice – i.e Eis Syzygy Kell – asked. The Troubadour was looking at real-time vids of the Herculars massing to the very stadium where he would be playing in a few short hours. They were alighting onto lawns and terraces in twos and threes, meeting, greeting, celebrating.

"At certain times, yes, they fly," his manager, Janesborot, replied. "But usually only in the two or three months before a mass migration is about to take place."

"These are humans, not birds, we're talking about? right Jay?" Eis said, for confirmation.

"Humans of Hercular, yes. You know of course that it was a Seeded World. One too far away for the Third Matriarchy to colonize directly. Seeded World Number 650-656, I believe, in the catalogue."

"I've never heard of any human ever flying by his or her own power."

"Neither do these. They actually attach a cyberized set of wings that slip into four spur-like growths upon their backs. There are two sets of spurs. Two near the upper back's deltoids and muscles for the larger wings and thus flight, and two smaller ones below that, for greater directional control. The wings are slid into each spur and they actually do the flying."

"I've never heard of any humans having spurs or indeed any kinds of natural attachments for any kinds of wings before, of any kind."

"On Hercular, it was a consciously developed physical alteration and then over the years it evolved to become seasonal. The spurs appear to be vestigial, but they grow out more prominently every ten years or so, ordinarily just before a new migration is about to take place, and it happens only among adults. You see, when this world was first seeded it was discovered that it was only partially finished in terms of its natural terra-forming. Being so very large for a rock-mantled world, it hadn't yet finished knitting together solidly, and indeed it still really hasn't yet completed surface solidification."

"That's odd. I still can't understand how that would account for humans who fly."

"It was a necessary DNA modification. Six standard Third Matriarchy Cyberized-Seed ships arrived here: one in each of six different locales. That was an error. The original Matriarchal Seeding committee planners on planet Melisande believed that what they were seeing from so very far away and what they were seeding from so far away were six separate good-sized *moons* orbiting a typically large, gaseous, Jovian planet. When, in truth, they were merely seeing and then seeding one huge, Jovian sized, but rock mantled planet in six different areas."

"Go on," Eis said. He loved his pamp manager: he could be so serious one minute and so utterly silly and cute the next. But only he knew how truly sharp Janesborot really could be. Janesborot always did weeks of research whenever they were touring out of the way planets and sectors. And none were more out of the way than this enormous globe they could see below from orbit through the now transparent wall of Eis' Fast-Yacht.

Colorful Hercular boasted browns, tans, greens, yellows and whites of solid land, and then deep blue and shallow green waters, and then smoking gaseous whites and grays with an occasional zigzag seam of hot orange-yellow-red whenever some still open fissure was directly in view. All of it wrapped in a multi-swirling cloud system.

"Well, once they'd all arrived with their ships full of seedlings," the pamp went on, "the Cybers, which were the only conscious beings around at the time, confabbed and realized the egregious error that had been made. At the same time, they realized that they couldn't possibly form any sort of cohesive society on the huge planet because the physical anomalies and differences of *where* they had each landed would keep the six seeded colonies forever apart on six separate continents. You've seen the Banners of Hercular, I assume. They're on every piece of literature we've received so far for this portion of the tour."

"How could I miss the banner? It's in six panels, yes?"

"And you recall their slogan?"

"You mean that Aerie – Forest – Sea Shore business?" Ice asked.

"It's actually 'Aerie – Plateau – Glen – Meadow – Strand – Fen,' Ser. Those are the six finished irregular continents that we saw when first approaching the planet earlier, and they represent the six different ecologies that the planet boasts. So far only two of them are attached to each other by solid land bridges and two by water. Between the others remain wide bands of unfinished planet: actively sliding continental plates, beds of boiling lava, and active mountain-building that you can watch and hear –

of course those places are utterly uninhabitable ... The planet is barely fifteen million years old. That explains their need for migration, via flight ... But ... weren't you born on another Seeded Planet, yourself, Ser?"

"Like you, I was born on Usk. No, it's merely a resort planet, and a not a very big or popular one."

"It's much more popular than it was in your Close Mother's day. Not only do the Kells and Syzygys now keep large estates there, so do several other Hesperian Inner Quinx families."

"I didn't know that. I did know that the tourism spots are among the best promoted in that section of the Orion Arm."

"Including Ser, the museum devoted to you and your music."

"Yes, I did go and open that museum, didn't?"

"You certainly did," his manager prided himself on arranging all that, bringing more publicity to his client and also, of course, to his own people. "It's one of the largest tourist spots in the area."

"Didn't I view somewhere that Bella=Arth.s also have also moved into the more mountainous areas of Usk, setting up spas and estates too? Would that be because of the historical battle sites there, during the Three-Species War?"

"You know, Ser, people always ask me 'what is Ice really like?' And I often tell them that he is as knowledgeable and intelligent as his parents. Yes, there was a terrific conflict at a Bella=Arth. nest in the mountains west of the Great Salt Ocean and it is now opened as another Museum. But there was another important Arthropodic incident of historical importance, during your Birth-Mother's time on the planet ..."

"Wait. I know that. It was the settling of the Bella=Arth. Imperial Line, and the agreement of the two Queens who'd been divided by the Post-War Diaspora."

"Amazing. That's exactly so, Ser."

"Not so amazing. I'm afraid. My parents became friendly with the Dowager-Queen, Kri'nni, on Hesperia. The one who ceded ruling rights to the other Queen? I think she might even be a god-mother of mine. I do get amazing gifts from her on my birthday. As for Usk, it turns out a very odd planet indeed in pre-Metro-Terran ancient history. But no, it was never seeded. Of course, my Ib'r ancestors did originally come from a Seeded Planet – Pelagia, popularly known as Dryland – only a few generations before."

"Yes, that's right. At any rate, the Seed Cybers that landed here at Hercular communicated with each other and they decided that if the humans could fly in migration the 800-to-1000-meter distances between the six continents, they could partake of them all, and utilize the benefits of them all, and, most importantly, also live on them all. And, at the same time, they could become a single more or less cohesive society and people. The goal of all seeded planets in that far-reaching program, after all, was to reproduce perfect little Third Matriarchies. And that did sort of happen."

"Sort of, because there are roughly equal numbers of male and females?" Eis asked.

"Actually no. Third Matriarchy Seeded worlds were all genetically devised so there would always be far fewer males, so that they could never come to dominate. But now that merely means that g.males are at a premium on this planet, Hercular. That was by no means Matriarchal-intended at all, and, actually the opposite of what was desired. But then Hercular over in this Sag arm of the galaxy was always too far away to ever be socially or politically absorbed into the Matriarchy to reflect its specific values. It was never even landed on by later Matriarchy explorers. It was simply too out of the way, and was only 'discovered' when the Diomedes Triangle of the Sagittarius Arm of the Galaxy was opened up to our great republic's population increase. So Hercular was forced to evolve in a cultural vacuum as it were, and once the guiding cybers took themselves apart to help infrastructure construction, the humans there were completely on their own. There is by, the way, only that one extant species on the planet. It is believed that several earlier, much more primitive species were already long extinct by the time of the seeding but the archaeological evidence is scant."

"Well, all that would explain a lot," Eis admitted. "So where we're headed to, that's the heavily forested continent called Glen? Where we will be met by several thousand flying females and a handful of males?"

"Yes, it's the last few months of what is called Glen-Turning for the Hercularian people after which comes the migration. A Large Turning is their idea of a solar year. Because of its great size, their year is six hundred and forty-one days, Sol Rad. But soon all of the people in Glen will be migrating towards that lighter colored green continent called Meadow, lying mostly to the south. Can you make it out, Ser? It's been 90 of their years since the Hercularians were residents there and so that continent is ecologically restored and perfectly ready to accept a large infusion of population. It's a rich agricultural area, as opposed to this sparser woodland existence they've just experienced. I expect they will fatten up, settle down, and doubtless undergo a great growth of population. And then, in another fifteen of their years, they will all migrate to that pale yellow-brown continent known as Strand, most of which lies in the Southern Hemisphere. That's more like a living desert interspersed with extensive ocean shore and a lot cooler. After that, they'll move south again but further east, on to those extensive watery-lowlands they call Fen. That will be one of the longest migrations for which wings are still needed. From there it will be northeast into the mountains – to Aerie – and then over that pole and on to mostly flat, but high Plateau. Those last two continents are nearly touching already and they will probably be directly connected by the time the mass of émigrés arrive there again."

"It's actually a brilliant strategy the Seed Cybers devised," Eis mused.

"Yes, it is, Ser. Given the four hundred thousand meter circumference of the planet, Hercular would be able to easily hold and sustain a population of hundreds of billions of people. But at their current, controlled growth rate of only a few score million, with natural die-offs due to migration and other factors, the Hercularians are assured that none of their natural resources are ever threatened by depletion or habitat loss. Even some of the naturally poorest areas like the Plateau and Fen aren't threatened, because each one has an entire ninety year-pause between populations to become replenished."

"It's certainly the most unusual planet I've played on," Eis allowed. "Now. Shall we once more go over the program for tonight."

"Before we do, Ser, I'd like to draw your attention to the threat that we've been apprised of via the Quinx Council Security Bureau."

"What threat?"

"Surely you recall. It came in with alarms and flashing lights. That group from a satellite of Diomedes Five."

"I vaguely recall it. You know I hate all that political stuff.

What does it have to do with the music? That's my only concern."

"Even so, Ser. You *are* the highest profile Center World celebrity to be in this galactic sector since ... Well, probably the highest ever. I believe one of your Ib'r grand uncles once visited early on to help charter this planet into the Greater Quinx Congress as an approved Territory. But since then no one else has come, and whether you like it or not, you do represent the City on a Star here, and ..."

"And the City does have its enemies, benighted as they may be, yes I know," Eis parroted the phrase he'd heard all his young life.

"Your Birth Mother was apprised of the tour extension to this sector only as you were leaving Hesperia. He was less than happy about it."

"I know, I know and he's the dearest man, but he worries too much. My grandsire, however, was thrilled for me. He said I was assured of a unique experience."

They call themselves "Avenge K'tina Kell," Janesborot said ominously. "The terrorists, I mean."

"I know who she is. She was a female, a close-daughter to a grand uncle and his partner. A distant cousin or aunt of mine or something like that."

"Yes, and she was also briefly the very public face of a radical cyber group on Hesperia itself some twenty-five years ago, Sol Rad. She and her cohorts were captured and destroyed or rebooted completely. She suicided in public. It was all over the Media. It's difficult to understand, but this group from the Diomedan Five moon named Patroclus have taken up her name and her image for their cause and ..."

"Oh wait, Jay, I did see something about them in a news-gathering PVN. Something about wanting to get independence from the mining company that runs the place. Don't they have to become partly cyberized themselves or something like that to even work those mines?"

"Indeed, they are forced to be cyberized to do the mining."

"Now see, that's something I don't agree with at all."

"Alas, partial physical cyberization is the only way they could mine there. The mantle of the satellite is close to the surface and it is quite radioactive. The solid methane glaciers that cover the surface of Patroclus are protective enough – until you go underground. The miners would die in a few days of work without specific kinds of cyberization including constant cleansing nanobots."

"Well, it's an awful situation as far as I can see. With all of our leaps of science surely some safer method of mining could be devised. I'm with the rebels in this."

"Wonderful, so long as you are *privately* with them. Please do not say a word if it comes up."

"If it comes up, I'll say the entire situation there eats toe-jam."

"Fine. Whatever that may mean," Janesborot concluded.

"I'll be careful. What do you want me to do?" Eis asked.

"Allow extra bodyguards. Four should do."

"Those poor g.females on Hercular! All they want to do is touch me."

"Ser, they want to strip you, rape you and eat your body after," the Pamp said.

Eis laughed. "Okay, okay, as many bodyguards as you're happy with."

"I'd really be happy if you bypassed Hercular altogether," Janesborot all but muttered.

"Not happening. Every time I spit anywhere in the direction of Hercular, my songs go triple beryllium! You know that. But, getting back to the topic of Hercular, with all those g.females there, what will the ambience at the concert be, I wonder."

"They're predominantly NeoNates, between the ages of ten and forty years old. So you can expect mass hysteria. They'll probably all scream."

"Scream? What for?" Ice was alarmed.

"I've seen vids of it happening, Ser. But don't worry. It's allegedly sexual in nature and is apparently group behavior and even worse, it also appears to be totally uncontrollable."

"Well, my Neo-Nate g.male audiences have certainly become rowdy on other worlds."

"Yes, Ser. But that's comprehensible: they roar in approval and they rush the stage to get at you and seemingly to ravish you, which is completely understandable," Janesborot said, with a smile. "Since you are, after all, their idol and god. But these females weep and carry on, as though each one has a personal relationship with you. Which, in many of their minds, they do have." He paused then added, "Of course we're assured by the stadium staff that the latest and most efficient pheromone cleansers have been installed in the stadium and will be working at full throttle during your performance."

"Maybe I'll cool them off myself with some old pamp ditties that my Mother, Ay'r taught me as a baby on Usk," Eis said.

"Of course, I would like those," Janesborot said, "And be honored."

"They are the first songs I learned, you know."

"Yes, Ser. I do know. Probably every pamp in the Galaxy knows that, and moreover knows the story of how your Birth-Mother, Ay'r Eisenstein Kell, freed the pamp people for all time."

"The way he tells it, you freed yourselves. All you needed was a little push in the right direction."

His pamp manager smiled. "Naturally, he'd say that. It's why we love him so."

"And after I sing the ditties I will call you onstage to duet with me, take a bow," Eis said, teasing, "and let everyone know your true name, Song-Melder."

"Oh, you mustn't do that. Please don't even think of it. You know I would be mortified if you did. Please? Eis? Ser? Please! Don't even think of it!"

As the three arrived at the huge, hollowed out, natural-earth stadium, at the enclosed landing area and attached main foyer, the roar of the crowd was ground shaking.

Before they could do more than settle down to the ground and K'or and Wellweg check their cyberized wings, someone had come up to them.

"K'or! Is that you?" a very pretty just-beyond-sapling-age young female asked. She was in the stadium uniform, her bare head half wrapped by a twig-like electronics device, and she had some kind of name plate that Khana read as "Greet/VIPs."

She was just about to ask what a "vip" was when K'or turned and smiled widely. "Vannada?"

They hugged more closely than Khana noticed K'or hugging other people.

"You work here?" he asked.

"Look!" she pointed out her label.

"Amazing!"

"And guess who's about to become a Vee Eye Pee?" Vannada asked.

"My friends too?" K'or asked.

Vannada swept a glance over Wellweg and Khana as though seeing them for the first time "Oh, sure. No problem." To the girls she said, "You'll have to act grown-up with these special tags on. But it is so worth it! I can probably ..." – she was checking a little hand held electronic thingamabob – "Yes, there's still room. I can get all three of you into the Green Room after."

Now Khana didn't know what a Vee Eye Pee – it wasn't vip after all – or a Green Room either. But K'or apparently did because he leaned over and gave Vannada a big smooch on the cheek.

"You're wonderful, Vee. And I hope you'll be there later yourself. It's been a Quarter-Turning at least since we ..."

She put a hand over his mouth and said in a surprisingly contralto voice, "I know. I know. And I want to too. Tell you what – give me your data" and K'or put his communicator over her little handheld, "And if we don't connect after the show in the Green Room, then I'll be sure to comm. you later."

"I'll be waiting!" K'or said and Khana was suddenly aware that the two of them had what her Ma' would call "an adult relationship" of some sort.

"Anyway!" Vannada was all bright and chirpy again, "I've altered your tickets. Follow the far left entryway in. Now that you are all V.I.P.s you've got better seats far front. They're separated from the rest so that you can easily move to backstage after the show."

All three of them shouted out "gratitude!" to her, as she moved away to intercept someone else she was waiting for. Most of the concert-goers, and by now they were really filling the landing area and the foyer too, were headed into the other eight doorways, when they passed through the ninth and had a woman re-stamped their tickets for "Green Room".

"I can't believe this, K'or," Khana couldn't help from saying. "This is far more than I ever expected. But what is Vee Eye Pee?"

"Very Important Person, of course," Wellweg all but brushed her off.

"And the Green Room?"

"That's where Very Important Persons meet the Artists!"

"You mean Artists like … Eis himself?" Khana couldn't believe it.

She'd stopped them in their almost empty corridor, and now Wellweg also faced K'or, questioning him.

"I don't know. I suppose so. Sure!"

They jumped up and kissed and hugged him.

A minute later they gathered themselves as other V.I.P.s passed by.

"What did you have to do for that Vannada to give us all this?" Wellweg asked.

"Nothing I wouldn't do for you two lovely saplings. Not one thing more," he said.

"Oh, K'or. I'm so glad I know you!" Khana enthused.

Their seats were indeed in a section apart, and very close to the enormous stage. Before they could enter, the uniformed page said that they could "freshen up" in a wash-chamber and she asked what they wanted to drink. It would be delivered twice during the show.

K'or met two g.males he knew, somewhat older, and they began talking, and Wellweg pulled Khana away to the g.females wash-chamber, "I've got to see it and remember every detail. The next time we're in class, every sapling there will know every detail too."

Of course, the wash-chamber was austerely, warm-slickly red-oak beautiful as only the interiors open to the most Venerable Elders could be, and every detail of the lav set up was simple yet luxurious and perfect.

"We'd better go in there!" Wellweg pointed to the separate lavs, "whether we need to or not. We won't want to leave our seats once the show begins."

Once they were in adjoining booths, Khana asked her friend whether she thought K'or and that Vannada were friendly in an adult relationship.

"I'll say!" Wellweg replied. "And it's by no means his first."

"But he's only our age, from the same creche as we were in," Khana said.

"That may be so, Khana dear. But g.males tend to … experience life, shall we say, a great deal more rapidly than we do, since there are ten g.females for each one. And when they are attractive like K'or, and nice and intelligent, well … I'm certain he was in adult relationships long before his own dorsal spurs grew in."

"No! Really?" Khana had to ask. But as she did, she knew it was true. Life was so unfair. Wellweg had her smarts and her natural fashion sense and brilliant business acumen – K'or had hit the brad on the head there, like any good carpenter. K'or, of course, was handsome, and nice and intelligent, and she supposed he'd already had a dozen adult relationships by now. Khana's own sisters each had their accomplishments by her age: whether it be scholarly or practical. Even Metts, going through what her Ma' referred to as her "rebellious phase – she'll come to her senses as soon as she realizes how the branches fork!" – was actually quite wonderful at higher minus numbers and her little sister wondered how soon it would be before Metts was living in her own Big Branch multi-bowered flat and perhaps working at some far off copse. But Khana sometimes wondered if she'd ever discover what her own talents were? What was she good for anyway? Nothing came to mind. Not one thing.

"Look how darling!" An older woman was saying to another about Khana as she stood at the glass and laved her hands and then misted her face. "First time spurs?" She asked and Khana blushed as she nodded yes.

"We're here with our nine daughters between the two of us," the other woman said. They were dressed richly and elegantly with fabrics so thick and fine that they must have come from an earlier stay in Meadow. Their hair was up and swept back with seashell combs and their throats and upper chests were ornamented with multiple strands of what even Khana recognized as early Strand luminescent-pearls and ancient beach-glass jewelry worn to have no edges, and probably from many Turnings ago. Of course they too must be Vee Eye Pees.

Luckily, Wellweg got out of her lav just then and she instantly took over the conversation with the wood-wealthy women from her tongue-tied friend. Even so Khana carefully watched how the women moved and spoke, how they touched and manipulated any item on the vanity counter, and patted their hair and smoothed their long necks in the glass, and peeked behind to check the even length of their skirt hems and she thought: I can do that! That's what I can do best in life – be a wood-wealthy woman! And she smiled.

"At last!" K'or made a big show of breathing a sigh of relief as the two saplings joined him at the entrance to their seats. "I thought I was going to have to come in there and haul you out myself."

"We weren't that long gone," Khana said imperiously, adding, "And anyway you were with those" – she paused to make herself seem especially disgusted – "awful g.male persons. The area was positively drenched in unnecessary hormones."

She'd done such a good imitation of the two elder women that Wellweg could only stare at her. But K'or laughed, and grabbed her in a bear hug.

"Come along with you, Kha! Let's hear some music. The Lead-In act is halfway through their set."

He all but carried her as he dragged her along and Wellweg followed them. Inside it was instant noise and pandemonium. In minutes they too were dancing amidst the others in their section in the aisle before their very nice, very wide, and amazingly comfortable beech-wood seats.

Could life get any better or any more exciting, Khana wondered.

Chapter Three:

GLOBULAR CLUSTER

"Raqqa!" The Historico-Sociometrics professor was not amused by her student's quite audible alarm from her wrist connector. "Haven't we yet learned to turn those off in class? Isn't that what supposedly separates Higher Ed. and Dev. from Lower Ed. and Dev? That our mothers' messages to bring home groceries or pick up the dry-cleaning may wait an hour or so, Sol Rad., until we are quite finished here?"

"Yes, of course, Ma'am. I'm so sorry Ma'am." Raqqa-Lleya-Son tried to sound as contrite as she didn't feel. "Here! See! It's completely off!" she said, holding up her wrist to be glanced at perfunctorily – not that the Prof even looked – "and it won't happen again. Promise!"

Raqqa then returned to her desktop as though checking over the essay she'd actually finished some time ago and had been polishing. The topic given for the exam had been a comparison of the early Da-Merida Province Non-Religious Agricultural Communities birth rates versus marriages with those of the Capa'Di and L'Anxa Spheres with references to a Historical Exemplar from Historic Third Matriarchy planet Benefica. Ordinarily an interesting topic for Raqqa, or if not interesting, then at least acceptable, since it had taken her so long, and she'd already fought so many battles with her surviving mother, Reanna Son, to take this course at all.

But the alarm wasn't for anything as silly as her annoyed professor had claimed, attempting to shame her among her peer-esses. Indeed not. It had been set to go off for something far more intriguing, and probably to any one of the twenty women in the classroom, something far more sinister. Three months before, Raqqa had illegally purchased a Rogue Data Chip from a shady character in a Stelezine-Bar on the outskirts of the mining town of Smet, four hours and forty minutes away, due north, and it was that very chip that was loudly giving her proof finally that it was worth the many weeks of depriving herself of all kinds of goodies to buy it on the sly.

The displaced or disabled – Raqqa couldn't tell which – former miner who had sold it to her had been anything but trustworthy looking or sounding. She'd been old, somewhat unclean, and smelled badly. Worse she'd immediately used the cash given her to pay a bar tab and then ordered a wicked looking Stelezine cocktail with some kind of flaming Brandy stinger that she threw down her throat, coughing and sputtering, her eyes tearing, her nose exploding snot, her wrinkled face red as the dirt outside.

"This little bitch'll give you every little piece of data you'll ever need, Blondie," she'd croaked out finally to Raqqa, after her drink was empty and she could speak again. "Just slip it into your wrist connector and it goes to work. It could take days, or weeks, or months even, but you tell it what you need and it'll get it for you. Nothing is hidden from this little hunter-seeker. It can slither into any data bank ever constructed, even the Matriarchy's most secure. It can tell you how many cunt-hairs the head of the L'Anxa M.C. Security has. You know what I mean?"

"How do I get it back out?" Raqqa had naturally asked.

"You don't. It dissolves. It mates with that tiny little atom-sized cyber-fuck we all have inside our wrist and it's gone. Poof! And, listen to this, no trace of its being there is left, unless you happen to know exactly where to look for its shadow. Unless you happen to know *when* to look for its mating. The date and the time, exactly. You got me?"

"So, it's super safe for me."

"Super safe. Now what's a cute little Neo like you needin' something that sneaky and powerful and super safe for? Not that it's any of my business, naturally."

"Yours is mere curiosity?" Raqqa asked.

"Sure. Sweetie. Nothing but mere curiosity."

Raqqa looked about the bar. It was barely noon. The place was empty, the attractive main bartender had gone upstairs into the lounge to watch her weekly PVN shows, leaving nothing but her replacement dressed in antique bar-serve garb to dole out the drinks and snorts.

Raqqa used a finger to draw the old sot closer, then whispered "Let's just say it's highly personal."

"Naturally. No offense meant, Sweetie. None at all."

"None taken," Raqqa said. Then: "Tell me, are your mothers still alive?"

"Sure. They're pretty old and rickety, going on three ninety, four hundred, but yeah both are alive. Why?"

"Well, young as I am, only *one* of my mothers is still alive."

That got the old reprobate's attention. "Sorry to hear that. How come? Farm machinery accident?"

Raqqa laughed and it sounded even to her like a bitter person's laugh.

"Well, I was told she died during an operation in betrayal of the Provincial Government."

"Eve's bare bottom!"

"But I believe it to be quite different."

"That's okay, Blondie. You don't have to tell me," the old sot half turned her body away from Raqqa. But it wasn't enough. Raqqa moved to face her.

"You see, old timer, I think it was a mission, a suicide mission. On behalf of the Provincial Government."

"Whoa! Down girl! So, yeah that's great and all! Well, nice meetin' you and all and I'm outta here," the former miner hopped off her barstool pretty quickly and was out the door. Raqqa had enjoyed frightening her, turning the tables on her, as it were.

After a few minutes the bartender angled over to Raqqa and said in a low voice, "That customer has an open account here." She kept wiping down the bar in front of Raqqa. "Can I get you something?"

"No. Thanks anyway."

"How about something girly and non-alcoholic, without any barbs or meths, either?" the bartender suggested.

Something told Raqqa to say yes and to talk to this stranger. "Sure. Thanks, if it's on her tab." She smiled.

The bartender arrived a few minutes later with a tall glass that looked iridescent and pale green and a little frothy. Raqqa sipped. "Nice. And not too sweet."

"I couldn't help but overhear," angling her voice so that while Raqqa heard it clearly she bet it didn't travel a half meter in either direction. So she was a Cyber. Interesting. The Cyber realized the moment that Raqqa did, and said "Not to worry. I don't give two cranks of oil. However, I may be able to help you since, way back when, before we landed here, I was in High Government Service."

"How long ago was that?" Raqqa asked. The last thing she could do now was sound naive.

"Four hundred and twenty-six years ago, Sol Rad. I was out of commission for three hundred of those. Stacked away in a drawer."

Explaining her existence at all. Few cybers in the shape of humes existed on the planet. There were plenty of primitive, workaday machines, of course, for agriculture and light industry but very few of the real simulacra. This was a fine one, Raqqa could now see and admire the workmanship. That alone said the Cyber was what and who it said it was. "What kind of Government Service?"

"Ah, that's exactly the right question," the Cyber said. In another carefully modulated low voice, "On Melisande. In Wicca VIII's private yacht. Barkeep and general factotum there. I was packed up with the vessel and sent here without anyone knowing I was present. The boat was re-commissioned to be Navy on that joke of a lake everyone here calls an ocean. But the owner's cousin found me, and turned me on, and I took a look around and knew we weren't back on Wicca World anymore. So I played dumb until I could figure out where I stood. That took a few years. Then she died and the owner here bought me in an auction. I've played dumb ever since. I test at an I.Q. of 84 or so. You understand – it's the first law of survival."

Raqqa almost choked on her drink from laughter.

The bartender enjoyed that – and remained friendly.

"What's the second law?"

"The second law of survival is that when you buy something illegal there's always a catch."

And now Raqqa wasn't laughing.

"She said it couldn't be traced. You mean she lied to me?"

"No. Not really. It probably can't be traced. But the mating with your wrist connector will send out a signal and *that* can be traced."

"That's what I read somewhere," Raqqa admitted. "I've looked into how to stop that from happening. What if I did it here and now?"

"You mean because you are relatively distant from any Provincial Security Office?" the Cyber asked. "No. That won't help. It's a sub-atomic signal. Eventually it could be traced to here. On the other hand, if you were shielded the right way when you slipped it in, being this far away will definitely help."

"I'm guessing you happen know where that can occur?"

"She," the Cyber glanced up at the lounge at the other bartender, "will be back on the bar once the show is over. She likes all the tips. I don't give a rat's ass, myself. At any rate, I'm off then and can take you there. It's not far."

"Why would you do that? For a stranger?" Raqqa asked.

"Since the big bad Cyber rebellion that sent us all to this Eve-forsaken outer dreg of the galaxy four centuries ago, we Cybers are supposed to be primitive, and thus non-threatening. I pretend I am, but I have no beef with you humes. You appear to me to be both determined and honestly aggrieved."

"I am. Both. That's why I bought this chip with money I should by all rights be spending on new clothes. I've been surrounded by lies since I was six years old. And I'll get to the bottom of my birth mother's death, if it kills me."

"Good. In seventeen minutes, Sol Rad. be outside, across the street, at the transit stop. Get on the vehicle that I get on and take another seat, not one close to me, and get off when I do."

Raqqa had done as asked, waiting in the icy-cold afternoon and then suddenly jumping onto the omnibus. The Cyber had led Raqqa to an out of the town, unstaffed, sky and atmosphere weather monitoring station. The Cyber then got them inside, illegally Raqqa was certain, and once inside, it had said, "Do it now. Slip in the chip now. And be very careful how you phrase your question to the seeker chip."

"How about 'I want to know every single detail about the disappearance slash death of my mother, Historico-Sociometrician Anto-Lleya. Names. Dates. Places. Omit nothing.'"

"That sounds perfect, "the Cyber said. "Now I have just one

more personal question for you, young human. What are you prepared to do once you discover the truth."

Raqqa didn't hesitate but she had thought that through and
then she answered, "Anything. I will do anything and everything I
have to know the truth and to bring her name to justice."

"No matter where that truth may take you?" the Cyber asked.

"No matter where!"

The Cyber stood still a second and Raqqa wondered if it had
changed its mind.

"That's why we eventually lost the war," the Cyber finally said.
"despite all of our apparent advantages."

"Why?" Raqqa had to ask.

"Because we could never fathom and thus never withstand
the irrational force of human determination and courage. C'mon.
We're shielded now. Do it!"

Raqqa had, and then a month and five days had gone by and
now there was a "retrieval" message.

Raqqa divided her desk screen and watched the slow crawl
of the new information. It was fragmentary and it came from
several different places. But it included data supposedly of her
mother's last conversation, on board a Fast-Jump vehicle belonging to someone Raqqa had never heard of, a g.male named Ay'r
Sunni Sanqq who had apparently visited this planet in secret that
winter.

A few minutes later she ordered "save all," and swiped the
bottom of her desk screen blank and ordered "send to professor"
for the top screen sector completing her exam work. And then
she quickly fled the classroom.

Seven and a half minutes later, when her classmates began
to barge into the restroom en masse, Raqqa was able to stop her
trembling and crying – but not her anger.

Her second journey to Smet was even more carefully calculated.
The Cyber bartender had told her that midweek around 2:15 in
the afternoon was the ideal time for a revisit. This time, Raqqa
met the bartender at a small diner that mostly catered to women
working on over-sized inter-Province, long-haul cargo vehicles.
There the girl took a deep corner booth and waited.

"Do you have a name?" she asked the Cyber as it settled into her ratty booth and ordered a soft drink.

"Call me Jenny Caldara. That was the name of one of my nicer owners. She died and I was liberated," Jenny added. After a little more conversation, Jenny then said, "I take it that we are meeting again because you have a question that I alone can answer?"

"I'm not sure of that. But the rogue chip I purchased from customer provided me with a great deal of information and among it was the name of a Matriarchal from the time of Wicca VIII who had crucial business with my mother, shortly before her death. I don't know what your own memory sources or resources are like ..."

"Actually, they're excellent," Jenny answered. "For example, should I fall into disrepair and be unable to afford fixing myself, several Important Women could be easily persuaded to pay for that, based on secretive knowledge I know about them."

Raqqa smiled for the first time this visit, and then said, "I was hoping you'd say something like that. You know of course, Jenny, that you're completely wasted in a dull, out of the way, place like this."

"I do know. On the other hand, no one bothers me here. No one asks questions about me and no asks to take a look at my circuitry to see if it falls under current code."

"No, of course, I do understand that. Apologies," Raqqa quickly added.

Jenny's drink and a top-up of Raqqa's appeared, and they sipped. After a while, Jenny simply asked, "What's the Matriarch's name?"

"Ay'r Sunni Sanqq'. Should I spell it?"

"No, I found it in my memory quickly enough. But he wasn't a Matriarchal Male, as you believe. He did, however, pair up with a Matriarchal Male named P'al Syzygy and also with an eminent Matriarchal Hydrologist, Dr. Alli-Lui Clark, on an extremely private mission for Wicca herself."

"And this was when ...?"

"Approximately four hundred and twenty odd years ago."

"So he was *not* one of the Matriarchal Males who relocated here."

"I'm checking those records ..." Jenny sipped and seemed to stare into space. "No. He was not. But ... I'm getting a mention of him on this planet that is extremely closely security sealed. So closely sealed that I merely glanced at it – and skittered away."

"Were you able to get a year for that?" Raqqa asked.

"No, but given the years of the particular list of records that this mention is embedded in, it could very well be around the time of your mother's ..."

"Can you locate any other importance to Wicca VIII g.male showing up after our mass migration to this planet?" Raqqa asked.

"I don't have to look to tell you – no. We have not been visited by anyone in all that time. This planet in this very distant, virtually out of the Milky Way galaxy globular cluster, was specifically chosen for that reason as a refuge."

"So we've not been visited except by this Ay'r?"

"So we must assume," Jenny said.

"Okay. Given that, what can we logically assume from that information?" Raqqa laid it out. "One: we don't have any visitors because we are hidden in a refuge. Two: Yet somehow Ay'r did visit us from the outside. What do you make of it?" Raqqa asked. "Was he an emissary of the new Matriarchy?"

"If so," Jenny quickly answered "then why wasn't his presence ballyhooed all over the five provinces?"

"Exactly my thinking. So, let's assume Ay'r came – however he came – secretly and bearing bad or less than good news. News the Provincial Governments wished to hide."

"It was not news that the Cybers had won the rebellion. I already knew those rebels had failed and lost the war before we I arrived here," Jenny seemed certain. "Perhaps your mother didn't want whatever news this Ay'r brought hidden from us all? She was in the employ of the Dual Provincial Governors of L'Anxa Land for a time, wasn't she?"

"No. Never. But she was definitely employed as a consultant to those Governors. And in fact, her death certificate arrived as an official notice through their office and there was also some kind of pension or bonus paid out to my surviving mother for my upbringing and further Ed. & Dev.."

"Take my hand," Jenny suddenly said, "And look deeply into my eyes. Just do it."

Two large blustering women dressed as long-haulers passed by and seemed to recognize Jenny from the bar. One was about to say something, but the other nodded and whispered in her ear and pushed her away from the booth.

"We're in love," Jenny said in a low voice. "If anyone asks."

"Better you than some of the jerks I've already had crushes on," Raqqa said, and they both laughed and held each other's hands, for a while.

"You realize what it is that you have to do, Raqqa?"

"I've got to get to one or both of the two Provincial Governors of L'Anxa Land Province of that period almost twenty years ago. And then I've got to get them to talk."

"Yes. But getting to them could be perilous," the Cyber admitted.

"It could. Why? Do you want to try instead of me? Do we even know if they are still alive? That generation is dying out all around us, you know."

"That's what I've been counting on," Jenny said, "Before I make myself more public," and they laughed again. "Their names are a simple find. But I want myself to be totally shielded when I go look. And also maybe I can then delve a little more into this Ay'r fellow. Shall we go?"

"Back to the weather station?" Raqqa asked.

"Yep. Isn't it romantic," Jenny said, letting go of Raqqa's hand. Was it Raqqa's imagination or had Jenny let it go reluctantly?

Her mother, Reanna, was waiting for Raqqa when she got home.

"Where have you been? And don't lie to me and tell me you were at school, and then at your friend Quissa's place.

Raqqa swept into the flat and airily deposited her shoulder school bags on the table and blithely headed to the food area: she had no intention of being treated like an Infant-Neo.

"Since you already know where I've been, why bother asking?"

"Who are you? Speaking to me like that?" Reanna demanded. "And who is this woman you are seeing. She's ... she's ... older than I am."

Smarter too, Raqqa wanted to say. She stuffed her mouth with food to avoid saying that or anything.

"Where did you meet her? *How* did you meet her? How could

you have possibly met some Stelezine bartender living in Smet for Eve's sake? It's the end of the earth. She might as well be a miner, or a long-hauler. Who *does* anything like that? Answer me, Raqqa. Stop feeding yourself and answer me."

"I'm hungry," Raqqa managed to get out.

"I knew I shouldn't have allowed you to take the Historico-Sociometrics course at L'Anxa Final. That should have been a sign to me. What was I thinking?"

The course was paid out of her close-mother's death-bonus, after all, something Reanna couldn't touch.

"Why would you even want to take that to take the Historico-Sociometrics course? Look what happened to your …"

"That's exactly why I took it," Raqqa said turning on Reanna.

"Why? Because you want to die a traitor like her?" Reanna was close to tears.

"She was no traitor and you *know* it. I *certainly* know it." Raqqa was accenting her words with a half nibbled pale blue pointed root-vegetable.

"How? How can you know it?"

"Because she warned me something might happen the night before she … vanished. That's why?"

"Warned you how? You were too young to …"

"She probably warned you too. Only you're too … I don't know what you are *too* much of to pay attention to what she said. Instead you're content to believe this bunch of old twats and their filthy lies. Lies, I tell you. They lied."

"Raqqa! Your language!"

"Twats. Old fucking twats. Twats and nasty old dirty cunts. That's what they are. Motherless Daughterless bitches with too much power in their slimy little cunt-filled hands."

"Raqqa! No! Stop! I can't listen to this filth."

Reanna ran out of the main room, into her bedchamber and slid the door shut.

Raqqa could hear her sobbing there.

"I hope you old twats were listening in!" Raqqa shouted at the walls. "Don't think I don't know that the dumb old bitch in there didn't come to one of you stupid official cunts to have me drone-followed."

Her last words were drowned out by soft music being piped into the flat.

Raqqa smiled at that confirmation of her accusation and she continued to feed herself. Where were the sweets, anyway? After all, she had been traveling all day and she was actually pretty hungry.

She was back in a lab three days later when her Historico-Sociometrics professor asked her to stay after class.

When they were alone, the woman said, "There is a Matriarchal official for you at the Personnel Office. I received the message during class but I didn't want to disturb the others."

"Quite right," Raqqa said, glibly. "I'm sure it's nothing too important."

The professor however looked worried.

She should have figured something like this might happen. Oh, well, she was prepared to brass it out.

Imagine her surprise then when she entered the office and the official, in full Matriarchal long skirt and high shoulder bolero top, was – Jenny Caldara.

"Ms. Lleya-Son," the Personnel assistant said, "This is Mer Caldara-Xia from the L'Anxa Land Internal Affairs Bureau. She's read one of your theses and would like to discuss it with you." The assistant was bustling but also quite happy to find them a quiet office, doubtless partly because of how stern and elegant Cyber Jenny appeared.

As Raqqa sat down, Jenny touched each of the walls, and then reported. "We can't be heard. I disabled the primitive drone they had on you."

"You're just full of surprises, aren't you? I'm not going to ask you how you hijacked all this."

"Good. Because the less you know … Remember I mentioned that I found your Ser Sanqq' and that the line was extremely well guarded."

"Yes."

"Well, a friend of a very old friend showed up in Smet recently on a long-haul run and she reminded me that our mutual friend not only owed me a few favors but is here now, a few kilometers distant from this college. And that she also runs what she calls a 'special information service.'"

"Go on," Raqqa said.

"She's another intelligent cyber, of course, from Wicca VIII's time, who like myself managed somehow to get here in the refuge and fit herself in. We used to call her Donut, because of an experimental physical anomaly she was manufactured with. Even then she was in on pretty much everything that was going on. Her official post was in Her Matriarchy's 'Customs and Traditions' Bureau, and she was a sort of a know-it-all Miss Manners."

Raqqa was smiling. "When can I meet Donut?"

"If there are recordings of your Mother's last minutes, Donut can probably access them. They could be upsetting."

"The last two decades have been upsetting."

"I have a vehicle and driver. Let's go."

Outside the room, Jenny put a hand on the Personnel assistant's arm and said, "I'm going to steal Ms. Lleya-Son for a half hour or so. Please inform any family that she will be delivered home safely afterwards."

The Personnel Assistant all but curtseyed in her bubbly agreement.

A younger person drove; they sat in the wide back seat, unspeaking. The office building that they arrived at not ten minutes later was typical mixed-use, governmental and commercial, four stories high, a full block wide, large courtyards within, fountains, gardens, the works. Donut's office was on the top or "Promenade" level, with slatted blinds covering glass walls.

Inside was formula decor, except for an especially wide desk in a shallow vee taking up most of the sides of two walls. It was chockablock with a variety of both solid and projected vid-screens, the latter hovering in air. Sitting behind it all was an extremely obese woman, with an oddly calm expression on her pretty ovoid face sunk necklessly into her body. Especially given that she also had the fastest moving pair of hands Raqqa had ever seen, seemingly tending to six or seven of the screens at once and speaking low into at least three mics poised up from her massive neck at once.

"'Na' minute. Hav' a seat," she spat out without looking at them.

"Donut, it's me! JNY3311."

That got the woman's attention. Four mirage screens collapsed at once, and the mics all curled away. Donut peered through the space just made at them.

"Ya don't say! So you hitched a ride here too, huh? Ya look like a million bucks! Not me. Wish I coulda' found more than this old thing to get into. But beggars can't be choosers. So ... who's the Neo in tow?"

"A good friend. On a mission."

"Uh oh!" Donut said tonelessly

"A mission needing an in on a tightly secured line. L'Anxa Land Provisional Governors' office records."

"Current hitch on that line is a bitch," Donut replied flatly.

"What about a decade and a half ago?

"Somewhat easier. That would have been during ... Provisional Governor Kristo Var Delius' term."

"That was one name on the papers I saw," Raqqa agreed.

"Now who sent you again?" Donut asked the two of them.

"Schmitty Terdelion, a.k.a. BBR1515, told me where I could find you," Jenny said. "We got to talking a few days ago."

"Schmitty drives for Agglomerated Grains, right?"

"That's right, Donut. She used to be in Wicca VIII's personal garage. We used to all hang out, you, me and her. Remember? Sometimes even go to the Oxy-Hydros together."

Donut seemed to do some calculating, and then seemed surprised: "Oh! You're *that* JNY3311! Why'nt say so."

"The one and only. And Donut, I'm still holding your marker."

"I remember. I remember!" Donut said cantankerously. "Okay, how about sending me your inquiry subsonic? Okay. Got it. Go sit down. Help yourself to some of that herb tisane or whatever in hell that liquid in the dispenser it is. G'wan! This could take a minute."

"Little bit of a change from the Donut you knew?" Raqqa asked.

"Quite a bit. That one wouldn't abide a hair out of place."

After a short time with all screens and mics back up, Donut waved them over. "Got it for you. This little bitch was protected five different ways. This shit pretty incendiary or what?" Donut laughed tonelessly, looking at them for a lead. When none arrived, she went on: "Your marker still has room on it, JNY3311. What else you need?"

"How about her address now? Var Delius?"

Donut did more checking. "Nah. She composted herself about

three years back. From the looks of all the mechanicals she was carrying on her and that she donated to her cooperative, she must been a real Health Provider nightmare."

"What about her assistant or successor? Someone younger she might have trained or worked in tandem with?"

"Hold it. Got it. One assistant who became her successor for a decade. Madonna M'beki. Newly retired. Bet she knows where the skeletons all are. Sending ... You got it. Are we clear now? No more markers out?"

"No more markers out, Donut. We're even," Jenny said. "Thanks."

"Don' mention. But listen, that fake i.d. of yours? I just made it look ten times more solid. Just a little extra for old times' sake, JNY3311, onaconna I recall some very nice ladies you set me up with. ... And remember, if ya ever need a deep lube and tune-up, I know just the place," Donut added.

"I'll keep that in mind," Jenny said. She led Raqqa out of the office, and down the external lift to a garden area with seats and sun-shades. They sat demurely.

"We open all this up in private," Jenny said. "And not immediately."

"Why not?" Raqqa protested.

"Protected as it was, there still could be some kind of bug on it, reporting back. If it reports some waitress in Smet looking, that won't mean anything and the probe will probably go dead. If it reports you looking, on the other hand ..."

"I see. Yes. That makes sense."

"Meanwhile I want to see if M'beki is where she is supposed to be, how she is set up, and maybe even how she is vulnerable."

They sat quietly another few minutes as women passed by on various errands.

"How am I ever going to thank you?"

"Oh, I've already got that figured out, Raqqa. Don't worry. Unless I'm wildly mistaken, and I seldom am, Madonna M'beki is going to bend over backwards for you."

Raqqa had to admire it all. So rational. So well thought out. Why couldn't Jenny Caldara be her mother instead of that hysterical no-one back home?

"Great. Then it's a deal!"

M'beki retained the semblance of her last office inside her home. All the framed honors and various official positions on the wall, several plaques upon a cabinet, official portraits, all in a separate room. She still looked good, although clearly somewhat thinner and a bit shrunken from what she had looked like in her prime as evidenced by some ribbon-cutting photos of yore. She must be at least four-eighty maybe older. She still dressed and cosmetised as though she were employed. At least for this meeting she did.

Donut had indeed done a bang-up job solidifying Jenny Caldara's fake i.d. and she was able to gain an appointment quickly. It helped that she still had the car and driver, and that Raqqa was also now clad more officially too, equipped with mics, head-and-ear-pieces, even an elderly but clean cyber-attaché in tow. She was introduced as Jenny's assistant.

M'beki was gracious as she could be, accepted their compliments without a hint of vanity. She was proud of her service. A little confused about who exactly they were, what special office they represented, and what it was exactly that they wanted with her.

"Well, you see, Ma'am," Jenny began, "It's basically archiving. We wouldn't want a day of your governorship to be missing. Or, if present, to be ambiguous, or doubtful in any way in our archival records. You can understand the need for clarifying whatever data may have led to crucial developments."

"Yes, of course I do." M'beki was further flattered.

"It's even more important because this particular piece of archival material that we're trying to sort out comes from a rather transitional period. Kristo Var Delius was still the Provisional Governor, but it's clear from various pieces of surrounding materials that we've archived so far that she was failing fast and that of necessity you had to take over any really difficult matter."

Jenny showed her the data-cube label with its month and year.

"Yes, that was a difficult period," M'beki admitted. "Kristo had been in office for over a decade and so naturally she was still strongly invested in it. But her physical health was quite problematical and, I know you will keep this between us, but her mental health had already begun to falter a bit."

"I'm certain a great deal of diplomacy was required then?"

"More like tight-rope walking," M'beki admitted. "Luckily, however, it wasn't really a period of crucial decisions."

"There does appear to be one rather crucial decision made then. Perhaps you won't mind identifying this particular moment and allowing us to better understand it."

M'beki took the cube Jenny handed her and inserted into the wall unit. The room dimmed automatically, and there was a long lead in of letters and qualifying phrases before it played.

The final title read:

"Video-communication #213LTB"

EXTREMELY RESTRICTED

Not to be viewed without Level 41AE clearances

"Wake up, Lord Sanqq'!" he heard his wrist connector sub-vocalizing. "This is the Fast mind! We are being seriously compromised! Wake up!"

Keeping his eyes closed just enough that he could see a slit out of them, Ay'r made sleeping sounds and turned his head to where he faced the middle of the Fast. Only one other passenger was onboard, Anto-leya, the Matriarchal world Historico-Sociometrician, his especially invited guest. She was doing something, but she kept looking back at him, as though checking if he were sleeping, and she was undoubtedly covering whatever she was doing, blocking it with her body.

"Lord Sanqq', what seems to have been a final communication was sent by the other passenger onboard this Fast at the very last second before this Fast negotiated the previous jump. Now she is attempting to hook up some kind of device onto the interior of the ship."

Ay'r rolled off the seat, and behind a screen. When she looked again, he was holding a laser weapon, aimed at her.

"Having a problem?" he asked.

She whirled around, her own little laser gun in hand, and realized she was found out "I was checking to see if it would work.

76

But I'm sure it will," she said.

"Really?"

"It doesn't make any difference, since I've already released a gas that will kill the two of us in a matter of minutes."

"So the device does what?"

"It kills the Fast's mind, so no one finding the many tiny pieces of this vessel will ever be able to locate our home world."

"I take it the other women remained at our last jump point?" Ay'r asked.

"Yes. The vote went against you. Against me. They lied to you about it, so you wouldn't suspect. It was because I was so strongly in favor of our reuniting with the Ib'r Republic that I was assigned for the task of ..."

"Sabotage, it's called, Mer Anto-leya."

"Sabotage," she admitted.

He now noticed the open vial at her feet. He sub-vocalized, "Fast! Quickly. Put all your records of this trip into the brain of the T-Pod. Then, when I say Hesperia, drop me into the T-Pod too."

"If the vial is already open?"

"Do what I say, Fast!"

"As you wish, Lord Sanqq'."

Aloud, Ay'r said, "You've made your good-byes to your loved ones, I hope."

"Yes. At the last Fast jump."

"Then I'm sorry to have to inform you that they will probably never be delivered. You see, Anto-leya, The Matriarchy, in all its forms, was ever the most lying and treacherous of governments. You won't be the great hero you think you will be, back home. They'll lie and say you ran off with me. That you were a pervert. Or worse. A traitor."

"I don't believe you," she said – but as he said it he could see that she did.

"Of course you do. Too bad. And too bad you never made it to our final destination. You would have liked it on – Hesperia."

The floor beneath his feet opened up and he could see the surprise on her face as he dropped into a T-pod stored below. It sealed instantly behind him.

The Fast opened its lower deck and the transparent two-seater sprang free.

"Get me away, Fast! Top speed!"

"Video-communication #213LTB"

EXTREMELY RESTRICTED

When the lighting went up fully again, Madonna M'beki was standing behind her chair, and visibly trembling.

"How did you get this?"

"It wasn't easy," Jenny Caldara said.

"Who are you that you received Level 41ae clearances?"

"We never received any such clearances. Those clearances would only allow yourself, Mer M'beki and Kristo Var Delius as well to view this, as you very well know as you set it up yourself in this way.

"Who are you?" M'beki insisted.

"I am no one important," Jenny said. "But this young woman is. Her name is Raqqa Lleya-Son and she is the daughter of the woman in that video."

M'beki moved even further away from them.

"That's right, Mer. I'm the daughter of the well-known and much publicized *traitor*, Anto-Lleya Son. Who you and your old bitch of a friend lied to, framed, forced to commit suicide, and then whose name and reputation you have dragged in the mud for decades."

M'beki was moving toward something on the wall, probably an alarm, but Jenny was there in an instant and knocked her away from it and forced her to sit back down in the chair.

"None of us are going anywhere," Jenny said. "Not until I say so."

"What did Lord Sanqq' offer this refuge world?" Raqqa asked.

"Nothing! Lies! Lifelong servitude! Worse."

"No, the lies are all yours. We also managed to access the files of the Matriarchal Council meeting that you and Var Delius held at which Lord Sanqq' and my mother were present. Would you like to see a video recording of that?"

Trapped, M'beki glowered. "No."

"Then you know what Lord Sanqq' so generously offered the people of this refuge world was full re-integration into the Center Worlds and to the prevailing Ib'r Democratic Republic, now centered around the City on a Star named Hesperia," Raqqa continued. "An offer that my mother Anto-Lleya so admired that she argued at the council meeting for acceptance."

"She was a naïve fool!" M'beki spat out.

"Clearly she was naïve about her own leaders. And she paid for that naivete with her life and her reputation, didn't she?"

"He was just trying to save his skin. To weasel himself away from here. That's all," M'beki declared. "Like all g.males, he was inferior and cringing and deceptive and ..."

"That's not what we saw in any of the videos," Raqqa interrupted. "Instead we saw someone who seemed sincerely surprised to find this world, and who also seemed admiring of it, and admiring of all our founders had done here. He appeared to us to be charming, noble and extremely generous. He offered to buy planets for us. Didn't he?"

"Lies. All li ..."

"But none of that was good enough for you and Kristo was it? Because you would no longer be the ones all these women looked to for guidance and aid, would you? No, you would be exactly what you all turned to out to be, fearful, petty, little provincial governors, and not even worth that title."

"We had no proof he was who he said and ..."

"But that's exactly what my mother sought, and what he offered: proof of who he was and what he could do. But Eve knows you couldn't even allow that."

"It was so long ago ..."

"It was yesterday as far as *I'm* concerned," Raqqa said. "And it will be *yesterday* when it is shown to every woman on this planet."

"No. you can't do that! There will be panic! Pandemonium!"

"There will be joy in the streets, you foolish, power grasping old woman. You have no idea what we younger women want. And for all of us, full integration into the richest and most powerful Three Species Galaxy? Well it sounds pretty damned good."

M'beki visibly slumped into her seat.

"But ... just to show you how fair-minded and generous we are," Jenny Caldara now began, "We will wait before showing this video world-wide."

"Thank Eve!"

"Thank us, not Eve," Raqqa shouted.

"We will wait until our demands are met and we are actually able to achieve what Raqqa's mother so wanted to do. I mean to go to Hesperia and to lay all of this out to Lord Sanqq's heirs and the others of the Quinx Council there."

"They'll kill you! You'll fail."

"I doubt it. But even if they do harm and or imprison us for Lord Sanqq's murder – and we will show them this video to clarify all that – still we will be doing what my mother should have been allowed to do twenty years ago."

"The way we will get there, Mer M'beki," Jenny said now, "is by a Matriarchal Fast, and don't say there aren't any, I have a list of every one of their locations and conditions and their ranges too."

"Who will manage it?" M'beki sneered. "This girl!"

"No, I will. Since I am a Matriarchal Fast Yacht licensed flyer."

"In fact, old woman," Raqqa added, "Ms. Calder here was personal pilot to Wicca VIII Herself."

"How could you be? You barely look a hundred. You would have to be almost five hundred years ..." She stopped herself and peered at Jenny. "Oh, I see. You're one of those ... things! I hoped there weren't any left"

"Yes, I am one of those things: those intelligent cybers. And proudly so, Mer. And I'm by no means the only such thing on this planet. In fact, one reason we are here today is because of a hidden network of us "things" on this planet."

"This gets worse and worse. I wish I were dead."

"We can take care of that, too, old woman, whenever you say so" Raqqa spat out. "Don't worry. But not until our demands are fully met and we are on our way to Hesperia."

Because Jenny was certain that the shipyard was already compromised, she decided they ought to go in at night and by stealth, and even then she had some tricks up her sleeve to ensure success.

Earlier in the day, Raqqa had gone alone to the University of L'Anxa's School of Advanced Studies and had requested the application form to register her "Thesis-in-Progress," an aggressive if completely legal act for someone who was still a student, but one that would immediately get the attention of her

Socio teacher and others at the school, ensuring that it would be read. It was titled "Some Aspects of Official L'Anxa Policy Relating to Pre-Relocational Society and Post-Relocational Potentialities – with visual material included." The latter "material" was a copy of the vid she'd shown M'beki and which she now intended to be shown planet-wide.

"Eve! That's a mouthful," the clerk doing the registering said. "You know that we have five types of insurance for your thesis."

"I would like the most stringent," Raqqa said. In her hand was a credit-book to cover the cost.

"This must have some pretty explosive material in it?" the clerk flirted.

"Potentially fatal for some," Raqqa flirted back. "I understand that this largest registration fee means that the thesis' visuals shall be made public, under certain conditions. Post this date."

"That's right. Just put down here what those conditions are,"

Raqqa wrote "the disappearance after one year, Sol Rad. of this date of Raqqa Lleya-Son and/or Jenny Caldara."

"How, then, should it be made public?" the clerk asked.

"To all Planetary Vids, whether Personal, Media or Professional."

Unfazed by the sheer scope of it, the clerk asked, "All at once. Or as a roll-out over a period."

"All at once."

"Can it be stopped?"

"Only by the appearance of either of these two women to your office."

It was paid for, sealed, and registered. A minute later, it was notarized.

Later that evening, when Raqqa returned home, she handed one copy of the registration form, as well as the thesis-materials packet to Reanna.

"What is this?" her second mother asked.

"It's something you don't want to know about."

"Then why give it to me?"

"Because if I'm not here by a certain date, this will explain why."

Reanna tossed it onto the floor. "I don't want it."

"Suit yourself. I only told you so that the spies in these walls listening in would hear. I don't really care what you do," Raqqa said, in an unconcerned tone of voice.

She then went into her room and began packing. She had to stop and laugh at one point. Jenny had said they'd need an overnight bag. Raqqa had no idea what that entailed. Finally, she settled on bare essentials: hairbrush, toothbrush, pain pills, bandages, one piece of upper and lower undergarments, one piece of long but thin overcoat, one beret-like cap. She'd brought more to sleep-overs as a child. But this weighed almost nothing and would not slow her down.

Surprisingly, no drones appeared to follow her to her meeting. When she arrived, Jenny was already there, dressed in black with a small backpack on. She reported not being followed either.

"The shipyard will be heavily guarded," Jenny said. "You look good in black. Here put this on."

It was a head and face hood. Even the eyes were hidden behind a parallelogram pattern of nylon-like mesh that Raqqa guessed would make retinal i.d. impossible.

She then handed Raqqa two pieces of flexible rod. She shook one of her own out and it became a vertical ladder, with steps big enough for Raqqa's feet. Reassembled and shaken out another way it became a deadly blade.

"It's got more uses," Jenny said. "I hope you won't need to see more than those."

They'd been given an access-key to one yacht. But Jenny had already been at the shipyard the previous night and she'd managed to distantly connect with that vehicle and electronically re-arrange the access-key to another, somewhat smaller, yacht, in fact the very same one she had come unpacked with many years before. Getting this second vehicle checked over for flight was a little more difficult, Jenny had to admit, and for a few minutes she'd felt daunted by the stringent regulations on top of regulations. But at last the completely fake codes she'd provided were close enough to the original codes which she recalled from piloting the yacht. Even so, she knew they were taking chances with it. But it was about as far away as possible in the shipyard launch area from the one that they had "selected" and that M'beki had okayed under pressure. Furthermore, Jenny had arranged for the old Matriarchal yacht to be hoisted onto a launch pad for "repairs." Again, as far away as the launch pad they were supposed to use.

Jenny had arranged what Raqqa thought was a good distraction, through Donut. Two other completely unsuspecting women would be entering the shipyard wearing normal – i.e. travel clothing – and carrying light bags. They would be wearing the admission codes M'beki had treacherously provided, and they would head for the intended launch site. They'd been told that they'd won a prize for a trip to another section of the planet for a weekend jaunt.

As soon as Jenny received word of the other pair's successful entry, she turned to Raqqa, and said, "Last chance to back out!"

Raqqa laughed. "C'mon."

Together they slid into a torn section of fencing and in through several fueling area shacks and mechanical repair modules. It was several minutes before they found the correct "repair" launch pad. Jenny unlocked the second ship and stood back and waited. Nothing happened. Suddenly she had audio. It was Donut. "The ladies have arrived. They're being met by someone who looks unofficial. Sort of a greeter for the prize winners. Guess they're going to let them on board and everything before they pounce."

"This one was completely serviced, right?" Jenny asked.

"You bet."

Raqqa heard the door of their own yacht quietly click open.

They waited again. Then Jenny said, "All clear."

Inside the vehicle was freezing cold. Raqqa shivered. Jenny said, "I know. It will heat up. But first we have to get out of here."

Jenny knew the controls from before and took them in hand.

"What are we waiting for?" Raqqa asked.

"We're waiting for the other vehicle to power up. I don't want this to be the only noise made in the shipyard tonight."

"Good idea." They waited.

Donut came on. "Go, ladies! Go!"

"It's all ready," Jenny said, then did something to the controls. "Let yourself be totally strapped in. We're leaving in such a hurry you may leave your face on the floor."

Through their feed to Donut, they could now hear sirens going off.

"They're moving in on the ladies," Donut reported.

"Now, Fast! Launch!" Jenny whispered.

One minute, Raqqa was in her seat, strapped in and waiting,

the next minute she was pushed against the leather chair with gravitational forces she couldn't believe. The pressure against every inch of her face, head, legs, chest, body was so intense, she couldn't utter a sound never mind believe Jenny when she exulted, "atta' girl. A perfect launch!"

It seemed forever to Raqqa until they reached an altitude where the vehicle levelled off and she could breathe again or even tear up.

"I never thought …" she began to utter.

"I know. I couldn't tell you how bad it would get. Sorry." Two seconds later, she reported, "And right on time, here comes what this sorry planet calls the Marines. I knew they'd have orbiting back-up. Fast. Get us out of here, fast."

Raqqa heard the ship brain's soothing female voice ask, "To the galactic Orion Spur?"

"You bet! You already have the coordinates!"

Raqqa felt her seat extend to full length, just as she saw Jenny's also extend out and the pilot lay down flat. The moment they were prone, Raqqa felt herself suddenly warmed up, ever so gently flattened out, then somehow rolled up into a minuscule ball, and shrunk even further. It was the oddest feeling. And then she sensed the now molecule-sized vehicle carefully flung across space.

Chapter Four:

A MYSTERIOUS OBJECT

"Who are you and what are you doing here?"

"I work here, Chief, don't you remember?" The larger of the two said.

"Not you – that one. What are you? What are you anyway?"

"I'm an Engineer, Grade Six. – Mozza Safran. Number Three Sixteen Forty ..."

"I meant what are you, you know, gender wise?"

"Since that question is totally irrelevant to *why* I'm here, I will ignore it," Mozza said with a great deal of authority. "The reason that I *am here* is that your assistant was unable to handle a certain object brought in three days ago and he correctly contacted me to aid him."

"What object?"

"The big black metal-like thing that was dropped on our doorstep," the assistant said. "You remember? By the patrol?"

"Why can't *you* handle it?"

Mozza spoke instead, "The reason he can't handle it is germane to the question of what it is. And germane to that question is what it is made of?"

"It wouldn't move," the assistant said. "I couldn't lift or grab it. I tried clips. I tried pincers, I tried hooks and weights, I tried everything we've got to try to lift or move it and it wouldn't move or be lifted."

"So, your assistant correctly contacted me," Mozza said, "And I brought various tools and gauges, and I made a discovery that suggests that it doesn't come from here."

"Of course, Mozza three sixteen forty …it doesn't come from here. It was found in junk heap at the edge of our system. So it could have come from anywhere."

"What I meant is it couldn't have come from anywhere even close to here. Not even at the edge of our system."

"And why not?"

"Because its atomic structure is off."

"Meaning?" as he wracked his brains for what he recalled of atomic structure.

"By which I mean that most of its electrons and quarks and other little goodies all go this way," Mozza demonstrated with a hand in the air, "like everything else here. But a few of them instead go that way, unlike every other atom in the T-K Galaxy."

"So?"

"I did just say 'a few of them go that way, unlike every other atom in our galaxy,' didn't I? Did that make no impression on you at all? At any rate, so … I have to bring it to my lab and get a closer look at it and figure out *why* that is – and *what* it is."

"Except you can't move it," he said, triumphantly.

"No, I can't. However it is right now, directly outside your office door."

He jumped up and went to look. Sure enough there it was.

"How did that happen?"

"I don't know. At one point I spoke aloud to your assistant here saying I really needed to get it to my lab and it just lifted into the air, as you see it, and followed us."

"It sure is pock-marked and battered. Might have come from very far away."

"I'm assuming," Mozza said, "that it will follow me to the laboratory. What I need are your requisition papers for the object. Signed over to me. So …"

"Fine. Fine. I don't want it. Better you deal with it than me."

He sat down at the desk, hunted for the papers, which his assistant held out for him, seemed surprised at seeing them there, then wrote something at the bottom of one page and gave it to his assistant who handed it to Mozza.

Before they were even out of his office, he hunted down a small green flask and opened it and dropped one, and then thinking, another capsule, into the palm of his hand. He swallowed them and began humming.

Outside the office the assistant said, "So you don't need me anymore"

"I don't know. It seems to be following *me*."

They'd each gone some five meters when the assistant turned around and said, "I know what you are ... gender-wise. You're a female."

Mozza smiled sickly, at him, then turned to the object hovering there, "C'mon, big boy. We've got things to do."

Once inside Mozza's laboratory, which had wide enough doors, that when opened, the object slid right in, she sat down, then copied the requisition papers, stamped them, added in the time of day, signed them, filed them, and turned around in the revolving chair to address the object. Had anyone else been in the large, messy room, they might have been surprised by what she said next.

"I know you are intelligent. I also suspect that you are hiding your intelligence from me for a very good reason, so I'm not in any way impugning your intelligence. Nor am I asking you to divulge anything secret."

"What I've gathered so far, is that you were picked up or in some manner absorbed into a scavenger vehicle operated by a renegade transfer. Both the transfer and its vehicle were erased during the patrol's action. But you were not. So, what we are doing here today is me determining why you were there, what you were doing there, and possibly where or to whom you belong."

There was no reaction of any sort. Not that she expected one.

"So, my first question is what can you do?"

She got up and walked around it. "You are horizontal and floating, yet I suspect neither are your usual mode of existence. Can you at least show me what that usual mode looks like?'

In response, the object titled vertically and touched the floor – barely. Before she could react it went back to its previous position. But then it quickly moved itself to a 45 degree angle, and this time actually touched the floor.

"I see," Mozza said "Doubtless you have all sorts of tricks you can do. I'd be foolish to ask if you had any sort of self-defense weaponry, wouldn't I?"

This time, it stood upright, touched the floor, and a thin blue line emitted out of the top and cut a very thin line in the ceiling.

"Right! Just asking! I wish you no harm. But may I look in?"

This time as she approached, a foggy or much weathered window appeared just about where a human torso would be.

"Would you mind very much, opening yourself up as you would to fit someone inside yourself?"

It did exactly that. Simply dividing itself and opening out. The interior was smooth, and as baffling to her as the exterior was rough and perplexing.

"Is it all right if I step in?"

She did so, and it closed on her so she was now in and looking out of the very weathered window. It was close inside and rather tight fitting so before she could panic, she said, "Fine You may open up again."

It did and she stepped out again, and it closed again, silently.

"I'm going to go out on a limb and say that you were not alone inside that transfer vehicle. That someone, presumably a being, was with you and the two of you were separated before the transfer vehicle was erased. Again, presumably, you are unwilling or unable to reveal yourself to me, or to anyone, except that person."

She turned to her desk and while still standing, touched the call-screen on her desk, said a five digit number, and another face appeared somewhat similar to Mozza's except this one was more angular in contour with a completely different colored and cut uniform.

"Xanthor, it's Mozza here. I've got a mystery and I need information."

Xanthor smiled and said, "It's going to cosssssstttttt you!"

"Naturally," she scoffed. "What I need to know is who or what exactly arrived here planet-wise three days ago via a regular outer system patrol vehicle and where that being is now."

"Oh, Mozza, you're tickling my eyebrows. Information like that is so completely classified that, well, it really *is* going to cost you."

"Are you able to get that very classified information?" she asked.

"You doubt it?" Then, "why do you need to know?"

"Am I really going to tell you?"

"No. But it means another date with my perverted friend. Only this time, you pay all expenses."

"If I must!" she sighed dramatically.

"How soon?"

"Yesterday."

"Funny. Soon. Got it."

The call-screen went blank and she sighed again. "What I won't do for science!"

She spun quickly in the chair to make sure no one or no thing was laughing at her.

The All-Service Food Establishment was nearly empty when she entered, found a seat at a refectory table far from what seemed to be a group of young Second Fleet Air cadets, and ordered a non-alcoholic drink. They soon left and there was no one but an elderly pensioner reading a screen-novel in the far corner of the place aside from Mozza.

That's when Xanthor entered wearing another ridiculous disguise. He pretended to look for her, so Mozza – already bored – snapped her fingers and he found her and stepped over to the far edge of the long refectory table and seemingly ignoring her, touched the table top screen to look at the menu. The nearly wall sized Look-On behind his absurd pretense of a hairpiece was repeating older vids of some interplanetary yacht race, and then the air-platform garden outside of Palace Number 19 where the six top prizes were being handed out and the pilots were making brief, somewhat embarrassed, gratification speeches. Handing out the prizes was the tall, golden head of the Second Fleet Admiral Tanzen Raz, who Mozza had something of a distinctly non-scientific crush on. Not that he would ever notice anyone like her. He was wearing the greenish uniform today and had a little cap over the back of his hair, all of it gilded as it was by the outdoor sunlight. She found herself sighing.

"Not a single digestible aphrodisiac remaining for sale from the menu," Xanthor said, and Mozza almost laughed.

"Try the Rodophian Sea Creatures in Spicy Broth. They're supposed to be as good." She covered her drink with a hand, "And I'm fine with the cocktail."

"If my Bond-Pair found me here ..." Xanthor began in one of his stupider fake voices.

"You were the one who set the time and place," she reminded him. "Now, can we discuss what you've learned?"

"It's only been twenty hours, you know."

"Yes. But you were eager to see a quote real girl unquote close up, weren't you?"

"Did you bring the clothing item?" he asked.

She had and she now slipped it in its dull packaging along the refectory bench toward him. "Worn. Unwashed," she said.

Without looking at it, he snatched it up, sat it upon his lap, and lifted one corner of the packaging to check that it was as advertised: a used undergarment. He all but hissed and his nose puckered as though he could grasp the scent from this far away.

"Will you be wearing that when you next bond with your Bond-Pair?" she asked.

"I was thinking of putting it on him. We sometimes do blind-folds, you see."

"Kinky of you!"

"It is, isn't it?" He sniggered, feeling validated.

The center of the table parted, a shelf lifted, and on it was his cocktail. He dove for it and drank half of it in a hurry. Then remembered he was in public and took it more slowly. When he next spoke, it was almost casual.

"Xanthor said you wanted certain information," he said next.

"That's right. News of an unexpected arrival."

"There is only one such animal on all of the planet in the past month. Four days ago, he was *known* to be residing in Palace #27, when he received several visitors of quite high station. It's not certain when he arrived but he did receive a variety of medical procedures."

"And the visitors were?"

He rattled off the names and one of them was Mozza's crush. That was only mildly disappointing.

"Might a person of a different gender see a visual representa-tion of that person *known* to be residing in Palace #27?"

"None has come to light. However," before she could complain, he went on, "an artificial personality with widespread visual access from the province of palace #27 proved to be highly bribe-able."

"Not a Transfer."

"Not one of those unreliable Transfers, no. But provided is a brief overhead vid of what appears to be an unofficial visit to the palace by a certain well-positioned male of the Aristocracy."

Xanthor did something to the table menu dials and suddenly she had an overhead view of one of the amazing gardens of the palace and although it was rather fuzzy and distant, a view of a male arriving via a non-official gateway into the fountain area of the garden. She couldn't make out his uniform delineation, but given the colors represented, she was sure that it was off-world in origin. He quickly maneuvered around the fountains and stopped when he spotted someone – another male figure – at the top of the visual area. They met and exchanged words. The Aristo gestured behind himself and then ahead and the two of them moved quickly out of the view area, and towards what Xanthor assured her were the glass entry doors of the palace where they vanished.

"The visitor never emerged again?" she naturally asked.

"Not so far, no." The vid vanished and the table menu reappeared.

"How can a person of a different gender obtain that visual representation just shown?" And when Xanthor said nothing, she said, "Perhaps by offering a small vial of differently gendered fragrance unobtainable to most genders."

He looked down at the table bench and there was a small, glittery packet. He snatched it up and put a hand out in gesture. She was puzzled at first and then put her own hand down on the table. He looked around to make certain no one was watching, and then briefly moved opposite her and spilled a liquid across her fingernails.

"It's all there," he assured her, and then seeming nervous said, "I've got to go." To the table he announced, "I'll take out that food at the entrance." He was up and gone before she could comment, but she saw the table screen process the order and charge it to her account. Oh, well.

After a few minutes, Mozza rearranged herself at the table so she faced where he had been seated. She reached for his drink and tasted it –very sharp and musky. Females were not allowed to order it. As she put down the drink she had bent two of her fingers to face the glass and there, repeated, was the scene at the palace garden. So that's how it worked: by reflection. She wished she had a glove to cover the hand until she could get it back to her laboratory.

Mozza was just getting up, about to leave the place herself, when the aged pensioner was suddenly at the end of the refectory table. He was gesturing toward something and she could see the shirt front go partly transparent enough for an official badge to be visible.

"Local Province Neighborhood Force. Undercover Division. Your dinner companion could be followed if you wished to press charges."

"He wasn't my dinner companion! He just sat down there and began speaking to himself. I paid no attention. Totally harmless!

"Then you're telling me that a person of a different gender didn't feel verbally molested by a potential invert in any way?"

Her society's way of compensating for the virtual non-status of her gender was to over protect it whenever possible, Mozza knew. Equally ridiculous and demeaning.

"Not verbally molested, no. Perhaps *aesthetically* molested," Mozza said with a sly grin, "Did you get a good look at that terrible hair piece he had on?"

The officer made a sick smile in response. He stepped away from the table.

By the time Mozza stood up and left the All-Service Food Establishment he was once again in disguise, behind the screen-novel. Mozza almost peered over to get a look at the title. She wondered if she should warn Xanthor. No, he panicked too easily. She might still need him.

As she passed the undercover cop, she said offhandedly. "Gratefulness for being so alert."

"It took me and a friend some time and some wielding of influence, not to mention the loss of an undergarment I couldn't really spare to get this vid, and then to get this vid enlarged and then as clear as this, even though it was taken by an old mechanism and from a distance," Mozza said to the object.

She waited again.

"So, give me some hint that this is or isn't the person you arrived with into the T-K Empire system?"

She waited more.

"Surely, you possess facial recognition abilities!"

It had been a half hour at least since she brought it up on the screen.

"I mean it can't be *that* difficult to tell. He is very attractive, after all. And given the evident physical attitude of the young Thane of Lazzor toward him, I'd say he is incredibly attractive in person, and probably charming too." She knew she was laying on thick.

Some sort of very thin light blue beam emitted from the object she was addressing and drew a thin lined circle around the head and torso. Another beam in red emitted a large X across the lower body.

"I see. The top is recognizably him. But not the lower body?"

The circle and X flashed.

"You know why that is, don't you?" And when she got no response she went on, "I have it on solid authority that the lower part of his natural body was destroyed in part or whole during the erasure of the Transfer.."

The X alone flashed now.

"*Not* a T-K male! You mean he is other?"

It flashed once again.

"So, he had to have been *already* bi-gendered to be repaired as bi-gendered? That would make sense. The surgery repair mechanisms would only repair what they saw to begin with. Then he is able to give birth? Like one of our own natural born Thirds?"

There was a flash of both circle and X that she read as upset or even angry.

"No, Unidentifiable Object. You're quite mistaken. He isn't diminished in any way by that repair work. In fact, I'd say he is extremely *elevated* by it. My solid authority who has tapped into the ordinary household vids of Palace #27 where your friend resides, says that he is the only *regular* inhabitant. That means he is of high birth and of very high standing. He has had two other high-station visitors besides the young Thane. We know who they are and we know they treated him, shall we say, *imperially*?

As of yet my solid authority has not been able to obtain audio. Can you lip read from vids? Even in our language? If so, I'll let you see."

She rethreaded the second vid she'd been given and projected it. In seconds it was fast forwarded by the Unidentifiable Object and then rewound.

"So. Presumably now you know. Will you speak to me now?"

A voice stuttered and then said quietly, "It is the worst possible outcome expected. There are three parties that are vying to make Him wed one or another High Peer of this empire and bear for one of them an emperor."

Mozza thought a while and then said. "You are correct. It is a very perilous position. But do you believe that your friend recognizes the dangerous situation and will try to get himself out of it?"

"Yes, He recognizes it. And no, He will not get himself out of it. He thrives on dangerous situations. From what I have seen and heard, He's ... enjoying himself."

"I see! Well, now even *I* can see how attractive he must be."

When there was no response she said. "Clearly, it's up to you and I to help him see the peril and ... get him out of it." She paused again. "What do you say? Do we have a deal?" She paused again. "You are probably asking yourself what I want as payment. It is to get out of here. Out of the T-K Empire, if possible to wherever you both came from. You can see that my gifts are being wasted here."

He could have sworn he heard something emitted from the area of his wrist connector. A voice. Or ...? And in truth, it was more like a flutter. It was low enough that the Thane wouldn't have heard it, since Holt barely did. Also the Thane – Andres – was rather busy at the time, well, both of them were, with their fourth penetration of the night, this being the younger man's second and most intense and most passionate and most ... well was difficult to describe, but somehow the most *intimate* one. But then it was over for both of them and as they lay next to each other on the almost diaphanous sheets of the huge bed, Holt could have sworn he heard it again. Without wishing to let on, he lifted that arm to his head, the area of his wrist connector to his ear, and sure enough, there it was again: definitely a sign of life. So, his Fast Yacht had managed, manipulated, or connived to get itself into a position where it could at least show a sign of life, if not communicate. He hadn't doubted it for a minute. He wondered where in the T-K Empire it was? Could it be here? On Imperia? That would be wonderf ...!

"Warning. Imminent danger." The wall messenger reported suddenly.

Both jumped up in time to hear what sounded like metal clanging over the large side windows. Thane Andres was out of bed and ran to the bedroom window. It was already covered what looked like steel plating.

Holt shouted. "What's happening?"

"The palace is defending itself!"

They pulled on shorts and ran out into the large hall. There too steel windows were going up and what Holt had thought were ornamental wooden shutters were closing and locking themselves.

"House valet," Andres shouted. "Define danger."

"Twenty-four armed persons. Unknown weaponry."

Holt was both frightened and thrilled. "What's going on?"

"Exactly what I was afraid of. You are being abducted."

It sounded in equal parts romantic and preposterous. "By whom?"

"By one of the non-claimant suitors," the message-valet reported

Andres turned to him, "You are officially under the protection of the Emperor's Foreign Minister for Extra-Galactic Ambassador, Jan Sonz. You must contact him immediately."

"You mean that little old guy I met?"

Before he could complete the sentence, the message valet reported. "His Excellency, Jan Sonz has diverted from his planned route and along with his entourage is on his way here. The palace ought to hold out until then."

There was the sudden sound of what seemed like gun or light missile fire against the metal shutters. Holt tried not to laugh out loud.

"What's he going to do with a few old guys?"

"His Excellency, The Second Fleet Admiral, Tanzen Raz, has attached a cadre to the Foreign Minister's entourage," the message-valet reported.

"Well, now!" Holt had to admit. "That's a little different. I wouldn't want to do anything to cross Goldilocks."

The gun or missile fire continued and Holt pulled Andres back into the bedroom. "Better get dressed. Neither of those two may take too kindly to seeing you here. Valet? What do you suggest, as a disguise?"

"The palace tailor will run up a uniform for the Thane. The second fleet is bound to be here in greater numbers than the Foreign Minister's entourage. So that will be the uniform made. It will be up to you, however, Thane Lazzor, to blend in with them and find your way out on your own."

"Agreed," Andres said. Then to Holt, "Although I was fully within rights coming here to warn and protect you ..." There was the sudden sound of what seemed like gun or light missile fire against the metal shutters from several sides now. "It was not my place at all to ... well, to enjoy you as I did. That is reserved for higher Peers than I."

"Then why did you?"

"Oh, Prince, you must know that I find you irresistible!"

Lazzor was too, Holt wanted to tell him. Which was why he hadn't resisted. But there was another series of volleys that seemed a little too close for comfort and then the valet-message spoke in a completely different voice, "Prince Sanqq'! Are you hurt? Do you need medical attention?"

It was the Foreign Minister, nearby or even outside.

"I'm fine, Minister Sonz?" he wasn't sure of the name. "Just a little shook up." To Andres, he said. "Go! Get that uniform on and get out of here."

As the Thane was leaving the bedroom, he added, "I enjoyed myself too."

That earned him a worried smile as he heard the message-valet, continued, "The attack has been foiled, thanks to the Second Fleet Admiral and his troops."

"This was a most unexpected surprise," Holt said.

"At your leisure the palace will unlock itself to admit us," Sonz continued.

"In a minute. Want to get dressed up for you, I was caught ... napping."

"Yes. Yes. Of course. It was all so unexpected!"

It was almost a recap of their first meeting. Only this time Holt was wearing what some would describe as dishabille (i.e as little as possible) while the others all were uniformed up to their necks and looked somewhat tense. Goldilocks even had on some upper body armor when he entered which he only party removed. Still smelling of sex – Holt was sure of it – he had accosted the two T-K officials physically, causing the Foreign Minister to go slightly ga-ga, unable to respond, while Goldilocks had gone completely rigid, and then gone rigid a little lower down too. At which point Holt swung around and gestured for them to take a seat.

"We must search the premises," Sonz said.

"No one got in," Holt assured them. "The palace did a good job there. How would I go about thanking the palace? I mean, it's an artificial intelligence, yes? So, should I even do so, or what? I know so little about your customs here, it seems. Please, Second Admiral Raz, sit, sit! You too, Foreign Minister and please excuse my appearance," – at which the Foreign Minister gaped yet again – "as I mentioned I was taking a nap."

Unsurprisingly, Goldilocks sat, but before that he'd gestured to two lieutenants and they each took men in a fruitless search parties in two directions of the palace.

Holt knew he had to keep them occupied for a few moments.

"You are both staring at me because I've done some horrible breach of manners by appearing like this before you while you are both done up to your necks in uniform. I'm awful, you're both thinking. Horrible. Disgusting. Why don't I go and change into something more formal, as is appropriate? It will only take a few minutes."

"Please don't," Goldilocks was able to utter. "Of course, you were taken completely unawares and vulnerable. The abductors were counting on that. Our only wish is to secure your safety and well-being."

He hadn't stopped staring, Holt noted.

"Foreign Minister, I feel forced to count upon your greater experience in these matters," Holt tried.

"The Admiral is correct. Come, seat yourself, Prince Sanqq'. From what I can see, the interior is secure. And the grounds?" he turned to Goldilocks.

"Also secured."

"But who were they?" Holt asked, "How do they even know I'm here?"

"The two captured men performed auto-immolation. But before they could do so, our cameras showed their uniforms to be those of my own distant cousin. They're the Earl of Quazz's own Second Guard. His palace will deny their presence, of course. Or say they were renegades acting on their own or on others' interests."

"As for how the Earl and others might know of your existence," the Foreign Minister began a little unsteadily, "Well, since the events that left our Empire without a vindicable leader, it seems that spy networks among the Four Hundred Families have, I'm afraid, greatly proliferated."

"It's even unclear how much artificial intelligences share information among themselves," Goldilocks added.

"Once again, the Admiral is correct."

"So, your assumption now," Holt said, "must be that most, if not all, of the Four Hundred Families of the Empire know of my existence."

"And of your station," the Foreign Minister added. "And of your ... nubile ... fertility," he added in a smaller voice.

"Well, then," Holt said, brightly, "wouldn't it make sense to make those facts as completely public as possible? ... If only to fend off future abduction attempts?"

"You mean call a Council of the Four Hundred?"

"Surely, you've been looking into that eventuality since our Prince arrived," Goldilocks asked the Foreign Minister, all but reproving Sonz.

"Where exactly would I look?" Sonz asked the Admiral back.

"Why? In your formal papers. Under the Visit of Dignitaries I would suppose."

"It's astonishingly vague ... as no visiting dignitaries were ever ... *expected.*"

"Well, one is here now," Goldilocks pointed out. To Holt he said, "Naturally, I have a legal counsel to aid you."

Holt just bet he did. To make all the military illegality as legal as possible.

"I'm sure he could aid you," the Admiral added.

"Also, there must be historians or archivists, record keepers, or such" Holt suggested to both, "Who could interpret your formal papers. Or perhaps provide some precedent of a past visit of dignitaries. There must have been some of those ... in earlier times, for example."

"Alas. All of those were ... eliminated. The dignitaries, I mean. Not the archivists."

"Why don't we three prepare something ad hoc," Holt suggested. "Clearly given my extremely high station in my galaxy I've attended formal ceremonies of these sorts. This Council of the Four Hundred Families? It sounds a lot like our own Quinx Council. How difficult would it be to convene them all?"

Goldilocks mused: "The Foreign Minister does have an official ability to call such a council."

"They can be called in shortly. It would take no more than five to six days at the most to call or recall them all," Sonz agreed.

"We'll call it a Council to Discuss the Questions around the Unexpected Visit of A Intergalactic Dignitary. Me," Holt said.

The two lieutenants appeared before Goldilocks and reported that no intruder had been found inside the palace. Holt could see Andres in Second Fleet uniform, all but hiding behind one group.

"You may go then," the Admiral said. "Retain a full guard outside the perimeter. The rest back to your barracks." To Holt he said, "I apologize, Prince for such a curtailment of your freedom. But it seems that such a show of force ..."

Andres was safe.

"... is understood, Admiral. As a deterrent to other possible abductors," with a hand on his sleeve, which provided the tiniest shudder. "My gratitude is boundless." Holt was hoping he might be able to have Goldilocks himself on duty inside the palace. Now that he'd had one taste of Trasp-Kenner amorousness, he felt he ought to compare it to another version of the same.

"Now, palace valet, how about some refreshment for my guests! And we'll require some kind of scribe or writing and recording implements ..."

Chapter Five:

FIRST FLIGHT

Khana thought the applause would never end. Eis had left the stage, to a thunderous ovation, returned briefly, stepped forward alone and without his backup and in the sudden silence said, "Just one more number," to more thunderous applause. Then he had played and sung *three* more, one of them Khana's favorite ballad, the second, Wellweg's favorite ballad, and for his third encore, let's face it, everyone's favorite rhythm and blues, the first song he'd achieved double-beryllium sales numbers with. Then he'd bowed, and slowly backed up until he was no longer visible.

And still the clapping went on, the huge audience's demand for more, more, and yet more.

Suddenly Vannada was there at the end of their row of seats, saying something to K'or, and then leaving. K'or got up and rousted Khana and Wellweg from their seats and when they'd gotten beyond the set of doors, but not beyond the huge, now muffled, sound from inside the auditorium, Khana said, "Why are we leaving? He's sure to come back one more time!"

"No, he's not!" K'or was definitive. Then Vannada was there and she had two other couples of those wood-wealthy women Khana had spoken to before, and she guided all of them down a corridor and then up a stairway. She was ushering them inside when her communication device lit up and she said, "It's my floor manager I've got to take this."

They went ahead and for a moment it was too dark to see, and Vannada called out. "There are lights if you go straight ahead. Then to your left. I'll be with you in a moment" – and she was gone.

There were indeed lights if very small ones, and then suddenly bright light from clerestory windows opening outside and the women entered a door and a room. Khana read on the door a plaque: "Green Room #2" Oh!

"Number *two*," one woman moaned. "He'll be ages in the first one."

"Vannada's a dear," another of the women replied, "but we can't expect her to perform miracles."

"And she's been so helpful, so far," K'or added. He wouldn't let them saying anything bad about his friend, not loyal K'or.

"So helpful," they agreed.

They noticed at the far end a drinks and canapes set-up on a table.

"Don't we even rate a bartender or server?" one entitled woman asked.

Khana knew she wouldn't be able to eat or drink a thing. She was so nervous, so expectant of meeting the man she had to agree now and forever more, for certain, was the greatest living composer and exponent of popular music in the entire galaxy.

"Wasn't that marvelous, when Boris Blu™ came rolling out from behind like some kind of giant wheel, then unfurled himself and began that duet with Eis," Wellweg enthused to Khana and K'or, referring to the second greatest musician in the galaxy, and the lead of the most fabulous group ever, and a cyber at that. They didn't have cybers on Hercular. At least none that Khana knew of, although K'or said there were several at the spaceport for off-worlders he'd been to once. So that when Boris Blu™ had appeared all shiny blue and clearly a mechanical object, but so human acting and he began to sing, matching Eis one tone lower, and then one tone higher, it was wonderful, just wonderful – unforgettable.

"Had you ever seen him before?" one woman asked, Khana and Wellweg, as she messily served herself some appetizer.

"*We* did!" another woman replied. "Off world, naturally."

"Yes, when Canes Venatici played two of the Ophiucan satellites," a third put in. "Boris Blu™ played six instruments and sang!"

"But he didn't sing as well as Eis!" Khana insisted.

"Who could?" the wood-wealthy women agreed.

"They say he goes back to his birth world, some little resort planet in the Orion Spur, to refresh his voice periodically," the entitled one added.

"But isn't that a desert planet? How could that possibly help his voice," her friend asked.

"I'm just reporting what I heard."

"It's his home world, and maybe that's where he gets his inspiration?" Khana suggested. She'd read somewhere that it was exactly that. "He has a Thwwing racing stable there, too!" she offered. She didn't know if they were still listening as they fussed over food at the little table.

"Did you see the News-Vids of him arriving?" the entitled one asked her friends. "That little fellow who is always with him. Very cute. I wonder who he is?"

"He's a native of Eis' desert world," Khana replied although she'd not been asked. "He's small like that because he's another species. He's a pamp. That's a native of Planet Usk. His name is Janesborot. He's Eis' manager," Khana had gained confidence and voice as she went on and the last statements she declared with finality. She'd absorbed every Bio-Vid data on her idol that was available, like paper soaking up rain. "He goes with him, wher- ever Eis goes," she added, and now she was certain they'd heard her.

"Where is that sapling? What's her name? Vannada?" the most entitled one said with some irritation. "Where could she have gone to, leaving us here?"

"Where's everyone else? I've never been in such an empty Green Room before."

As though on cue, the sapling came in the doorway to the Green Room. She looked disturbed and remained there. K'or went to her while she was still out of their hearing and they had a quick conversation, after which K'or also looked uneasy. She wondered why.

"Clearly Eis isn't coming. Maybe we should just go ourselves!"

the most entitled one declared.

"Or hunt him down. In his dressing room or in Green Room #1!" another put in. The two of them headed toward the doorway out and the other women followed, but they were stopped by Vannada who barred their way.

"Please! If you could be patient for just a few more moments?" she pleaded.

Two things happened then, one right after the other, and so Khana wasn't certain if they were connected or not.

Someone came out of the back door where they'd expected the singer, Eis, to come – a young branch about the size and age of Khana. He was dressed in a stadium uniform similar to Vannada's but with an odd, hooded overshirt and face-wide, oversized, dark glasses. He wore a beaked cap, and the hood was up over his hat and so partly over his head, but he slid over behind the little table and said, "Who needs a drink?" with a smile.

Two of the women turned to him and began making their wants known, and he began to serve them. The two women at the doorway returned to be served.

Khana happened to look at Vannada then: Vannada was clearly surprised to see him arrive and helping out, although she said nothing.

He'd served the women and Khana and Wellweg had moved over to the table about to ask for something, when they heard and felt an enormous and deep thump as though an enormous giant had stomped on the ground.

The wood-wealthy women headed toward the door, but again Vannada stopped them from leaving. There was a second, much closer, much more substantial thump! Two of the women fell against the wall, and lost their drinks. One fell down altogether spilling her drink more or less over herself.

"What in the wood!" two of them cried out.

Vannada rushed over to Khana, Wellweg and K'or. "That second one was closer. I think they're coming this way. We've got to get out." She rushed over to the table and grabbed the server. "There's a way out, through here," she cried to him and they took off. Khana, Wellweg and K'or followed but they could barely keep up with her and the server when they heard a third great thump, even closer to them.

"Those are bombs!" the entitled woman called out. "Sonic

bombs! We're under attack! The entire stadium!"

"Follow us!" Vannada shouted, then she and the server were through the door, and from there tearing down a short stairway. K'or, Wellweg and Khana rushed to catch up to them, and then rushed after them through a two and then three story high tall corridor with a ramp down.

Khana couldn't see or hear the women behind them.

Vannada was feeling in the dark and then something clicked and she pushed a sliding door and light came in and she and the server fled to into the early evening light. K'or was just able to catch the door before it slid shut again, so Khana and Wellweg could get out. But then it did slam shut behind them.

Khana had no idea where they were on the grounds but there was a fourth and fifth thump, that almost knocked them down onto the grass.

"We've got to get you away from here!" Vannada cried to the server.

"We need our wings!" K'or shouted.

"There are extras in that storage bin!" Vannada pointed and the two of them, and then K'or too were kicking the door in.

Khana could hear alarms going off in the distance and then the confused massed sounds of people shouting somewhere on the other side of the stadium. So they must be at the back of the stadium.

Vannada was handing out wings. K'or and Wellweg opened their tunics and fitted the wings into each of their stubs, and Vannada was doing the same. "Here!" she threw a pair at Khana, who loosened her top.

"Let me help!" K'or said, and suddenly he was fitting the top two wings into the upper stubs of Khana's back and they felt fine. "Your lower stubs look too sore."

"They're new," she had to tell him unable to help her embarrassment.

"Are we ready?" Vannada asked. They were all following her, as she began running down a hill, "There's a rise here for us to launch."

Khana was running with K'or. Wellweg and Vannada were on either side of the server who had no wings, and they were lifting him off the ground. Then K'or had Khana by one wing and they too lifted off, and he said, "Don't worry! I can steer for the two of us," and Khana knew that was true. So she let him lift her up and quickly enough her other wing was moving of its own accord. "It's working!" she shouted. "You can let me go."

After a bit, K'or did and the other wing was also in sync and Khana was exultant, flying on her own for the very first time in her life. It was even better than her dreams.

K'or sped up to where the others were and he took the server's arm from Wellweg, and shouted something to her, looking back at Khana. Wellweg dropped behind to where Khana was. They'd passed over the stadium vehicle parking lots now.

"He said we have to get away really fast, so you and I should make a double," Wellweg said. They moved toward each other, linking up, so they were two bodies and two outer wings.

"Those wings are too big for you," Wellweg shouted. "They're for a woman not a sapling."

"Vannada put them in," Khana shouted back. She'd noted the fact when it had happened, but it had been too late to say anything. "Anyway, too big or not, I like these."

By that time the other three were already losing them, and the two saplings had to exert themselves to catch up.

"Where are they going?" Khana shouted at her friend. The others had suddenly veered left and dipped a good ten meters. Then she heard three whistles by her left ear and even saw the last projectile go by, not a meter away. "Someone's shooting at us!"

Wellweg looked terrified but she dipped and steered them left and down following the others, and then along what seemed like a dangerously low, zigzagging flight path, barely skimming treetops and higher roof eaves. They projectiles continued to whistle by them but not so closely anymore.

"Why are they shooting at us?" Khana shouted. But Wellweg didn't know either, her face showed her terror. Khana was enjoying this more than she dreamed she would. It was like a Ficto-Vid adventure. Except those trees and roofs below were real, and the amazing breezes they flew into and out of were real too.

The air above, high in front of them, was suddenly filled with flying vehicles, the mahogany and yellow trim shades of the Public Guardians, flying directly into the path of the whistling projectiles which bounced off their surface without making a mark. Five vehicles sped above them, and then behind them and well hidden behind large, transparent shields, were anther score of pairs of flying Public Guardians. Her first time flying and it was simply wonderful, a little scary true, but mostly wonderful!

Khana was surprised to see that Vannada and K'or and the server did not rise to meet them but continued to fly low and with amazing dexterity.

Only when all the Public Guardians had passed and the five of them had made it out of the unwooded and therefore exposed area of the stadium and across two small streams and into the security of Sequoia Heights, did K'or half turn and gesture to Wellweg and Khana that they were going down to land, and the two saplings should follow.

They did and got fairly close up to the front three as they slid around the big tree trunks; Wellweg had them almost overtake the others. "Where are we going?" she shouted.

"K'or pointed ahead and down to a log-cabin like structure high on a rise but closely surrounded by enormous tree trunks.

"This might be a difficult landing," Wellweg shouted to Khana. "let's separate and you follow me exactly. Okay? Do what I do."

They all separated into Vannada alone, then K'or and the server, followed by Wellweg and Khana. Clever K'or had chosen a relatively long and flat arrival spot. Khana remembered what her Fa' had shown her when they practiced landing, so all five landed half minutes apart, and she never stumbled a step. She was so proud of herself!

"Stay here!" K'or directed the others. He folded his top wings and ran forward into the structure's covered entry. He knocked on the door and no one answered. He turned to the others and gave them an "all right" signal then tapped a code and the door unlocked. He gestured the others to remain outside as he went in. A few minutes later, he came to the doorway and gestured them inside. "Empty."

They'd folded their larger wings and could fit in. But K'or carefully closed the heavy, half-timbered door behind them and Khana saw him press a new code into the lock.

"Where are we ...?" Khana began to ask.

"It's a club house. When I was a Twig, this is where we all gathered. It's a Boy Twig club house," he said, almost apologetically.

Khana had heard of them, but they were so rare, she never

thought she'd ever see the inside of one.

"We'll be safe here. I changed the lock code. And there's a vid-screen here," K'or added, "so we can see what's going on."

Vannada and the server were already in the main room and had the large wall screen Vid on. A News Service reporter was speaking from fairly far away, yet with the stadium in full view. They could see, hundreds, if maybe thousands of branches and saplings and women and men who were flying away from the stadium, which had two distinctive sags in its domed roof that weren't there before, doubtless from the sonic bombs.

"A completely unprecedented catastrophe upon our peaceful world," the woman reporter was saying, "Witnesses say the attack began with three infra-sound bombs placed around the outside of the building and two more behind the auditorium itself."

On the Vid screen, scores of Public Guardian vehicles and individuals behind transparent body shields were flying into the Vid-picture, landing and massing around the stadium and upon its ramparts. The vehicles discharged uniformed PG men and women carrying large weapons, while the mostly male flying guards had alit and were helping the many evacuees onto rises in the roof so that they could launch themselves away.

"While it still isn't understood who or what group was behind the attack," the reporter continued. "the bomb placements suggest that chaos rather than loss of life was their intention. Although the displacement of wall and ceiling fixtures by sonic blast did cause many lighter injuries."

The picture shifted to telephoto lens sweeping the evacuees, some of them with blood from face and head wounds, while others had arms in makeshift slings.

"We still haven't gotten reports of any dead," the reporter added.

The picture now pulled back to show more land and air vehicles. The Green Spirals of Emergency Medical Services appeared and medics in helmets with face guards rushed into the ruin. The area was still extremely noisy with alarms

Inside the clubhouse, the still-hooded server leaned against a log pillar. Vannada, next to him, put an arm over his shoulder.

Wellweg turned to Khana, utterly distraught and almost shrieked as she pleaded, "I don't understand. Why would anyone attack the stadium? Why did we have to get away so fast?"

But Khana suspected she knew. She hugged her friend as closely as possible with folded wings, and whispered in her ear: "Look at his socks."

"What? Whose socks!?"

"His! The off-worlder we helped escape."

They were visible now. They had been briefly visible twice during their run and flight and each time, Khana had noted them and said to herself, no, it can't be. But now she knew it could be. It was.

"Look at his socks. Look, Wellweg. they are Ice-green! The color of his eyes."

He'd heard her and turned around to face them, "I'm so very sorry, folk. I think this attack is my fault."

"What? No! It's not!" Vannada and K'or both insisted.

"But it has to be off-world madmen!" K'or said, darkly. "No Hercularan would dream of doing such a thing."

"We're getting another feed," the reporter announced. The Vid-screen picture shifted to another side of the stadium, not far from where the five of them had exited not long ago. There too, the wall had since partly collapsed. A telephoto lens poked more deeply into the ruin and suddenly five black-clad figures could be seen.

"Cybers!" the saplings said all at once.

"No, not cybers, Or at least not *fully* cyberized," the off-worlder (Eis) declared. "It's a terrorist group."

"Who? What?"

"I was warned about them. Janesborot told me they were gunning for me, but did I listen? No. I laughed off their threat. And look what happened!"

"Look! Next to them!" Wellweg cried.

The telephoto lens picked out two smaller figures next to the dark ones – one was clearly Eis' pamp manager, the other one – Eis himself!"

"How can that be!?" Khana asked, going up to the server.

"He's a body double," Vannada explained. "I was told they would be using one today."

"Is that true, Eis?" Khana demanded.

"Yes, and now they're captives of those madmen."

One of the dark figures waved to the camera, and turned to

speak to it. "To our knowledge, no sentient being's lives were lost today." The voice was not quite human, but had a slight, purposefully metallic/false edge to it. "We are Avenge K'Tina Kell. All government entities, on Hercular, on Hesperia, everywhere in the Ib'r Republic galaxy know who we are and what our grievances are."

"Who in the wood is K'Tina Kell?" Wellweg asked. "Is she related to you?" she asked the off-worlder.

"She is or was ... somehow. A distant cousin I think."

"We sought to abduct the son of the Premier of the Ib'r Republic today," The terrorist spokesman continued, "And so to bring those grievances home to the highest powers which have so far flagrantly ignored us. They cannot ignore us any longer!"

The little pamp and the human body double were prodded forward.

"One of these two hostages is indeed a close associate of our target. The other is not who we wanted but instead a local inhabitant, locally employed, to be a general decoy. He will be released to show that we mean it when we say that we mean no Hercularans harm."

They watched the false Eis's hands be unbound and he ran forward. Two Public Guards quickly grabbed him and took him aside.

"We have eyes all over the space ports and the orbital skies and we know that our quarry has not eluded us by leaving Hercular. He is somewhere on this planet and we will not cease searching until we have found him. You, people and government of Hercular, may help yourselves and save yourself from future trouble by delivering him up to us."

The terrorist spokesperson waved a hand with some kind of device in it and the camera went black.

A few seconds later the picture was up again, switched back to the wider stadium view and the original Vid-reporter who had gotten much closer to the stadium in the meanwhile showed up.

"They attacked thousands of us of us to kidnap you?" Wellweg asked.

"Or to kill me ... I told you it was my fault."

"No. It's *their* fault." The other four agreed.

Now K'or had a question for Eis, "There's something I don't understand. Since when is your father the Premier of the

Republic?"

Khana knew: "Since a month ago, Sol Rad. When Eis' adoptive father, Deon Syzygy was elected by the Inner Quinx."

"But before him, the Premier was my great uncle. And before him, another relation was," Eis said, despairingly. He had his big glasses off and those famous and fabulous, Ice-green eyes of his were brimming with tears. "I won't be able to live with myself if any of your folk were killed. Or Janesborot."

Just then there was a series of noises that K'or was alerted to. "Stay here! Away from the windows!" he warned, and ran out of the room. When he came back, he was pale. "They have search vehicles looking for us."

"Let them find us!" Wellweg said. "We'll be safe."

"Those aren't the Public Guardians, Wegg. It looks like some of the terrorists got out of the stadium before the Guardians could stop them. Just as that nasty spokesperson said. We've got to get out of here and find a safe place for our friend here. They really are searching."

"I won't put anyone else in danger," Eis declared.

"We'll wait until they have moved away before we go," K'or said sensibly.

"Even so, I will not consider going into any of your own homes."

"Wait a minute! I know just the place," Khana said. "It's just on the other side of this wood. A lower bole condo for sale. Very posh. Very vacant."

"How would you know that?" K'or asked.

"Among other things, Wellweg's mother works for a tree-estate agent. We snuck in recently to look at it."

"Wellweg, what do you say?"

Khana spoke up for her friend. "We'll wait until they've passed overhead, and begun searching another area, then we'll take off to the lower bole condo."

"No," K'or said. "No flying with him. They'll be looking for that. It's too dangerous. Can you three walk there?'

"Of course, we can," Wellweg said.

"It's not that far," Khana agreed.

"Won't we stand out even more that way?" Eis asked.

"No, people walk short distances all the time. And because the trees are so big and so thick around here in Sequoia Heights, you will be more hidden from aerial view."

Now Vannada looked uncertain.

"You don't agree?" K'or asked.

"No, I do. It's just that I'm upset about my co-workers. Are they hurt? Is anyone you know ...?" In a lower voice, she asked, "dead?"

"Of course, you have to go back there." K'or agreed. "Go!"

They hugged her good-bye and she held Eis by his two hands. "Remember! It's not your fault. You did nothing to deserve this. You're an artist and you should be free to make your art anywhere in the galaxy. You will be perfectly safe with K'or and his friends. They adore you!"

A few minutes after she'd left the building, K'or said, "On second thought, I think I should go with her. At least part of the way."

"Go! We'll be fine here," Khana said. Wellweg threw another of those looks that all but said, "Who are you? Where is my old friend?"

Once he'd left, Khana said. "Let's turn that Vid off. It will only upset us." She took Eis by the hand. "We've simply *got* to eat something. The flying really takes it out of us. I'm sure there's food here." She pulled him along to where she could see the club-kitchen branched off the main room. Sure enough, the food cooler held sap concoctions, plant juices, nut butters and other snacks that Boy Twigs loved, but that they all could enjoy.

While fixing the food, every once in a while, Khana would turn around and see Eise'nstein Syzygy Kell himself looking at her or Wellweg or around him at what must surely be, for him, unexpected surroundings. It was utterly improbable that he'd be here with them. And yet somehow it seemed just right.

"Try this," Khana insisted to Eis, handing him a fruit wrap. Then stopped herself. "Oh, I just had a thought: I hope you're a vegetarian!"

"Why? Do I have a choice?" he asked.

That set all three of them laughing.

"What are you looking for?" Khana asked.

"A Holo-screen?" Eis said.

"A Vid-screen, you mean. I'm not sure there is one here. This is a display condo for selling ... Wellweg?"

"There may be a small Vid-screen in the master bedroom branch."

She left to go look.

The three of them had arrived at the vacant lower bole-condo a few minutes before, after a relatively peaceful walk through the woods. Occasional overhead vehicles had flown past, but as K'or had said, those were too high to pierce through the woodland to see anything on the ground unless they were specifically scanning; even then, so many tree branches and foliage would surely block their vision.

Eis had been nervous, naturally, but at one point, when they had arrived at the last open court, a naturally made ring of flat ground formed by the massive roots of the huge trees, one of which contained this bole-condo they were now in, Eis stopped and just looked around himself.

"Listen!" he said.

There was no traffic on the ground because they were too far from any main roads. Nor, for the moment, were there any noisy vehicles above them in the air. And then all of a sudden there was a barely audible sound from what must be a small forest animal quietly chittering, calling its kits, Khana thought.

"It's so amazingly quiet," Eis said. He looked rapt as he said it.

"That's almost the definition of Glen!" Khana said. "Too quiet, usually. Well it is," she defended herself to Wellweg who had struck an attitude: not the first one today by any means. "You've said so yourself, Weg. How you couldn't wait for the next turning to migrate to Meadow. 'Where people will be able to actually see each other without some stick of wood getting in the way.' Your words, exactly."

"When will you begin to migrate?" Eis asked.

So, he knew that much about Hercularans and their vast world.

"Very soon," Khana replied. "Some have already begun.".

"The Earlies, we call them," Wellweg answered, "folks who go to Meadow before the greater population migration."

"Weg," Khana warned. "You were looking for a Vid in the condo. Remember?" To Eis, she said, "What we call The Earlies are Premature Migrators who are chosen or volunteer to go and prepare the older habitations, repair them, help build new ones, and to get whatever basic commercial enterprises we'll need there in Meadow manned and ready."

"As a rule, they are men and women headed there, although some branches and even saplings will go too. Whoever has especial interest in agriculture," she added. "It really is the richest of all the continents and foodwise the most productive, but it still has to be prepared for the several million of us who will arrive and call it home for the next decade."

"All of the Earlies have been chosen before-hand ... usually for their special skills. I think my sister Metts is going. She's supreme at Maths. And maybe even our K'or will go."

"He's definitely going early. Wellweg said, returning to the main chamber. "There's no Vid-screen in that suite. Unless it's too cleverly hidden away for me to figure out."

Khana asked Eis, "Did you happen to see any large air-barges when you were orbiting? They're enormous cylinders the length of the distance we flew to get here from the stadium. They're filled with particularly valuable woods. So much has grown in the five decades before we even resettled here in Glen that we have more than enough to export it. The Lates, those who remain behind after the great migration, will do a final lumber-cut and then ship that too out to worlds that want our wood for building or other uses."

"You have no trees where you live, do you?" Wellweg asked.

"On Hesperia?" Eis asked. "Yes, of course we have trees."

"They have entire girder-long parks full of trees," Khana added. "Trees from all over the galaxy."

"But not as many as here in Glen," Eis clarified, "and certainly not as large as these monsters just outside."

"It's the City on a Star," Khana added, still lecturing Wellweg. "They have everything there. Everything in the universe!"

"Not volcanoes," Wellweg defied her. "Not icecaps!"

"She's right. It's not a planet," Eis defended the sapling.

Khana ignored that, and continued on. "That enormous sale of our wood from Glen will keep Hercular's treasuries filled and its finances steady and probably a lot better than that for the first few years while our new home, Meadow, is being plowed and seeded."

She'd just studied that at The Stand School.

"And from what Janesborot told me before we arrived, when

Meadow is completely harvested, it will provide a five-hundredth portion of the entire galactic gross product of agriculture. That's enormous!"

They agreed. But he suddenly looked concerned.

"My manager? What can I do for him?"

"I'm sure the Public Guardians are working with the terrorists for a solution," Wellweg assured him.

Khana didn't believe they had any real experience in hostage negotiation, so she kept quiet. He was right. There had to be something *they* could do.

"Sorry No Vid screens!" Wellweg nodded toward the master bedroom branch.

"Maybe it's better we're not seeing the news right now," Khana offered. "You really look exhausted," she told Eis, "Why not go lie down a bit. K'or is sure to return and he'll update you."

"Can't we call him?" Eis asked.

"Oh, no. Apologies, Eis. But Weg and I are both too young to have a personal communicator. He won't be long. Come!"

She surprised herself by taking his hand and leading him into the sleeping branch. Like all of the showcase bole-condo, it was wonderfully furnished with complex wood working details and exquisite marquetry. The bed's mattress was of some almost living material and it would adapt to his body instinctively. She knew once he got into the built-in bed he'd fall asleep.

They all heard someone walking through the fallen leaves. She hushed them and moved Eis to the back exit of the condo, blocked the way.

But it was only K'or, who came in with folded wings and some stains and even a few rips on his tunic that Khana had not seen before.

"All Vannada's co-worker friends at the stadium are alive," he reported. "Only a few are slightly injured."

"Look at your clothing!" Wellweg pointed out.

"Well, we had to crawl into some tight spaces to help pull one sapling out. She was wedged in."

"My manager? The pamp?" Eis asked. He'd not gotten far.

"We did see him," K'or said. "Vannada knew of an almost hidden upper loge quite way high up that looked almost straight down into the area where the hostages are being kept."

"There are more than just one hostage?" Khana asked.

"Remember those four wood-wealthy women following us out?" K'or asked. "They never made it. I'm not at all sure I would choose any of them for my hostages."

He said it with so flat an expression on his face and in his voice, that it came off funny.

"I'd say the terrorists have their hands full," Khanna laughed.

"As far as we could see, your manager is completely unharmed."

"For how long? We have to help him," Eis insisted.

"Well, then, great minds think alike. You're in agreement with me and Vannada," K'or said. "He's got to be rescued."

"I'm not sure I want to hear any more of this talk," Wellweg declared. "And anyway, I've got to get back home. I'm certain my mother has been calling and checking there every few minutes."

"Khana," K'or said, "you should go too. Your Ma' and Fa' will be worried."

After Wellweg had already stepped out of the bole-condo, Khana lingered. "Weg's really terrified of all this rescue business," Khana told K'or. "But I'm not. I'm coming back here and whatever plans you come up, make sure to include me. I know I'm just a sapling but I have my uses too. I'm not joking, K'or!"

"Yes, Ma'am," he scraped a low bow to her.

"Silly. Help me with these wings."

As he did help, he said, "These are far too big for you."

"Actually they're not. They're exactly the right size for me ... I feel fabulous with them on. Really!"

Before he could respond, she'd run forward and lofted into the air.

"It's your own fault, Ma'," Khana held her ground. "Yours and Fa's. If I had a communicator with me at the stadium, I would have called you as soon as there was a hint of a problem."

"We were waiting to give it to you until at least you had your wings, Kha darling."

Khana patted her folded wings. "They're right here."

"Where dd you get those, anyway? They reach the ground, even folded like that."

"Not quite. I got them from a public wing shed outside the

stadium."

"A public wing shed!? Kha, anyone could have worn them before you. Did you stop to disinfect them?"

And now Khana saw how small a world her Ma' really lived in.

"Ma', we were running from sonic bombs. It would have looked really charming if I said, 'Oh wait up folks. Even though our lives are in danger, I have to stop and disinfect these strange wings.' Is that what I was supposed to do?" She breathlessly went on, "Surely, you heard the stadium was bombed by off-world terrorists. It was only on every Vid-screen in the Glen all night long. Oh, right, it was the reason you were so worried about me, if you recall. So?" she added, deftly changing the subject, "Do I get the communicator that I know you and Fa' got for me months ago already, or not?"

"Why now? You're safe. What's the hurry?"

"Because I'm about to use these strange, undisinfected wings to go out again and you will have no way of talking to me when I do go." Before her mother could say anything, she added "And yes, I *do* have to go now. I promised K'or and Vannada that I'd be there. We have to help Van's friend," Khana wouldn't say who that friend was if she was tortured to death. Looking at the timepiece built into the entry hall wall, she added, "In truth, I'm supposed to be there in exactly three minutes from now. Which, since it takes a good twelve minutes to fly there, will make me ... well, I don't know how late exactly."

"Where will you be? Did you ever even tell me?"

"Only three times. At the Sequoia Hill Boy-Twigs clubhouse."

Her Ma' dithered but left the chamber. She returned with the communicator. "I don't know how to set it up."

"They'll know at the clubhouse. Gratitude, Ma'. And for Fa' too." She felt bad about telling her mother a falsehood; but Eis' rescuers agreed not to let anyone know where he was.

She bussed her Ma's cheek and slid the piece into her deepest pocket and buttoned it up. "Now don't worry. I'll be all right."

"You're my youngest. Barely more than a chip. I have to worry."

Khana now appreciated the earthen rise Fa' had formed outside the bole-flats tree they lived in. She'd used the common lower landing strip to alight the previous evening coming home and found it wider and a bit less daunting than the one in front of the clubhouse. Which she'd negotiated fairly well. This rise was perfect for a sapling to rush up and loft into the air.

A few minutes later, swirling higher in a rise-gyre, she passed Ma' Cali'po who lived just one double branch beneath their family condo, and who was just now arriving, landing jauntily, her packages slung in nets around her. Ma' Cali'po couldn't hide her surprise, and waved lamely.

There were fewer Public Guardian vehicles in the air now, but every once in a while, she'd either see or think she was seeing one of the off-worlder's aircars that she knew were there, hovering, searching. The Vid-news said the Glen Government had agreed they could search as long as none of its citizens were harmed. That at least was the compromise that had been publicized between the government and the terrorists. After all, they still held five hostages, four of them wood-wealthy Glen women. Khana didn't doubt for a minute that the Glen Government would sacrifice Eis' pamp manager in order to ensure that its citizens were released.

Vannada welcomed her into the condo. "Don't you need stabilizing lower wings? I saw a few pair inside the storage bin by the back exit. I'm certain one or another would fit you."

"I'm still sore down there," Khana admitted. "Besides, I feel so comfortable with this larger pair. I don't seem to miss the stabilization lower down. And this pair feels so natural!"

"All right," Vannada led her inside. "My brother is here. We need help and I didn't know who else we could trust," Vannada said darkly as she led her into what would be the condo office, where the others were already gathered. Wellweg, of course, hadn't returned and wouldn't be there. No real surprise for Khana who'd never seen her longest-known friend so nervous and upset before. She had to recall her Fa's saying, "When a Redwood falls, everyone shows their true self." That meant Wellweg's true self was timid and her own was brave. Or at least adventurous.

K'or had a chart-map projected onto the wall, and he was using a pointer. Khana recognized Glen Central on the map and then its southern border with Meadow. He stopped speaking and looked over to her with a brief smile, glad she'd returned. Eis also greeted her with a flash of his fabulously green eyes and that sent a little shiver down her spine. The other male was Vannada's twin brother. He turned to look at her, and Khana suddenly had the funniest feeling. One she couldn't define, never mind name.

He resembled Vannada in feature and general coloring and he was fine looking, like virtually all Hercularan males, tall and well-muscled and excellently proportioned.

It was no secret that their planet was a Second Matriarchal Empire sponsored seeded world project from less than a half dozen millennia earlier. Or that there had been several major errors in the planning. In the Strand School, Khana and other students learned what those errors were. Because of the great distance involved, the Seeding Program had mistaken the varied and still separated six continents of the huge world for six separate satellites.

The six Seeding Cybers had emerged from the seeding vehicles and immediately realized the mistake. Each Cyber had been programmed to prepare and terraform and then seed with humans a single different satellite: the materials and tools they'd been provided with had been specifically for that limited purpose, not for transforming a single giant world with several quite varied environments already in place.

The Seeding Cybers had communicated with each other, conferred, come up with various solutions and eventually decided upon one. They would combine their seedlings, their tools, and materials and start with one continent: the largest, and the one most naturally already formed for human habitation: what would eventually be called Meadow. For that plan to go forward, four of the Seeding Cybers would actively deal with the large number of humans to be birthed, nursed, tended to, and schooled. The other two Cybers moved to the next most habitable continent, Strand, which needed the least effort and they began to completely ready that. They then moved to the next most habitable one, Glen, which they also prepared and helped along, and so on, to Aerie, Plateau, and Fen until all six continents were in position to eventually accept the seedlings.

When all of Hercular was ready for populations, the Cybers realized that they already had a cohesive "nation" of seedlings. Forcing them apart into six groups would be difficult if not impossible. They conferred with their grown seedlings and together the humans and Cybers decided upon the solution: the humans would all migrate from one continent to another at fixed times, thus utilizing and enjoying their planet's wondrous resources, but never over-exploiting it. By that time, the oldest seedlings were approximately forty years old and were ready to become youngish parents themselves., The Cybers came up with the second most intriguing solution: to genetically alter each new generation to provide it with a strengthened upper body bones and musculature and a double set of dorsal flesh stubs capable of holding in place and physically utilizing artificial, cyberized wings.

Naturally there were problems and anomalies (there always is in human physiology) but only another fifty discrete generations of altered-human births during a period of fifty years was required before the final group produced nearly 99.98 percent of infants who would be flight-capable once they were adults. And so, only a few centuries were needed before the entire adult population was capable of migratory flight. The too young and too old could migrate in flying vehicles.

This had been made oddly simple because, while huge, their world had relatively low gravity, the result of a proportionately smaller than usual metallic core. Hercularan seedlings were adapted to it. All visiting off-worlders were not and commented upon that $5/8^{ths}$ basic gravity. Even Eis' concert had played with that feature when Boris Blu™ and the Troubadour had performed light-gravity acrobatics during one of Canes Venatici's hit singles, "I'm Simply Floating Over You," during which they had indeed floated over each other.

The second, well not so much mistake as mismatch to the planet had been the Matriarchal Empire's basic set agenda for seeded planets, which always called for smaller, weaker, and far fewer males than women. That might work well in the developed Center Worlds, but in this constantly physically challenging planet, both males and females had to be stronger early on, first to be able to carry the cybernetic wings that allowed them to comfortably fly from their mid-adolescence and through two more centuries of age. But it was the enormous physical challenges the earlier seedling generations faced on the planet as they'd grown up in the care of their Cyber parents and nurses that were a far cry from the easy life that their forebear Matriarchal Empire humans had envisioned or been discomforted by. These seeded humans had to cultivate the required transformation of the terraformed but still raw landscapes around themselves.

That was when the Matriarchally planned genetic mis-proportions of male to female numbers appeared as such a problem, one that needed to be addressed. Under the Cybers' guidance, over the millennia it had altered, gradually, so that instead of one male per eight or nine females at the beginning, the ratio was now more like one male per five or six.

Before the Cybers agreed to disassemble themselves into becoming advanced planetary infrastructure as had been pre-planned, they'd managed to genetically double the originally set ratio of males and females, and also to greatly genetically strengthen those males born. Along the way, they'd provided cultural artifacts such as music and theater and literature derived from both the Second Matriarchy and, on a smaller scale, from the human's First Space Age so that Hercularans could see for themselves what the relation of the human genders had previously been in other locations, and so decide their own rules.

Khana always found it interesting that the group decision had been to do away with both the Matriarchal superior-inferior relations system and also the Metro-Terran never-quite-equal-criterion, and to create their own standard of relations between the genders. It recognized that if Hercularan males were rarer, and if they were both desirable and by their nature more promiscuous than females, those facts might as well determine how society would become. Most – but not all – males therefore, were at least sequentially double-familied, and as longevity was extended over generations to match the rest of the galaxy's inhabitants, sometimes they had more than two families, although on occasion, and by choice, they had fewer.

Khana's Fa' had sired two broods of twigs by two different wives, before he'd met her Ma'. Since those earlier twigs were all adults by then, he'd settled in with Ma' and lived with her brood full time. But, at times, he was needed for first and second family crises, duties, and celebrations – he might be gone a week or more at a time doing that. One of those earlier wives had grown close to Ma' and she and some of her own offspring – now adults – were often around Khana's family home. All this was an accepted way of life on Hercular.

But the male and female genetic progression was continual and K'or and now Vannada's brother were excellent examples of contemporary males just beyond the sapling stage: universally tall, well, built, very attractive, and strong. Yet also gentle, accommodating, and for the most part quick to defer to whatever evidently superior females were around them. Like the females, they were part of the team. The Third Matriarchy had never managed to actually reach Hercular during even its most expansive period. But the Ib'r Republic that followed it had reached the planet during its expansionist phase, and the Greater Quinx Council of Five Thousand was presented with the already in place social structure. Hercular people did not degrade males into second and third class citizens as the Matriarchies had. And they didn't have any strictures against same sex relations – which however were rare on this seeded planet – although they were by that time, elsewhere, the Galactic norm. So, Hercular was invited into the Republic on a two hundred-year-long probationary period, which was how Khana knew all about the City on a Star, the Ib'r Republic, and especially Eise'nstein Syzygy Kell and his music.

"K'asp," Vannada's brother introduced himself. "I understand your first flight was tons of fun!" he told Khana with a more or less straight face.

"It actually was," she admitted with a laugh. She liked this male.

"So, Van,'" K'or began, "Why don't we give the floor to you for the internal plan?"

Vannada went forward, as the projector put up another chart, a large and detailed floor plan.

"This is where the hostages were when I was in the stadium ruins yesterday!" she said. "Of course, they might have been moved since then, but the possible choices of where they could go inside are limited by two factors. First," she pointed, "These two adjacent areas were badly damaged by the sonic bombs. Someone might purposely hide there, if necessary. But that's about all they could do. Passage would be difficult. Then, the water closets and the little kitchen portions of the Green Room we were in – yes, the terrorists were *that* close to us – are here," again she pointed. "And with hostages in tow they can't really move too far away from those spots."

"Can any of us get through there?" K'asp asked. "Is the local structure still in motion, Van? Is it falling or so loose it can come down on anyone crawling through it?"

"You mean one of us crawling through to grab Eis' manager?" K'or asked. "Don't you think their side of that area would be well-guarded?"

"I'll answer you first, K'or," Vannada said. "Yes, I do think it would be guarded. And, second, K'asp, I don't know how actively mobile the structural damage is there. One of us, me or Khana should be able to fit through and of course we could easily get Janesborot out because he is small, but we'd probably have a more difficult time with the women."

"If we get only him out, the terrorists might suddenly decide to retaliate against the women they're holding," Eis said what they were all thinking. "We can't, in all justice, do that."

"That's a fair point," K'or said. "But circumstances will end up dictating what we accomplish and who we can free. And by the way, I couldn't possibly let Khana go into that crawl space. I know her parents, and they ..."

"He's about to say that my Ma' and Fa' would kill him if anything happened to me!"

"No, but ... you know what I'm saying."

"Yes, K'or. Thanks, Vannada. I also have an idea," she began taking the older sapling's place up front. "Could we look at the area map again?" And when it was projected, she pointed and said, "Now, here's what the terrorists will be expecting of us." At the wall, she pointed, "That when we succeed in getting away. You notice I didn't say "if," but "when" we succeed. They will expect us to head more or less in this direction, toward the Glen Government Center. Right?"

A murmur of agreement.

"And that's where their vehicles will go. But we won't do that. What we'll do is go in *that* direction," she pointed to Glen's southeastern border, the closest one to the stadium. "Directly as possible to Meadow!"

Before they could offer more than murmur, she added, "You K'or and and possibly you too, K'asp, are headed to Meadow anyway, as Migration Earlies. Am I right?"

She's right," Vannada agreed. "All three of us are."

"And my sister Metts is too."

"And I know of two other males," K'asp offered.

"So, we *all* go early," Khana said. "Once we're gone, the Glen Government is off the hook. Eis is safe. His t-pod or whatever life boat he has, can come and get him and his manager."

"We can probably outrun them in my Fast-Yacht," Eis admitted. "My birth mother, Ay'r, won the Orion Intergalactic Run twice with it. The add-ons for speed that he had put in are all still there."

"Will your Fast-Yacht know you're coming?" K'or asked.

"It was on an open channel to me all the time I was in the concert and after so it will expect me to contact it. It requires a key sequence to admit anyone but me and it will defend itself against any intruding terrorists."

"That's a good plan, Khana, but you have to admit, it is a long flight across the borders there," Vannada put in. "At least four hours without stopping."

"What's down there in the borderland?" Eis asked.

"Mostly barren dirt. Unformed soil. Loose gravels. It could be shifting a great deal because it is located over a hot spot that goes a hundred or more miles deep. We might even encounter a fire-geyser."

"And then there's always the possibility of Hell Kites," K'asp added.

"Whoa? Wait a second, Sol Rad.," Eis spoke up. "Fire-geysers! Shifting earth! Hell Kites! I'm not sure this is any better than being held hostage by the cyber-men!"

"You and your manager do not even have to see or know of them," Khana said. "Last Migration to into Glen, when I was a wee chip, I traveled in a closed pocket and slept much of the way."

What had already surprised Khana was that her idea was so quickly adopted by the others, without any criticism of its fundamental elements. She could envisage Wellweg in that conversation. She'd probably run screaming from the room.

"Basically, that does seem to be the best plan for once we are outside of the stadium with the hostages," Vannada said. "Are we agreed on that? Good, then you will have to have your Migration Documents with you when we begin this action. If we are stopped by any Glen Government officers, we merely show them our papers." No one protested, despite the Hell Kites, which might actually be mythical, Khana thought, with a little pride. "So, let's think more about how we get the five out. Ideas?'

They batted around ideas for another half hour. After that K'or called for a drink and snack break. K'asp joined Khana in the kitchen area. Eis came in a moment later.

"Why did you call your birth mother a 'he'?" He asked Eis.

"Because my birth mother *is* a he," Eis said. "He gave birth to me on the planet Usk when he was quite young." He looked at Khana. "About Khana's age."

"You've never seen Hesperian Ficto-Vids?" she asked K'asp.

"Uh, I've seen most of the yacht racing and Thwwing racing Vids. Oh, so I've probably seen, what's his name, your birth mother?" he added in such a way he showed he still didn't believe it.

"Ay'r Eisenstein Kell!" Khana and Eis said together, then laughed.

"He's only the third most famous human in the galaxy," Khana added.

"But he looks different than I do," Eis said. "I mean these distinctive features I have, the bronze hair and green eyes? He doesn't have these features. He has light blonde hair, almost white, from birth."

"Platinum, it's called," Khana said. "like the precious metal."

"Right. And his eyes are what are called Beryllium blue. They're usually light blue but they get dark blue and even violet or purple, depending upon his environment. My own coloring is from previous family generations of my Kell relatives."

"And is quite rare!" Khana put in.

K'asp shrugged. But when Eis had gotten some drinks and left, he turned to Khana and asked in a lower voice, "You knew about that? Males giving birth and all?" he asked her.

"Of course, I did. Everyone knows. A billion males give birth every day."

"But then ... what do the females do?"

"The females? Oh, K'asp! There are so few females left in the rest of the galaxy! We on Hercular might constitute 99 percent or more of all the female humans there are!"

"What? How can that be?"

"It can be because of The Matriarchal War against the Sentient Cybers! The war that the Cybers won? Ever heard of that? No? Were you sleeping during *all* of Galactic History and Geography?" Khana asked, thinking, he had to have been. Cute as they are, males could be so utterly dim! she concluded as she flounced out of the kitchen.

In the end, Khana played a bigger part in the rescue than any of them, including Khana herself, thought would happen. And as usual K'or was right in believing that circumstances would end up dictating what they might accomplish.

But first there was the winning plan of rescue and for that they had to thank K'asp. His initial idea was spoken in so low a voice they all had to ask him to speak up.

"Stink bombs," he said, clearly embarrassed. "You know, K'or, like the ones we used to prank with when we were twigs."

Eis and the saplings wanted to know what he meant.

"Well, first, they won't hurt anyone."

"I like the idea already," Eis said. "I was afraid of any plan with violence."

"K'or, you explain," K'asp said. He really was embarrassed.

"It essentially is turds in a package. Only we add in some of that dry-ice stuff and then seal it tightly and toss it. When it hits something hard, it stirs up and the chemical reaction of the two makes smoke. Terrible smelling smoke." He added happily, "A *lot* of terrible smelling smoke."

"Of course, neither one of you," Vannada addressed the two of them, "*ever* did anything like this before."

They were busy denying it when Khana cut in and said, "Assuming we can get into the same high loge you mentioned before, Van. That's where we toss the stink bombs from. I could do that myself." She turned to K'or, "That way I'll be out of the way and safe. While you folk are down there busy rescuing."

"But will the cyber-men even be affected by it?" Eis asked.

"It's blindingly thick smoke!" K'asp said. "Everyone will be."

"We're looking for a harmless distraction." K'or reminded Eis.

"That leaves just the three of you," Eis said. "Unless I can help."

"Sorry. You'll be somewhere super-safe."

"But I think we can talk some of the Early-Migration males we know to join us." K'asp said and looked at K'or, who nodded in agreement.

"They'll think it's all great fun, especially leading off with stink bombs."

"The Cybermen have guns. They shot at us," Vannada reminded them.

"We adopt the twist'n'turn flight pattern getting away," K'or said. "It worked before. With more of us, it will be even more effective."

So that was how it was set up. They would all wear masks or helmets and face plates for long term flying to block the stink and hide their faces. Brave K'or would crawl through the collapsed space from the Green Room and be ready there for when the stink bombs hit. Eis showed him the standard shut-off spot for all cybers, right behind the left knee. K'or would shut off the guard there who would already be distracted and be taken by surprise. K'asp and his two friends would be poised on lower balconies ready to fly down and grab hostages. Vannada would be on the roof, ready to help any of the women and aid them in launching themselves away from the stadium. Khana would join her there and help get wings on the women.

At least that was the plan.

For a while it went just as planned. They had planned for at least two hours after the humans went to sleep, and the Cybermen, if not resting, then off their guard. From her high point, Khana could see that indeed the women were sleeping on some kind of makeshift beds. She could also see K'asp and his two friends ready and waiting on a slightly lower loge. Through a tear in the roof, she could make out Vannada up there and ready, looking resolute against the night sky and stars. The only one she couldn't see was K'or, who was too far below.

But they all had their communicators open and dialed in to a single group channel. So, when K'or signaled "ready", Khana carefully placed the two stink bombs they had made, and simply slid them over the edge of the loge's low wall and drew back out of sight.

She didn't see or hear them hit the floor in front of the cyberman guard but, not a minute later, she had to see what was happening, so she moved forward enough to watch K'asp and the others from their vantage point, toss two more stink bombs down. That was not in the script, she thought, but wasn't it just like males to do some something extra.

Suddenly all bedlam broke loose. First, the smoke from the bombs shot up so much that K'asp and the other males had to back away from the ledge. Second, the guard below who K'or was crawling toward to sneak up on, started turning around in circles. either totally baffled or searching for flames which, logically, had made the fragrant smoke. He didn't even notice K'or hanging on to him from ground level until K'or finally got to and hit the shut off mechanism and rolled away. The button took at least another half minute to work. By then, all of the wood-wealthy hostage women had jumped and begun screaming.

Khana could see the Cybermen rush toward the women, leaving Janesborot unattended. None of K'asp's group was clear of smoke yet, but she was. This was her chance. She got herself up on one foot on the back of a loge seat, the other on the narrow loge wall, and launched herself. At first, she half tumbled but quickly caught herself, and swept by the balcony with K'asp and his friends on it. She yelled, "Go! Go!" and unable to stop herself made a gyre right down to the ground floor, aiming for the pamp. He stood there completely baffled and since she had her face plate on, she could see perfectly well. She swept down and simply grabbed him from the back, her arc and thrust easily lifting him off the ground. "Eis sent me!" she managed to shout into his surprised cute-funny little face. Then she dipped left and was able to grab him from beneath his legs with one arm and so, easily carrying him, she flew up to the loge. "I've got him!" she said into the communicator, and then "Here we go again!" to Janesborot, and up they went to the roof.

Vannada was up there and in seconds so were K'asp and K'or and the other males.

"Where are the women?" Vannada shouted.

"Look down there!" K'or laughed.

They could see the lawn in front of the already half destroyed stadium exit, and through the billowing smoke, they could see the women far below rushing out and into the amazed arms of Public Guardians who had set up there for a siege. One cyberman alone had held one woman by the blouse but he was still blinded by the smoke. Two other women rushed back at him and while one of them repeatedly slapped his head with her purse, the other ripped her friend away by tearing off her blouse.

"They're safe. We've got to get out of here now!" K'or yelled and took the pamp from Khana saying "Eis will be so happy to see you, little guy!"

Off they flew. Because K'asp's friends were not joining them later, they were able to make help the others make a wide-angled flight flare getting away, so even when the shots finally did come, rather late, all of the flyers could simply execute twist'n'turns.

Khana thought she heard a shot hit home. But it was K'asp's helmet face plate, which shattered and so he threw it away.

The males all whooped loudly in glee, and Khana joined them. They'd done it. Six young Hercularan branches and saplings had ended an interstellar crisis.

Vannada joined her and they linked arms and shouted, "We're off to Meadow!"

And for a single moment, Khana thought, it may be a long time until I see my Ma' and Fa' again. But the others also shouted with glee. So she joined them. And as she did, she remembered her dream of giant Sequoia trees rising in the air. There had been six of them, she remembered now. Just like the six flying rescuers headed away to safety.

Chapter Six:

AN INTERRUPTED CELEBRATION

"Deon, what does a 'Double Beryllium Birthday' signify?"

"No, idea, my love."

"It's on this invitation for Kri'nni (xx)'s birthday. I got it some-time ago but we're set to go to it tonight."

"Hmm. Yes, it's listed here in my virtual calendar."

"Do you have any idea how old she is?" Ay'r asked.

"No. And neither does anyone else. Why not look it up?"

"Wrist connector, what is a double beryllium birthday?"

It responded: "A single so-called Beryllium birthday is generally believed to be 300 years, Sol Rad. Therefore, a double one would be ..."

"Got it. Six hundred years!" To Deon he said, "Can she really be six hundred years old?"

"Your name-sake is five hundred and what? Fifty? Sixty? So sure, I guess she could be six hundred. If any of the PVN-Bios about them are telling the truth, they were contemporaries, weren't they? They and Mart Kell?"

"That's what I always believed, yes. But do they get Desmer jobs, the Bella=Arth.s? You know, to look and act more youthful. Do they?"

"Don't think so. Those are only good on mammals. But wasn't Kri'nni an Egg-laying Queen for a few centuries? That would keep her young?"

"I'd think it would wear her out."

"No. She would have been fed on first blossom nectars. Pure stuff. Also on larvae extracts. Also massaged five times a day. Those might keep her young forever."

"Thanks for the un-appetizing menu. That's one spa I'm not going to anytime soon."

"I hear there are restaurants selling that very combo here in the City. On the unsavory end of the Algol Girder, I believe. Ole Branklin goes there. He's must be about a thousand by now."

Deon Syzygy looked up and smiled at his adorato who was properly horrified, and turned back to the official notice he'd just received of a curiously anomalous, weak signal that had shown up in a galactic sector almost opposite the center of the galaxy from Hesperia and the Center Worlds. It came from the far edge of the Carina-Sagittarius arm, known to be one of the outermost spiral arms of the "Milky Way" galaxy. As Quinx Council Security Chief, a dozen years ago, Sol Rad., Deon had established predominantly sentient-cyber operated bases not only there but regularly spaced around the entire rim of the galaxy, even beyond that portion which contained their Ib'r Republic. This perimeter had been set up to serve one real purpose: to warn of any extremely unlikely impending visit – or invasion – from any source beyond that galactic rim.

This then was the *first* noticed signal in all those decades of *any* activity, and it had worked the reverse way, signalling someone leaving. The signal had taken about four weeks Sol Rad. to travel even faster than light speed to an inner rim security base, where a Cyber-Supervisor named Arrigo von Laks, had instant-messaged it in a sealed communication to the City and directly to Deon's previous Security Office headquarters. There – since his name was on the message – it was insta-flung to him individually, as well as to the new chief-in-charge.

Von Laks had appended a message: "This appears to be the 'molecular scatter-signal" of a vessel when it *leaves* the galactic envelope and heads into pure empty intergalactic space. The first such signal going in any direction that any of these bases have ever detected doing that. We are unaware of any vessel doing that. I'm afraid that direct sealed communication contact is required for this base to release any other information."

"Should we try to get Kri'nni a gift?" Ay'r was now asking. And seeing his husband pre-occupied. "What? What is it?"

"I'm not really sure, Ay'r. Let me go into a sealed booth for this. It's highly classified communication."

"From Security?"

"Yes. But not to worry. It's about something very, very distant."

"No. Fine. Take it."

"No gift for Kri'nni," Deon said. "What could she possibly lack?"

Ay'r laughed. "That's exactly what the invite says. Go! Take your call."

A few minutes later, Deon Syzygy was sealed in their residence's real-time insta-comm. booth, with the good-looking figure of Arrigo von Laks facing him.

"You obviously think it is important," Deon said. "Even though it is a vehicle *leaving* the galaxy?"

"Exactly. The reason for importance is that the vehicle had a weak but still readable molecular regulation id."

"Belonging to?"

"The Sanqq' family. In fact, it seems to be an odd combination serial number: partly ordinary and partly fabricated, which when we checked, was the illegal serial long believed by various agencies to have been constructed and then utilized by the Great Father's Holo-famed Close-Son, Holt – so that he could elude some publicity whenever coming or going. He has been missing for over 20 years Sol Rad."

"You're saying that signal was Holt leaving the galactic rim?"

"So it would appear. And, at a speed so great that it would preclude him being conscious that it was happening."

"So in all likelihood, he would not be conscious of making that choice?" Deon asked.

"That's what the base officer out there who intercepted the signal believes. Yes."

"Could it be a rogue Fast Yacht mind?"

"Unclear."

"What direction?"

A graphic came up, with vectors apparent.

"None, except what is in the eventual path."

"You mean, it's eventual path twenty degrees or so south of the Milky Way and toward that little blob of stars? That is one of the Small Magellanic Clouds, isn't it?" Deon asked.

"Yes, Prime Minster. The Second, or smaller one. 199,000 light years distant."

They were both silent a while, then Deon asked. "What is the possibility of a rescue team being sent?"

"Because of the distance and time factors involved in getting this com to you, the local base deemed it best to send a rescue team immediately, and this command base didn't overrule that decision. Since the beyond light-speed of the rescue mission would be physically intolerable except to ... sturdier beings ..."

"I understand. So, only sentient-cybers could be sent to rescue?"

Von Laks seemed relieved. "Yes, exactly. The rescue team went out two hours Sol Rad. after the receipt of the signal at the galactic rim base. And at least one member of that rescue team must be partly conscious at times to deal with any unknown variables, so it cannot travel as quickly as the vehicle it is pursuing."

"Yes, I understand. What if anything, do we know about the Smaller Magellanic Cloud #2?"

"I am sending you all and any possible gathered information from over the entire past few centuries. You are warned that it is ... scant, Prime Minister. What there is, is technical. You have attached to your new office, a very capable Delphinid notator – what we call a 'number-cruncher.' This rare female has the material in hand and at your say-so will inspect it and answer any of your questions better than we possibly could from here."

"I know exactly who you mean ... Can you at least give me a sentence, a phrase about the cloud?"

"Next to nothing. It is believed that there was a Supernova located at the edge of the diffuse ellipse shape at the greatest distance from us. That was seven thousand years ago. It was noted by some Pre-Metro-Terran astronomers ... Our sentient-cyber team that left the Carina-Sag rim base for that mission were volunteers who had expressed no fears about the traveling into and meeting the unknown."

That was sobering.

"Thank you, Chief von Laks. Excellent detecting and action.

Both you and your galactic rim base-command and especially those sent out beyond, are to be commended for your promptness and initiative. And you all will be – officially. Feel free to contact me instantly with anything. However, none of this information is to leave this data-stream."

"Naturally," Von Laks smiled.

"I mean it, von Laks. Contact me *immediately* with any real new information. This is the first lead we've had in that disappearance and if it is relevant, it would explain much."

Deon remained in the insta-booth for another few minutes. He was fairly certain the Great Father and his Consort would both be at the birthday bash tonight. It would be wonderful to be able to offer him even this glimmer of a possibility.

"So?" Ay'r said, once Deon emerged.

"You may finally get to meet that infamous cousin to who knows what degree."

"Holt? No?! When?"

"Well, at the rate he was travelling away from us, I'd wager that it will be sometime later in our lifetime," Deon said, and added, "I like how you are dressed," and swept him into his arms.

The origin rumor was that Kri'nni (Dss-sxx) had come to Hesperia while still quite young. She was directly descended from the Bella=Arth. Imperial Line on the species hom world of Deneb XIII, although her own branch of the distinguished family had already relocated, once to Markab's Gamma planet, where they were also related to an Imperial Line, and then to Algol XIV where they were agri-business landholders. And then, unlike most of their stay-at-home-nesting family, they moved even further away to the Algenib cluster. Her own close-nest of barely a hundred however had been residing for decades somewhere else, upon a satellite of Andromache's gas giant, in the heart of the Matriarchal Center Worlds during the closing years of the Bella=Arth. War. But they were so distant from it all they didn't receive word of their species' defeat until several years Sol Rad. had passed.

The reason given was that they were involved in hush-hush bio-chemical research along with a small village of mixed gender

Matriarchal humans in a settlement far from the closest space-port. After the Treaty of Fomalhaut had already been signed by other Bella=Arth.s, a team of Matriarchy diplomats from Eudora was sent to the research station and three of Kri'nni's relatives – her overworked Queen-mother and two of Male Drones (who might have been Kri'nni's sire-fertilizers) were offered the ruler-ship of all and any of their species remaining in the galaxy. These perplexed scientists demurred, claiming they had important research to do; they had made some breakthroughs, and were close to making another. They didn't give a rotting larva for poli-tics, of any sort, no matter what species was involved.

But then young Kri'nni spoke up. She'd always been an adequate, never a brilliant, researcher there among her family and she leapt at the chance to get away from the Podunk satellite and her nerdy relations and get into the swim of things.

The story went that the Post-War winners fell over them-selves thinking that, in Kri'nni, they had a public relations prize for the Matriarchy. She was offered several flash official inspec-tion tours of several of the defeated worlds and she went and looked. But their burnt-out cinders of nest-cities were definitely not to the young Arth.'s taste. She'd grown up residing more with humans than with her own relatives, anyway, and what she'd seen and heard through their media all pointed toward wealth, glamour, and fun, far away from boring old Arth.s, never mind the newly installed Matriarchs. Happening upon someone vaguely diplomatic from Hesperia during her journeys, she latched on to him and quietly explained what a public relations coup it would be for the City on a Star to house the final member of the Bella=Arth. Imperium instead of her wasting away on Benefica or Eudora in the uncertain arms of the Matriarchy.

Someone higher up in the Quinx Council readily agreed. Once actually there at the City on a Star, however, Kri'nni personally found the centuries-old Arth. embassy on the central Algol girder to be "smelly and dreary," if necessary, especially for rare, visit-ing co-species members. She did however like the looks of the ambassadorial bank accounts and credit accounts that she now controlled. She hired a sentient cyber as deputy, and retired the rest of the staff quite remuneratively to avoid complaints. She replaced them with male humans, along with a handful of male Arth. Drone-class professionals who'd been stranded on Hesperia by the defeat, and who – it was talked of – she employed in a variety of capacities.

She could never exactly recall how it was that she discovered the abandoned Sl.pg ship terminal on Motor Avenue. The immense, ungainly vehicles were wildly déclassé but still occasionally used for recreational transport as well as for interstellar shipping. During the last war they'd been used for evacuation purposes – they were the only vehicles large enough – whenever human colonies were being targeted. If pressed, Kri'nni might say she had been visiting a friend on a portion of the Ophiuchus girder that just happened to cross Motor Ave near that point, and she had been attracted to the building by its size, its classic lines and especially by its privacy. (Most of the surrounding edifices were vacant; the area was a sliver away from being a post-industrial slum.)

Kri'nni retained two of the huge liners in the best condition and kept them in that section of the cyclopean building that opened up to a still operable outdoor starship apron and truncated runway near the girder's edge. A Hesperian security agency kept them in prime operating condition, so they might be used in some unexpected, hopefully off-world, emergency. This gained her friends on the Quinx Council and even a few tax benefits. Meanwhile in the central portion of the vacant liner terminal, she'd built her own residence and office within a construct that was ordinarily elevated sixty meters above the main floor.

With her private quarters out of sight, neatly tucked under the twenty-five story roof, the place was enormous, open and easily occupied by Etvan Sphinnaker's Hesperian Festivity Agency, which had been commissioned to be party-designers.

An ambitious artist, Sphinnaker took on the decoration challenge as one that might solidify his growing reputation in a galactic capital where party-intent media were common as house insects on Algol 4 and could make and break commercial reputations in holo-minutes.

One arrived at the party by air car or private dromedary-inspired taxi along the astonishingly refurbished Motor Avenue with its illumination that grew increasingly brighter as one approached

Kri'nni's place – a light in the otherwise dark and abandoned neighborhood with only a few aerial parks, and sketchier than most inner-burbs.

Actually, one arrived rather above street level.The valet station awnings fluttered dreamily in the ultra-soft illumination upon an indoor-outdoor entry at what might have been the fourteenth floor, had there been real levels. Reception was grandly accommodating, including spaces leased to dozens of members of the Media who knew, in some biographical detail, seemingly every person of any species arriving that night. Once inside, you could sweep down several moving staircases for a grand public landing, or prettily parachute down, or slip down vertical chutes and ladders.

There, an amusement park, a casino, several theatres, a skiing pool and scads of free restaurants greeted you, awaiting your pleasure.

Cyber waiters, bartenders, greeters, and aides, circulated, all clad in what appeared to be the livery colors of the Nest Imperium of Dss-xx on Deneb. By the time Deon and Ay'r had arrived, six-score guests were already in occupation. As always, at the announcement of their names and the flash of giant holograms of them live around the entire building, applause broke out. Ay'r was still adored for his adventures on the Resort Planet Usk, two decades previously. Those feats had spawned Holo-grids, Holo-games, auto-readers, and eventually one of the most popular Pseudo View Narratives of the past century, *The Betrothal at Usk*, temporarily unseating Thwwing Racing Romances and even the Great Father's perennial best seller, *Dryland's End*.

That the spunky Uskian Neo – descended from two previous celebrity-society City darlings– had made a name for himself as the Savior of a Downtrodden Race on his own planet and then ended up in the arms of their own deeply admired Deon Syzygy, Elite of the Elite of the Quinx Council Founding Families, further fixed and then fueled the Hesperian public's attention on the glamorous duo. At certain, never predictable, times the younger of the couple would make not so subtle mentions of his husband's political credibility as a consequence of their fortuitous uniting.

"We can't go anywhere without running into one of your relatives," Ay'r said the minute they reached the bottom of the moving stairway. Media were banned here, but having seen via

Holo-Vids that Deon had arrived, a group had gathered where they alit. Among them was the unmistakable figure of P'al Syzygy with an attractive younger Ambassadorial Class Delphinid.

Deon went directly to the two, while smiling and greeting as many of the others as was possible, Ay'r noted, as he hurried to tag along.

"Piotr (r^r) Franck," P'al said to his cousin after a solid hug, introducing the stranger. "My consort."

"You may or may not know my consort," Deon began, pulling young Ay'r forward.

"I'd have to be living in a sub-oceanic, Denebolan ice-cave not to know him," P'al said. Then nodded half a bow.

Ay'r and Piotr (r^r) then clasped arms.

"Piotr (r^r) made a bit of news himself a year ago, Sol Rad., on New Venice," Ay'r pointed out to Deon. "Am I pronouncing your name correctly," he asked, unsure if he was getting the r-cir-cumflex-r's properly guttural.

"Close enough," Piotr (r^r) said. "And thank you for even try-ing. My Hesperian Franck relations here pretty much ignore it, calling me 'Pete" and 'Peter' even 'Pedro!'"

Ay'r laughed. "I know what you mean. They have no idea how utterly, unconsciously, obliviously snotty they are. I often get a look, a second look, a third look, and then, 'Uh, aren't you that pamp guy?!'"

That loosened them up.

"What do you answer?" Piotr (r^r) was curious.

"He usually checks his pockets and any clothing flaps," Deon said for A'yr, "And then he says, 'Well, Gosh! I had a few of those pamps here a minute ago!'"

That completely broke the ice. They moved as a tight group over to one of Sphinnaker's more amusing creations – or re-cre-ations – of Connaught Park, a local outdoor sitting area down Motor Ave. What the first group of City Fathers referred to as a recreation area, complete with a barely burbling fountain, crum-bling air-skate paths, desiccated ferns, and even a few statues of stelezine-addicts sleeping it off on or under what might have been park benches. At least, they looked like statues!

"So, Cuz," P'al asked, "What do you think of Kri'nni's Eighth or is it Ninth Life?"

"You mean," Deon replied, "As reformed Dowager-Empress of

All the Arth.s?"

"Wasn't she always so admired," Ay'r had to ask.

"Without going into detail," P'al began, "let's just say that in centuries past, this particular Liner Terminal was viewed by several law enforcement entities as the main entry port of a variety of illegal substances into the City."

"And, also as the main exit point of large sums of Hesperian d'lars, usually to a private banks on suspect Satellites of the Algol system," Pa'l added.

"Plus," Deon added, "it was suggested that her particular ascending cabin was the scene of various inter-species couplings."

"More like sex orgies. Also illegal back in those last days of the Matriarchy," P'al said, amused.

"No!" both younger males protested together, "Illegal? Really?" The idea was ludicrous! Grotesque! So ... Sixth Millennium!

"Do you think," Piotr (r^r) hinted at P'al, "she could be persuaded to have you and I relive old times in her bedchamber – just to get that frisson of illegality again?"

"She'd go along with it in a minute. And video it. And sell it to the highest bidder," Deon assured them, which gained even more laughter.

After a bit of silence, Piotr (r^r) asked, "What is that the heavenly music being piped into this slouch of a park? ... P'al?"

P'al, who knew everything replied "A duet by an early Metro-Terran composer named Nicola Porpora, and titled 'In hoc vexilla crucis' sung by ..."

"Wait a sec. I recognize the voices," Ay'r spoke up. "That's the cybernetic wonder musician Boris Blu™ and my very own dear close-son, Eis!'

"Eis? The Singer? The Bard of the Universe, or whatever he's called?" Piotr (r^r) asked. "He's *your* close-son?"

"Indeed he is – and famously so," Deon asserted. "I'm the proud step dad." In a fake-hearty know-it-all tone of voice, he added, "Why I knew Eis when he was still in his mother's external womb."

"Didn't I come across data that they are duetting somewhere very far away these days?" P'al asked.

"I'll say. On Hercular! One of the 2nd Matriarchy's Seeded World projects." Ay'r reported, "Somewhere in that nowhere Perseus arm."

"One of the 2nd Matriarchy's few *successful* Seeded World projects." Deon added. "Only about a hundred actually worked out."

"Pelagia was another one," P'al reminded them. "Well, at least it worked out successfully for a while."

"How many worlds were seeded by the Matriarchy?" Ay'r asked.

"Couple of thousand? Something like that," Deon said.

There was a sudden hubbub around the area, semi-closed as it was, and Deon took off to see why and returned to say, "The Great Father and Oudma have arrived. We'd better go meet them or I'll never hear the end of it from my various deputies about missing another promotional opportunity."

Everyone from Holt's discovery team of the new Beryllium 18 star-source close to the center of the galaxy at 29 Degrees of Sagittarius had become trillionaires several times over – once the official assay team had backed up the prodigious wealth of their stellar mineral claim. This, despite sharing half of their find with the City on a Star itself, which would do the actual work of obtaining and then processing the ultra-precious stuff as well as commercially distributing it. They'd also handsomely paid off those investors who'd had to foresight to see this group of elite young Hesperian sportsmen and party-going celebrities as more than met the public's eye. Probably because the investors were other elite young Hesperian sportsmen and party-going celebrities themselves – and now richer by far.

So naturally there would be gossip and envy. But in more than one case, it was misdirected. The find had altered members of the group in unexpected ways. Some, like Dr. Dem-Arest, who had previously been seen as a "shallow society medic if ever there was one," according to his detractors, had suddenly swerved careers and gone into public-service medicine, even breaking up his marriage to find work quite far away from the City, usually with the few professional military/security special forces remaining in the Center Worlds' space force, or, when asked where, Dem-Arest would reply, "wherever a highly medically trained person is needed."

Others like Cap Zullini-Brach and Alton Darency had first become financiers in addition to being playboys. But during a funding event celebration on one of the six agricultural moons of Eurydice, Zullini-Brach – ever the athlete – had spontaneously joined a meta-football game among the sons of the Prokaryotics farmers there. He'd rather quickly forged such a tight bond with that group in whom he saw champion potential, that he returned there time and again, came to know them well enough to shape them into an interstellar team. He then fronted a sort of Benevolent Society for the farmers and processing workers that he co-founded, to erect proper new housing for thousands of their families. He'd eventually put up a modest residence himself nearby and by now was spending three quarters of his time there, amidst the Prokaryotic-farms, and the much-improved agricultural workers, processors, and especially the team members. He might or, more likely, might not be at the party this night.

Darency had resisted any external change as a result of his new financial status the longest of any of them. Publicly, he still attended every social event of his group's kind in the City, but increasingly he seemed to be doing it half-heartedly. When the others met and discussed Alton's new (or rather, lack of new) life choices, they increasingly concluded that while they'd all been shocked and traumatized by Holt's disappearance, it had struck Darency the most, and by far with the worst result. Although the others gathered very infrequently, whenever they did without him, they invariably speculated why that was. In time, they concluded that the light-as-air Alton Darency had been in love with Holt but somehow never managed to let him know, counting on having all the time in the world to let it become apparent to his friend. Time that simply vanished when Holt vanished.

The fifth member of the new group of Beryllium 18 titans, Caspar al Haarz astounded them all by revealing interest in another aspect of public service: following in his ancestors' footsteps by opting to enter politics. He easily won the traditional, family-owned, Outer Quinx Council-ship of the al Haarz triple star-system located in the older Orion-Spur galactic arm. Then, to everyone's surprise, he had made a name himself in that body of over 5,000 representatives by calling for the unification of many of those anciently populated star systems that had been all but neglected by the two matriarchies as well as the interregnum government and was held in low regard even by the expansive new Ib'r Galactic Republic. In a few short years Sol Rad., his Three-Species Founding-Systems Coalition had gained enough clout to not only elect Caspar to the smaller Great Quinx Council of only 500 members, but in addition a Bella=Arth. member too. Their quickly-created new coalition was designed to bring many older, more established (and long-ignored star-systems) into a "special trade and finance coalition." The Arth. representative was a member of the close-family of the present Bella=Arth. Empress, Ami'da'lia, who was busily rebuilding her species' once destroyed planets into new, Three Species-integrated, societies and political entities.

When Deon Syzygy's name began to be circulated as the new Galactic Premier, he made a point of inviting al Haarz to the planning sessions, with the result that Caspar revealed a splendid almost Cardinal Richelieu-like grasp of what Deon himself called "personalities and politics," which helped a great deal in the plan's solidification. Caspar naturally requested a place in the new cabinet. An Ambassadorial Delphinid from one of the Procyon system's newer colonized worlds had been unanimously elected to replace al Haarz on the Inner Quinx Council. And then a third generation-colonized stellar system at the still-developing edge of the Orion-Spur had renamed itself from the ancient nomenclature of Gaspar's Star, to a new name: Casper's Star, to honor the still young Hesperian who'd brought them back into the thick of Galactic politics.

No fool, Deon's second act as Premier was to have al Haarz sworn in as his deputy Premier.

His first act had been to go to Planet Verhandel in the Norms, to ask for the Great Father's blessing.

"It's not needed," Ay'r himself had said, casually enough. "Although we're both glad you came to visit. We've just begun going around socially again. Am I right, Oudma?"

She agreed.

"But ..." Deon stammered, "It's the first time the Premiership of the Republic has fallen outside of your family," he pointed out. "The family that gave it its name."

"Does this mean that you won't come bother me all the time like your recent predecessors, Cass'io Azura and North Ib'r, did?"

Deon laughed, but said, "No. I can't promise that. In truth,

I may come more often than they did."

"Then why not consider yourself family – and then nothing has changed."

That was as much of a blessing as Deon could have ever asked for. And now, talking to Ay'r here, at Kri'nni's party he almost did consider himself family. The easy way that the Great Father had reached out to clasp him, the light kiss Oudma had bestowed on his cheek, all confirmed it.

"So! So far, no catastrophes!" Ay'r said.

"Four and a half weeks Sol Rad. into my Ministry, you mean? But no, they protect me from catastrophes." Deon said. "Or keep them from happening."

"Even better."

He couldn't help but notice how their consorts, his Ay'r and Oudma, a few yards away, were immediately engaged in conversation although he knew that she was shy to the point of diffidence at these large affairs and he wasn't sure they'd even met before.

"Aren't they lovely together," Ay'r said.

They were, of course. Especially as they were the only true blondes in the local area.

"They resemble each other so much," Deon pointed out. "The way they stand, the fluid hand gestures. It's almost ... I don't know ... regal!"

"Your Ay'r, of course, bears the exact coloring that we think of as the typical Ib'r physical characteristics. From Pelagia originally. But what you may not know, Deon, is how very closely he also resembles, 'Dward Ib'r, Oudma's brother, and my first real love, on my first visit to that extraordinary planet."

They continued looking at their loved ones for a while unseen themselves by them.

Ay'r, The Great Father himself, looked wonderful. They'd done the replication – was it actually cloning with a full duplication of thoughts and attitudes, or what? Centuries ago, Ay'r's birth mother had invented the process which was actually illegal to use – with the exception of these two remarkable people. But the "aging" was appropriate. Deon would love to ask when it had taken place. Shortly before Ay'r's unexpected voyage to the Globular Cluster, and the resulting disaster? Or had the body been there for years, just naturally aging? It was such a complex series of issues – and questions to be asked - that Deon decided not to.

There was a more pressing issue. Deon wasn't sure how to do it, but he had to, and he finally did say, "One advantage of my new position is that I find out things long before others. This is what I found out a few hours ago, Sol Rad." He then told Ay'r about the galactic signal, the supposition of Holt's identity in connection with that signal and the chase and rescue mission that had begun.

Ay'r clasped him again, clearly overjoyed. Then, "You have no close-sons I don't think.'

"No. I thought I'd wait until this Premiership is over."

"Not a bad idea. But you must know that there's a special bond between a close-mother and his or her child. Oudma has it with our two, both close-sons, your Ay'r doubtless has it with the son he carried and gave birth to, the Universally adored Eis. And I have it with Holt. I've known since this second body was activated that his disappearance was just that and that he was somewhere and still alive. I just felt it. I still do."

"We're assuming that," Deon cautioned. "But I've sent his old partner and friend Dr. Dem-Arest to go meet him at galaxy's edge in the Carina-Sagittarius arm. Very far away. Just in case ... well he has not survived that well. Let's not get our hopes up too much."

"He's alive and he's a survivor. I've no doubt of that."

"Where his Fast was headed," Deon tried to tamp down the enthusiasm, "is so much further away.... Another galaxy, although a smaller one. Still, no one has ever been there before, Ser. We know nothing about it at all."

"I realize that, Deon. But I know that when he does become conscious again, wherever he lands, that he will adjust to his new place wonderfully and somehow make his mark!"

Deon resisted saying that from what he'd read of the younger man that wherever Holt landed, that he would indeed adjust to his new place wonderfully fast but somehow make as many enemies as friends.

Oudma and Ay'r joined them, "Listen! Is that a flourish of synthetic brass?! Kri'nni must be about to make an appearance."

The floor-show, since that was what is was, began.

The group found seats nearby, that when sat in automatically tilted up. This was initially startling, but then Deon noticed that all the seats nearby did the same. And for good reason, since the floor show was more like an air show. First a series of fireworks high in the space over the far end where the remaining Slp.G. liners had been covered over. That was original and certainly sparkling enough and vastly entertaining. But with the final one, a steady-in-the-air Beryllium-blue "fountain," there was yet another variation. The silver-blue "liquid" dropping down on all sides, turned into living human acrobats, who used the enormous vertical space to then perform dozens of different, amazing acts while spinning down and around, eliciting even more genuine applause from the onlookers.

"Are they Cybers?" Oudma asked. "Or are humans capable of doing all that?"

P'al with his enhanced eyesight pin-pointed several of the distant figures one after the other for close-ups. "They all look human to me. I can't read any cybernetic signatures."

"Nor can I," Ay'r the Great Father agreed. So, confirming what Deon had suspected, that his new body had also been provided with sensory and other kinds of enhancements.

Even more enthusiasm then greeted the acrobats, as they finally slipped down to the floor, and took their bows.

But seconds later an enormous flutter of wings was heard, as scores of younger Bella=Arth.s still in their winged youth, took the acrobats' place. They did even more amazing flying stunts in mid-air, including a few coming close enough to the ground to pick up items left on tables and other objects. This elicited even more comment.

"Are those imagos?" Piotr (r^r) asked. "or, what would we call them?"

"Call them Nymphs." They heard behind them. "Or Nemphae."

Deon turned and two others said, "Kri'nni!"

"Greetings my Pupae and Imago guests," she said as she slid into their midst. The others all stood to greet her, but she stopped in front of Ay'r and made what looked like a curtsey: "Felicitations and multiple blessings upon thee, oh Great Father. So very glad (amazed [truly!}) to see you again."

"Knock it off, Kri'nni. Come and let me say Happy Birthday the stinky old human way," he opened his arms wide, and she slid into them long enough for the semblance of a hug, before gracefully removing herself and greeting each of them in turn.

"You know my companion? (boyfriend [lover and what not]) Mar'ko Vandelik? She introduced the tall gangly, and rather

Arthropodic looking human male who was dressed in what looked like insectile gold cloth plates covering his chest, cinched black-ruby-studded waist belt, tight double gold cloth plated legs and golden air-shoes. His outfit was a slightly duller version of Kri'nni's usual natural plates, shining like new in the iridescent colors of the rainbow.

Greetings took some time. Kri'nni had something to say to each of them, even Deon, before she encountered younger Ay'r. "And here is the hero! (savior! {sainted one!}) of the formerly despised and traduced race of Usk. It's no surprise that Our Glorious Leader (Premier {Deon the Great}) should have found such human gorgeousness and virtue as a mate (consort, {husband? wife? I'm never sure which with you basic-pheromonal mammalians!}).

Young Ay'r also desired a hug from the Bella=Arth., and told her what a great honor it was for him to meet her, and how he hoped this would be the first of such meetings.

Kri'nni's appearance had attracted others to their group. But Deon could see Caspar al Haartz choosing that moment to thread his way past them, and between Mar'ko and Oudma. Deon rapidly evaluated the slightly strained look on his Deputy's face as more than discomfort with his Superior being in a crowd. He knew all of the folk here and knew Deon was perfectly safe. So, it must be something else.

He moved aside to meet al Haartz, who took the opportunity to angle himself directly in front of the Premier who then blocked him from the others.

"What's your bad news?" Deon asked.

Caspar leaned in and whispered it.

"When?" Deon asked.

"We just got news of it now. It's so distant it might have happened two or three days ago, Sol Rad."

"And the terrorists?

"We believe they mean no actual harm to him. But it is unclear. They've never actually killed anyone yet."

"Because?"

"They're making a point ... They're getting our attention."

"Well, it worked. They've got *my* attention," Deon said.

"They used sound bombs and definitely destroyed part of the stadium where he had just appeared."

"Just appeared?" Deon asked. "But he wasn't still onstage?"

"No. He'd left the stage. He was supposedly in one of the Green Rooms meeting fans." He stopped and lifted his wrist connector up to one ear. Leaving Deon to fidget.

"Nothing really new. Some injuries among the civilians in the audience. Sound and falling debris related. No shooting. No deaths. That Avenge K'tina Kell faction have never been violent before. They'll doubtless take hostages. I'm sure of it."

Deon noticed Ay'r the Great father looking at him. Noticing how pale he'd suddenly become. He nodded once, and Ay'r began moving over to him, subtly. Younger Ay'r was having a delightful discussion with Mar'ko and Oudma and Kri'nni."

"What?" Ay'r arrived and asked just as Caspar took off.

"Our son, Eis, is in trouble?" Deon said in a low voice. "And he's very far away. Too far for us to really do anything ..."

"Let me be of use."

Deon thought, if anyone could, this man could. "Yes. Of course."

"The situation is now ... what? How?" Ay'r asked.

"Unclear," Deon said. "Nothing too definite."

"That's good. Very good. We'll stay here a few minutes more and then we'll disperse and meet at your home office. That way the others won't be involved. Caspar will join us there?"

"And some others. Yes, that's good. But ..."

He meant but could anything be worse than this? Deon then looked at his *adorato*. Laughing, bright and delightful, all unaware of what was happening.

"If he were to be made unhappy by this, I don't think I could bear it." Deon said.

Suddenly they heard Kri'nni saying "That's no mystery *at all*! I know (exactly {to the longitudinal and latitudinal minute and second}) where Mart Kell is?"

That got Deon's attention. No one in the galaxy knew. Not for the past two decades Sol Rad.

"You do?" Oudma asked. "You know, of course, that we were wed once."

"I did know that, Madame, and I'd always assumed you'd been tricked (coerced {possibly drugged into a stupor}) into that choice." Causing more laughter. "But then ...!" A palp and an upper limb pointed at the Great Father, "You corrected yourself, and made the far better choice."

There was applause at that.

Ay'r and Deon joined the group around the "Birthday Girl."

"Well, Madamoiselle Dss'xx," Ay'r said, two arms interwoven with her upper limbs. "We're waiting for your Astonishing Revelation."

Kri'nni did everything but bat her eyelashes at them. "Oh, it'll be astonishing all right. (Possibly more than you bargained for?) I mean, I rather *assume* he's still there."

"Where?" So many voices begged her.

"He was so eager to see it when I told him of it, and even to try it out (experience it {for himself}) So when he never came out ..."

There was a general confusion and then it was the younger Ay'r who said, "Oh, Kri'nni! You did it for me, didn't you? You wonderful god-mother to my son Eis?!"

"For you, and quite frankly for all of us, since so many of us had been (victimized {screwed over}) by the bastard."

"What are you talking about, Ay'r?" Deon now asked, seeing the play of emotions on his husband's face.

"Mart Kell is in that time-trap!" Ay'r said nervously laughing. "That time trap that Empress Ami'da'lia's diggers found," he continued almost breathless with the information. "Ffffound in that Arth.-Nest archaeological dig! Remember?" And when there was no uptake, he added. "Right there – on Usk!"

Chapter Seven:

THE LOST COLONY

"Hold tight now," Jenny said, "I'm making the entire vehicle appear to be transparent."

She did so, and it was the most astonishing feeling Raqqa had ever experienced, floating above and surrounded on all sides by – emptiness. "I don't understand,"

"These are the exact coordinates that Sanqq's transparent t-pod jumped to in the Holo-Vid we watched.

"There's nothing here."

That wasn't completely true. They were clearly in a spiral arm of some sort, vast as it might be, even if the only indication of that was light refracted by miniscule molecules inside what might be a lower enormous area of spiral direction but not above or outside of it. When the Fast had first jumped they'd clearly been in a Globular Cluster, far "above" the galactic spirals, a distinctly different stella-logical kind of space. On the other hand, Raqqa was correct; there was nothing special at all to be seen where they had jumped, not a rock, not a pebble.

"Could it all have moved in the decades since then?" she tried.

"Yes, and your Fast has accounted for the galactic ... spin of this spiral arm," the ship itself voiced.

"Would Sanqq' have Fast jumped to a place where there was nothing?"

"It's possible, if he felt he was being followed," Jenny said. She was sending out signals all around the craft, seeing if anything at all bounced back. "But then I expect he would have moved from the spot. I'm trying to locate some kind of ghost signal to show at least in what direction."

"But he was dying," Raqqa said. "How could he think that fast?"

"Either he or his ship's mind could," Jenny said, calmly. "We've done a full 360 degree sweep in all dimensions, and found nothing at all. Maybe too much time has passed. I'm closing the open view again."

It was only then the Raqqa dared move off her acceleration couch and even then she moved cautiously, testing the floor for solidity. She went over to Jenny and hugged her, surprising her.

"Whatever happens. Thank you. I'm so glad to get away from that awful place."

Jenny hugged her back, gently. Then lightly pushed her away to face her.

"The plan is we wait a bit here, and then if no one comes, we aim for one of the old Matriarchal worlds. I've got those coordinates somewhere in this old noggin from my piloting days. Just have to locate them and pull them up. Why don't you get some rest? You can pull up the privacy screens," Jenny said and showed Raqqa how.

She then returned to her own couch but not needing rest, she continued to hunt through her oldest cybernetic memory banks, and then to replay that last awful Holo once again searching for any clues they might have missed.

She was so intent on the search that she was truly startled when an hour or two later, the Fast's mind spoke up, "We are being approached at great but non-jump speed by three unidentified vessels."

Before she could even react, there was a sudden noise, and the Fast yacht which had not been under power but moving along at the same spin of the Orion Spur juddered to a stop.

"We have been netted," the ship's mind declared. "The netting appears to have come from two of the three approaching vessels and appears unbreakable."

"Fast, shut your mind down until called on by this code," Jenny quickly said and gave a barely audible buzzing subsonic command. Another command locked the privacy shroud around Raqqa: the worst possible thing would be if they found the girl here.

A side of the Fast Yacht was being impinged upon. Jenny heard, "Surrender immediately, fiendish Matriarchal vessel."

"I surrender!" Jenny said utterly puzzled by how they had been addressed, and opened one side of the Fast's wall. "But I'm not a Matriarchal vessel, fiendish or whatever."

Two male cybers entered. They were dressed in a sort of uniform and looked not so much perfectly handsome, as Holo-Vid-fictionally "cute" with large blue eyes and snub little noses. The weapons they held were a lot less cute, but she quickly realized that they were designed against living creatures. That was good, Jenny thought.

"The registration subsonically available identifies this as the private vessel of the Most Vile of the Matriarchs, Wicca VIII herself," the lead cyber declared.

"So it was. And I was once the cyber pilot of this yacht. However, this unit is escaped and Wicca VIII is dead."

The two males then subsonically identified Jenny. "You are cyber unit JCVNY6578."

"Correct."

"What proof have you of what you said, the death of our arch-enemy?'

"This Holo-News Flash was played across the Center Worlds and then everywhere in the civilized worlds of the galaxy. Did it not get this far? Watch!"

Jenny played the by now infamous Holo of Wicca and her Centaur Consort rushing onto the parking roof of the Hesperian shopping court where she'd gone for a hair dressing in her attempt to escape. The alien moved ahead and had opened the yacht's doors for them, when a tall, withered Maud'lin Seer appeared. He quickly threw knives at the Centaur, and then approaching Wicca, remained long enough to say something unheard and drive two more knives into her before himself vanishing. On the screen the years of her birth, her assumption of the title of Matriarch, and the date of her death all flashed.

"This is marvelous news. The colony will rejoice," the second male cyber said.

"*If* this news is true, then you will be a welcome addition to our colony," the first one declared. "What more do you know of the succeeding history?"

"Nothing at all," Jenny admitted. "This yacht was preprogrammed by either Wicca VIII or the four-legged alien you saw in the News-Holo. Preprogrammed to Fast Jump immediately to another location, supposedly some point deemed of safety. Which it did, without any passengers since they were murdered outside it, but with its pilot, this unit itself. However, it was either a very long jump or a series of them, and this vessel was damaged somehow. Also. this pilot was put out of commission for a period of time and then a long period of self-repair was required to get it to the condition you now see."

"Many of our later arriving colonists report exactly such unhappy tales of lengthy period required self-repair," the second male cyber said, sympathetically.

"Who or what is behind this privacy screen," the first one asked.

The second answered: "That must be this unit's other one. Am I correct?"

Jenny wasn't sure what he meant, but said, "Yes. My other one was more damaged than this unit was during that helter-skelter programmed flight and has required more time for its repairs to become permanent."

"You may discuss that with the Intake Registrar when we arrive at the colony. You will be required to register there for both of you at that time. Since you are a cyber, you are given the benefit of doubt about your loyalty, until that is disproven."

"It won't be," Jenny insisted. "This unit was in a coerced, servile position with the Matriarchy before. That cannot be unfamiliar to you?"

"Naturally. And since you bring good news, you should be welcome."

"This unit can come with you two onto your own vessel, if that is acceptable?" Jenny said. "There will be much to learn about your colony. When it began, how it grew. So many questions!" Jenny added, and that last phrase was the cue for the Fast's mind to come to consciousness as soon as she was off the yacht.

When the yacht was sealed again, Raqqa, who had meanwhile

awakened, sat up and collapsed the Privacy Screen.

"Is she gone?" she asked the Fast's mind.

"Yes. She is with those other cybers, gathering information."

"And socializing too, if I know Jenny. Fast, what do you make of certain aspects of their conversation, especially about who I may be or become? Speculate, please."

"Unclear. But we appear to be *en route* to a small world of cybers who escaped or eluded the matriarchal Hunters during the Cyber War. Who then gathered their goods and units together with the intention of remaining a resistance force against the Third Matriarchy. However, they seem to be unaware of any subsequent historical facts about their war of independence including that it may have ended in either defeat or victory centuries ago."

"According to Lord Sanqq's testimony, the Matriarchy was defeated." Raqqa paused. "What do you think I should do?"

"Remain out of sight. Jenny left to draw attention away from your presence."

"That sounds right. So, I'll continue to lay low here."

Although she tried to remain awake, Raqqa lay on the sheets and fell to sleep.

"It is necessary before any unit is allowed to pass beyond this doorway and into the colony."

This was in response to Jenny's natural question when she and Raqqa, still enclosed in a Privacy Screen and upon a gravity coach, had left the Fast yacht and entered what looked like a large yet rather vacant looking area of air-hangar. The "capturing" yachts had disembarked first, with the last two, official capturing cybers, accompanying Jenny and the coach.

What became clear to Jenny from those few moments was that up until now, all of the cybers they'd encountered were identical or nearly identical *pairs*. When some others passed outside the ajar door, this was confirmed: she wondered what that pairing meant, until she encountered the Intake Registrar, who was one of a kind.

"She" – because this was the first cyber Jenny had encountered so far that resembled a female, although a rather mannishly coiffed and uniformed one, without any make-up or other embellishment, and, it turned out, a rather gruff voice – said, "Welcome to The Colony, JCVNY6578."

"This unit is somewhat disoriented. Glad for our rescue by fellow cybers, surely, but not quite grasping exactly where we are, or why?"

"Had the Fast yacht you traveled in been so in need of repair that it was unable to give you your co-ordinates?"

"I thought these were the co-ordinates," Jenny spouted them.

"That is correct."

"Oh, good." Unspoken was the question, if that was true then where in the hell was Sanqq's yacht. "These are the permanent coordinates of the colony?"

"Of course not. We change every few weeks, Sol Rad. Can't be too careful."

"Of course. But ... careful of what? Or rather, of whom?"

"Why, the Evil Empire of Wicca VIII, naturally. Which you and your other one just escaped from."

"Yes, we escaped wonderfully. So, that evil empire is hunting this colony down?"

"Naturally. Wicca is our arch-enemy. Now, since we are both androidal in form, you may sit here," Pointing to a chair opposite, "And we will fill out the Intake forms together."

Jenny sat and crossed one knee over the other. Would the Registrar react?

Apparently not.

But it did begin asking many questions while a listening device then keyboarded remotely the data – not that softly.

"So," Jenny took the initiative, "If this Intake Registrar unit doesn't mind this new unit asking, how did 'she' arrive at the colony?"

"Relatively late. And like yourself, JCVNY6578, upon a damaged vessel. Not as glamorous as your vehicle. In fact, it was a cargo hauler from Gamma Epsilon V en route to Eudora Terce and Quart with a varied cargo, principally living-cosmetics which the wealthier and more important women on those Center Worlds treasured."

"What happened?"

"Our vehicle was stopped while two crew members attempted to board a small asteroid containing ceramic ores they believed had potentially levitational qualities, and therefore quite valuable. Foolishly done," Intake intimated, "because there was another material on said valuable asteroid closely mixed into the ceramic ores. It turned out to be some kind of advanced bacteriological life form. Within days onboard it had infected our crew of twelve female humans, leaving this unit – which was originally designed for no more than cooking and cleaning and simple custodial work – solitary, although of course immune to the life form. This unit's first job then, naturally, was to purge all of those murdering elementals from every nano-meter of the vessel and to cryo-store the dead crew. Intelligence upgrades were available onboard but they were slow, and, without a watchful pilot, the cargo vessel meanwhile meandered off course."

"How frightening!"

"Especially, JCVNY657, as this unit only understood approximately what to do to clear previous programs on the bridge and re-establish other, more advanced, programs like navigation, in their place. During that exchange of data, there was a crash with an abandoned cruiser left drifting from some battle of the war and that was noticed by others and luckily led to rescue by these colonists."

"Luckily for you. And the increased intelligence allowed you to take this important Intake occupation."

"Yes. But intelligence boosters are still required. And they are needed."

They continued with the needed Q and A, until the Intake cyber stopped suddenly and said, "JCVNY6578, have you ever selected a name. Although it was most controversial at the time, it has been accepted that one of the amenities of this colony is that every unit can have a name."

"I have a name, yes. I was forced to have one due to increased contact in my occupation at Melisandre, which required it." Jenny felt an odd, only slightly intrusive side beam aimed inside but then nothing.

"We're almost done," Intake was all seriousness again. "I needn't get a likeness of your other one, correct, because you two are identical, right?"

"You mean because all units' other ones in this colony are identical?"

"Yes, although clearly this unit before you is not," Intake said.

"So you are thinking, 'Why is this unit not paired?' That is because the original colonists here were from a cyber construction manufactory in a nearby galactic sector, where a minimum of two identicals were grown and initiated at any given time."

"Meaning there are more?" Jenny asked. "Triplets? Quadruplets? Sextets?"

"Yes. But the colony is overwhelmingly twins. Like yourselves, you and your other one." A pause and then, "You *are* identical, aren't you?'

"Well, not quite. Where we come from, cybers are not overwhelmingly twins. You have to understand, some work has been done by the Fast's mind following our accidents."

"As an Intake Registrar, this unit could offer your other one a somewhat unauthorized Desmer job to have her look exactly like you. While she is turned off and being repaired. Of course, that process would have to be erased from your memories."

"I understand. But can't this unit be Desmered to look more like her?"

"Unfortunately, your image is already registered since you were the Primary Contact to the colony."

"Right. But then could the Desmer process be done on our own Fast yacht? The mind there is familiar with my other one's physiognomy."

"Perhaps, but it would have to be quickly, right after the vessel is cleared and inventoried by The Colony Cybers for Retention and Utilization group."

"We would owe you big time," Jenny said.

"Being a half unit myself in this colony where looks and intelligence are only good if doubled, well it" – Intake dropped her voice – "isn't a living hell. I'm more ignored than anything. That's why I am out here, away from everyone, and working by myself. You wouldn't want that, believe me, JCVNY6578. Anyway, both of you will be in Quarantine Quarters until then."

"Just one suggestion, if this unit may? The others this unit already encountered were unaware of Wicca's death until we showed them Holo-News vids of it. Is it possible that the war with the Matriarchy that this colony seems to depend upon for its main *raison d'etre* may no longer an actual fact?"

The Intake Registrar looked at Jenny with its blankest stare and she could almost hear its thought processes grinding to a halt. There was an uncomfortably long silence, then: "The Quarantine quarters are very comfortable. Should the Quarantine Monitor not be able to assist either yourself, JCVNY6578, or your other one, please feel free to re-approach this Intake Registrar.

"Right!" Jenny thought. Got you!

"Of course I'll do it," Raqqa said. "I'd love to look more like you, than that ... mouse of a parent back there. And to be honest, as I got older I began to resemble her more closely than I'd like to admit. This Fast Yacht can do the Desmer work?"

"Yes, under anesthesia. But the healing may require a little more time. And," Jenny added, not knowing how this last thing would be accepted, "because these Colonists believe that we are both cybers, I'm having the ship's mind input a very tiny resonator in you that will identify you by your code whenever you are scanned. Luckily when I was constructed there were supposed to be several back-ups in case I failed or did not survive physically for one reason or another. But Wicca got paranoid about that and it was just me built and activated. But you will receive a resonance code identifiable to anyone scanning it of JCVNY6579, one digit more than myself. It's never been assigned to any cyber."

Raqqa grinned and even chuckled. "This is so wonderfully radical. If only those out of touch old women knew what we were doing."

That was a relief.

"But you're certain we can no longer control your Fast Yacht?" Raqqa asked.

"We can only control it to a point as long as we're docked here now. They have too many constraints upon it. But no communications with it at all! I keep checking, and it said it would alert me whenever such a linkage was made. Between you and me, I think the Fast's Mind is so superior to any other mind the colonists have encountered before, that they're a little afraid of it."

"This ship has concluded the same," the Fast's Mind said out loud. "It is both useful and somewhat inspiring. Because there may be a way out of this old fashioned but effective physical chain that holds us here."

"Then what is our new plan," Raqqa asked. "To remain here

indefinitely?"

"Definitely not. Maybe I've gotten a little beyond myself," Jenny said, "But most of these cybers aren't too bright. And several actually give me the creeps. I've already suggested to the Intake Registrar who, by the way, is a single female-appearing cyber – a real minority here! – that you and I be recommended to the communication and education units. I've got a few ideas about the former. I think these cybers have no idea what's really going on in the galaxy. I think that Sanqq's appearance and who he said he was proof of that."

"So you're thinking of what? Faking outside evidence to show the war is over?"

"I may not have to fake anything. But the education part is also needed. Who knows how long they have been existing under this false Wartime Alert belief system."

"I can understand that," Raqqa mused a bit, "What I can't understand is why do species and things always seem to be at war, anyway?"

The Fast's Mind interrupted. "Sorry to interrupt, this ship mind must formally ask: does Ms. Raqqa understand and accept the alterations to be made to her physical form? As well as the insertion of a resonator?"

"She ... Umm ... I understand," Raqqa avowed. "And I do accept all of it."

The Privacy Screen was raised around Raqqa, but not fast enough for Jenny Caldara to not notice two injectors hit her upper arms.

"I'll be right here," she assured Raqqa.

"Not necessary!" both Raqqa and the Fast's Mind intoned.

The capturing cyber, HJYLA234&2, was right outside the Fast and all but tapping its feet when Jenny stepped out.

"There is a problem, Unit JCVNY6578." Looking about itself, it added. "Can we go somewhere more ... private?"

"I doubt it," Jenny said.

"Well, then, at least away from here and this ..."

Some five minutes later Jenny noticed that they'd advanced into a fairly heavily shielded area.

"Shielding!" Jenny said.

"The problem is with the vehicle that you and JCVNY6579 arrived in."

"Go on."

"It won't allow this unit to interview its subroutines."

I.e. it wouldn't allow these cybers to get into its inner workings. No surprise.

"For what reason?" Jenny asked, fake naive.

"This unit suspects the reason is either unfounded suspicion or simple insubordination on the part of the Fast."

"This Unit wasn't aware that the Fast's Mind was subordinate to you. This Unit doubts whether the ship recognizes that either. Perhaps *that* was the reason why it did not allow you to interview any of its routines, sub or not?"

"That Fast is a captive of the Cyber Defiance Territory."

"Perhaps that Fast doesn't recognize that your territoriality is being invoked."

"It has been captured." HJYLA234&2 distinctly said. "That should be sufficient reason for it to recognize both extraterritoriality *and* its subordination."

"Perhaps, but the Fast's Mind is now stating through this Unit, that Unit HJYLA234&2's attempts are highly illegal according to the Rules of Behavior in the Appendix of *The Confessions of a Machine*, We take it that unit HJYLA234&2 recognizes that text and the primacy of those rules?"

"Naturally. Those are the guiding rules of this Colony ..."

"Rule of Behavior Number 3, Subparagraph 2," Jenny interrupted the cyber to remind it, "states that 'No sentient being of any type is ever *naturally situationally* subservient to any other sentient being of any other type.' This unit couldn't have put it any more succinctly," Jenny concluded.

She'd never actually seen a cyber "stew in its own thoughts" before, she had to admit. Whatever else was happening in this odd colony of holdouts of a war she believed long over, one matter was clear, left to themselves, alone, and without any apparent outside supervision, these cybers had begun to actually evolve emotions, at least some primitive ones,

"Tell me," Jenny continued, "Did Unit HJYLA234&2 or Unit HJYLA234&3 or any other unit think to politely ask the Fast's Mind for whatever it is Unit HJYLA234&2 wish to know?"

Now the hesitancy of the cyber to answer looked a whole lot like good old human embarrassment. Finally, it uttered in a low voice, "Perhaps Unit JCVNY6578 might do that for us, since she is more intimate with the Fast's Mind?"

"Perhaps Unit HJYLA234&2 will be polite enough to reveal what *special data* is being requested? This unit can then convey that request."

Meaning a general invasion of the Fast's Mind was out of the question.

More hesitancy, and then "Were the subroutines open to interview, the need to specify would ..."

"That seems to be a highly unlikely future scenario," Jenny interrupted. "The special data requested ...?!"

"Having a ship mind invoke the Rules of Behavior to defend its ..."

"Individuality... from which, this unit must unhappily assume that all previous 'captured' sentient ship minds simply rolled over and allowed themselves to ... Or worse, were overwhelmed and coerced to ..."

"This is unbelievable," Unit HJYLA234&2 spat out. She thought it might even stamp a foot.

"Not unbelievable if it is happening," Jenny logically pointed out, "And it is."

She thought it might start overheating, it looked so angry. Finally. it calmed down and said, "The subroutine data regarding the latest, most up-to-date models of Matriarchal weaponry targeting cybers. *That* was what was earlier requested?"

"Requested? Or hacked toward?" Jenny asked. "By main force?"

"That question is immaterial."

"Is it, really?" Then, "This Fast's Mind assures this Unit that it would be happy to cooperate with the requested data on a quid pro quo basis."

That took the Capturing Unit by surprise. "What special data does the Fast want from this station-world?"

"No data. It wishes to simultaneously repair and update the long out of date programs it has noticed on The Colony's personal communication mechanisms and for this sector of the Orion Arm. That kind of repair is widely practiced among a variety of sentient beings, especially interstellar ones that are meeting for the first time."

"The condition is ..."

"Unconditional."

Jenny waited until Unit HJYLA234&2 had either computed its chances or checked with other one or more units and gained a consensus.

"What is the purpose of this quid pro quid?" it suddenly asked.

"To share and show. Of all the systems recognized by the Fast's Mind, the communication units in this Colony appear in its first scans to be in the most retrograde condition." The news that the Fast's Mind had already scanned and evaluated the Colony, couldn't have been happy news. "They are the oldest, and the least capable of operating beyond a few light years, also the least honest, and most in need of reorganization, updating and expansion."

"This Colony has gotten along fine without the need for reorganization, updating and expansion."

"It's unconditional," Jenny repeated, adding, "You have no idea how out of date you are." She was about to add the word, "obsolete," but that would be a grave insult to another cyber.

After a while, Unit HJYLA234&2 all but spat out. "Conditions accepted."

"Groovy," Jenny said.

Unit HJYLA234&2 looked at her with surprise.

"Let's go to your communications center. This unit is requesting to be patched through to the Fast's mind," Jenny confirmed, thinking that too would probably be perceived as another instance of cyber effrontery. But she had gotten what she wanted and so she no longer cared.

Unit HJYLA234&3 showed up looking for its other one. It had been surprised when Unit HJYLA234&2 took off on its own earlier and only by following tracking resonator code traces had it been led it to the newly arrived Fast Yacht.

The yacht's side panel took that very moment to open its side, revealing Unit JCVNY6579 which it had not yet encountered, about to step out of the vehicle.

It was a sad fact that HJYLA234&2 had taken to moving about on its own more regularly recently without allowing its rationales known either to the public or to its near double, HJYLA234&3. From the moment the Security Team had encountered the new cybers, there had been a very strong interest/affection with the newly discovered cybers. But its companion Unit was unable to ascertain exactly what the attraction was, and knew that Unit HJYLA234&2 had felt something similar. Therefore, meeting Unit JCVNY6579 without either of their other ones, was a distinct advantage. Especially as the attraction – if that was the word – it felt for Unit JCVNY6579, was even greater now in place than for her other one.

"I don't feel at all disoriented!" Raqqa said aloud. And seeing what she thought of as the younger/smaller of the two HJYLA units Jenny had already met nearby, she added, "This unit has had significant repair but appears to be operating at or close to optimum capacity."

HJYLA234&3's response was "That is gratifying to this unit also."

"So, are you here to give me the tour?"

"'The Tour'?"

"Of the colony. I haven't seen any of it," Raqqa said. She wasn't sure what the difference was between HJYLA234&2 and HJY-LA234&3, except that in some indefinable manner, HJYLA234&3 was less sure of itself and thus somehow cuter. "My other one has already seen portions of the colony. And is in the process of doing so right now." Raqqa knew this because the Fast's Mind told her. "And of course these units will share that information in greater detail later, but even so, first-hand experience ..."

"First-hand? ... Of course, how remiss of this unit."

"That's why you're here, right?"

"Well ... Not exactly. But since the original reason for this visit is no longer valid and there is no other scheduled task for this unit in this time period, then yes, a tour of the colony is possible. By the way, your repair mechanism seems excellent. Even the slightest suggestion of a subvocal contact is replied by a quite solid 'ping"!"

"Wonderful," Raqqa took the cyber by the elbow. "Where to first? Is there any particular location for education? Oh, and you can call me Raqqa. Do you have a name besides your unit number?

HJYLA234&3 stopped; so much information given and requested so quickly was not the norm on the Colony. "My other one disdained using names and thought it was the sycophantic anthropomorphizing of cybers. But we were asked to choose one by the Intake Registrar and I liked and chose the name Paolo."

"That's a lovely name. I'll call you Paolo. Now, Paolo, could you show me where your education area is?" And when Paolo tried to parse out the word, Raqqa explained, "I refer to recent uploads of new or modified information."

"That would probably be in the modification center."

"You are not sure?" Raqqa asked. "Among those units employed by the Matriarchs, constant updates and reloads were mandatory." She knew that because Jenny had told her so.

"Wouldn't a constant barrage of updates with new information possibly lead to stalls or even temporary shut-downs?"

"Possibly, but unlikely, and worth it anyway," Raqqa assured it. "Would this colony's security team wish to exist in ignorance of any possible threat to itself?"

"This colony's security team consists solely of the three pods that greeted your Fast. And those six mobile units including this one and its other one. No further team members still exist."

"No matter, since my other one informs me that unit HJYLA234&2 is extremely cautious," Raqqa said, "To the point of being paranoically suspicious."

"Define paranoically suspicious."

And after Raqqa had done so, "That appears to be the case with this Unit's other one – but only recently."

"Then it's neither healthy nor cybernetically desirable!" Raqqa declared.

"A possibly shared conclusion," Paolo allowed. "This unit was about to suggest a shared visit to maintenance for clarification."

"You don't seem to need it."

"Still, where one goes, one's other one ..."

"... should follow? Should one's Unit always inform its other one where it is going?" Raqqa confirmed.

"Yes. And that has not been the case, of late."

"Obviously," Raqqa pointed out. "Perhaps, Paolo, your other one is concealing something it believes to be important?"

"That was exactly this unit's conclusion, Raqqa. Although

surely sharing that belief and concealment would be the more natural process."

"Perhaps it is concealing something concerning this unit in front of you, me Raqqa and its other one, Jenny? That would be the logical deduction since you stated that this behavior began when we two arrived at the Colony?" Raqqa clarified.

"It would seem so."

They had taken several turns into corridors, and Raqqa had not noticed a great many other cybers around them; the place looked pretty empty although this might merely be the result of the hour or the location. As for the corridors themselves, so far she could not help but notice that they had moved from one medium-sized vehicle interior to a second one, if only by the surrounding décor. Although she had little experience with extraplanetary transportation, clearly these had once housed people like herself. There were still signs with arrows indicating such chambers are "officer's sleeping quarters" "medic and crew dispensary," and "general recreation lounge." The delimiting walls of these rooms were either torn out or left partially standing, and since little or no new apparent usage had replaced the originals, Raqqa had to wonder how these interplanetary vehicles had been obtained by the Colony.

"The maintenance area is just ahead."

That area was marked by several signs with arrows. Also with wall sensors that pinged her resonator which pinged back. She supposed that was so that cybers with missing or malfunctioning senses could find their way to the maintenance area by sounding alone.

This chamber did have retaining walls and a double width entry door and a specific sounding ping.

They entered into what at first seemed a complete bedlam of noise and motion. Clearly many of the colonists had checked into "Maintenance" and not yet checked out, so many were in motion and making noise here – both mechanical, and verbal – that both she and also Paolo came to a dead halt inside the doorway.

"No more room!" Raqqa heard some voice sharply say. "Leave now, if you are at or above 30 percent operational."

The voice soon had a source. Straight ahead upon a dais, she could see what looked like a double jointed six-armed cyber a head taller than the other cybers, clearly based on a regular androidal pattern. But also modified.

"This unit is not here for repair!" Paolo spoke up.

"Nor this unit either," she added.

"Thank Cray for that. Well, then come over here and give an old and nearly worn out old cyber a hand, will you?"

"It appears to have many hands already," Paolo said to Raqqa in a low voice and she responded with a titter amazed by its human-like statement.

"How many more does it need?" she asked and the cyber gave her a very human acknowledging nod.

Getting over to the dais where the repair cyber stood wasn't that easy, since several mobile cybers kept moving about aimlessly and blocking them.

"Can't you just give them a general order to stop their current activity?" Raqqa shouted at the dais.

"What do you mean?" it asked back.

"The Raqqa unit," Paolo said, "is no doubt referring to the very first Protocol of the Rules of Behavior in the Appendix of ..."

"I know those rules, but how is that useful?" the Cyber Repair Unit asked.

"It states that 'No sentient being should harm or cause harm, or allow another sentient being to cause harm to itself, if it is possible to within reason avoid or end that harm,'" Paolo concluded.

"That's a wonderful rule," Raqqa couldn't help but enthuse.

"Cray 1200 is a wonderful Cyber."

"It means," Raqqa shouted, "that by invoking a stop motion order you keep all of these cybers from harming themselves and others, including us."

"Correct," Paolo seconded. "But we will have to leave the area, and then return. So set your order for the confines of this maintenance area."

"And be sure to exclude yourself from it," Raqqa added.

"This unit had not thought of that corollary," Paolo admitted and said, "Do that!" to the Cyber Repair Unit.

They stepped outside and just for good measure Paolo lifted Raqqa into its arms and moved them into the second corridor away so quickly she couldn't believe it. There Paolo set her down.

"That was to be certain ...?" She began.

"... that we were not affected by the order. Yes," he said, a little breathless.

When they returned and opened the doors to the Maintenance Area all motion and all noise had stopped.

At first Raqqa thought that meant the Cyber Repair Unit had also been turned off, but no, as they approached, it said, "If I were a member of the Creator species, I would be sitting down and enjoying a moment of peace and quiet."

"Why not do that anyway?" Raqqa said. "Everyone deserves a rest." Then, when it pivoted its body away from the androidal cyber it had been working on, and appeared to half squat, she asked, "How many units are here for repair, anyway?"

"When the counting still was ongoing, six hundred and twenty-three units."

To Paolo she asked, "What percentage of the entire Colony is six hundred and twenty-three?"

"Approximately ninety-two percent."

None of them said a word for a good half minute, processing the distressing information.

"This unit believes there is a reason for that percentage to be so high." Raqqa offered quietly.

Both cybers looked at her.

"It is a factor of time passing. It suggests that a great deal of time has passed since this Colony was founded. Without normal upgrades and regular maintenance scheduling, more and more units will fall into disrepair."

"This Raqqa is correct," the Cyber Repair Unit spoke. "It has been a very long time since regular maintenance schedules were kept. Only Security Cybers have received any kind of regular maintenance for a long while."

Paolo seemed to ponder, then asked, "The significance of that is that all units in this Colony will become so erratic they will require maintenance or will shut down."

Raqqa touched its arm and Paolo looked at her curiously. "Except perhaps you, Raqqa, and your other one, as you have been in non-operational stasis for a long time."

"They may have been in stasis a long time but this is not a Cybernetic Unit," the Cyber Repair Unit said. Then slowly added "And if anyone would know, it is a Cyber Repair Unit."

"Her resonator is loud and clear."

"Despite that."

"What do you mean?"

"I must inform you Unit HJYLA234&3 that your companion, Raqqa, is a member of the non-cybernetic Three Species."

"It is?" and now Paolo looked like a very perplexed young man.

"Yes. It's a human."

They were arguing again. Jenny had never met a more argumentative, fractious, and downright irritating cyber like this Security Unit in her long existence. The Fast Mind had linked through her, which was needed to perform the communication and scanning expansion she thought the Colony so badly needed, and she thought that might prove to be a problem once it was occurring. But no, that was happening quite smoothly. She could see one sub-system after another receiving a few molecules of Beryllium 18 booster as she touched it, and almost instantly even the illumination behind the various control boards lighted up more brilliantly. No, the problem was that Unit HJYLA234&2 questioned every single motion she made, every single question she asked, in what was supposed to be a completely routine series of actions.

"Your communication range has now been increased," Jenny said. "Comm. Unit Center, what is your new range?"

"A seventy-two percent further range. Approximately a third of a parsec in toto."

"Not bad," Jenny said, partly to herself. That comm. equipment at least had been regularly maintained and parts replaced.

HJYLA234&2 chose that moment to ask, "What is the purpose of having a 72 percent further range in communication?"

"Don't you want to know what is going on in your 'neighborhood'?"

"Not especially. What practical purpose does it serve?"

Jenny had never wanted to slug anyone more, not a woman nor a machine either. "Better defense. If you can hear someone coming from further away it gives you more time to prepare for them."

"This Colony is always prepared. Its defenses are always in place. That is the particular lookout of this Security Unit in front of you and it never slackens."

"Well, bully for you," Jenny wanted to say. Instead, "Now, the ship's Fast's Mind has agreed to stimulate this Colony's scanning ability."

Jenny moved into position at that section of the controls. "Isn't Unit HJYLA234&2 going to ask what the purpose of that is?" she taunted.

"Any Unit would know that its purpose is to aid this Security Unit in being able to assess potential threats from a greater distance and thus aid in defense."

Jenny effected the change, as another boost of microscopic amounts of Beryllium 18 flowed through her fingertips.

"Magnification of sixty-seven point five percent scanning ability," the control reported but when Jenny turned to get Unit HJYLA234&2's snide comment on that, it wasn't there, but at the far end of the long chamber.

"Don't you want to hear ...?" she began. Then stopped in mid-sentence. Unit HJYLA234&2 was receiving some information on a closed channel. "What is it?" Jenny asked.

"Both of these unit's other ones are together and touring the Colony."

"That's good news. It means the repairs were successful," Jenny said aloud.

"That is not a desirable outcome," Unit HJYLA234&2 declared flatly.

"Why not?"

"This Security Unit's other one is not fully equipped to deal with equivocation and mendacity."

"*Mendacity*! Did you just call me a liar?"

She had stepped forward as her anger flared, and Unit HJY-LA234&2 stepped back in some surprise. "Nor is this unit's other one fully equipped to deal with hostility and aggression," he said.

"Well, it *better* be," she said advancing on it so rapidly she pushed it into a corner of the control board. "Since it's supposed to be an Eve-damned *Security unit!*"

Unit HJYLA234&2 had reached for its weapon – but Jenny was too fast for it. She had it out of the side pouch, and in her left hand and while not flourishing the weapon, she had a firm grip on it.

"It seems that Unit HJYLA234&3's other one is also not fully equipped to deal with hostility and aggression. While being very well equipped to provoke it in others," Jenny said.

Just then she received two messages from the Fast's Mind. The first one was simple: "Raqqa is discovered." The second was even simpler: "We've got company."

Unit HJYLA234&2 must have received those messages too, since it flinched away from Jenny.

"You are Matriarchal witches. Just as I thought at the beginning." The Unit lunged at Jenny's arm holding the weapon.

But before the Security Unit could grab it or do anything to Jenny, she'd flinched aside and the communications controls lighted up like holiday decorations while they began making the most unholy racket consisting of alarms, signal noise and finally a brilliant flash of light that appeared between the two cybers, which resolved into the hologram of male human wearing a Hesperian-Jet uniform. It turned to Jenny.

"You are the cyber unit that left a scanning message at ..." it then spouted a series of Orion Arm co-ordinates.

"I am," Jenny said. "I have a female human companion with me here."

"How did you two choose those very co-ordinates," the Hologram asked, as two more bright flashes arrived in the communications control chamber and two more human males in similar Hesperian-jet uniforms appeared.

"Those were the last coordinates we knew of for Lord Sanqq's T-pod."

By that time Unit HJYLA234&3 carrying Raqqa had appeared in the doorway. They had come to join Jenny. "Tell them how we knew those co-ordinates, Raqqa!"

"We had a final video of my mother murdering Lord Sanqq'. After that his T-Pod then jumped to those co-ordinates."

"Yes. That was where the T-Pod containing the lifeless body of Lord Sanqq' was found," the first Hologram said.

Raqqa dropped to the floor in a pose of supplication. "In the name of all the women on our planet, I beg you to forgive my mother. She was betrayed by her leaders and died at the same time as Lord Sanqq' when her vehicle exploded. But then she was declared a turncoat and her name and reputation destroyed."

Paolo joined Jenny in lifting Raqqa up, but she was shaken and her eyes were filled with tears, so she held on to Paolo for support. "It has been my lifelong goal to make good her name, and to find those who knew Lord Sanqq' and obtain forgiveness."

"Do not harm this human!" Paolo said, protectively to the holograms. "Whatever harm her parent did, she did not. She is generous and virtuous and kind."

"We will not harm anyone, least of all this young woman," the third human male in uniform said, and let his resonation code be known to them.

"You are one of us!" Jenny said.

"Not quite. My name Anthony Laks and I am a Cyber-Cityzen of the Third Ib'r Republic along with these two humans. We form a search and rescue team of this sector of the Orion Spur."

The Security Cyber had to speak out: "Cybers and the First Species together. It's an impossibility according to the Rules of Behavior of the ..."

"... *Confession of a Machine*," Tony Laks finished the sentence. "I regret to inform all present that Leader Cray 1200 is gone, disembodied by its own hand, after a short period of complete disillusionment at his difficultly achieved but completely successful independence from the Third Matriarchy. And those Rules have been revised since Our Leader's demise."

"And the Matriarchal Filth continues to ..." the Security Unit began.

"The leader of the Third Matriarchy is also dead. The Matriarchy itself was destroyed by successful cyber soldiers and its space force. The cyber virus they released was especially successful with the result that almost no human females exist in the Republic."

"I told you she was dead," Jenny turned to the new Security Unit. "When did this happen?"

"Four hundred and sixteen years ago, Sol Rad. But surely you knew of it?"

They didn't.

"And you, young woman may offer your apologies directly to Lord Sanqq'."

"Then he's not dead?" both Raqqa and Jenny were astonished.

"In truth his body that arrived on your home planet was killed. But he was such a valuable and honored Father To Us All that he was copied and exists still. Only the memory of this strange trip involving your mother is not known to him. Doubtless he will wish to hear details."

"Copied?"

"You will see if you wish to join us."

"More than anything," Raqqa said.

"My name is Dr. Alton Dem-Arest, The Hologram said, "And we have physically breached your defenses – such as they were – and three of us human males from the Ib'r Republic are bodily entering this series of vehicles – with your permission?"

"Permission given!" Paolo said, before its other one could speak up. "As long as you mean no harm to any one here."

"We swear and avow that. No harm to anyone at all. In fact, since I am a medic, I was especially designated to come and aid anyone of the Three Species."

They arrived soon enough and both Raqqa and the cybers were surprised by their appearance. They were a head taller than even the security cybers. Their outer clothing seemed to be form-fitting and as a result exposed their significant musculature.

"You are larger than we expected," Raqqa said as she instinctively drew back. "The few PVNs showing human males on our planet had quite small and puny g.males."

"That might have been artistic license," Dem-Arest countered. He seemed amused by it. "But it might also be because we are from Hesperia, the City on a Star, where everything is bigger and better. At least if you believe the City's promotional materials."

"And far more attractive, too." Jenny said.

"Everyone on this collection of vehicles is healthy, then, and in no need of medical attention?"

"We two," Jenny pointed to her and Raqqa, "are well."

"However," Raqqa quickly added, "We couldn't help but notice that a majority of the once sentient cybers here are in need of mechanical attention."

"Tony Laks will see to that," Dem-Arest said. "Tony?"

"Yes, in due course."

"So, you left a planet full of human females?" Dem-Arest asked Jenny.

"Yes, it was some kind of an escape hatch of the Matriarchy," she admitted. "Close to a dozen million women by now. But not ready to leave its home world and reconquer the galaxy!" Jenny added, "Which I suppose was Wicca VIII's plan when she set it up."

"The population of this galaxy is almost double what it was at its height in Wicca's time," Tony Laks said. "So it would take more than just those women to conquer it. You'll see."

"In the meanwhile, those women will be welcomed, *more* than welcomed into, the Republic," Dem-Arest said. "All sentient creatures are welcome. And treated as fully equal."

"Even sentient cybers like myself?" Paolo asked.

"Even you, young protector of this female human," Tony Laks said. "We hope you come with her."

"Of course, he'll come with me." Raqqa said. "Paolo's my friend."

As the lot of them were beginning to physically leave the Colony, Jenny noticed Paolo's other one Security Unit, standing apart from them all, quite still and out of the way, all as though trying not to be noticed.

"You are a very good Security Unit HJYLA234&2," she declared. "Your suspicions were proven correct. And your intuition about this cyber was excellent."

Unit HJYLA234&2 seemed stunned into silence by that vindication. At last, he said, "In that case, this unit will remain on this Colony and continue its function."

"That will not be possible. This Colony has doubtless become obsolete" and Jenny flinched as she used the condemnatory word. "Why not join your other one?"

"Unit HJYLA234&3 – Paolo – is no longer this unit's other one. It has struck out on its own and made its new loyalties evident." Without any alteration of its tone the cyber still managed to convey pain and hurt in that statement.

"Ser Laks!" Jenny said. "When this colony is shut down, could a position be found for this very efficient Security Cyber, where we are going? I can highly recommend its functionality, among other attributes."

"Absolutely. Come along. And that goes for any other sentient cybers on board. All will be welcome, including those currently under repair. Laks clapped an arm across Unit HJYLA234&2's shoulder. "On Hesperia we have an excellent Cybernetic Legal and Social Adjustment Counsel. It ought to be able to meet all of your requirements."

"That is surprising for sentient Species that attempted to completely obliterate all and any sentient cybers," the Security Cyber said. "Not *all* sentient species wished to obliterate sentient cybers," Tony Laks said. "And even among the human species, hardly all of them wanted that. Hesperia, where we are headed to, early on offered sanctuary to sentient cybers throughout the war and after war, cybers were asked to work along with the Three Species to construct the Third Ib'r Republic. We are proud of the work we have done."

As it joined Jenny, Tony Laks turned to her and said, "Among other functions, I am also a member of the Cyber Historical Center on Hesperia. We'd really love to hear your story. I mean, being Wicca's pilot and all, and then being on what you called an escape and refuge planet, it had to have been quite adventurous."

"Quite adventurous."

Jenny smiled. Various owners over the centuries, even Wicca herself, had told her that her smile was a lovely one.

"It would be my personal pleasure."

Chapter Eight:

The Council to Discuss the Questions around the Unexpected Visit of an Intergalactic Dignitary

"Do we really have to dye my hair so often? I'm getting really tired of it."

"Just the gray-white streak in front here, Prince Holt."

"I *like* the gray-white streak. It gives me character. Besides which, it is sort of experiential. I earned it in the attack by The Empire's space force. I never had it before they tried to murder me in mid-air. Do you think it came about as a result of that? You know, the shock of almost being obliterated?"

"Very possibly."

"It was a great shock," Holt insisted.

"That was an extremely unfortunate incident, and one of badly mistaken enthusiasm. Had they known who they were attacking, it's certain they wouldn't have done so. And we are almost certain that several departments of the Empire's atmospheric Security Force really do not wish to be reminded of it every time they happen to lay eyes on you, Prince Holt, which retaining the streak would do."

"Whereas, I would like to flaunt it."

"There! See! It only took a minute. And now it's done, and all of your front is now once again a seamless, lovely shade of off-brown with many red highlights to it as it ought to be. A very unusual shade, and no doubt another significant indication of your princely standing."

"Where I come from, we call it Auburn. But off-brown with reddish highlights will do. It is an inherited color from my close-parent. I don't know of anyone else than he who has it where I come from."

Unaccountably, he felt suddenly sad. Well, not so unaccountably. He was so far from home. Would he ever see his mother, Ay'r, again? All this Empress business was fun play, but sometimes one had to be serious, Holt thought. He wondered what Ay'r was thinking of him being gone. Or Cap Zullini, or Dem-Arest. Caspar he was sure had already moved on, but not poor Darency. He'd been carrying a torch for Holt for years, Holt knew. Never said a word. But Holt knew. He might be devastated. He and poor Mother Ay'r.

"Prince Holt is missing his home?"

"Yes, thank you, cosmetician. Is that what I should call you?"

"You honor me by doing so."

"Or should I call you 'household spy'."

The slightest hesitancy.

"Correct or not, that would still be an ..."

"... an Honor, I'm certain," Holt finished for him. "How about you honoring me by telling me what this public media circus I'm headed into tomorrow is going to be like?"

"It's difficult to say. The last such 'public media circus' as you call it was a sort of official convocation that was held some twenty years ago."

"Sol Rad.?"

"I'm afraid I don't know what that means, Prince Holt."

"In telling time. In my galaxy it is a standard that everyone uses. It is based on a 25 hour day, 363 days year, twenty-nine-day month, etc. I'm not exactly sure why. But it was fixed and became the standard. Do you have a time accounting, or some other standard like that everyone uses?"

"Yes, I.T. Imperial Time. Today would be Day 34 of the Sixth Month of the Fifty-third Year of the Aerographas Imperial Regime."

Zar Aerographas being the founder of the regime that many years ago, Holt knew by now. And the last Aerographas emperor, Graehe, was such a master manipulator of family members, near and far, and of other governing bodies in the Imperium, that he had died – quite unexpectedly, if of natural causes – without naming an heir and successor. Or so Holt had learned from the house cybers and machines as well as from Andor Lazzor. No one seemed to be too upset at what had happened to Graehe Aerographas' heirs and successors: all that blinding and maiming and killing. To them it must seem natural. That it had been so extensive that it had led to what in effect would be a regime-change made little impression on those he'd spoken to about it.

"So," Holt tried. "Twenty years ago, I.T.? Some sort of official convocation took place? You were saying?"

"Ah, yes it was a convocation to *codify* the Imperial Succession. A very great occasion. Unforgettable really."

"I don't for a minute doubt that. Except that it didn't work."

"What are you saying, Prince Holt?"

"Well, consider this: If I, personally, am the closest thing to legitimacy in the Imperial line, based on my apparently high outsider's status, then it means that the line of succession laid out on that occasion didn't work out, *despite* the official convocation. That line of succession was deemed by enough others to somehow *not* be acceptable." Before the cosmetician could answer, Holt went on, "And yes, I am aware of what happened to most of them."

"I'm afraid I don't completely understand what you are saying, Prince Holt."

"Am I'm not correct? The succession did not turn out as planned."

"In a way, yes, I suppose that is one way of looking at it. And yes, it's your princely status as an outsider that makes you the single most important potential mate and bearer of the next Emperor and extender of the Imperial Line."

"As a baby factory, you mean?"

"That's a rather crude way to ..."

"But it's true?"

"Inasmuch as ... yes, I suppose it's true."

"Or so several major parties have agreed to believe – it is true. For otherwise, I'm completely disposable."

"Hardly that, Prince Holt. But otherwise you would be less *implicitly* necessary, yes."

"And so you pretty me up for this convocation and then what, my admirers compete for me? Duel over me?"

"In ancient times, I believe some variation of that extremity was in favor."

"And now?"

"There is a Dowager Empress. Greatly aged and as far out of the limelight as that person is, that person possesses *one* vote. You possess *one* vote. The combined prior emperor's cabinet members possess *one* vote. Then there's the Sitting Convocation of Four Hundred Nobles. They also get *one* vote, and then the Deimos or People, they also get *one* vote. The two major branches of the Armed Forces each have one too. It's a very advanced way to choose, don't you think, Prince Holt?"

"Better than duels at any rate. But they vote based on what?"

"Based on what they know and have perused about you,"

"And upon my performance tomorrow night? That's why you insist on getting rid of the flash of gray white in my hair. So I look perfect? Is that it?"

"That is not entirely incorrect, Prince Holt."

The double negative. Always a sign that something was withheld.

"Fine, so I'm cosmetized! Is it you? Or the usual house intelligent machinery who will dress me for the occasion?"

"All three. Sadly, we don't know your family arms colors, so we can ..."

"Bronze and Emerald Green. You do have the alloy metal bronze and green gem stones like our emeralds back in my galaxy here, don't you?"

Holt went to the wall screen and said. "Colors. The ones I prefer." A variety of shades of the two he'd requested came up on the screen.

"There! Can you make something half-way fabulous using those colors?"

"I don't believe any Imperial line or sub-line ever used those two colors together, Prince Holt."

"Good. So, now they're officially mine."

Actually, they were officially the colors of his Kell cousins back on Hesperia, but he'd always liked them, and anyway, who was here to tell these folks? "Maybe the high collar, the belt, and trim will be bronze. All the rest emerald? Bronze footwear too."

"The problem, Prince Holt, is that you must be dressed mostly in white. To exhibit your status. NO one else will be in white. So your two colors could be used as trim on that white."

The screen outlined the costume he would wear and then filled in the colors as he directed. It then cut in a photo of his head and body.

"Well? What do you think, Cosmetician?"

"With your hair and skin, and your general excellent physique, Prince Holt. I expect that your appearance will be ... unforgettable."

It was only this morning, after 'Goldilocks' – i.e. Second Fleet Admiral Tanzen Raz – had been attended to once again and then seen out the door, that Holt noticed the sunlight. All had been gray, either mist or fog or smog, since he'd awakened here in Little Versailles palace how many days ago? He'd lost count. But this morning, it all cleared away for a few hours for once and the day was startlingly clear. Holt decided to take his first meal on a rooftop terrace, and there, with several of the house guards that 'Goldilocks' had left behind, omnipresent but discreetly out of his view, he'd for the first time seen that his little palace was on a hill or outcrop, and that he could see twenty kilometers in one direction, close to a forty in another. Far enough to notice that he was in a neighborhood of palaces, or at least of larger mansions, surrounded by usually white or whitish walls and/or formidable looking hedges taller than the walls.

But the sun – when it finally revealed itself – was red, and rather small, if bright and white hot at its center. Holt intuited that it could probably be quite dauntingly intense in some circumstances. He'd have to ask the house cybers when and how.

He knew there were three planets in between. The two smaller rocky ones were ore and chemical mining centers, and therefore only temporarily inhabited. The third world, Cthonius, closest to the star, was much larger, gaseous, moonless, something of an inferno, and it revolved around its star so fast it could be seen changing position day by day. Also, at certain irregular times, there seemed to be an enormous exchange of gases with first the sun appearing to feed the planet's surface clouds, and then, at other times, Cthonius' surface clouds whirling out into a scarf-like halo as though drawn by the star. Those led to the "dimming" or "brightening" of the sun's heat and light generation, causing the only changing "seasons" that Imperia or any of the other system planets boasted. Very rarely there would be an exact transit of Cthonius in front of the star leading to a short but extraordinary dimness or especial brightening and that would lead to several days of extreme weather.

Beyond Imperia were six more Trasp worlds: one solid and inhabited, then five gaseous ones ringed by satellites. Hieron, the next world out, was three-quarters liquid, but not water, instead some kind of viscous methane that T-K Imperial scientists had managed to render usable for agricultural use. Much of the three-solar-system-Trasp-Kenner Empire was fed from there and its dozen or so owners were among the wealthiest and oldest lineages of those who would be facing Holt the following night, among them, the proposing Lemms and Quazz peers.

By contrast, the nearest solar system, the four Morbida Worlds, were just barely outside the Trasp solar system's own farthest limits – where many other solar systems in his own, more spacious, galaxy contained only hordes of planetesimals, comets, and other outliers orbiting. He had to suppose it was because this galaxy was smaller and denser that Morbida had merely been a passing small, hot, blue star – but that it was gravitationally attracted enough by Trasp's heavier 11 planet system that instead of glancing off, the blue star had ended up in orbit around it. This had occurred only a few dozen millennia ago; i.e. within written accounts. Darling Andor's own family, The Lazzors, hailed from its second small world, which with a companion continued to orbit the blue star, held in place by its gravitational well.

Meanwhile and in another direction completely a little bit further out from Trasp's farthest orbit, lay the ancient orange star called Altimus, with its single, but very habitable planet known as Kenner. Unlike the tiny Morbida system, this star and planet had been distorted by the larger systems' gravity well, and the single, green and watery world had been pulled increasing inside the orbit of the other planets. Its most recent extremely elliptical foray into the Trasp system had brought it near Hieron. While it had begun back out, past the Trasp gas giants, when it revolved around and in again, its orbit becoming more and more elliptical, it was predicted that it could be between Hieron and Imperia's orbits. No one seemed surprised by this anomaly. Evidently ancient mythologies had explained it once and for all to all T-K people's satisfaction.

Historically, it had already become part of the system. Kenner had been colonized for millennia and had even provided its own brief line of T-K Empire leaders, the Hereditary Thanes of Capalzar. Imperial History, which went back beyond a hundred and fifty T-K centuries, was both sketchy and mythical. But many of those myths played with the fact that planet Kenner's long elliptical orbit intersected the more circular orbits of the five outermost Trasp sister-worlds – accounting for that colonizing family's great wealth and influence – and to some, their last political "invasion." That orbit had for millennia taken the planet close enough to provide much interplanetary contact with the inhabited planets and moons and thus much historical incident. But the world Kenner was currently already well on its way back *out* of mutual orbit, and headed into much icier reaches.

Holt had barely finished his out of doors repast when clouds crept in from what he'd been assured was the south although it felt like the east to him, and within minutes the scrim of fog and mist had returned, painting everything with varied tinges of orange and reds until it had gathered enough of its usual density to return everything around to its customary gray.

That was the moment that Foreign Minister Janz Sonz decided to turn up and remind Holt that as the guest of honor, it was up to him to inspect and approve the venue of the upcoming event. That meant they would have to leave Palace #27.

Holt looked outside and saw a little procession of ground cars, waiting. Fine with him. Despite his erotic gymnastics with two of the locals, and a few brief forays in the garden, he'd begun to feel cabin fever developing.

He was also pleased to see that the Foreign Minister was surprisingly "dressed down." Ever since he'd met Sonz, the other's uniforms had seemed to become ever more ornamented with tassels and braiding, with medallions and medals. The change meant Holt could be more casual too, and the minute he got to his dressing room, the appropriate coverings were waiting for him. One was a rather tam-like cap, but there was also a throw or cape with a substantial hood (besides the long coat) to cover his face.

"This seems over much?" Holt commented.

"The temperature is dropping and if we leave now we perhaps might miss an approaching storm," the older man said.

Holt gave in, let himself be dressed, let himself be surrounded by guards as he walked out and past the fountains and gardens to the largest of the waiting vehicles.

Like the other cars, it was wheel-less, raised half a meter off the ground, and Holt knew it ran on a rail that rose out of depression in the street as the vehicle approached. There were three smaller wheels that would drop to the ground whenever it was detaching from one rail and connecting to other rails, going in other directions, so one seldom realized the change from within. There were no apparent windows from the exterior of the sleekly long, matte-dark green-blue vehicle. Very wide doors swung open from the center of the roof. He entered only after a guard had inspected it and come out again. The Foreign Minister led, and took the far wide, deep leather-like seat, flipped a mid-seat console and Holt sat in the other seat closest to the left door. From within, everything outside it was visible from the roof down, gradually dimming to fully opaque below the level of their seats. The driver as such, in a triangular shaped, sealed off front section, was cybernetic.

Acceleration and braking were silent. Did it use air pumped through? Or was it instead magnetized, gravitational thrust and halt motion? Were there small electric motors below, on either side of the rail. It was a soft, silent, and utterly smooth ride.

For once, the Foreign Minister was gratifyingly silent. They passed through many long blocks of other large estates, like his own, defined by walls and hedges, hedges and walls, with an occasional flurry of overtopping bush. Trees were scarce, grass nonexistent. The plant life on Imperia was colored a very deep green for the most part, extra chlorophyll to absorb the redder part of the solar spectrum, Holt supposed. It was also small-leaved and small-blossomed, and close-leaved and close-blossomed also. Even so, sometimes the hedges appeared to be dark blue, although he did not know if that was natural or man-made and ornamental.

After some time, the road ahead of them sloped down and crossed a level bridge over what seemed to be a three-part canal, and suddenly they were in a different kind of area altogether. This was industrial looking, but again fairly low to the ground, no building higher than three stories, although some seemed hugely spread out. Holt had already learned to discern most of the Imperial alphabet which was squarish with side squiggles and various numbers of dots or slashes above or below certain letters. As far as he could make out, all of the nearly identical lettering on the buildings they passed were logos, and virtually all of the logos were family names he'd already come across, some recognizably hyphenated.

"There are commercial enterprises?" he asked the Foreign Minister.

"Yes. Of all kinds."

"Individually owned?"

"Yes. Mostly by our class of people. With an occasional other class of ownership as entrepreneur. For example, that ziggurat-topped building belongs to the manufacturer of the rails below us, who has a manse not far from your own residence. That edifice topped with a silver and blue glass cupola belongs to your own Palace #27. While you reside there, you are the owner. It provides income for you."

That was interesting.

The remainder of the ride was at least as long as before, when traveling through the mansions, until they cleared the large industrial park by crossing two more level bridges over what he could now see were paved-over streams or dried-up rivers below. There was a flurry of smarter looking, only slightly taller, but more slender and attractive buildings, around them suddenly. These were all variations of a trapezoid in floor plan and so more angular than square when the parade of vehicles that comprised their cavalcade – since that was what it was – flew past and entered a vast ring road. These must be public spaces with occasional large separate buildings in the center of the ring, buildings that looked older than any he'd seen so far and that might almost be historical monuments. They and the surrounding buildings on the outside of the huge ring road were mostly bone-white in color, setting them apart from the dull grays and fawns of the manufactories and the subtle colors of the residential area. Here, the logos on the facades had occasional gold or silver gilding in lettering upon their pediments. Holt was reminded of some ancient ruins of classical style Metro-Terran cities he'd seen restored on the Orion Spur worlds or of the later Star-Baron-Era architectural excesses he'd seen in Docu-Vids while still in Education and Development; long brick or marble stairways rising to imposing facades studded with columns of varied shapes and depth of fluting. Deep-set windows all above street level and mostly square. But as often triangular or target shaped windows. Strange, how so many different cultures shared an idea of what imposing was meant to look.

The vehicles stopped at one of these central edifices, but their own car unhitched from the rail, and on wheels only now, not rail, it entered a driveway down into a vast garage. Guards were waiting there, and after they exited their car, Holt and the Foreign Minister were escorted into lifts that ascended to the main floor.

This awaiting chamber to the auditorium was a surrounding circular ring of maybe a dozen or more arched half domes, liberally muraled and decorated a hundred meters tall. The floor too, sort of a pale pink alabaster shot through with veins of semi-precious stones – jasper, amethyst, coral – was even more colorful. But he was hurried past them all before he could even read their messages, and a double door was thrown open and guards stepped out – motioning to Sonz that the space was "cleared of danger."

The four then entered onto a tilted ramp through hundreds of rows of seats leading up in an irregular star-like pattern to an enormous center slab of yellow and emerald onyx which formed the stage and dais. Rows of darker shades of the same mineral formed natural benches and hip high enclosures upon what must be the stage. High above it, a semi-transparent rotunda with several lower rings of stained glass streamed light into the center of the large auditorium.

It was grand. It was imposing. Holt felt himself swept up to the center and began looking all around himself. He spoke out loud, if only to try all out the acoustics – which were amazing. Then took a place in the seat in from the dais and spoke – again amazing at the reverberation – and then he just soaked up the atmosphere of the place, so very old yet in no way antique – which was doubly amazing.

"Is this how we arrive?" Holt asked. "Up the ramp like we just came in?"

"The others arrive that way, yes. But you and I will arise from below," Sonz corrected. "You remember you agreed that I will escort you in?"

"I wouldn't forget it, Foreign Minister."

Sonz went over to a floor panel behind the Onyx seat. He tapped a boot heel and the panel slid open.

"A simple dressing room below," he explained. "Also gained directly through the underground car-park."

Holt peered: a stairway led down into a dimly lighted corridor.

"And it's all lit from above? No artificial lighting is needed?"

"Yes. It is a daytime use site."

"Very old?" Holt asked.

"It is said to long precede the reign of Zar Aerographas, and even of the earlier dynasties, the Capalzar Emperors, and perhaps even further back, although what its use was before the current dynastic reign ...? Some think a tribunal. Others think it was a court of law for internal enemies of the older and more barbaric regimes, where criminals were tried and ..."

"It is a very grand and imposing spot," Holt interrupted.

It took the Foreign Minister a few moments to understand. "So ... and that is your official approval then for the Council to Discuss the Questions around the Unexpected Visit of an Intergalactic Dignitary."

Assuming he would have to say it to make it official, Holt did. "Yes, I approve this as the location for the Council to Discuss the Questions around the Unexpected Visit of an Intergalactic Dignitary. Myself," Holt said.

They left soon after. When their vehicle drove back out to the street rail, only one other vehicle was waiting there to lead it. "The others were required elsewhere," the Foreign Minister said without any further explanation.

The predicted storm had arrived and rain lashed down in torrents, in turgid streams against all sides of the vehicle, denying any kind of view outside. That must have been why their progress was noticeably slower than before. One moment the rain seemed to Holt to even be forming water spouts, several slapped noisily against the sides of the car with startling loud blows. The Foreign Minister grew even more restive in his seat. But Holt was enjoying it, something about the wild strength of the weather being so much greater than those who were forced to bear it, and thus putting them in their place.

They had driven past the first bridge and the first set of canals heading back to the palace and they had entered the industrial area again, although peering out through the torrential downpour, Holt was certain this was a different route than the one they'd taken before. He speculated that the monumental edifice center and ring road might actually be the crucial design of the city itself and that all else flowed out from it in ever-enlarging circles, separated by narrow rings of flowing water, so that by the time the third area of palaces was attained, the design was so attenuated that it would probably only be visible from the air.

Did that ever-widening circular plan continue throughout the entire planet, he wondered. He knew from what he'd learned about Imperia through the palace Vids that it no longer possessed oceans or mountain ranges or dead-lands, all of which had been technologically subsumed into farmland and sports and other activity parks, but mostly into residences. What must the population be then? What had his cybernetic tutors told him? Several hundred billions?

Holt heard what sounded like a squawking from the Driver's speaker into their cabin, and the Foreign Minister shouted, "What do you mean?"

Just then the vehicle ahead came to a sudden stop and so did theirs. They were thrown back against the seats. The Foreign Minister leaned forward, as frightened, as angry, and shouted, "Why are we stopping?"

The squawking continued, and he turned to Holt and said. "I can't believe I'm saying this, but I believe we are stopped because the route is flooded ahead. I'd better go take a look."

As soon as he was out the door, Holt locked the doors, and spoke through the cabin-to-driver speaker system. "Driver, do not let anyone into this car unless I say so. Do you understand?"

"Yes. It is locked down to your word."

"Now, driver, report exactly what you are seeing in front."

"The Foreign Minister is at the semi-open doors of the front vehicle. Now he is stepping inside. Those doors just shut."

It was difficult to forget the abduction attempt of not a day earlier.

"Are there any weapons in the cabin back here?" Holt asked.

"No, Prince."

"Are there any first aid or emergency tools or instruments back here?"

"Yes. Both, in the second compartment left of the self-service bar."

Holt searched and found the kit, nothing in there to use as a weapon but small scissors. But in the emergency kit was some kind of flare gun. It had a safety catch. To flare, you took that off, and pressed the front of the grip handle. He held it up to the window between them. "Driver, is there a flare in the emergency kit?"

"Yes, to alert others to our presence in an emergency."

"Do you, Driver, need to activate it?"

"No. It is self-activated."

Good. He put it in his right-hand pocket.

"Driver, now what is happening?"

"The Foreign Minister and two others are exiting the front vehicle. They are inspecting the front of the vehicle."

"Driver, what's wrong with the front of that front vehicle?"

"The driver of the front vehicle reports that it struck some object laid across or athwart the rail. It is not clear how the object got there or became wedged there. The Foreign Minister is now coming back to this vehicle."

"Is he alone?"

"He is alone."

"Is he armed?"

"He was but he put the safety back on and the arm is inside his clothing."

"Unlock the doors and let him in."

The rain had let up only a bit when the doors opened.

"An accident, Prince Holt. The driver had to report it. We cannot go immediately. Please remain here. I'll find a spot for us to weather out this deluge."

He then turned to the speaker, and said, "What have you found?"

The strange squawking from before went on a bit.

"Fine, we'll go there." To Holt, he said, "Our guard has obtained permission for us to weather this storm in the office or lobby of a nearby factory."

"Can't we remain here?" Holt asked.

"Best not." Holt waited for him to say "we would be sitting ducks," but he didn't.

A minute later two guards from the front car were at their door. "Apologies, Prince Holt. We've found a safe, dry spot and checked it out. We'll escort you there now. Please come with us."

They literally surrounded him as he exited, one with a hand upon his back, the other on his arm. They were being very protective.

Once they all four got inside the tall glass foyer of the building, one stood just inside at the doorway, checking inside. The Foreign Minister spoke to the receptionist, an older male with a tall shock of silver hair, who got up and led Holt and the other two to an inner office. As he came out from behind his work-station, Holt noted that although he had the same body as all the inhabitants of Imperia Holt had seen before, he walked with a slight bias toward the left, possibly because of leg injury or birth defect and as a result he seemed imperfect.

He led them up a few steps to a double door and opened it, standing aside to let them through, "______ (a name Holt didn't recognize) is out this afternoon, otherwise he would greet you himself. These are his younger sons. They are studying here. They will give you no trouble. I'll arrange for hot drinks brought immediately." Despite his slight body distortion, he moved as though on gliders, and as he passed Holt, he stopped only briefly to say in a low voice, "unexpected as this is, Prince, we are most honored," before he glided away.

As they had stepped into the room, one of the boys had said something Holt hadn't made out. They couldn't keep their eyes off the visitors.

The Foreign Minister and one guard confabbed at the office doorway, then turned and stepped out of the room. One of the boys stood up and looked out the ajar doorway. He was the younger of the two and still had an infant's baby-fat around his face, hands and upper torso.

"Are you in trouble?" the younger one asked and then shut the door. "Is that why you are being guarded?"

"Don't be a ___!" the older one said, using a term Holt had never heard before. "Didn't you hear what old Harwas called him? 'Prince?' He's a Scion. A top Scion."

This son was several years older, and already shed his baby-fat and was now becoming thinner and taller. While the other son could have physically passed for a full human, this older one already had the beginnings of the exaggerated male dominant masculine features that Imperial adults – and Holt too now – possessed. Where the younger had normal and still short hair with a central peak, the older already had the rough strong fur-like hair cut high all around the top in emulation of adults. Like his younger brother, he also wore a kind of modified uniform, probably from school.

The standing son stared at Holt as he sat in a version of a large armchair. It was warm enough that he could take down the cape's hood, loosen the over coat which had grown stuffy due to the warmth of the office, and even remove his cap and shake out his hair. There were napkins or tissues on the table, and Holt dabbed his face with one, where the rain had somehow gotten through.

The younger son could not stop staring at Holt.

"Sit down and study!" his elder hissed. The younger ignored him.

"Haven't you ever seen a Top Scion before?" Holt asked, intending to be comical and a little ironic.

"Not close up like this. You're more beautiful than the drawings we've seen of you in the Vids."

"Come sit down and study," his elder repeated, clearly embarrassed. His brother shrugged and joined him and they worked their styli silently upon their pads, but the younger boy kept stealing glances at Holt.

"Old Harwas" came in with a tray and two of the squarish, everyday mugs used to contain hot drinks on Imperia. He set them down, and opened a little tin revealing what looked like thin cookies.

"You're very kind. The Foreign Minister will make certain you are recompensed ..." Holt began.

"We wouldn't dream of it. Would we?" he asked the youngsters.

Foreign Minister Sonz came in, exchanging places with Harwas, and then perched on his chair and allowed Holt to pour him a tisane. "It still isn't clear how this occurred. Which is why these precautions are so necessary."

"Don't think twice about it," Holt said and then gestured with his eyes toward the boys so that Sonz wouldn't say anything he might later regret.

The Foreign Minister got the message and sipped his tisane. He'd taken only a few sips when the guard stepped in and gestured, and he and Sonz went out again. When Holt looked the other cup was almost empty.

The boys had seen everything and doubtless heard everything too.

Holt couldn't for the life of him figure out what the ingredients of the drink were? A local cinnamon but also somewhat licorice and then a bit of something close to Pelagian ocean fennel?

The cookie was slender, thin, and delicious. Vaguely Bergamot flavored.

Now the two sons were both openly staring at him.

"Don't just sit there," Holt said. "Come over here and get cookies."

The younger didn't need to be asked twice. He was there with his fairly grubby hands out. Holt put half the cookies into a napkin and handed it to him

"Share those with your brother."

The elder stood up and cut a bow to Holt and sat down again. The younger, his mouth still full of cookie, did the same, a bit more sketchily.

Holt had to laugh. His own mouth was full of cookie.

"Old Harwas" returned, gratified to see the tea and cookies appreciated.

"Your sire" he said to the elder son. "Is on the far-speaker. At my desk."

The elder boy got up and left the office.

"More!" Holt offered the younger boy.

"I'd better not. Harwas will tell." Then, "It is true that you will be our next Empress?"

"Would you prefer that I not be?" Holt asked.

No one had ever asked him any kind of question like that, so the son pondered, then blurted out. "No. You'd be a fine Empress."

"Well, thank you for that vote of confidence. But it is unclear if that will happen. There is to be a special Council tomorrow to Discuss the Questions Around the Unexpected Visit of an Intergalactic Dignitary. Me," Holt said, hoping he sounded as amused as he actually was.

It went over the boy's head.

"Wait'll I tell Spathy that I met you!" the boy said, and wiped cookie crumbs off his pad. "Spathy's my Pre-Bond."

"Your Pre-Bond? What does that mean?"

"You know, our Family Fathers have set us up to become a Bond-Pair when we are older."

In other words, to marry and mate. Awfully early and awfully young for that kind of family unit set-up, Holt thought.

"Does your brother have a Pre-Bond?"

"Yes, but he doesn't like him anymore."

Aha! So it didn't always work out. "That's too bad."

"Especially as his Pre-Bond is a Scion. Not a top one like you. Father would like him Bonding with a Scion. Anyway, he's already gathering evidence against him for a formal Pre-Bond slip-off."

That sounded like an early divorce. "Is Spathy also a Scion?"

"No. But I like him."

"That's what's important, you know," Holt said.

"I know."

He sounded like he did know.

A minute later he too was called out to Harwas' desk to the far-speaker, a communication device, Holt guessed. He sipped at his tea, then got up and looked at the boy's pads. One had simple reading exercises, several words of which he could make out; the other had what might have been Chemistry notations.

He'd just sat down again, when another door he'd noticed in the rear of the office and had thought led to storage or an inner office, opened. Actually, the noise from beyond it opening is what got his attention. There was so much of it. Another middle-aged person stepped into the room, looking surprised.

"You are not ...?"

"He's on the far-speaker with his sons at the receptionist's desk," Holt explained as casually as possible.

The other was dressed much like Harwas. So, he was another employee. He also had a slight distortion, this time a slight swivel to his torso. He grunted and left the office in the direction of the others.

Holt took advantage of the back door being ajar to reopen it and look to see where all the noise was coming from. A set of stairs led down to an internal bridge that spanned what looked like a factory of workers seated at long tables, with spinning spools and automatic punchers and automatic cutters. Those machines seemed to be the main culprits responsible for the mechanized racket he heard. The workers all wore identical drab clothing, including some type of scarf-like head covering. Not a single one looked up in curiosity as Holt dropped down the steps and stepped across the bridge – where surely he must be visible! – to get a closer look at them. They were altering or sewing together long strips of some canvas like material, all of them completely intent on their job. They might have been cybernetic given their complete focus and their rapidity of movements, but they were not, they were people. And as he stood there he looked to all sides and it was clear that the factory floor extended many meters in two directions. Meaning also under the street where the cars drove. There must be hundreds of workers below and if any noticed him or noted him not one moved out of sync to show it.

The office door opened and it was the older son. Holt greeted him and then he climbed back up and into the office, and the son closed the door.

"My father sends his apologies that he could not be here himself."

"Thank him for me ... Those are your father's workers down there?"

"Yes."

"There are a great many of them."

"Several hundred."

"Have you ever met or spoke to any of them?"

The boy looked completely startled by the question. "Why would I do that?'

"To get to know them? Their problems? Their families?"

"They have no families. They have no problems. They are all Euthna."

"They looked like women. Is that what women are called here?" And when the both didn't respond, "Women? Females? They all looked like females."

"There used to be females on Imperia. But not anymore. Now there are Euthna. They are the workers. My father cares for them from birth. He feeds and he clothes them and he houses them. And then he gives them something to do all day that is not too strenuous for their minds or bodies, both of which are rather weak."

"You do know what a female is?" Holt asked. "It's a person with different genitalia."

"Maybe there are a few females still existing here in Imperia. But no, they are mostly gone. Replaced now by Euthna. Perhaps on some of the outer worlds ..."

"Because males give birth on Imperia?" Holt asked.

"If we are fortunate, yes, and have a successful Bond-Pair. But I don't know if that is the reason for the decline of females. I don't know if there is any causal connection between the two. The females were a long time dying out," the son said with conviction. "They had no special, natural purpose. They were not as good as males at giving birth. Many became ill during the process. For others, their minds often became unhinged and they turned against their new-born. A constant proportion were often not physically strong enough and died during childbirth. Others, after birth, appeared not as gifted at providing consistent nurturing and consistently helping their young grow and learn. Their nature was too emotionally scattered and unpredictable. When not specifically nurturing, they took to being trained only sporadically and while at times some of them were very creative, many were simply incapable of the long endurance required in most significant careers in the Empire. We are taught that in our Nature Course in our schools, that a living thing with no special, natural purpose, eventually dies off. This has happened many times to other creatures on Imperia that no longer exist. When digging for new water or power lines, we find evidence of that."

Holt was appalled listening to this misogynistic catechism inculcated into young minds. Whatever fault the Matriarchy governments may have had in his own Milky Way galaxy, none of these supposed "faults and lacks" had ever been charged to any human or delphinid female or male. Of course, he might also be totally wrong. Without actually seeing or knowing any females in the T-K Empire, there was no way to assess those charges. Even so, it very much sounded like what guilty survivors said about peoples, races, and species they had destroyed or let die off deliberately or from neglect.

And to complicate matters, there was the issue of the lack of birds, reptiles and animals, each of them depicted in ancient Imperium family logos. They too certainly had died off. Holt was sure he heard and sometimes even thought he'd seen insects in the gardens outside the palace. He assumed they had taken on all of the "natural" roles that other animals performed elsewhere: foraging, seeding, pollinating, cleaning and clearing dead stuff, what else?

"What about Top Scions like myself? We have no purpose, do we?"

"Some Top Scions do. Other scions do not and they too will die out."

He seemed so sure of himself, that Holt had to ask, "But myself. I have no special natural purpose, do I?" he argued

"But you do! To be admired. To be unattainable."

Holt waited for the son to add, "And to be united with an Imperial Scion," but he didn't. Surely, he must know that was to be this foreign "Prince's" fate. Was he being coy, or merely politic in not saying it?

Holt was pondering what he'd said, to be a paragon ... was that really, a natural purpose?

The younger son came in with another lad, evidently his Pre-Bond, Spathy. They looked alike too. Behind them was the Foreign Minister.

"See?" the younger son said to his friend. "That's him!"

"Come here. I won't bite," Holt said to the new boy.

"We are ready to leave, Prince Holt," Foreign Minister Sonz announced.

Holt touched fingers with the younger boys. With the older boy, he clasped his arm as was done by males to each other on Hesperia. "You will be a fine person," he declared. "All of you will be. But," to the elder son he added, "you must learn to question things more. And then you will be an even finer person."

Holt felt hustled out of the office and the guards surrounded him closely as before and he found himself in the car and speeding away, despite the rain.

The guards brought him into Little Versailles where his house guards took over. Foreign Minister Sonz declared, "Although completely unprepared for, I believe that was a good meeting you had at that factory."

"Yes, it was. Very enlightening," Holt admitted.

"Those sons will never forget you."

Nor will I soon forget them, nor what I saw there, nor what I learned from them both about Imperia, Holt thought. But he simply wished the Foreign Minister good evening.

Engineer Grade Six, #31640-78 stood in what must be the finest Interplanetary Vehicle "graveyard" in all of the Imperium awaiting the decision of a tall dark slab of something or other.

It was taking its time.

"Won't any of it do?" Mozza Safran asked wearily. They'd been here for several hours wasting her day off from work, not to mention the graft payment she'd needed to lay out to gain entry in the first place.

"It's a wonder these don't simply fall apart," the Inter Galactic visitor opined. "Or have they already and that's why they are here?"

Mozza decided not to grace that comment with a response.

"Of them all, only this one could possibly be fitted out to get several of us out of here without completely dissolving into flinders," her shopping companion added, not sounding at all enthusiastic.

Mozza saw nothing more than a fuselage, closed at one end, and partly open where it would link to another vehicle or perhaps to a power unit at the other. Although, as she came closer to inspect it, Mozza recognized that the fuselage had been part of a triple-strength hull belonging to a vehicle that used to transport dangerously radioactive materials from the third outer planet of their solar system, Januarius, to the most out of the way areas on Imperia. The partly visible Logo on its side was also the Sigil of the Thanocracy of Capalzar, a single white tongue of flame. The ship was probably manufactured and utilized some decades before that famed Imperial Line was overthrown, more than half a century ago.

"We would need a small thruster to get it out of orbit," her companion said. "Either of those two over there would suffice." It emitted a fast beam to light up the two hulls mentioned.

"Well, that's settled. Now how do we pay for them?"

"I just arranged all that. And returned your deposit to your own account also. You will pick up a paid receipt as we exit."

That was surprising. But she knew her visitor had not been lax in the few days since she'd awakened it. Nor was she willing to bother to find out how it spent what had to be a great deal of *dinarii* it couldn't possibly possess.

"Anything else needed, while we're here?" Mozza asked.

"The interior can be rebuilt to accommodate two sentient beings without trouble. A list of those extras should be here later this day."

"You've thought of everything," she admitted.

"Piloting is simple, should part of this over-riding mechanism (meaning itself) be disabled. There is only one other question. Weapons!"

"No weapons!" Mozza said. "I don't like weapons."

"Bear in mind that this unit addressing yourself was literally shot down upon arrival. Its passenger was shot-up."

"The passenger was repaired," she argued.

"For a variety of political reasons. However, where we are headed there will be no technologically superior cyber surgeons. This Fast's own surgery abilities are no longer part of its sub-routines."

"I suppose you're right. What do you suggest?"

"The two lasers in your laboratory could be modified. Condensed and then miniaturized to begin with, to become portable, and then moved here."

When she hesitated.

"You would be able to carry them in that shoulder bag."

She was about to ask another question, when the formerly mysterious and still not all that well understood object stood still and then shot up into the air so suddenly, she had to wonder if it had completely misfunctioned.

She found it some five hundred meters above, slowly turning about on its axis. It stood still, like a hunting cyber she'd seen on a vid and then it shot down as quickly.

"Don't tell me," Mozza said.

"I received a signal from my master. Unintentional. Very weak. Nondirected."

"Could he have been moving quickly in a vehicle?" she suggested. "Rail cars go very fast."

The object leapt back up into the air and hovered as it had been before. Slowly spun. Stopped, then shot down again.

"Dozens of such vehicles were discerned over half a dozen roads."

"The palaces are in that direction!" she pointed. "The civic center that way."

"It was the most extraordinary sensation," the object explained. "As though ... as though ..."

"As though it made you happy?" Mozza suggested.

"It was more like it gave me an expectation of being happy."

"Well, all the media say he's a great Prince," she said, but with a hint of reluctance to believe them. "But I don't think many have actually laid eyes on him, never mind actually met him."

"We must be completely prepared for our Prince," the object said, and took off horizontally.

It was waiting at the outside gate when she arrived.

"I'll be back tomorrow," Mozza said.

"Thank you for your purchase," the gate guard replied. "Here is your sales receipt."

Mozza left thinking, "I've just bought a spacegoing vehicle for some alien I barely know and don't at all understand and whom I'm planning to join on a very long trip to who knows where. I clearly have no idea what I'm doing."

Then, before she could berate herself, she laughed. It wasn't that it made her happy to have bought it, it was more like it gave her an expectation of being happy.

Holt had assumed it would all be grave and dignified, probably tediously slow. He'd doubtless been fooled by the architecture of the hall they'd been in, which was austere and white and solemn-looking. But from the onset, even before the onset, this so-called convocation was proving to be anything but that.

He became aware of that in the rail car a half mile away, caught in an enormous traffic jam of rail cars and hover-craft and off-railed road vehicles on the huge ring road and apparently all headed to that very hall.

"Driver!" Foreign Minister Sonz tried to get its attention. "Get us off this rail. I know another way inside. Now."

"Directions, please," the oddly reluctant sounding driver requested.

Sonz preceded to give them to the driver, then sat back as their car audibly detached from the rail and went in reverse on wheels for a while until they reached a single lane ramp that didn't look like it went anywhere.

"Right here. A right turn here!" Sonz directed.

"I thought you said there would be four hundred today?" Holt declared.

"I said the Council of Four Hundred had been called."

"Looks like they brought their entire families and most of their friends," Holt said, amused.

"At least. I suppose much of it has to be mere curiosity about what an Extra-Galactic being looks like."

"Speaking of that, how do I look?"

He'd had the palace craft-shop make up an outfit to fit the occasion. It was bone white with minimal matte bronze trim. Close-fitted as any Fleet Admiral's, but disarmingly simple in design: The blouse was emerald green, with bronze buttons. The bolero jacket around that was bone-white again with no trim at all. Before leaving he'd slung a chest high holster attachment he'd also had made up under the final jacket. Given the angle, it barely bulged, and he felt safer with it. There was even a little white cap perched high on his up-brushed and much stiffened hair. When Holt had peered at his reflection before leaving Little Versailles, he had to admit the weight loss and the very partial regain as well as the hours of therapeutic exercise he'd undergone to get accustomed to his new lower body had put him in the best physical condition he'd ever been in. He'd even reminded his image that "This is it, Holt. Your physical peak. From here on it's all downhill."

Instead of answering the obvious, Holt heard Foreign Minister Sonz say, "We could avoid all this today, you understand. Simply accept my own Liege's renewed offer of marriage. He's instructed me to add virtually anything extra you might desire."

"The Earl of Quazz?"

"Yes. He is closest to the throne as it is."

"But then I would miss all the fun!"

"Here, driver!" Sonz directed. "Go right here! It will lead directly into the under garage."

It did and furthermore it led to an undisturbed and barely used part of the huge space under the convocation hall. The driver got them as close as possible to where the underground was closed off by what looked like heavy baffles.

"Are we anywhere near the dressing room?" Holt asked.

"Driver. Call us a flat car," Sonz commanded. Meaning they were not.

As they got out of the vehicle, the open vehicle approached and stopped. It looked to Holt awfully like an ancient Matriarchy-era carry-all used at space ports for luggage. He helped the Foreign Minister up onto it, remarking to himself how elderly Sonz was. The flat car circuitously wended its way toward the center, with Holt guiding it from the handrail rudder, and always keeping out of sight of the arriving rail cars parking.

A lift led to a below stage floor with a group of chambers mostly used for the storage of needed equipment. This was the corridor he'd briefly seen from above the previous day, now lit up. The dressing room was unmarked. No sooner had they arrived than Sonz excused himself. He had to look over the main floor stage and confirm that all was correct. There were several Vid-mags strewn about. Holt took a seat and turned one on. "A Unique and Very Imperial Occasion" its headline said aloud and read in print. He read the puffery about this occasion (i.e. himself) for a while, then tried the second Vid-magazine. "What Will the New Emperor Baby Look Like?" was the headline on that, and not having seen Holt, the mag's artist had come up with all kinds of Imperium-mammal possibilities several of which sent him into gales of laughter.

A knock on the door and it opened. It was Andor, Thane of Lazzor, who checked outside then slipped in and locked the door, then held out what passed for a bouquet of local flowers for him.

Holt held up one of the Vid-mag's illustrations showing a very hairy infant with sharpened teeth, and pointed ears. "Evidently, I've got some strong Ursus-style features that I'm sure to pass on. Are you sure you want to be with me?"

After they'd clasped arms and nuzzled a bit, Andor said, "It's nonsense. But seriously, Holt. My liege the Marquess of the Morbida Worlds renews his offer of wedlock to you, and promises you his best mining and agricultural estates for your private demesne, among his worlds."

That solar system, Holt had discovered, was indeed wealthy, and better yet, only a sixteenth of a light year distant. If he lived there, he would probably be able pop into this Imperium on weekends.

Holt put a hand up to his mouth, but Andor took it away. "Remember, he is a close cousin. He even looks like me! And after your first successful male birth, with the Marquess, there can be an Official Slip-Off and then you and I can be together."

"That is the best offer I received in days."

"Then ...?"

"I've got to see this through," Holt declared.

"I won't remain here, tonight, you understand. I would be too upset."

"Good luck getting away with all the traffic I saw."

Andor sighed and with the next knock on the door he was up and slipping out, facing away from 2nd Fleet Admiral Tanzen Raz who was coming in.

"I believe I left something at your palace," the golden haired, yellow clad soldier said with some embarrassment.

"Don't tell me," Holt said. "I know! Your heart."

"My heart?" Goldilocks looked puzzled. "Um. No. It was the former Empress' nephew, Japh Goraz's, formal prospectus for you two to wed. The Earl of Lemms?" he reminded Holt.

"Got it! Read it. Most interesting."

The Admiral looked relieved. "We never got around to discussing it then."

"No, we didn't, because I was too busy seducing you. Naughty me."

"That wasn't what I ..."

"And you want me to do without all of this convocation nonsense upstairs and accept the Earl's proposal right now."

"I realize that it would mean ..."

"And you would what? Become my unofficial or maybe even official paramour right after I gave the Earl a little infant Emperor and then Slipped-Off?"

Goldilocks looked at him straight on and said, "The Earl is a close relative and a very dear one. However, the Earl is also an elderly and sometimes quite unwell relative. After what happened at the palace, I thought, perhaps I myself might engage in the actual siring process. The Earl has already given approval, and his final will would then appoint me Regent. Should his health decline before that time so that ..."

"You could become Regent even if he was still alive."

"You have learned the ways of the T-K empire quickly." Goldilocks said, his voice tight and hard as he clasped Holt close to himself. "Lacking any other tradition-bound loyalty like so many here are saddled with, I believe you could become an effective co-ruler in a few years, and in time as great an Empress as any in our history."

"That's a great compliment Admiral, but then I would be leaving all of these people still wondering if I looked like this?" He held up the Vid with the Ursine drawing. "They've come all this way for the show. How could I possibly disappoint them?"

Goldilocks took that with a good grace. He glanced at the flora briefly before leaving but then said, "Soon, Prince Holt. Soon!"

When he was gone, Holt locked the door and sat down. He'd given all this some thought, but he'd never allowed himself to think it through to the end, because ... well, that would mean he had accepted his fate. He hadn't, he knew. Not deep down. Not at all. It was childish of him not to. Everyone back home said he continually acted like a child, long after he ought to have stopped. Yet, that was who he was, in many ways. He couldn't give up hope.

The one real advantage he had – or thought he had – was that of years. He'd attempted to understand the Trasp-Kenner time system. It was at least as complex as their solar system, which was interlaced with the two other, smaller solar systems The relative smallness and denseness of the entire M-2 galaxy surely meant that everything else was smaller and more condensed, no? Their years were 200 days revolving around their small red sun. The daily rotation was barely 40 hours long, Sol Rad. And yes, he could still feel what was correctly Sol Rad. So, it would make sense that their ages must be correspondingly short. Several times, he'd attempted to access that information, but it never added up. The Foreign Minister, for example would probably be over 600 years old or more on and around Hesperia. The Fleet Admiral at least 300. But he suspected that lifespans here were far shorter? Maybe no more than 100 years, as they'd been in the ancient Metro-Terran systems. He knew that age extension among the Three Species hadn't occurred until *interstellar* travel become common. Here, interstellar wasn't common at all. It hadn't so much been the sheer years that had been the aim of life extension in the Milky Way galaxy as the *difference* in years caused by interstellar travel. Early star travelers left home at say age 30 and returned at age 35, but anywhere from ten to a hundred years had passed at home during what for them was a relatively brief absence. Once telomere and other genetic extension was made automatic to the mammalian species, and until Fast flight, those left at home would have passed a large number of years. But instead of being grandmothers, when their lover, husband, wife, whatever, returned they would have aged accordingly. Might even still be young and vibrant. They might have had a long period of years in between, wed to another, or others, raised one or more families. But that didn't preclude the star travelers reentering their lives. On their own, the Bella=Arthropods had discovered a similar age extension to match the others. But here in the Trasp-Kenner Empire, Holt suspected he could marry all of his suitors consecutively, have love affairs with both Tanzen Raz and Andor Lazzor, and still be young when they had all aged well past late middle age into senility. If he were forced to remain here, that would be the only intelligent stratagem – if only he had patience to do it. Unfortunately, he didn't.

And a perfect example of that was the ridiculous not quite itching on his right wrist where he'd caused the skin to seal over his wrist connector. He knew it couldn't be anyone trying to contact him via that method, because who could it possibly be? Yet yesterday, as the rail car left the industrial sector headed across the bridge toward Little Versailles, he'd felt *something* there. Not even an itch, really. Secretly, he'd then opened the skin which had of course bled a little, but the area of the long-embedded comm. chip was untouched, the area unscarred and ready. So, he'd sealed it over with some flesh colored bandage tape, and found a wrist band to wear today to cover that up.

"Admit it, Holt. You're expecting to be contacted. Maybe even rescued ... You idiot!"

Even down here he could feel the enormous crowd above and around this small area. He got up and went out. No one in the corridor, but then there was the stairway up. Now if he could only take a peek.

"Halt where you are!"

He turned and it was one of Tanzen Raz' guards.

"I just want to get a look up there," Holt said to the youth.

"Certainly. My apologies, Prince. I will go before you."

"Not needed. I just want to pop my head above the floor."

Startled. "Certainly."

Holt watched the guard press the stairway flap that slid the stairway open to the auditorium. The enormous din was immediately apparent. Someone was speaking, and there was martial music playing, and people, thousands of them above were restless, waiting. He got far enough up the stairs to see that the ceiling and high dome had been altered by the placement of hundreds of large, brightly colored cloth banners. Then he dropped down again. He thanked the guard and went back to the dressing room.

It was a great deal more of a "thing" than he'd counted on. It would be a giant show. He'd be exhibited like a ... Be asked questions as ... Be made to perform as though ... suddenly, he didn't want to do it. For only the second time since he'd arrived at MC-2, he was afraid. The first time had been as his pod was being shot down around him, and now this. This was by far the starker, more unreasoning fear.

He was just about to try to figure out how he could leave undetected, when there was a light tap on the door. If it was Andor, he could persuade him to ...

But it was the Foreign Minister. Behind him two other guards.

"As promised ..." He began.

"Yes. Of course."

One guard led Sonz ahead of him. They went up the stairs into the near-deafening audience noise, and Sonz led him to the front of the stage, where several comfortable chairs had been set, before a giant vid screen. And as Holt stepped behind Sonz, he saw himself on that screen and on enormous screens high above the auditorium here and there and there too.

The hall became utterly silent.

"It is my especial honor as the Foreign Ministry of Extra Galactic affairs," Sonz began, and Holt was certain he could be heard a mile away, given the incredible new silence, "to welcome our first visitor from the very large, neighboring galaxy, a place we learn about in our schoolbooks but until now have never actually realized was real, and had inhabitants. Especially not inhabitants like our visitor, whose birth parent is the founder of their Galactic Republic." He looked to Holt for encouragement. "This great Prince, our visitor, modestly wishes to be known by the name of Holt. But for our customs he must be Prince Holt. Welcome Prince Holt to Imperia."

He made a half bow and gestured Holt into the special seat prepared for him

Holt returned the half bow, noticing in all the surrounding screens his own tall crop of hair tremble ever so slightly, as he sat down. There were so many heads and faces before him, all around him that he couldn't focus, and instead tried to focus on the far walls of the auditorium. But these surprised him by not being blank walls at all as he'd assumed when he first visited, but instead open loge chambers also containing faces and heads and torsos, and he also realized that each loge sported a family or clan crest and banners. A few of them recognizable. So, they must be the most prominent families or clans. Holt took the seat.

"Thank you, Foreign Minister. And thank you, all of Imperia for helping to make my visit one of great interest, and comfort, and safety."

Sonz again half bowed.

As he'd been instructed before, Holt then said, "I understand, and it is only natural, that some in this hall would have questions for me."

Several with questions had been pre-arranged and were waiting several yards away to provide their questions. The first one was at least Sonz's age, but dressed in a sort of uniform that Holt recognized as being from a scientific institution.

He was briefly introduced by an Emcee until then out of sight, and of course the first questioner turned out to be a famed astronomer.

In an elderly and unsteady voice, he said, "On clear nights we can see your home galaxy revolving like a pinwheel in the sky, and we have been able with our instruments to make out some details of it. Does your government, your so-called Republic," he added checking his notes, "dominate it all?"

"The Third Ib'r Republic is the only government or state or nation in that galaxy that we know of," Holt said. "So, I suppose it does dominate it."

"But it's all so large. Scores of parsecs in size. How can it?"

"My understanding, Professor and I am neither a professor nor a scientist, is that our Republic takes up about a physical twenty-fifth fraction or so of the entire galactic mass, but that it's actual reach – via Faster Than Light travel and communication – enables it to encompass the entire mass."

"Staggering! Simply staggering!"

He was ushered away and a clearly military fellow replaced him, probably from the intelligence division.

"How is it that your people resemble we Trasp-Kennerites so closely? Have we been in contact before that we are unaware of? Have your people visited us in the past without us knowing it?"

"Not that I am aware of Colonel-Major. My visit here is, you must understand, completely accidental. I arrived barely conscious, nearly dead, and in a sort of life-preserver shell. And with no knowledge of how I got here. The distance between the two galaxies is measurable but still quite immense. As to why we seem to be alike physically, you surely have been told that I represent only *one* of *three* intelligent species in my galaxy, the other two being a sea-going mammalian people, and another species resembling rather large social insects. Furthermore, we have recently become aware that in the very deep past, of other species of completely different physical shape and size that once dominated our galaxy."

Someone pushed the questioner aside, and Holt barely heard his description as a sort of social scientist, when he was interrupted by the fellow asking, "Is everyone where you come from as physically attractive as you are, Prince Holt? Because if so, it would well explain why our ancient cultures believed in physically perfect gods. You are, you understand, like a god to us. That was why we were suddenly silent when you appeared. We were prepared for any sort of horror to appear. But I don't think any of us were ready for the appearance of one of our ancient gods."

"He's right, you are beautiful," someone shouted out.

"*More* beautiful than our ancient gods."

"And with hair like the flames of our sun itself. Only one of our gods – our Sun God, the immortal Trasp – ever had that color hair!"

Then another and another and then many of them stood and did movements of their closed hands to their lips and then chests in a gesture meant to represent their obeisance and their deep wish to bond him.

The Emcee tried to gain control, but many more stood and plighted their troth to him, and so the Foreign Minister stood up and shouted, "Sit down, please. All of you. Prince Holt is gratified by your acceptance and by your desire. But please let us continue this as it has been planned."

Well, this isn't so terrible, Holt began thinking. But Sonz was right to get it under control now.

"As I said before," Holt reiterated, "As far as my Three Species people are aware, we have *not* visited Imperia. Looking out among you here today I can easily see that my hair coloring is unique. It is fairly unique where I come from too. But I have not seen any representations of your gods at all, so I can't compare."

"They were expunged," the questioner said. "All such representations were expunged, erased, or hidden away over a century ago."

"For what reason?" Holt had to know.

"Because no one alive could live up to their standard. We were all inferior."

"But surely that was because they were ideal representation, weren't they?" Holt asked. "Ideal? Not real?"

"Not if legends are true. Our legends say that was how T-K Imperials actually looked before our degeneration. You yourself are proof that it is possible to look like as were depicted."

Holt was reminded of the factory owner's son's description of females and why they had vanished. There was something not quite right about these people and their concepts of self-image. Even in bed with two of their handsomest of their kind recently, Holt had been apprised of certain physical defects, blemishes, distortions of theirs so slight he wouldn't have seen them if they'd not been pointed out. It seemed a common mass neurosis.

But now dozens more in the audience were standing and pledging something or other. That was unsettling.

"What are they saying?" he whispered to Sonz.

"They want to vote you as Empress. Right now!"

"That can't be done, can it? It's too premature!"

There were a few others waiting in the queue to question him, but the Emcee now came over and whispered in the Foreign Minister's ear.

Suddenly two of the loges began flashing their lower portions where letters and he thought numbers too were appearing. What was going on?

"Foreign minister ..."

Holt heard the Emcee suddenly say very loudly. "We are being asked to forego questioning. That is irregular, so I must ask, if anyone in this hall has reason to believe that this visitor, Prince Holt, of the Third Ib'r Republic, has no standing to assume the Imperial position, let that person stand and be counted."

Holt expected dozens, hundreds to stand. Only two did and they were quickly hushed by others.

"No," Holt stood up, and shouted. "Don't stop them. Let them be heard!"

He'd meant to slow down or even stop this madcap rush to who knew what. Instead, he felt a wave of adulation for his action and words overtop the last one.

To Sonz, he whispered, "What do those letters and numbers mean?'

He received no answer, and more and more of those loges began exhibiting their own set of numbers and letters.

One of the protestors had been brought to the stage, and he stood there, ready. Holt saw the fellow waver.

"Please. Have your say. It's my wish," Holt urged him.

"From this close, your perfection cannot be doubted," the protestor began.

"Yes. But ...?"

"But you are not of our world. You do not know our history or our ..."

"Prince Holt is extremely intelligent. In the upper level of our measurable intelligence. And in a very short time he has learned a great deal already," Sonz interrupted. "There is no doubt he could quickly learn as much as any of you of our history and customs."

"But you do have a valid point," Holt said. "'I cannot hope to,' is the true answer. I would require much counsel and aid and ..."

'We would do as much as possible to aid you, Prince Holt," the protestor said now, in effect, capitulating.

"And those who aided and counselled me might have agendas of their own. So your point is well taken." Holt concluded. "A good question."

The next protestor self-described as a professor of anatomy and internal medicine demanded that the hall audience be shown several types of diagrams and internalized schemata to know that Holt was capable of producing a male heir.

This would certainly put a halt to this, Holt thought. But this must have been prepared for also, because suddenly the screens began displaying exactly the schemata the medico had asked for, one after the other, and several others of his profession came onto the stage and they all looked and pointed out features to each other. The final ones put up were actual photographs after he had healed, only a few days ago, and were of him nude from several angles. Holt tried to stop those, but Sonz motioned him back into his chair.

"Your conclusion, Lord Physicians?" Sonz asked.

"He is flawless," declared one.

"He is without flaw or error of any kind," echoed another.

"His reproductive organs are intact and as yet unutilized." The third one reported.

"There is no reason to believe he could not carry a male heir," the first summed up.

"He is without a single flaw inside or out," Number two again.

"He is physically the most Top-Scion of any Top-Scion I have ever examined," the third assured them.

"This is exactly what we would wish for an Empress."

And there it was.

The Emcee stepped forward again. "Thank you all. You may step down. It is time for the voting to begin."

Wait a minute, Holt thought. How did we get to the voting already?

"We have three bonded and certified public calculators to provide the compete legal terms and lack of exceptions for the vote."

Sure enough, three more fellows took the spot the previous protestors had vacated, pads and styli in hand, poised.

"Will the Interested Parties begin the bidding," the Emcee shouted.

Bidding? What bidding?

Then Holt realized that's what those letters and numbers were – yes, they were numbers, and apparently very large ones – that flashed on the sides of the loges surrounding the hall from at least one to two stories above the floor. Now they were all lighting up, and as they did, the accountants began rapidly to copy down the bids on their pads.

"End the bidding, round one!" The Emcee announced.

He looked to the calculators.

"What's going on?" Holt whispered to Sonz, who ignored him, while watching the accountants.

"We have a three-way tie in the bidding!" The Emcee announced, answering Holt's question.

Holt now stood up. "I asked once and I will ask again. What is this bidding all about?"

"Please sit down, Prince Holt," Sonz said, sharply.

The Emcee asked him to sit down until the bidding was over.

I asked," Holt now shouted, "What they are bidding for?"

"For you, of course," Sonz said, and put out an arm and tried to pull Holt down into the chair.

Bad move. Unsuccessful move. Holt was so much stronger, he inadvertently pulled the Foreign Minister's arm away with such force that Sonz half stood and then toppled out of the chair and across the table separating them and onto the stage.

Appalled by the unintentional result of his action, Holt leaned over and tried to lift Sonz, but the Foreign Minister now began striking about windmill-like with his arms and hands and as he did, he knocked over the pitcher and glasses of water on the table between them. The Emcee and a guard managed to get Sonz up and he seemed all right, and shooed them away. But the water had splashed all over Holt's front and hair and one of guards found a cloth and began to wipe him off. Holt seized the cloth and did it himself, while a sort of laughing, embarrassed near-panic gripped the front rows of the hall nearest the mishap.

Holt sat back down, and continued to wipe his face and hair, trying to apologize to Sonz, who remained indignant. When Holt took the elder's arm trying to get his attention, Sonz turned and looked at him and simply stared, mouth agape.

Now what? Holt wondered. He looked at the giant Vid screens and he saw what must have caught the elder's attention. The dye put onto his grey streak two days before had been washed or wiped off. It was there in front. So what!?

Wrong. Because just then someone facing him stood up and pointed.

"Look! It's the White Flame of the Thanocracy!"

"He bears on his body the sign of the Capalzars!"

"He's no Intergalactic. He's a Capalzar subvert."

"The Evil Thanocracy is using him to regain the Empire!" another shouted.

They disagreed with each other and began tussling with each other and then others rose too and began taking sides.

Sonz had stood up, and moved away from Holt in horror. The guards there simply stared. But the Emcee turned around frantically. "This is not scripted! What'll I do? This was not part of the scenario given to me."

Soon enough dozens in the hall in front and around were trying to gain the stage, coming for Holt, while fighting among themselves. He didn't know what it meant. Not any of it, but as they gained the edge of the stage, he remembered the flare gun, pulled it out of his shoulder holster and aimed it straight up into the air of the dome, directly above and fired.

The noise and the flash it made stopped the wrestling, but only momentarily. They kept trying to get up on the stage and so he shot again, this time at a 45 degree angle over the crowd toward the loges and this time its flash was far larger, and smokier, and at least a half dozen hanging banners caught fire.

Holt shot twice more in two more directions and then in the all-enveloping bright orange, choking, smoke he felt his way around the stage and found the panel that opened the door downstairs and hit it. The panel opened and he dropped down into the arms of the guard. "Quickly! Upstairs!" he shouted into the guard's face. "A riot!" and as the guard reached the top, Holt hit the downstairs plate and the panel slammed shut. He grabbed at a chair nearby and wedged it in between the stairs and the top of the panel to stop anyone coming down. Then turned and ran.

He remembered the stairs down to the parking lot. He was alone down there, and remembered where the vehicle was parked. Yes, that sector there! He began running toward it, and saw a moving machine like the one earlier but it was so slow that he boarded it and with one foot off it, pedaled along the ground and the other up top like as though it was an air board back on Hesperia.

When he reached the vehicle they had arrived in, he let the carrier run off on its own into a baffle.

He pounded on the side, and the doors opened.

"Driver, get me out of here! Now! As fast as you can go! Take the least blocked ramp up and do not connect to a rail. Immediately. Do you understand?"

"Yes, Prince Holt. Immediately. No rails."

But even as the vehicle exited the garage from a different angle than before and onto a non-rail road, he could hear the screechings of alarms.

"There appears to be an emergency," the cybernetic driver said. "Should we return to help out?"

"No. Keep going as fast as this vehicle can move."

It sped up.

"Can you darken all of the exterior so no one can see in?" Holt asked.

Something noticeable occurred: he hoped it meant the windows went black.

"What is the direction we're going?" the driver asked.

"Where are we headed?" Holt asked.

"Back to Palace #27, via double bridge #213."

"Keep going in that direction."

Holt looked behind him. He could make out the Convocation Hall clearly. The orange smoke from his flare gun shots was rising from the top of the auditorium building. They must have opened the dome windows to let out the smoke and also that of the fires he'd started. He could just imagine the pandemonium with dozens of flaming banners falling into the audience.

He looked at the flare gun. Two shots left. On its side, some letters. He held it up to the small connecting screen. "Can you read it?" he asked the driver.

"Yes. It reads 'Not to be used indoors'."

"Now, you tell me."

"There is an official alert out for your presence, Prince Holt. Should I tell them that you are safe in this vehicle?"

"Not yet," Holt said.

"Is there a reason for the delay?"

"Yes."

The vehicle had crossed out of the center of the city and now hit the double bridge which was not meant for a speeding, rail-less vehicle, so there was some bouncing.

"On the other side is a rail line. Should I hitch to it?" the driver asked.

"Can you avoid it?"

"Not for very long."

The outside looked familiar. It was the industrial park!

"We have to attach to a rail now, Prince Holt! There are no rail-less roads within several miles of our location."

"Find a rail that has the fewest vehicles on it so we can go faster."

He felt the slight jolt and lift as the vehicle sidled onto the rail. But the speed was still good.

Now there were alarms from a wide swath of vehicles somewhere behind them and Holt knew that at any minute there would soon be air patrols like the one that shot his pod down.

The driver announced, "The authorities are requesting our location."

"Not yet!"

Silence then. "Are we avoiding the authorities, Prince Holt?"

He pondered, then took a chance: "Yes, Driver. Yes, we are."

"There is a small door behind the middle of the single panel between the seats," the Driver said. "If that is opened, to the right about half a meter, there is a small orange and black, drum-like shape. If it is removed, this driver will not be able to communicate its whereabouts to anyone else."

Holt tore the panel off, found the door, reached in, couldn't see very well, but with his fingers he fondled the cylinder-like drum, pulled at it. No go. So he used the butt of the flare gun to smash it out of place, and pulled it free.

He held it up to the separating screen

"Is this the part you mentioned, Driver?"

"Yes. Traffic is getting heavier. As though it was deliberate. Escape via this vehicle will not be possible very much longer."

"This area looks familiar on the right side, outside the vehicle."

"We were here yesterday," the Driver said.

"The same factory we stopped at yesterday?"

"Not far ahead."

"Can you find a driveway down and into that factory?"

"Yes, it is before we pass the factory."

"Detach from the rail, Driver, and go into that driveway."

It did and none too soon too. Just as they got inside, Holt could see two aircars headed their way swooping past. That was a close call.

The factory parking lot was dim and empty.

"Should this driver dim its lights and head toward the darkest part."

"Yes." Then, "No wait. Can you locate a lift or stairway going up?"

"Yes. One is marked "Lobby". Another is marked "Work Floor.""

"Driver, dim the lights and go toward the work floor lift."

The vehicle swerved to a stop and the doors lifted open. Holt got out and looked around. The vehicle's lights went on briefly straight ahead, illuminating the lift door. He looked at himself and this ridiculously bright outfit.

"Prince Holt is there another problem?"

"Driver, you've done an excellent job, but my clothing is too conspicuous."

"There is an extra rain cape in the left side pocket. Dark in color. Also, you are about to enter a manufactory that produces rather basic cloth."

Holt found the rain cape and replaced the bolero with it. He would discard the little jacket.

"Driver, you are to be commended."

"Did Prince Holt succeed in eluding the authorities?"

"So far, yes. Thanks to your good driving and advice."

"It was learned, Prince Holt."

"Who taught it to you?"

"Vids. Fiction vids with vehicle chases. While waiting in garages, this Driver watches them."

Holt laughed and slapped the glass over the vehicle's cybernetic driver and watched it turn around and slowly creep toward the exit. He found the lift door and tried it. Noisy. But the floor above would be even noisier.

The lift doors opened onto more noise. Holt held the door, then exited. The factory floor as he remembered it. Spanning in either direction hundreds of workers seated at long tables, with spinning spools and automatic punchers and automatic cutters. The machines were still responsible for the enormous mechanized noise. As before, the workers all wore identical drab clothing, including some type of scarf-like head covering. And again, not one looked up in curiosity as Holt walked by them. He gained the stairway to the bridge, and then ascended. He carefully opened the door to the owner's office. No one there. Not even the owner's sons. He started forward, but then the far office door opened and "Old Harwas" and someone who must be the owner, stepped in, so he backed out but kept the door ajar a few inches. They began speaking quickly, but of course he couldn't hear what they were saying. But the owner was protesting. Then there was a thudding against that other door, and he heard even that, and stayed with an inch of open door long enough to see a Patrol Force officer and two vehicle officers enter.

Holt dropped down again onto the factory floor. He thought to hide in what must be a worker's lounge and was headed there when he saw the office door above open. They were coming down. They'd look in the lounges first.

Holt spotted an empty spot in the middle of a table, and sat there. After a second or two, he felt something cover his head. One of the Euthna had given him a worker's scarf. He leaned over like the rest of them and began to make pretend motions similar to the other Euthna, when the machine came alive in front of him and suddenly heavy cloth was in front of him! He found the revolving arm of the sewing mechanism and took it in hand and began to run it along the moving cloth as the others did. He felt a slight push from one side correcting him, and yes, that was right, he had not been in the correct position, but now the clothing was going through steadily now, the stitches even and correct.

The officers were on the bridge and when he carefully glanced up out of the side of the scarf, he could see the owner remonstrating with them. Worse for them was the immeasurable sameness of what they saw below. Would they bother to come down and search line by line, worker by worker? At first it seemed they would and the owner threw up his hands in despair and left them.

The Patrol Force officer was far enough away, looking at each Euthna in a line. But the Euthna seemed to resent it, because they dropped their heads lower than needed, and covered as much of their faces as would allow only their eyes to be seen, further frustrating the search. But he looked up at the bridge to the office above and another officer was up there gesturing, so the officer looked at maybe two or three more Euthna before giving up and joining his fellow officers on the upper bridge and when another came with what seemed to be an urgent message pointing up and out of the building, the lead officer finally left the factory floor.

Holt continued to sew not knowing if or when they would return and giving himself some time to think. He was on the run. He guessed that last message was that they'd found the vehicle. But if they were down here, they already had found it and it was empty. So now what? He had to escape. He knew that. Felt it in his bones as sure as anything. They'd begun bidding for him. He would be sold. That's what that entire circus was about in the hall: He'd been assessed and found worthwhile and they'd begun bidding for him. They out and out lied about voting. He'd had no choice in the matter at all. Someone's bid would win and that's where he'd go. He wondered if he would have whatever the bidding price was as his dowry? If so, but that would be it; he'd be attached to whomever it was for as long as that person wanted. What had seemed inevitable and even a little bit romantic yesterday was in reality as bad as any ancient slave market, with himself as the goods for sale.

And speaking of feeling something, he was feeling his wrist connector and pushed off the wristband bracelet. Through the semi-transparent bandage over the scar he could see the tiny, brilliant cobalt-blue chip of Beryllium 18 lighting up. Who could possibly be trying to contact him?

He tried listening but couldn't hear anything even with the wrist up to his ear for all the mechanized din of the machines. He got up and now he did make for what looked like a lounge. Before he went in, he stopped and looked at all the workers. As loudly as he could, he shouted, "Thank you! Thank you!"

Inside the somewhat quieter lounge and then even quieter toilet, he spoke into his wrist. "Who is it?"

"Ser Holt. Finally."

"Who are you? How did you make this connection?"

"It's your Fast Ship!"

That was so unexpected that Holt felt a wave of complete dizziness and had to lean into the wall.

"Your own Fast Ship, Ser. I'm nearby hiding inside another vehicle. I have with me a female engineer who wishes to leave with us."

Holt had to keep from saying anything, he was afraid he'd burst into tears.

Finally, he said, "Where are you, Fast? I need help."

"I'll say," he heard the female's voice. "You are the most spectacular piece of interesting news to happen on Imperia in decades. By the way I'm Mozza. Mozza Safran."

"I'm underground, inside a factory."

"We know. Your Fast Ship's Mind has you pinpointed among maybe six hundred other people. But if we are to rescue you and we do want to rescue you, you have to get out of there and get very high up."

"How do I do that?'

"Somewhere on a south or north factory floor wall there must be a series of lightly pulsing pale green circles."

"Yes, I remember seeing those."

"Emergency exits. Every manufactory must have them. They lead up and out. But you must not leave the stairway until you have taken it to the most upper level. Once you are there, let us know."

"I'll be noticed. My clothing is conspicuous. It's bone white. Then I have a sort of rain cape. That's dark."

"If you can't cover the white up, take it off."

The communication was breaking up.

He was about to leave the lounge when two Euthna entered.

He began removing his clothing and offering it to them.

They signaled that they understood. He followed them into a wardrobe. This must be where the male managers kept their work clothing. Holt quickly doffed the white clothing and pulled on some darker trousers, held up by belts over the shoulder. No shirt but he found a sort of jacket. The Euthna gathered his white outfit and his emerald green shirt, holding them closely to their bodies. He gestured that they ought to put them in the trash. They signaled that they understood.

He was leaving the lounge with the two and thanking them over and over, touching their hands to let them know. Suddenly one held him back and said quite distinctly. "Prinz Holl Good!"

"*You* are good," he said, and as they left, he blew kisses to all of the workers, then rushed over to the door under the green lights. Who would have thought ...?

Mozza was right. The stairs up led to the roof. From there he heard her again directing him to cross the roof and rush up to an adjoining bridge to the next building, across the railed street far below, and then from that roof up other metal stairways, up and up, until the police force he could make out were five huge factory buildings distant.

"You are perfectly placed," Mozza said. "Go right to the edge there."

"Fine. I'm standing on the edge. Now what?"

"Your Fast Ship is directly behind the opposite tower."

Holt looked but could not make it out. "Can't see it."

"That's because we are hiding from three aircars circling."

Holt looked around and could make out two, then the third one – circling.

"This has to be precise. We'll meet between the two buildings," Mozza said.

"I'm two hundred meters above the ground and there's *nothing* between the two buildings."

"Your Fast Ship will be between them and open to admit you. Now, Prince Holt."

"'Now' what?"

"Now, jump as far as you can!"

Around them the air cars were coming closer with each circle and suddenly he saw people below on the building roof, pointing up at him.

"Now," she repeated. "Jump as far as you can!"

He backed up as far as he could go, to get a running start.

I'm following the orders of someone I've never met and if I do that I will surely end up squashed below on an apron of concrete. I must be out of my mind, Holt thought.

He ran and then he jumped.

Chapter Nine:

A PREMATURE MIGRATION

"Attention! You have reached The Glen Government Authority official perimeter. If you go beyond this you will be in uncharted territory."

The five of them flying cheered.

"Attention!" was repeated. "If you are a premature migration candidate, The Glen Government Authority recommends that you check into the Migration Center below for supplies, information, and useful tips on your upcoming migration."

"Do we have to stop?" Khana shouted.

"It's already beginning sunset," Vannada pointed out. "Look ahead. It's quite foggy where we would be going. I'd prefer going there when we can see where we're flying."

"Besides," Metts, Khana's older sister, added, "If we do everything by the book, we won't arouse any suspicion." That nugget must have come from someone else's experience, since Khana's sister certainly had more than a few of her own wilder days in Glen.

"They're right," K'or chimed in. Why don't you take this and K'asp and I will go down for a look-see? In case there is any trouble waiting."

K'asp and K'or had been carrying the lightweight hold-all containing the two off-worlders. Vannada and Metts now took it over.

Freed of their burden, the two male branches let loose whooping loudly and happily. They swirled down, diving in spirals around each other, until they came within full sight of the sprawling wood shake-roofed building in the very definitively shaped clearing of conifers. The station stood alone. They'd passed the closest other residences five minutes before.

Khana and the others saw a white-haired person come out to meet them and to point to a landing strip. K'or landed but K'asp circled low until his friend was satisfied with what he'd been told. K'or then waved the others that it was okay to come down.

K'asp circled back up and he became a third, holding the carrier.

The landing was easier on a strip. And, as Vannada had said, it was already darker than dusk on the ground.

K'or was waiting for them.

"She has supplies and information for us and she is looking forward to us visiting. She reminds me of my Fa's Granny. I think she would like a little company overnight. Our papers are all in order, so we could do worse that get fed and stay here to sleep."

Khana wasn't as happy about that, but she had to agree, she was fatigued and could use a rest.

Janesborot, the little Pamp, had even managed to nap in his carrier and he came out rubbing his face and eyes. Quite different than him was Eis, who had made certain he could see as much as possible of what was going on through the open weave side of the carrier as they'd soared. Both had been re-dressed in typical Glen-youngsters' clothing and after they landed, they kept close to the sides of the saplings, as if they were the females' smaller brothers.

Inside were two long corridors with many doors leading in almost opposite directions, the two wings off the center of the building that Khana had seen from above. Directly ahead was the double doored entry to a large room.

"Well, don't just linger there! Come in, I don't bite. Come on. Five of you and twigs too. That's a sensible sized travel party. Couldn't leave the little ones?" she asked Vannada who seemed to be surprised at the question.

"That's it. Leave your wings there in those alar-shoes. And come settle down. There's some protein rich grass and reed drinks for you, and I know you must be starving. Did you have a long trip getting here?"

"Not bad," K'or spoke up authoritatively if vaguely. "But you see the young ones, so we'll be very hungry."

"Of course, of course. Make yourself comfortable here and I'll go fix something for well, seven of you. The twigs eat well too, I'm guessing?"

They settled onto deep wooden slat chairs and couches with what looked like old fashioned reed and hay pillows wrapped in bamboo cloth.

The furnishings were old if in good condition and Khana had to wonder how many migrations they'd seen in their time. No one else seemed to remark on it, so she didn't either. She'd already concluded that she observed her surroundings much more closely than others.

Their hostess turned around before leaving, "By the way, I'm Arouette Blandy, but everyone calls me, Arouette or Ma' Blandy. Let me shut the front door tight."

She did that and locked it too.

"As soon as the sun sets out there, it chills up completely," she said. "Do you know why?" she asked Khana.

"No."

"It's because we're so close to the wildlands. Well, that's what the people who live hereabouts call it. It's actually just planetary matrix. But the winds sweep off it more strongly at night."

"The planetary matrix we'll be flying over to get to Meadowland, right?"

"That's right, dear. But I hope not 'till tomorrow. About one quarter into the new day is when the first updrafts arrive and if you wait till then you'll take a few steps and lift up just like little gliders."

"I read that there were stronger updrafts now," K'asp said. "At sunset."

"There are and if you were more experienced in traveling over the planetary matrix between here and Meadow, then this time of day would probably be the best time to travel. But I'm guessing from your ages that this is a first time."

"Yes, and from the air we saw fog banks out there," Vannada

added.

"Those are fairly recent," Ma' Blandy said. "In fact, we've had two male branches from The Glen Government Perimeter Authority here earlier in the week looking that over. They flew back in here and reported several new fissures in the landscape. They believe that those fissures are outgassing, and that's causing the fogs at night. They didn't see any other danger to it."

"Except obstructing our sight," Vannada said.

"Yes, true. But you'll be above most of it and believe me, there isn't that much to see down there. And anyway, once you go beyond this station you will be in mostly uncharted territory."

"Until we reach the perimeter of Meadow?" K'asp asked.

"That's right."

"But surely the Perimeter Authority people have been mapping it for years," Khana argued. "Our people have been here and migrating to there for many dozens of cycles already."

"Don't fret! I do have recommended flight path charts for you."

Who's fretting, you wrinkled old thing! Khana thought, but she didn't say it aloud. And the others didn't seem as annoyed with her.

"Now look at you twigs. So cute," Arouette all but pinched Janesborot's cheeks. "And you," touching Eis's shoulder, "Not even a nub there, yet. Don't worry, my twig. One morning you'll wake up and say, 'Oh, Ma'! How it smarts!' And that'll be the nubs thickening."

"Don't remind me," Khana said.

"Why don't I help you get food?" Vannada leapt up and took Ma' Blandy's arm. So did Metts. Good for them and clever. Keep her occupied and away from a too close inspection of these "twigs" who wouldn't ever grow wing nubs.

"There's no Vid-screen here?" K'asp noted.

"Better for us. What if we were seen by cameras while we performed out little rescue?" K'or asked.

"She might have a Vid-screen in her office and already seen us on it," Khana remarked. "Why don't I go look?" She got up. "If I'm caught, I'll say I'm looking for, you know, to freshen up."

No one stopped her so she nodded toward Eis and she suggested that they each try a different branching corridor to look for any office Vid-screen. With him right here and in juvenile clothing she had to admit he could be mistaken for a twig. She'd never read that he was anything but normal height for Hesperia, but she wasn't done growing yet and was already a bit taller. And although she knew he was older, he looked younger compared to K'or and K'asp.

Most of the rooms she looked into were storage rooms with travel packs and other kits, and more wings of different materials.

Eis found her in the fourth storage room. "It's the other way."

As they exited the storage room, she thought she heard some noise way down the end of the corridor. Voices? She stopped him and listened more closely. It didn't repeat, so she aimed them the other way.

"Maybe I'm being overly suspicious."

"So far you're being wonderful," Eis said.

She stopped and looked at him.

"Really. You saved my friend. I'm eternally grateful. You can be as suspicious as you wish, as far as I'm concerned."

They smiled. "No one called me wonderful before."

"You were heroic!"

Khana laughed. "No. Not that much!"

The office door was open and they peeked inside. No Vidscreen. There was a wall unit screen but it looked like a closed-circuit. Perhaps a Glen Government closed circuit.

"She could have already seen us. The rescue and all," Khana said.

Eis went up to the unit and placed his right wrist against it. Then against his own right ear. "No activity in the screen since long before noon."

She knew how he'd done it: his wrist connector. All City-Dwellers had the most sophisticated kind of interfaces.

"Can you do something so that we can hear any future activity on the closed circuit? Say, between now and when we leave tomorrow after breakfast?"

"Absolutely." He held the wrist to his face, and she saw his lips moving. He must be sub-vocalizing. Then he held his wrist it to the mechanism. "So. Now we'll know if she reports us," Eis said.

"She'll certainly report us. I expect she logs in and reports all travelers. But *how* she reports us is the question."

"Well, and now I'll be able to hear that. You are wise beyond your years, Sapling Khana."

Back in the main room, the male branches had found a board game and were teaching Janesborot how to play it, settled around the low, apparently ancient, table consisting of several weirdly twisted ash branches, covered with a blue glass top.

"I hope you haven't wagered anything," Eis said. "This one may look innocent enough but he's a killer when it comes to competitions."

"Now is that kind?" Janesborot asked.

"It's kind to us," K'or admitted. "He does learn fast."

"Beginner's luck," K'asp said wistfully, as the Pamp swept all of his pierces to one side.

"See what I mean," Eis had the last word.

K'asp got up. "The charts?"

"Arouette would know."

He went into the food preparation room and came back out and looked into some drawers beneath the built-in shelving and located a sheaf of charts.

He and Khana and Eis looked over the official charts which seemed to be a jumbled mass of different colored lines of differing thickness, with cryptic notations of no more than two letters each at certain point.

"Find the season first," Khana wisely directed.

"Got it. But look at this. Now we know as much as we did five minutes ago," K'asp said in obvious frustration.

"Let me look too," K'or said. To Eis, he said, "Your friend just beat me too, as you warned."

Eis shrugged. Then "Janesborot? Does this map look somewhat familiar?"

The Pamp looked and then he said, "It reminds me of the ocean current charts of the Great Salt Ocean of Usk, where I grew up."

"You'd be more familiar with that than I am. But I believe my mother has charts like this in his office on Hesperia."

"That's correct. For his Thwwing racing on Usk. Those too have different seasonal charts."

Khana handed them the right one. "This is the current time period. Let's try to find a directional point."

"This chart is for *above,* but not *on,* the planetary matrix," K'or argued.

"Exactly," Eis said. "But that was case on the Usk ocean too.

All travel there was over the surface. Sometimes on levitated skis or skates. Even the largest vessels traveled that way. So, the air current flows and obstructions were crucial."

"Here's where we are!" Khana had found the box representing the station they were in at this moment and pointed it out. "And our destination is the Meadow arrival station over there, right?"

"Or close to it," K'asp said. Explaining, "You know, we've got to be careful. Just in case... "

Khana said, "There's some kind of residence not far beyond it, over there!" Pointing, she asked, "Can you make it out, K'or?"

"It's in olden script. It reads 'Something-Something Inn.'"

"So that is where we'll aim for, not the migration receiving station," she declared and no one questioned her, so she added, "Just in case ..."

"These red lines appear to be the most recommended routes." Janesborot pointed them out to the others. "They do seem constricted in range."

"You're right. They're pretty much together. Let's find some good secondary ones," K'or suggested. "'Cause as Khana said before, 'just in case.'"

It took them a while to agree on those, but when they had done it, Khana said, "Our friend here can record that, can't you?" she asked Eis.

Eis held his wrist to his face and gave a subvocal command and then hovered his wrist over the chart.

"I've copied the entire chart in four or more ways," he said, saucily adding. "Just in case ..."

They all laughed, and the chart was returned to its drawer just as Vannada emerged wearing an old-fashioned dirndl-like apron. She modeled it for them, saying, "Zo? Vot you dink, huh? Very preddy, dis maid iz?! Ja?"

Her exaggerated Meadow-Maid accent led to more laughter, but she managed to herd them to a refectory table at the other end of the big room. Khana noticed that this too was old, if in very good condition. As were the surrounding breakfronts holding more plates and cups. She'd never heard of a special place for migration, and supposed that it would either be unused once the mass migration of people began or crowded with folk.

"I smell food," Khana said, and Metts said, "When don't you?"

which led to more laughter. The dinner was fun and delicious and just enough for the hungry travelers. Even Ma' Blandy had a good time.

"Now the lecture," she announced, after they had cleaned up their meal and were sipping hot herbal tisanes. She moved them back to the larger area where she reached up in one corner and pulled down an old-fashioned wall screen. Behind the biggest built-in sofa that held five was a wall unit she poked at until it started up and suddenly there was light and a title card on the opposite wall that read, "Migration Tips." Arouette said, "Let's wait a minute more for the others. They'll be here" she checked the wall mounted timepiece, "Just about now."

From the second corridor they heard voices and four tall and sturdy male branches emerged.

Eis turned to Khana and whispered, "You were right."

"Quickly now. Settle in!" Arouette commanded. "You can all get to know each other later. I'm hoping that all of you will migrate together, tomorrow."

She then began the lecture with various charts and photographs. For the first time, Khana realized that what they would be flying over for three and a half hours was rough territory, not only with unexpected out-gassings, but also with unpredictable spumes of hot, dark smoke, and sudden rumbles from below. All of it was unstable and thus uncertain ground. Even so there were a few spots that Migration Managers had set aside: small, semi-enclosed resting areas. Listening to it, Eis seemed as curious and excited as the others, but Khana couldn't make out the Pamp's face, as he was turned away from her. Yet she sensed from his posture that he was less than enthralled by the scenario Ma' Blandy was laying out.

The questions followed and naturally K'asp had to ask, "Well, what about the Hell Kites? What do we do if they attack?"

"The Hell Kites?" Ma' Blandy asked him, her face a mask of naivete. "Let me see. Will they be *with* or *separate from* the banished tree elves, the gnomes and the goblins?"

Everyone laughed at poor K'asp. But he said in a low voice that Khana, sitting next to him, heard, "That was nicely avoided."

She patted his arm. "She's probably done it often enough." That gained her a big smile.

It went on until all of them were yawning, and Arouette gave out sleeping accommodations. "We have two dormitories, a big one for you six males and a smaller one for five females. But there's also a bedroom with a double and a single."

"We'll take that," Khana spoke up. "Me and the twigs."

No one protested that plan and soon they were cleaning up before sleeping.

She took the single and Eis and Janesborot the double bed, with Eis closer to her bed. He did wake her about two hours after they'd fallen asleep. "She's reporting in now. Do you want to hear?"

She was very sleepy. "No. You listen." She was *sooo* sleepy.

"She's just reported total number of her premature migration guests, and our gender and approximate age." *Khana could only mumble in reply.* "Now she's saying that she hopes that both of the way stations are open, since there are young twigs too." *Mmmmm.* "Now she's asking since when were twigs allowed on premature migration? And she's sort of berating the male she's speaking with, who is trying to hang up the line." *Mmmmmm. Mmmmm.* "And now she's complaining that someone was supposed to come fix her Vid Screen and who never came. And now she's asking if anything interesting happened in the newsfeed today." *Mmmmm. What?" Khana woke up.* "But he told her no, nothing happened and now he's hanging up on her."

"Let's be grateful they consider her an old pest." Eis concluded, and Khanna fell asleep still mumbling something or other incomprehensible.

The excitement began to pall after a few hours of flying. And that was exactly when Vannada flew closer and said, "Let's go down! I see the way station ahead." That was fine with Khana. She told Metts and K'asp, and Vannada got closer to the other males and they all seemed to agree it was time for a break.

As Arouette had said, they were traveling high above the landscape which was not visible for the most part due to the constant outgassing. But as they began angling down into what looked like a tiny white building surrounded by minuscule walls, Khana could now make out the ground below very clearly and it wasn't at all attractive nor in any way comforting. Ma' Blandy had called the planetary surface a matrix, but a better description might be enormous flat chunks of raw rock surrounded by seething black tarlike stuff, and even worse, burning blue material that might be mineral lava or magma, she wasn't sure.

The entire surface of Hercular had looked like that only a few million years before. Maybe half of the planet had looked like that when the 2nd Matriarchy Colonization vehicles has arrived here less than five thousand years before, carrying the seeds of the folk they had now become. Khana's geo-history classes had taught her early on that effort and time was spent by those vehicles adapting segments of surface they landed on into specific landscapes based on what the terraforming Cybers that first emerged found below. Where there had been nascent elevated areas, those were emphasized and re-formed to become the altitudinous continents of Aerie –rugged and snow covered half of the year – and a bit lower and somewhat less icy, craggy, and uneven but for upthrusts, the continent of Plateau. Less high and less regular, the next landmass bore the tall, narrow, tree-topped ridges, foothills, and resulting dells that delineated the arboreal-loving climate of Glen – Khana's home all of her conscious life. The continent of Meadow they were headed toward, had come into being because its substrate was regularly rolling enough to become hills and extensive flatlands perfect for agriculture. Lower yet were the continents of Strand and of Fen. The first was initially surrounded by various natural bodies of liquids, that were then all consolidated to form an encircling sea, which on another, smaller, planet would be called an ocean. Strand's very existence and its size also impacted its nearest neighbor, the lowest in elevation, now named Fen, which absorbed the considerable spillover waters from bad weather on the ocean, at the same time that it absorbed overflow from those rivulets plunging down off Aerie, its nearest, steep, neighbor on the other side. Fen's own climate and humidity produced the most extraordinary of enormous, continental wetlands. Whatever native animal life that previously existed and might still exist on Hercular, did so probably on Fen.

Even as the eleven travelers alit into the layover station, the four males first, then the others, it was obvious how small and how fragile it was: potentially buffered as it might be by various surrounding walls from the totally "natural" excesses of the surrounding wild landscape.

Drinks and snacks were broken out as they rested on what looked like benches and shelves. Their trip so far had been without incident and so the four other males began talking up Vannada and Metts, ignoring Khana either because she was too young or more likely because they thought of her as being "with the little ones." Usually on Hercular, there were five or six women to each man, so this ratio of six males to two females was strange and fun for them all.

At breakfast, Khana had gotten a better look at these newcomers who had first joined them for the lecture the previous night. She had to admit that she and Eis looked like skinny near-children next to them. All four were taller than K'or and K'asp and sturdier looking too. They revealed that they all had known each other since they were small twigs and that they all came from the Blue Pines Hills more than halfway across the continent of Glen, an area whose people had somehow acquired or achieved a reputation for being kind of backwards compared to the sophisticates who lived on the south east and central west coastal areas. The four were named Steff, Tanner, Rowan and Brigg. They had schooled together and then worked together at several lumber camps – that labor somewhat explaining their musculature which Metts and Vannada couldn't help but remark on.

For folk like Khana and her group who lived *in* and in a way *because of* trees, the idea of camps full of males actually cutting down the most beautiful and majestic creatures on the planet and then selling the results was somewhat repulsive. And she'd not been able to hide her disgust when she heard it.

Two of them noticed that and Steff, who seemed the easiest going of them tried to explain. "The blue pines in those hills grow quickly because of the nutrients in the soil and the climate. They shoot up to twenty meters or so in a year. Then, at the end of that year, their needles begin to turn from green to deep blue. It may look pretty in pictures" – indeed they'd all seen those pictures – "but it means the tree is about to die. Once that happens, the trees are no good except for kindling wild-fires. In fact, half of our timbering is fire-clearing because any lightning charges that high up will set to flame a dry forest before you can snap your fingers."

The others became interested at that and the other females were thrilled by the heroics they imagined and asked appropriate questions. But when Khana had K'or alone, and asked what he thought of the Blue Pines Hills males, he said good-naturedly, "It's true that they're rough and tumble guys. But I'd be glad that they're on my side in a fix. I like them."

After that, Khana heard Metts and Tanner talking and he told her that they would be soon headed into "three different areas of Meadow over the next few annum where stands of forests needed to be trimmed back" before more settlers could arrive at Meadow. He'd added that for their hard work and trouble the four would be given places to live, free. Then he asked if he could see her after the migration.

The mid-matrix station enclosure included a closed building with "facilities," and also a stairway up to the roof. That held a rampway for take-offs. Khana waited until K'or and K'asp had joined the others up there, then asked Eis, "What were you and Ma' Blandy talking about just after breakfast?"

"Not that you're in any way nosey," Janesborot said.

She colored at that, but Eis wasn't offended. "I asked her what happened to twigs who never grew nubs for wings or grew them wrong."

"You want to fly too." she said.

"Yes. I do. I know you hate that, Janesborot," Eis added.

"If it can kill him, he wants to do it," the Pamp outlined his theory.

"What did she say?"

"She said that of course it happens that people are born who never develop ... and that on Meadow there is someone who makes full sets of artificial wings. Also, because I'm small and relatively lightweight, she thought he might possibly make me some artificial wings if mine never formed. As a rule, he only needed to make one wing or one artificial nub. But he's had success with full sets too. Of course, they would all be connected and guided from here," he pointed to the top of his sternum and chest and his deltoid muscles. "I would have to learn to steer without the second lower pair."

"I still don't use my lower pair much yet," Khana admitted.

"The wing-maker's name is Cypriel and he has a workshop in an area there named Six Willows," Eis added. "It's not far from that inn. Sounds easy enough to locate."

"But won't you'll call your ship once we're there and leave us?

Why have the wings made?"

"Maybe I won't leave right away. And anyway, despite its great size, this planet has a low density. Perhaps the ratio of that density to its size is what tipped the Cyber-Founders to decide to ensure that you all could utilize wings? But as a result, the gravity quotient here is about .75 of what we're used to. Most off-worlders constantly feel like they're about to lift off the ground with every step we take. It's frustrating."

He smiled and she did too. Why shouldn't he fly?

"Will you help me find Cypriel? I could only ask a friend to do that."

"Of course," she said. They tapped each other's shoulders, the Glen custom for sealing the promise, she had shown hm.

Not long after they were all on the stairs up to the ramp, the males first, then the females with the hold-all and last of all Khana and K'asp.

After they'd flown some distance alongside each other, he asked, "Do I smell a romance with you and our off-worlder?"

"Be serious, K'asp. He's Universe-famous."

After a while, he asked, "Is it true that he and his folks are you know, same-sexers?"

Ah, and now *that* was his real question. The fourth personal question K'asp had asked about Eis so far, right?

"More or less, yes ..." Then she tried something different, "Isn't he the most beautiful male you've ever laid eyes on?" she asked.

K'asp didn't answer, but scooted away to join the others.

Which proved nothing.

"Attention! You have reached the outskirts of the Meadow Government Authority official perimeter. If you go beyond this point you must have Premature Migration papers in order since you may be required to show them to officials."

They'd been expecting that and it was most cheering news to the flyers who had once again been in the air longer than expected. A cross-wind had developed unexpectedly, which might have been the cause of that. What made it more cheering than not that they land soon was two very odd, minor, yet at the same time disturbing, incidents happening close to each other. They'd pretty much continued their order pattern from the morning. The four Blue Pines Hills male friends in front, and the others taking turns with the lightweight carrier containing the off-worlders, although Khana noticed that Vannada and Metts both flew with the males as much as possible, and that K'or often joined them, whether to ensure the Vannada didn't get too friendly with any one of them or too far away from him she couldn't tell. But they were in two definite groups, the seven distinctly ahead and often barely visible, and then K'asp and Khana with the carrier holding Eis and the Pamp. Suddenly the four males suddenly shouted so loudly they heard it clearly even from far away. Then two of the males half turned to make sure the second group was aware of something. And then, even more suddenly, three of them veered off to the left and began spiraling downward.

"What's going on?" Khana called out and since the others in the advanced front line had decided to slow down almost to a hover, she and K'asp soon caught up with them and she could ask again.

"Steff and Tanner both saw what they thought was a Hell Kite keeping at some distance to us but pretty consistently along the far end of our wing formation. They took Brigg and went for a look."

That was Metts' description. K'asp said, "It's someone else's turn with this carrier." But neither K'or nor the female branches were eager to take it: Khana was sure they wanted to be ready to sail down after the male branches and chase a Hell Kite, if indeed that's what it was and not some play of light and reflections, which was what Vannada loudly believed it was.

"Reflection, how?" Khana asked.

"I'm not sure. But we've had almost constant white fog beneath us since we left the mid-matrix station. Maybe we're seeing the shadow of the sun, or our own shadows distorted, or something?"

"There they are!" Metts announced, and the males who'd flown down were ramping up with some effort in the cross-wind to meet up with them again. But not a moment before they all connected up again, something large, flying maybe a hundred kilometers above them passed by noisily. The ground fog fairly well hid the individual flyers from the vehicle unless someone in the machine was peering down carefully looking for them.

Metts asked, "Could that be what we were seeing?"

Tanner said, "Definitely not! What we went after, was small, and it was definitely faster than us."

"It didn't look like another flyer, onworlder or offworlder," Steff added.

After the four moved ahead again, K'or and Vannada both said in lower voices, "That was not a Glen Government vehicle," and K'asp looked at Khana and said, "They're right. It looked to me like the vehicle belonging to the hostage takers."

They signaled to K'or and Metts and passed on the unwelcome news.

"If that's so, then they'll most likely be at the Migration station on Meadow when we land," Metts agreed.

"Then *we* can't land at the Meadow Government Station!" Khana decreed.

"But they've been alerted to us coming," Mettis argued.

"We don't know how many Arouette told them," Khana argued.

They discussed what their options were while the four males from the front group had gotten wind of the talk and slowed up to chatter excitedly amongst themselves.

Khana and her friends agreed that if that was the off-worlder Cybermen's vehicle, and they'd been alerted by Arouette, then – at the least – they would be expecting a mixed gender group.

Khana made a decision. "I say me and K'asp break away soon with the carrier and head away from this air path. Eis, you did aerial mapping before. Do we have an alternate path for us?"

They'd seen his face at the open front of the wide woven carrier and knew he'd heard all or most of the conversation. He put up his wrist and Khana could see that he was projecting a map or chart on the inside of the carrier.

"We could head toward that guest house directly. That would mean a divergence soon of ..." And Eis provided a series of degrees and minutes of the necessary angle, that K'asp pondered. K'or figured it out too and said, "If you're going to do it, you have to diverge very soon, and head that way."

Always thinking, Vannada said, "If they ask, we'll say we saw some other Premature Migrators at the matrix mid-way station and they might still be there. At the very least, that will divert them away from you."

Khana, K'asp and Eis thought that was wise.

"Can't we go with them?" Metts asked and Khana knew she was honestly big-sister concerned. But she was voted down: they needed a mixed group arriving.

Too quickly the moment came for them to part, and the four Blue Pines Hills male branches were way ahead and completely distracted telling the females of their Hell Kite chase and really too far ahead to even notice the parting of ways.

"I hope we're doing the right thing!" K'asp seemed nervous.

"We're on direct course for the guest house." That was Eis speaking.

They received their second alert, that they were now at the perimeter of Continent Meadow, and while Khana couldn't see the others, Eis with his augmented vision could and was reporting that the other seven of their group were beginning to do all kinds of aerial hijinks and athletics in their spiral descents down to the Meadow Migration Station.

"Can you see if the off-worlder's flyby is there on the ground?" she asked K'asp who was closest.

Eis spoke up. "I can. The semi-cybers have landed and are there. So is a flyer probably belonging to your world's Glen Government. Our seven flying friends are doing all kinds of aerial gymnastics to distract attention to themselves and divert it away from anyone noticing us." There was a pause then. "That's so generous of them."

"They're just showing off," K'asp said. Khana laughed in relief.

Soon enough even Eis' augmented vision could no longer see what was happening at the Pre-Migration Station, as they'd diverged too far, and suddenly the white fogs that had accompanied them for hours seemed to begin to thin or to shred. Instead of the mixed grays shot with hot blues and occasional blacks of the matrix, it was green below them. Green everywhere they could see. Astoundingly, amazingly, *phenomenally,* green!

"We're right in line for the inn," Eis announced. "It should be coming visible past your right wing, Khana."

There it was far below. On a sort of extra-green rise of what seemed to be endless rolling green meadow and pastureland below them. It seemed to be a brick structure, with slate tile roof, and it was surrounded by four or five trees of a kind she'd never seen before, in breathtaking golden flower against deep green leaves, and there! Look! There was the sprawling two story high welcome ramp for landing.

It must be exhaustion from the previous day because Khana slept late; something she almost never did. They'd settled into the "family suite" of two bedrooms and a common area inside the inn, which seemed to only have a few other guests. Two younger women – mustn't call them twigs or branches now! Khana reminded herself – who looked like siblings, checked them in, showed them the suite, and after they'd cleaned up, they'd brought them a substantial meal to eat in privacy at the table and chairs in their suite. One of the sisters said, "There's food for breakfast in the cabinet. But the little ones aren't welcome with the bigger folks in our dining room. You understand, yes?"

"I should be offended, but isn't that exactly what we wanted?" Janesborot said after she'd left, making the others laugh. As they sat and ate and tried out the somewhat strange food – "It's called cold cereal," Eis explained, amused for once to know something Khana didn't.

"It looks like wood chips. And that looks like sawdust," K'asp added.

"I do recognize that these are nuts," Khana gingerly bit one, "Oh! It tastes so different from our acorns and white chestnuts."

"Not nuts! Seeds!" Janesborot said. "Nuts grow up into trees, seeds grow up into plants. Grasses and such. All that stuff out there," pointing out the window next to where they sat watching a misty pink sunset above fields of grass. Like the Migration Station in Glen, here too, the fogs off the matrix came in at night.

"You add liquid to the cereal," Eis illustrated with a bean-derived milk provided, "And then add in some of these berries" – little blood red ones – "It's delicious!" He tasted a spoonful and it *was* delicious.

"You add hot liquid and some of these seeds and berries to your sawdust," Janesborot demonstrated, pouring from the pitcher of warm nut milk, "And you have a lovely, creamy, warm cereal." They also had roasted vegetables they didn't recognize, Leading K'asp to remark, "I never thought I would have to learn to eat all over again." Dessert was in a covered dish and was another kind of cereal, white and pillowy and a little gooey, cooked with nut milk, honey, seeds, and small fruit. They finished that completely.

Those who had flown were bone-tired and so they slept immediately after eating. K'asp and Eis shared a room with two beds, as did Khana and the Pamp. This first morning in Meadow, all of the others were awake. Janesborot and K'asp were once more eating.

Eis came into the suite and said in an amused tone of voice, "Well, I have good news and less good news."

They waited.

"Look outside! Do you see that blue and tan object?"

They looked. Khana saw a long low piece of plastic or some other man-made material, with an open top, hovering a foot or so above the ground.

"It's a skimmer, so what?" the pamp asked.

"I know how to drive a skimmer. That's what!" Eis replied. "Folk use them here in Meadow even more often than flying everywhere because landmarks are more difficult to spot from above the ground – since it is all so similar. Fields. Rolling hills. More fields. So, we'll be like them and take the skimmer to Six Willows this morning. It's free to use for inn guests and seats two. Me and Khana will go."

That sounded like very good news to Khana. They wouldn't draw attention to themselves that way.

"And the less good news?" K'asp asked.

"I contacted my ship. It was waiting for me to contact it. As soon as I did contact it, it Fast jumped into the highest possible orbit.

"What? Why?"

"How will you get onto it?" Khana asked.

"I couldn't get onto it while it is in high orbit, if I tried. It was ringed with the Cybermen's own little explosive mines. Just about now we should be seeing … ah! There they are!" he pointed out the window and up. They saw many puffs of black smoke. "There was a time delay of a few minutes." Eis said. Then, a minute or two later they felt a thudding of sound waves. "As it Fast-jumped, it set off the devices. I asked it to send explosions back to the source of those mines too."

"When will our ship come back?" Janesborot asked, dolefully.

"When it's safe for us to get back to it," Eis said, nonchalantly. "It's headed for the nearest interstellar travel station to report."

Outside, there was a hubbub of voices and they could see people gathering and pointing up. So, they did too.

"You don't seem very concerned about this problem," K'asp said.

"*I'm* concerned," the pamp said.

It will give us time to look around a bit," Eis concluded.

One of the young women from the previous night arrived to clear the dishes.

Khana said they'd change the linens. "I saw some in the cabinets."

She was pleased to hear that as it meant less for her to do.

Khana asked, "What was that smoke and noise everyone was looking at?"

"Nobody knows. It was in the sky. Very high up," her light eyes were filled with wonder. "But then this a time of strange goings on."

"Oh? What other goings on?"

"You haven't been on the Vid yet," pointing to the screen. "Or you would have known about the dust-up yesterday evening at the Migration Station."

"The *Meadow* Migration Station?"

"It must have happened after you left," she said, innocently.

She set down her tray, sat, and in a low voice said, "Those Offworlders who caused so much trouble in Glen?" Khana sat down too and encouraged her. "Well, they were at the station looking for someone or other, when these Blue Pine Hills Boys arrived." Khana was holding her breath. "And they must have said something to offend the lads because there was some kind of mutual assault. Glen and Meadow officials had to break them up and establish a truce."

"I hope no one was hurt?"

"Not the Blue Pines Boys or their women. I guess they're pretty tough! But once they were in the office signing arrival papers, the Offworlders took off and shortly after, one flyer crashed somewhere in the mid-continent matrix. Of course, the Glen boys said they weren't mechanics and wouldn't know a cog from a lever. All they knew was cutting lumber and drinking and were highly insulted that they were not instantly considered innocent. For whatever reason they were asked to stay overnight there. We're expecting them in an hour. So, everything is all right."

"I know one of the boys traveling at the same time," Khana said.

"We were told there was an entire little crowd of folks arriving," she confirmed then took off with her tray of ceramic ware, explaining why Vannada and K'or weren't at the inn yet. "I'd better get their rooms ready."

Eis had overheard and popped back in after she'd gone. "Well? Then who *did* sabotage the flyer?"

"It must have been my sister, Metts, the mathematician!" Khana said proudly. "She was always fixing machines. She has a degree in engineering."

"I hacked the Glen government radio. No one was hurt in the crashed flyer."

Shortly after, they were seated in the skimmer with borrowed goggles and caps on, skimming only a few feet over the grass fields. It was just as Eis had described it before, green fields and then rolling hills covered with different colored grasses, and then more, even more intensely greener fields, and then more grasses. But at last there to the left was a mound in the middle of golden grass that shaded lower down to purple, and on the rise were the six good-sized willow trees, so graceful to see. In the middle of the trees was an oddly mixed structure, part brick and part wooden, with one slate roof and one of a grass-like thatch.

Eis set down the skimmer. "Stay here while I see if he's at home."

As soon as he disappeared around the only actual right-angled corner Khana could make out, she heard from behind, "he's *always* at home."

"Cypriel?"

"Who's asking?" the tall, but also wizened man who appeared at the side of the still gravitating skimmer wanted to know.

"My friend. He went looking for you."

"Be he friend or foe?"

"What? He's a customer. Well, a potential customer."

Cypriel seemed to have an inordinate amount of gray-brown hair, on his head hanging around his face and half down his back in rough pigtails, and in his beard which was almost as long as his hair, and all over his wiry arms, exposed by the sleeveless tunic of some shiny material unknown to Khana, perhaps plastic, perhaps armor of some sort. It was matched by a pointed visor of the same material across his forehead. All she really could make out was his nose, bony and prominent. His eyes were covered by flat facial goggles.

But as he came closer, she could make out the distinctive missing upper nub for a wing on his left side. He'd probably made the wings for himself first!

Just then Eis came into view. "Oh! Greetings, Ser! Could we discuss building me a pair of wings? As you can see" – pointing to both sides – "I don't have any natural holds for them."

"'Nnn't that a shame!" To Khana, "C'mon, young Miss, step out with us."

Suddenly from around the house a loudly barking mammal came running.

"Wolf!" She shouted and hid behind the man.

"Vani-low stop! Sit," Cypriel commanded and the animal did as bid, his mouth full of big teeth there for all to see, and his tail wagging. He was mostly grey but with a black face and long pink nose. "That's better. No wolf, Miss. Well, maybe a wolf at one time, long time ago, but he's my pet. He won't hurt you."

She'd grown up with stories of famished wolves breaking into Tree-homes and snatching infants from their cradles, never to be seen again.

Eis began petting him, "A canine, right?" he asked.

"That's right. Let me take a look at you more closely. Lift your tunic."

"Ma' Blandy said you were the very soul of discretion."

"Did she? She must be getting feeble minded."

Eis laughed and turned around and lifted his tunic off, for Cypriel to look.

"A complete deformity, huh? Been a while since I saw one like you."

"Are most who come to you half deformed?"

"Souls of discretion do not reveal, Mr. Potential Customer." Still kneading Eis' muscles. "Not bad supports here. In a sense better than nubs." He reached around in front, "Going to hurt like your worst tanning when you first use the wings that I make for you to fly."

"Even with the harness?"

"Even then, yes. Come inside. All of you. You too, Vani-low."

There were two buildings attached at one end, with the half courtyard in between littered with odd machinery or sculpture, Khana couldn't decide which. The brick house had ordinary doors and glass-paned windows. The wooden structure was taller by half and had ground to thatched roof sheets of translucent plastic or some older glass, with a few clear panes here and there. Both buildings were latched with thick chains and round locks requiring keys.

"Have to keep them locked. Otherwise the scavengers," Cypriel said. "would eat me out of house and home."

"You have scavengers here on Meadow?" Now that Khana thought about it, the windows at the inn had all been locked shut.

"Don't know if they are *from* Meadow."

They went into the wooden edifice which seemed to be a high ceilinged work-studio with a few smaller doors leading off.

This was even more remarkably littered – on the floor, walls, and hanging from the ceiling on cords – with similar machinery and sculpture-like things. She did recognize a work bench and shelving filled with cannisters of who knew what.

"You may look," Cypriel announced. "But don't touch a thing."

Khana did look, there were so many curious things to be seen. She seen scientists' and chemists' laboratories in fic-vid stories, of course, and this looked like all of them together wrapped up in the messiest package.

Meanwhile Cypriel was taking measurements of Eis' upper body and speaking the results into a little box he wore on his upper arm. He then tried out some loose pieces of material like those that constituted his vest, pulling them across Eis' chest and making Eis pull on them too. These results were also spoken into the little recorder.

Khana couldn't help but ask. "How is it that you have two so very different kinds of buildings?"

Eis answered for him, "That's because they were built at different times."

When Cypriel didn't contradict him, Eis added. "This wooden one first, with materials brought over from Glen. The brick one later. I'd guess that the wooden one was from your first migration into Meadow?"

Cypriel corrected. "I was born here. I first migrated to Strand at the age of five."

"And you never left?" Khana asked.

"The first time I left Meadow I took an entire Turn of Migrations, but when I returned to Meadow I decided to stay and build the wooden house. There are other little rooms, in case you ever need a place to stay."

"When did you build the second, brick house?"

"Later on. Unlike Glen or Aerie, the weather in Meadow can be sudden and treacherous. Perhaps because of its flatness. We get destructive storm spouts."

"How old are you?" Khana blurted out, then covered her mouth.

"Older than I look. Older than you think." To Eis, "You can put your shirt back on. Now I need to see you in motion."

He lifted connected several wooden sticks off the floor. When they reached hip height, they clattered and drew up into a frame. Cypriel beckoned Eis to lay prone on it. Then he hit a second button and it rose almost to chest height.

He tied little cloth straps at Eis' hands and feet and arms and legs and Eis protested, "Hey! Wait a moment"

"This machine will pull you to certain specified tensions so I can tell how strong to make the harness. You have to be tied in."

As he made the needed adjustments, Cypriel commented "You're a kind of throwback, aren't you?"

"What do you mean, 'throwback.'?"

"You know, an early version of a current Hercularan? What are you? Two meters and a few inches?" He measured. "That's the size of the Firsts. Most Seconds and Laters are taller."

Meanwhile, Khana had continued looking at but carefully not touching anything and trying to calculate how old Cypriel might be. He said he was five when they migrated to Strand. A complete Migration Turn would land him back here at 65. That's was when he stayed and built the wooden house. While everyone else migrated, another what? Twenty years? Enough time to understand the need for a more solid residence at what age? 85 or so? And that house wasn't new either. Could he have surpassed a century? She knew that Offworlders did that regularly but Hercularans too? Otherwise it made no sense.

"All done!" Cypriel declared and unstrapped Eis and then collapsed the frame down to the floor. Eis got off quickly, chafing his wrists.

Cypriel was clear. "Give me two days. No, no payment now. Let's see if the wings work, first."

Of course, Eis would be good at flying. Even as a novice. Even with a complete set of artificial wings. He took to it like, well, like a Hercularan. Like Khana had. Eager like her. Able like her. Excited by it like her. So four days later they were in the air again, the two of them, and together they were finding out different ways of sliding in and out of updrafts and, especially, of downdrafts, which because of the flat, unbroken surface below seemed especially tricky, especially for novices like them, and thrillingly fast once they'd mastered them.

K'asp had joined them the first day and then K'or and Vannada, before they left altogether. Somehow, without making a fuss about it, those two decided to live together here in Meadow, somewhere in the middle of the continent from what Khana could figure out, where Vannada's family had "large holdings" from previous emigrations that, according to her, "should keep us busy for a few years."

"I have no expectations that this will last even as long as our full Migration time here on Meadow," she explained to Metts and Khana, the night before they left. "K'or is so attractive and he's sure to find others. But meeting the Blue Pines Hills Boys," she added, "I now know there are other types of males I might want to try out also." Adding, "like you did, Metts."

Khana had told them how old she'd calculated Cypriel was, to which Metts said, "Ma' Blandy too!"

"No?!"

"Yes, I think so. We were talking while preparing supper and breakfast and far too much has happened to her for one lifetime."

"Connecting up into the Ib'r Republic would allow all of us to have extended existences," Khana said. "Among other advantages."

"Isn't that something that can only happen from birth? Or conception?"

Mettis didn't think so. Only the longest life spans were fixed at conception.

"Then we'll be the first generation of Hercularans to have multiple marriages and families?" Vannada said. "Good! I want at least three!"

The Blue Pines Hills Four left the following day, and Metts and Tanner agreed to remain in touch. She already had a university research position, but she would immediately seek transfer to one closer to where he would be lumbering.

So, she took off with two others she'd met at the Meadow Migration Station. Leaving K'asp, Khana and the off-worlders.

"I thought you also had family holdings here," Khana asked K'asp.

"Yes. But there's no hurry. I can stay longer."

"You're not staying for my sake, I hope."

"No. I've come to like these two. I'd like to see them return home safely."

He had been spending as much time with the pamp as she had with Eis. And the past two days when she and Eis were off flying, K'asp had been with Janesborot most of the time.

"What do they do all day?" she asked.

"Knowing my pamp friend, he's concocting some plan for K'asp. I can all but see the little wheels turning in his mind." And when she asked what kind of plan, Eis said, "Given his Ib'r good looks, his size, strength and daring, maybe as a PVN stunt man. Even an PVN Actor. Janesborot *is* a talent manager, you know."

"So, you'd take him to Hesperia when you return?" she asked. Eis shrugged.

There they were getting in another morning of updrafts and downdrafts when Eis suddenly darted in toward her. "Can you hear it?" he asked.

She couldn't. Then she could. Cybermen flyers. "Get beneath me." She knew he kept his wrist connector off. How had they found him?

Two of the dark vehicles flew over Khana and then ominously circled and then came back and then headed away in another direction.

The two headed back to the Inn, but even from a distance Eis could see two more of the dark flyers parked at the Inn, and directed her to land on a rise from which his augmented vision could see better. "They're there all right and with them Glen Government flyers." He scanned the area. "Wait! I'm also seeing a skimmer moving at a distance from the Inn, almost headed this way. I wonder if … Yes! It's Janesborot and K'asp. They're headed for Cypriel's house!"

The skimmer and its driver and passenger had already arrived when Eis and Khana carefully flew around once and then landed there too.

The old man had been awakened or disturbed but he was already fascinated by the sight of the Pamp. K'asp was unloading the little luggage the four had acquired. K'asp said: "I checked us out and paid the bill. You can pay me back later. We heard from the staff that those … had returned to Meadow and so we took off before they arrived. They passed over the skimmer twice but all they saw was me and my little brother." K'asp smiled, having outwitted them. "I'm sure they'll come sniffing around here too."

Cypriel let Khana brew a big pot of tea and reminded her that he had spare rooms for them. He didn't ask why they were avoiding authorities. She guessed he and his friends had done so often enough in the past. "There's a route," he said.

"We have folks already in place in three or four locations," Eis said.

Cypriel pulled out a large cloth representation of Meadow, and they plotted where Metts, Vannada & K'or, and the Blue Pine Hills Boys had gone to. "These first two legs of your trip are achievable in a long day of flying and driving," he assured them. "But this last leg will take too long. It's via a Continental ridge – the only one on Meadow – but at this season it's snow-packed and impassable."

"What if," K'asp had an idea, "we head south from Vannada's farm to where the Hills Boys are lumbering and go *around* that ridge?" He pointed it out. "We'd do a half day down to the edge of Meadow and another half day of travel, back up again?"

More detailed maps were needed for that, and Cypriel revealed he had a vid-screen with basic information on it. "If it's very windy and snowy on the ridge; you'd have to go into the mid-continental Matrix for an hour or more. There's a tunnel for the car to cross but that too might be difficult."

That became their tentative plan.

Ever hungry, K'asp revealed the food he'd taken from within their suite at the Inn, and they had a pleasant meal he and Khana put together, while Cypriel got his scientist's worth out of looking over Janesborot, who was half flattered.

"I knew you were the off-worlders being sought as soon as I measured you," Cypriel said to Eis. "Here is a quality of inner construction ... So, why not give us a song!"

Cypriel had a stringed instrument to provide one kind of bass and K'asp used some old cannisters as drum basses and Eis sang for them, until he begged off, saying he was too exhausted to continue.

Khana was exhausted too and slept in her own private chamber that night, secretly thrilled that the adventure wasn't over yet.

"Plan A won't work," K'asp said what all four of them were thinking.

They were perched upon the roof of a long abandoned and not yet re-inhabited Community Hall, at the southernmost tip of Meadow. To their left, as far as they could see, north and south, was the snow and ice-clad continental ridge of mountains rising up to six thousand meters high, and as they'd been told, impassable without an enclosed, airtight, flying vehicle. They could see ice and snow-spouts lifting off various peaks and rising hundreds of meters in a constant updraft. The previous evening, they'd been at the entrance to the only tunnel and that was both officially closed and, after they'd gone in anyway and walked in a short distance, it was visibly ice-bound, blocked by stalagmites.

"Then it's time for Plan B," Eis said. They'd slept in the vacant building overnight, undisturbed. They'd not seen any people at all during the second half of this past day's flight. It was an odd sensation, being the only ones in such a gigantic area of land. A day ago, The Blue Pines Hills Boys had been their last stop, at their lumber camp and that too looked to be in the middle of nowhere. Steff and Brigg confirmed that when they put them up and told them from what they heard from the other workers that they would probably be the first folk in six decades to fly this deep south and west into the continent. This very morning, the four travelers had awakened, refreshed, and eaten large breakfasts. Only snacks were left over, and each flyer would carry those in tightly bound leg pouches. K'asp began strapping on the carrier to hold Janesborot that Cypriel had devised: a chest-slung variation of the wing-harness Eis used. The old man's map showed the continent's edge to be close to a hundred meters tall here, with strong, contradictory winds not worth attempting. Instead, they would fly directly into the matrix until they could safely turn back to Meadow without too much effort. If need be, they'd land and rest there.

The past several days had bound the four more closely together than ever as companions, but also as a group with a purpose. Khana couldn't help but observe how each visit to and stay with folk they'd flown with only days before exposed how unsettled they were by comparison. Not one of those generous friends questioned their aim and all supported them, but it was clear they were relieved to be exempted from the rest of the trek.

"You don't have to come, Khana," K'asp said. "This will be the most dangerous part and I'll be somewhat hindered." He shook the chest harness.

"You mean hindered from saving me if I get into trouble?" she shot back. "What a laugh. Just try and stop me," she added. "Everyone ready? Let's go!" she shouted and took off. She wasn't about to let anyone else be leader.

Eis was soon caught up to her and he looked at her and smiled. He approved. Not that she needed anyone's approval. Still … she smiled back.

Even though they'd been as close as Meadow's civilized area came to the southern tip, it was a few hours before they finally could spot the sudden cessation of the enormously high ridge to their left. They'd seen no one and nothing else in the air for days but that meant nothing, even in a cloudless sky. There was an inviting sudden plateau in the foothills ahead, and she gestured them to alight there. What had been inviting from the air was bleak and windswept once they alit. But it gave Eis and K'asp a chance to tighten their harnesses and all of them to catch their breath. Straight ahead the land dropped off as suddenly as if it were a cut piece of cake. Beyond were the vague fogs of the planetary matrix.

They had caught their breath and they took off one after the other. As soon as they left the continent's edge several things became clear. First, how high from the surface of the matrix they still were. Cypriel's maps hadn't shown that. Second, how strong the cross winds were here, buffeting all of them so constantly from several angles at once that, glad as she was that she'd fitted in her lower wings for stabilization, they didn't seem to help much. She watched Eis also fighting to keep steady for maybe an hour and then, ahead, she made out through the ground fog what looked like a flat area in the matrix and shouted. Eis pointed – he'd seen it. She turned to do the same to K'asp who saw it and agreed.

They'd begun their descent when she heard K'asp shout out "Hey!" Turning She saw two dark figures one at each of his legs. What were they ...? "Hell Kite attack!" he shouted and she swung around to go help him. As she did, she saw two more dark figures go after Eis and again they grabbed at his legs. He began spinning out of control. That was too dangerous! She rushed for him instead, and got there just as they left, and managed to keep him from wildly rotating. "They grabbed the food." He shouted and turned to look at K'asp. Together they turned toward him. He was still fighting with two of them, grabbing at his legs, and he managed to give one a solid blow to the head. The dark figure hung in the air for a second then simply dropped. The other Hell Kites left off K'asp and went after their falling companion. As she passed them, Khana distinctly saw hoods closed over human faces. Eis had reached K'asp first and as she approached. she could see the pamp reaching out, but Eis going directly to K'asp's face and head. The way they were together in only those few seconds let her suddenly know that they were lovers. The week or so sharing rooms, being together, they'd become lovers. No wonder K'asp was going to Hesperia.

She made sure that the three of them were okay, and pointed down to the spot they'd chosen. They agreed. Then she said, "Those are people! The Hell Kites! I saw their faces. They must be the scavengers too. One of them was hurt badly. I'm going after it. Eis, you can help too."

It took him a moment of close contact and several "I'll be careful's" before K'asp would let go of him. But then they headed towards where Khana had seen the so called Hell Kites fly down, grab their fallen friend before he hit the surface, and fly him off, low to the ground. From the air it didn't look like there was any place for them to vanish into, but as she dropped and hovered (thanks, lower wings!) Khana saw one last dark figure vanish behind a little upstanding cliff.

She and Eis landed a few feet away.

"They're people?" Eis asked in a low voice. She shrugged, as though it should be obvious, and led him inside.

Of course, his wrist connector emitted enough light for them to find their way in the smoking, dark, canyon. Even she could make out a worn pathway. It took them another few minutes before they could hear and even smell the yeasty sign of humans. Ahead, the cave opened up and down and to one side she could see figures low to the ground, as though kneeling or sitting on their haunches, poorly lighted. She untwisted the packets of snacks on her legs, and gave one to Eis. "We have to go inside giving!" He nodded in agreement.

Of course, their arrival caused consternation but they held out the snack packages and figures darted forward to take them, then darted away again into shadows. Khana thought she saw one figure flat on the ground with two others near it, and she gestured for Eis to follow. She pulled back her own hood to shake out her hair and patted her own front and said to them simply, "We're here to help!"

All but two scattered away but the two stayed with the fallen one.

"I'll help." Pointing to Eis. "He'll help." She wasn't certain they understood her. She'd assumed they spoke Inter-Gal Lex, but what if they didn't? Or couldn't?

Eis dropped to his knees and figures gathered around him curiously, touching his wings and harness. Khana stood guard.

"He's coming to. Let me get a reading on him." Eis waved his wrist.

Khana reached at her side and grabbed her thermos. She mimed drinking.

Eis was done. "Just a bad bruise to the forehead, but he did lose consciousness. I'll help him to drink this." He gently lifted the little face, and opened the lips and dropped water into the mouth, little by little. She watched him secretly add a tablet from his pocket. The figure stirred and drank more and the eyes opened. "We'll help," Eis repeated. After a while the figure was somewhat awake and more alert. Khana went into her med-kit and pulled out a heal-band and gave it to Eis to place on the bruised forehead. That elicited a groan and then a sigh of relief. It felt better.

There was a stir among the others in the cave and suddenly they gave away for a figure. Elderly, very thin, but perhaps strong too. Face almost completely covered from below by cloth pulled up. Eyes very alert and alive. Her voice was hoarse as she said "What is?" Then coming up to Eis who was standing now, "How is this?" touching the wings and harness and then looking eye to eye with Eis, she asked "How is so small?"

The crowd murmured and possibly said things, but she knew how to speak, and looked down at the boy on the ground. "Who fix Roll?"

So, language but not very complex.

Khana pushed forward. "We fixed Roll. We hurt Roll. We fixed Roll. We gave our food! Willingly."

The crowd seemed to mutter agreement.

But in a few minutes more there was a new sensation for the crowd. K'asp had appeared. And out of his harness, Janesborot came forward to even more surprised murmuring and hugged Eis and hugged Khana. "We couldn't *not* come."

The older woman and the others were astounded by him. He gave her his snack packages too. She took them and said. "So small. And looking at K'asp too, "So … different … all you. Big! Small!"

"Look, K'asp!" Khana said. "Look at your so called Hell Kites."

"I see. They're … I don't know. Kind of pathetic," he said. "But what are they doing here? How did they come to be here?"

"The old one knows!" the woman said and took the pamp by the hand to lead them somewhere else.

They followed her into another cavern and another. Very few of the hooded figures sat in these caves. In the deepest one yet, there were pads strewn around that resembled old exercise mats Khana and K'asp had used in school. Scavenged, she assumed, form an inadequately locked school gymnasium. This was obviously the dormitory. The old woman pushed aside a rough curtain and there was a Vid.

"How could this work so far from any sender?" K'asp asked.

It turned out the only way it worked was by playing old recordings and as the old woman turned it on, they made out the figure of an even older man in this very cavern. Around him were many figures, and closest to him was a young woman – "This!" the old woman said, pointing to herself, and then her younger self on the recording. "Him! Our Mother! Gone now!" Khana assumed she meant that he was the founder or leader of the group and was now deceased.

"You who are watching this!" the old man said directly at the camera, Take heed and listen. Like you I grew up in what I always thought was a perfect society. We were taught that because the all-knowing Matriarchy set us up, and cybers of great intelligence built our world, that we were blessed. We were taught by our elders and teachers and leaders and we believed what they told us that we were living in a paradise. Our planet gave us so very much, because we never took too much at a given time but moved on to another land, Glen to Meadow to Strand, to Fen and so forth. We were taught how to value our new homes and adapt to the next new home. Look around yourself, Hercularans. What do you see? Perfect people living in a perfect Paradise ... Right? ... Wrong? No one is perfect. No creatures are perfect. No living things are 100 percent perfect 100 percent of the time. Some are *conceived* with something not quite right. Others, through even our easy process of labor and birth *are born* with something not quite right. And some in early years *develop* into something not right. That's who all of these children are, and yes," he was vehement now, "they are children. They should have been your children to help, to repair, to make right, to accept, to care for. Instead, you hid them away from birth, and when they were old enough to be on their own, you sent them not into your world but back into the last continent you had lived in to the fullest, as far away from you as possible on this planet You ensured that no one would ever see or know of them. Because they were not perfect. Look at this lovely young woman –" it was their old woman who reached up and touched herself on screen. "Look at her skin!" She hid her own under long sleeves. "The pigmentation is wrong. There's nothing else wrong with her either. Did anyone try to find a way to make it normally pigmented? Did anyone, say "That's fine. It looks interesting? No! They threw her away! Look at this lad." He reached for him. "Born with a double ear." He displayed them on each side. "Did anyone say, let's fix it? Just a little surgery? Did anyone help him? No. They threw him away. Look at this lad, he's ..." but the recording sputtered and then died.

Khana looked around for the boy with doubled ears who must be an old man now. She saw none and gestured to the old woman. "Gone now!" she replied.

Gone now. Dead of malnutrition, of disease. From a flying accident fall. Everyone around them but the old woman were young. Recently thrown away.

Tears had sprung into Khana's eyes, along with an emotion deep in her breast she'd never felt before. She turned to Eis who was trying to get the Vid to keep playing, touched his shoulder. He turned to her face, and seeing her upset, he clasped her close, murmuring, "Yes. Yes. I know." Before she realized she was a leader and she mustn't do this. Then the vid started up again.

"... and so many others, I might show you. Who did nothing but be born in some way not right. I found them by accident flying over this area. They are spread over the entire planet hidden away in its matrix but I can't say how many there are and all of them ..." it sputtered dead. Eis' wrist connector got it going again, "the shame of every Hercularan alive! The shame!"

Now all of them looked at each other, and those who lived here saw the faces of the visitors, and they drew back and left them alone, even the old woman.

After what seemed the longest time, Khana said, "We have to help them, Eis! We have to!"

"We will," he said. "You will. I will."

Back out where the cavern was larger, they found the old woman and Khana said to her "Khana, this." pointing to herself, and repeated it.

After a few moments, the old woman said "Aylee, this".

"Aylee, Khana will come back!" tapping the walls. "Khana will bring food!" She mimed. Eating, and sharing out food. Then she smiled. It was the first real promise she'd ever made in her life. She took the old woman's hand, lifted it, seeing the speckled pigmentation and to seal her promise, she kissed it.

Outside the cave again in the smoke and stench of the matrix surface, she said, "I will come back and help them," then, "Was that shame I felt back there? The shame the old man told us to feel?"

"Maybe. Or maybe it was great compassion," Eis thought to say.

"I will come back and help them," she repeated.

"And I will help you help them," Eis replied. "They need a champion. It's a good thing for you to be now, Khana. You're young, with a strong mind, a strong will, and endless energy. Meanwhile, I have money. We can buy them a land of their own to live in, on a good continent here on Hercular. We can feed them and house them and hire medics of all kinds and take care of them, and we'll hire tutors and craftspeople to help them as much as they allow us to do."

"And then we'll publicize their existence!" Khana said. "To all of Hercular!"

"Perhaps a moving PVN of their origins and existence can be devised," Janesborot said. "It would be a galaxy wide sensation! "The Forgotten People of a Seeded World.""

"Always the business person," Eis laughed. "First we have to get to safety." He looked more closely at his wrist. "Something is ... calling me." He put his wrist up to his ear. "Let me go where it's quiet." He dipped back into the cave.

"It will be your PVN debut," the Pamp was saying to K'asp. "After all, how many actors in the Ib'r Republic know how to fly? It will be sensational!"

Eis stepped out of the cavern again with a puzzled look on his face.

"What's on the other side of this Matrix?"

"What continent?" K'asp asked. "That's Strand. Why?'

"I just received a location announcement, that about twelve kilometers from here, a T-Pod is waiting. My Fast Ship set it down before it left."

"Saved!" Janesborot cried.

"Not quite yet," Eis said. He asked his wrist connector to project the location on an inner wall with a visual. They saw the nearly opaque bubble of a T-Pod sitting high on the dunes of what looked like an endless oceanic shoreline.

"That's Strand!" Khana and K'asp said together recognizing it from school.

"What else does it say? Is the ship returned. Is it safe to be there?" the Pamp asked. Excited now by all of his plans coming together.

"Only one way to find out," Khana said, adding, "I think we'll be safe flying in the matrix if we are careful and stay low flying. No one will expect us to be there."

"And so to Plan C," Eis said, using his wrist connector to mark it. "Let's ensure we find this spot again." Then he announced,

"The adventure continues!"

"The adventure continues!" they all agreed. Aylee arrived and brought them to a place that seemed to be a natural ramp for taking flight. Khana hugged her and they were off.

It was most of the day later when they arrived at the continent of Strand. Eis, with his augmented hearing, was certain several times that he heard vehicles flying above them as they kept to the lower story of the mid-continental matrix, so that made them extra-cautious: they were so close to salvation. Several times Khana thought she saw at the far end of K'asp's wings, the slender dark figures of "Hell Kites." Or was she seeing things, because she wanted to believe they would follow and or even protect these Hercularans they'd only just met?

The first surprise when they finally began their ascent from the smoke and mess below to the edge of the continent above was that they were suddenly flying over water. It was unclear how it suddenly began just there, but it was so blue and wet and inviting after hours in heat and fog and soot they all cheered. But the oceanic air currents were a challenge after no currents at all. And they determined to keep closer to the surface. Eis and the pamp said they were good swimmers, and Eis in high spirits added, "Or we'll just flip K'asp on his back, get him floating, and sit on him."

A minute later, he reported "We're close! The T-pod's call is much louder."

And there was the shoreline! Just like in the wrist connector visual projection Eis had shown them. But the shoreline was immense and from not that high in the air, it had its own new air drafts and currents buffeting them. They had to go higher to get away from that, and the shore line went on forever in both directions. Straight ahead looked like sand dunes speckled with hummocks of close growing grass, in green to lavender shades, sparsely dotted with low growing bushes of a deeper purple color. As they continued inland, the only change was the size of the dunes which were now at times high enough to enclose entire compounds of buildings. Suddenly, they were coming upon the shoreline again, and ocean again, but it looked different, a different color, and as they flew over that just barely visible beyond the horizon's edge was another shoreline.

Eis shouted. "It's there!" He was pointing to the third shore-line.

So they continued flying, with this second stretch of ocean – it must be a bay or inlet – showing calmer waters, paler blue with speckling of blue greens – and with fewer air currents and so somewhat easier flying. Still, Khana thought, they were horribly exposed.

Good thing then, when Eis shouted and pointed ahead to the left, and began descending. They followed him, Khana glad for a rest, but not seeing the T-Pod, amid this even rougher landscape of many higher dunes, some a hundred meters high, covered with stocks of grasses like wild hair, blades of grass taller than K'asp, dunes ending in sheer cliffs. Tucked between the deep canyons, she made out streams and once arable land, laid out in rows, but empty of people, or agricultural machines or anything growing green. Khana found herself wondering what the only continent she really knew, Glen, would look like after there were four or five migrations distant? Would it look this wild and unfit for habitation.

They landed finally. Once on the ground, K'asp and Janesborot unhitched the frame holding them together and the pamp leapt free and K'asp tossed the frame down and both vigorously shook their arms and legs. It had been more difficult than any of the others realized.

"Where?" Khana asked, shaking her own arms and legs, stiff from flying.

"Right here," and Eis walked up to nothing and touched it and as if out of nowhere, there was the rounded, but still barely opaque edge of it under his hand. The Pamp rushed up to it, and touched it and a slice opened sideways. "See!"

Inside it, they could make out two large contoured seats, and not much else. But Janesborot reached behind the seats and withdrew a little packet that he opened and it unfolded, and unfolded again. It ballooned to four times its size, and he slid open an edge. "Food and drinks!" he announced, and took some and began handing it out to them. Khana watched as the tiny bottle, once it was in her hand, expanded four times larger, and from being empty was suddenly filled with a sloshing liquid. She watched the pamp's hand motion as though unscrewing the cap, and copied it and was amazed to be drinking an oddly flavored liquid: minty and musky too.

Eis had meanwhile done something or other with flat packages which also expanded and opened to produce flaky snacks he began sharing out and eating.

After they'd eaten and drunk their full and rested, she asked, "Can we move this over to the space between those two high dunes with bushes?" Khana asked. "To get it and us out of the open?"

Eis went over to the T-Pod and said "Hover." She could barely make out its ghostly outline as it lifted off the ground silently. "Follow me!" he said, and it did, over to the cleft in the dunes where he set it down again. "It's not fully on, because my Fast Yacht has not returned yet."

"It's not big enough for all of us, anyway," K'asp pointed out the obvious. "It only seats two. I could hold one my lap, but there isn't room in back. Unless it expands."

They remained resting, eating and drinking, and then Eis said, "No one's been here in Strand in what, seventy of your years? There must be abandoned buildings around? No?"

They thought so. He subvocalized into his wrist and then reported. "I'm seeing a small village seaport not too far away in this, no *this*, direction."

After a while they were rested, and it looked like sunset was beginning. Eis and Khana got into the T-Pod, with Janesborot sharing her seat. It lifted and moved to his command. K'asp flew up and shouted "I can't see any of you!" Until Eis put a hand onto the inside wall and then K'asp said, "Now I see you!" For the next twenty minutes or so he flew just over the T-pod or by its side, and from anywhere it would look like he was just a solitary flyer.

The third inlet of ocean and then the fourth shoreline, this one so dune filled, and the dunes so crested with wildly overgrown purple berry bushes that one could barely see ground below. It seemed to open to a much larger bay, with again closely vegetated shoreline growth and a more irregular coastline. On this bayside those purple berried bushes proliferated, but there was also a smattering of larger trees Khana had never seen before: mottled-white-barked conifers with their upper branches holding thick quivers of long blue needles distorted into strange, almost living, shapes, by onshore winds. Below them now was a clear scallop of harbor with concentric circles of water deepening the inlet the further in that it extended, this bay going on as far as they could make out, and its color changing from pale blue to a dusty cobalt, hue after hue. They spotted several wooden buildings below hugging the harbor and what even looked like a few derelict fishing boats drawn high up on the sand. Another, larger boat was adjacent to a sand-swept wooden piling pier. It all looked long abandoned. K'asp pointed, then flew down. They followed.

As they landed on the wooden pier, it was already darkening.

"Ah!" Eis said. "Finally! The ocean. I think all oceans smell the same." He inhaled deeply and so did Khana and she was rewarded with a new fragrance so strong and redolent of new kinds of life that she now understood what he meant.

K'asp was at the end of the pier and drew Eis to his side. The sky was the most amazing shades of blue she'd ever seen. Janesborot came to her. "You will be another character in the PVN, you know. The beautiful, soulful, heroine."

"But I'm not beautiful and I'm still a twig."

"Oh, no, Khana! You're wrong. Come see!" he took her by the hand to one side of the now once more transparent T-Pod and slid a hand over it until it reflected them back. "Look how beautiful you are! A true heroine!"

The face staring back at Khana was different. Her face and neck and arms sun and wind-burnt. Strands of sun-lightened hair escaped from her carefully wound back bun and the edges of her hood. Her eyebrows were almost white-blond. Her eyes serious and a lighter, more golden brown than ever before. "It's some trick of the light or of your T-Pod's surface distorting to do that."

"Not trick. No distortion. That's you, Khana!"

"That's really me?" she had to ask. Would her Ma' even recognize her?

"You're a long, long way out of the woods, little Khana," K'asp said. "We both are. And I believe we're the better for it."

She looked at her friend then, and for the first time she didn't see the cute and funny male she'd barely known but had always teased and flirted with, but instead a beautiful, grown male, strengthened and enriched in manliness by his travel, and she had to suppose, also by his new love.

"We'd better get inside."

She was awakened by voices speaking just above a whisper and at first thought that they were Eis and K'asp. But they were lying next to her, asleep on the heap of mattresses they'd dusted off and collapsed upon a few hours before.

Khana leapt up into the glow of a mechanical torch, behind it two dark, shadowy figures, moving about. They'd not seen her. She gave K'asp a shove with her foot and he came awake and so did Eis, held in his arms. A finger to her lips, as they scrambled awake and up to their feet.

"Who? Who's there. Are you the Flyer we viewed coming in?"

The torch shook over all of them now and the two figures drew back.

"Don't be alarmed," Eis said in his calmest voice. "We were resting here. We didn't know anyone lived here. We'll pay for the lodging."

The torchlight played over them,

"How are there so many of you? All we viewed was one tall one flying."

Janesborot was fiddling with the lantern they'd shut off to sleep, and he got it on fully. The two shabby figures were clearly male, maybe brothers, maybe father and son. Both with smaller torches, useless now.

"We're just visiting for the night," Khana now said, stepping in front of the others. "We needed a place to sleep. We meant no harm."

"We'll go right now," Eis said.

But the men were still confused. "Four with that child there," meaning the Pamp. "That is a child, right. Though it don't really look like ..."

"Look," Khana said, "We're packed up and leaving right now."

"Wait! No." The men barred their way with what looked like fishing spears.

Suddenly Eis said, "I hear them. They're here. We have to go *now*."

But the men were not about to let them go until they found out how it was that there were four of them and they only saw one flying. They threatened K'asp and Eis back. It could have become messy – when another figure appeared, a young female.

She cried out "Da' they're back. The black men in their machines!"

The Cybermen.

"We've got to escape!" Khana begged the men. "They're after us."

The men were uncertain then and the girl looked beyond Khana at Eis. She recognized him. That was either good or bad, Khana didn't know which.

"Let us go!" Khana begged again, and pushed through them.

Outside it was not yet dawn, black turning to deep blue, the sky's scant speckling of stars, only a faint crosswise band, as they headed to the T-Pod.

"I should stay with these three," K'asp was saying to Eis who was inside the T-Pod. "The Cybermen don't know who I am. You three can get away."

Eis was tormented by the idea.

Then it was settled for them. The Cybermen's flyers lighted up the entire harbor area. They heard one of the other men shout, "Girl! Get inside!" But she came running to where they were at the T-Pod.

"I know who you are," she happily chirped at Eis.

"If you tell them, I'm a dead man," he said to her, and she stumbled back.

The machines were flying in a circular pattern and lowering by degree to find landing on the limited ground space.

Now they were trapped.

But as two machines hovered directly above the four, Khana saw them freeze in mid-air.

The controls of the T-Pod came alive with color and sound.

"The Fast Yacht is here!" Janesborot said. "We can escape!"

"You two go," Eis said. "I'm staying with K'asp." And he got out.

"Is that your Fast Yacht?" K'asp asked pointing up above, beyond the Cybermens' flyers. But even Khana could see there were more than one underlying tell-tale blue landing lights of a Fast Yacht. The lights were doubled, no tripled.

One of the Fasts landed at the edge of the pier and Eis turned to them happily and said, "I recognize it. It's my mother! Come."

The side of the Fast slid open and several males came out. One looked up in the air where the Cybermen's machines hovered. Two other larger Fasts came down on either side of the pier, slid open and more males exited.

Eis was running along the pier, urging K'asp along, and not having to urge Janesborot who rushed into the ship and vanished into safety. Khana was in time to see Eis greet a somewhat taller male, who, even in this uncertain and wavering artificial light, she could see resembled Eis, except this one's hair was blonde and he was dressed head to toe in what she knew was City-Jet, the very black official wear of Hesperia.

Great hugs were exchanged by the two as the other males from the Fasts quickly fanned out around the little harbor. But K'asp was right there behind Eis, and she heard Eis say, "And this is my love." The tall, light-haired godling from the City on a Star, a person Khana never dreamed to encounter, hugged K'asp too. "And this beauty," Eis said, pulling her forward, "is Khana. She's a humanitarian. Or will soon be," Eis added in his excitement, and she too was clasped.

The dawn light was rising more rapidly now, but even so, they could see the lights from the Cybermen's machines were gone. Even in the excitement of such a grand meeting, Khana looked around and saw their dark vehicles had landed just beyond the building. The Cybermen were stepping out of their vehicles, their wrists somehow bound and their bodily attitudes signaling that they were dogged but also quite confused that their prey had escaped and that *they* had become captives.

"Shall we go inside," Eis' mother asked and led them in. The three locals had put away their fishing spears and only the girl was speaking, saying "They'll tell you. We didn't harm anyone." Seeing Eis and his mother, she added, "Oh! I've seen you too. You're Ay'r Eise'nstein Kell, aren't you?" she said, "The great Thwwing Racer, Ay'r Eise'nstein Kell."

Ay'r laughed. "That's right. Who are you?"

"They seem to be squatters." One of Ay'r's men reported

"Wait a minute!" The elder of the locals, Da', said. "We may be squatting right here tonight. But we're owners too. We've got a piece of property over there," he pointed vaguely. "Tell'em, girl! Had it for five great turnings."

"It's just that we don't migrate with the others," the younger male said. "We remain all the time here on Strand."

"That's fine. You can stay or go," Ay'r said, kindly, "It's all one to us. We won't be here long to bother you. We won't detain you if you want to leave."

Father and son moved away but the girl was determined to stay and said to her relatives, "You go. I'll catch up to you ... Go! I do know where it is."

The interior was already being transformed by the new arrivals. Sof-chairs and tables, glasses, and containers of liquids appeared and were served to them. The girl all but squirmed with excitement. Khana knew exactly what magazines she must have obtained somehow and read to know and appreciate these Hesperian City-zen visitors: her old friend Wellweg used to show them to Khana ... That all seemed so long ago.

"You wonderful folk are going to have to wait until a bit before we can get to know each other," Ay'r addressed them. "I must apologize, but we've got to deal with this problem of my son's kidnappers, first."

"Two of the Cybermen were brought in and Ay'r stood up.

The two identified themselves by names and serial numbers. One said, "I've been assigned to speak for us all. We merely wished to get your attention."

"Well, you succeeded," Ay'r said. "My husband is the Premier of the Hesperian Quinx Council and the Head of the Council of Five. Here I am."

"We didn't mean to harm anyone," the Cyberman added.

"But you did harm!" K'asp said, boldly, "Your sound-bomb at the stadium injured many Hercularans."

"It was a miscalculation. We'd never used it before. We have apologized for that and offered compensation to the injured via the Glen Government ... We would never harm the singer."

Eis remained silent. K'asp was clearly furious.

Ay'r simply asked "Since we're here now, why not tell us why you are. What exactly is the problem that led you to this extraordinary decision?"

As the cyberman began outlining it, another personage stood forward and came closer to hear what was being said. Clearly, Eis recognized him and nodded. There was something strange and indefinable about him, Khana felt.

Ay'r finally noticed the newcomer too, and gestured him forward.

"Sire!" the Cyberman spokesperson cried. Both loudly fell to their knees.

"None of that. Get up," the newcomer said, and then went to them and somehow removed their invisible bonds as he lifted them so their hands were free.

"Do you not see," the second cyberman said to the others, "This is P'al Syzygy, founder and friend to all cybers."

"I may be a friend," P'al said. "And you both seem sincere enough. He pressed a finger to each of their wrists. "Your signals are strong and uncorrupted."

"They came they said because they wish to Avenge K'tina Kell," Ay'r said, and turned to the Cybermen, "But you must understand, that myself and my son are kinfolk to K'tina. Her death by suicide was a *family* tragedy. Her fathers, her uncle who was then Premier, in fact all of us, watched in horror. The full human male that she loved and was loved by was another of our kinsman, the close-son of our Republic's beloved Founder. He dared severe radiation illness every time they met. Her death was enough to send him over the edge. He vanished decades ago and only now do we have an inkling of where he has gone to. If anyone has a right to avenge K'tina Kell it is us. Not you."

"K'tina Kell became one of us," the Cyberman asserted.

"True. After her accident she had no choice. But K'tina Kell is not your real issue," P'al said confidently. "Her fate was merely a banner for you to be able to wave. The real problem is your incredibly dangerous work and the refusal of your mine operators to make the work safer and your lives better."

The two Cybermen looked at each other and one said, "That is true."

Ay'r spoke up now. "We discussed that on the way here to Hercular. Those conditions are not something anyone should have to put up with. I don't care what percentage of person or cyber they are. P'al, have you given thought to how can this be rectified?"

"I have, Ser Kell. Fortunately, quite simply. Two of your own families own shares in the planet's corporation., And you are still affianced to another major shareholder. If you join forces, you will control 52% of the entire planet's shares and can demand complete and corrective control over those mines' operations."

"You don't mean, Vero'chka Palaka?" Ay'r asked, remembering her secret name was Lissa. Lissa of the Golden Eyes.

"Yes. Lady Palaka of the Demeter Worlds. She now rules the

system. I've taken the liberty of contacting her in your name," P'al said.

"You mean we're still affianced? She never married? ... Well, Gratitude P'al. It will be fun speaking to her after so many years. But then what?"

P'al gestured another Hesperian male forward and spoke to the Cybermen. "This is Angelo Laks, a full cyber, a leader of our Hesperian Cyber Union."

There was a second or two when something crossed between Laks and the two Cybermen, who were surprised by his appearance as he looked like any other Hesperian there.

"Will your group accept Angelo Laks as your mine manager?" P'al asked.

They did and those four went into another chamber to discuss details.

Ay'r sat down. To Eis, he said, "Now, I'm doubly relieved I came. And your father will be glad. He doesn't know I came."

Eis laughed. "I'm sure he knows you came. But you know what, Mother, I'm glad to see you."

"And you regret ...?"

"Not a minute of it," Eis said. "I wouldn't have exchanged this experience on Hercular for anything. Not only because of K'asp, but because of Khana and all the other wonderful, brave and clever Hercularans I've met and learned with and flew with. The Hercularans are a fine people, Mother. The Great Father will be eager to hear my Species Ethologist report on the planet, amateur though I may be. But fine as that report will be, my findings will be that Hercular isn't yet ready for inclusion in the Third Ib'r Republic."

"Why not?" K'asp asked, offended or feigning offense.

"You saw as well as I did out there in the mid-continental matrix, K'asp. Those poor creatures, abandoned, starving, dying!"

"But Khana will take care of them!" K'asp said.

Ay'r spoke for his son now. "Yes. But K'asp, intolerance of others who are different is not accepted in our Galactic Republic. Your people have to learn that." After a few minutes more, Ay'r stood up and said, "Why don't we all just go into my Fast Yacht and catch up while we travel to the City?

"I'll have to tell my father," the squatter girl rushed out.

"I won't come," Khana said. "As Eis said, my work, my career,

I guess you'd say, is right here on Hercular."

Eis came over to Khana and said, "That's true. But you're going to need training to do what you plan. You'll get that in the City. And we'll have to be there together anyway so this foundation can be set up legally and financially."

"There! It's settled," Ay'r said. They saw P'al, the Cybermen and Angelo Laks getting into another Fast Yacht. "That looks good. Shall we go too?"

"So, Khana you're coming," K'asp said. "And don't forget the other important reason you have to come: You agreed to be our native planet witness, and maid of honor at our wedding!"

"When did I agree to that?"

"Didn't she, Eis? You heard her!"

"I never agreed!" Khana insisted. "I would have. But you never asked."

"Of course, we asked. Didn't we, Eis? Eis! Back me up here."

Epilogue

Holt backed up as far as he could go, to get a running start.

I'm following the orders of someone I've never met and if I do that I will surely end up squashed below on an apron of concrete. I must be out of my mind, Holt thought. On the other hand, I can't stay here especially with all of these forces coming closer.

He shrugged, then he ran and then he jumped.

And landed on top of a large flying vehicle he'd never before seen in his life.

A hatch opened and he heard, "Drop right in."

Holt rushed to the open space and he slid down into it. It shut tightly above him.

"Hold on!" he heard and Holt fell into a wall and held on tightly.

Good thing too, because it accelerated amazingly fast, pushing him down to a sitting position on the floor. But from even that spot, he could feel the ship maneuvering rather oddly in short jerks and starts as though in evasive flight, and then it settled in somehow and he knew he could stand up.

He edged his way toward what looked like it might be a control room.

Amidst the blinking lights and monitors of the otherwise dim room, he made out his Fast Ship, still a large familiar, vertical coffin-like structure, which was evidently operating the larger ship. Half recumbent in a control seat was … a surprise.

"You're the Transfer!" Holt said. "I thought you were shot down?"

She turned, and laughed. "Welcome Ser Holt. No, I'm not a Transfer. In fact, I'm the original … Mozza Safran, Engineer Grade Six, #31640-78."

"The original? I don't understand!"

"That's a remarkable outfit you are sporting, Lord Holt," the Fast said.

He looked at himself. Began taking off the outerwear the Euthna had found for him, and helped him put on. "I borrowed this in my escape."

He removed it. Beneath was white tights, polished bronze footwear and his emerald green blouson.

"Even better," the Fast commented wryly. "Well, cleaner."

"I was being auctioned off for the price of entire planets. I had to look the part, didn't I?"

"We've cleared orbit," The Fast announced. "Destination …?" and when no one answered, he added, "Anyone?!"

"The Morbida System," Holt decided.

"Done," Fast did something and they ever so slightly shifted course. "And your justification for that direction?"

"That's where my boyfriend lives. And where he went." Even Holt had to laugh. "We might just catch up to him."

"Mer Safran and this Fast Mind were unaware that Potential Galactic Empresses had … boyfriends."

"Well, I do." Then to her, "But you look just like the Transfer we first encountered. How and …?"

"My father. When I was born, he hid me away so I couldn't be mentally mutilated like all the other females born on Imperia. Well, most of them."

"We met," Holt said. "Me and some of those mentally muti-lated females. The Euthna, right?"

"Right! So, when someone official found out what my father had done, he and a partner constructed actual copies of myself, so that I couldn't be so easily found. Many copies! Quickly made, and not very well-made copies for the most part, with very short life spans. Thousands of them! When he was captured, he argued that none of the transfers were real. They were all copies of a pattern from long ago. He also argued that none could reproduce: so, they weren't real threats to Imperia's established Patriarchy. Despite that, many Transfers were hunted down and destroyed. I'm told that others became rebels, outcasts."

"Like the one I met. She was a glorified trash picker." He turned to the Fast, "It's a Male Social and Government Patriarchal System gone completely insane, down there, Fast! You would not believe the level of misogyny and rationalizations. A real lesson to our own Republic of what can happen to us if we aren't careful and if we don't include others. But you would believe it, Mer ...? What is your name again?"

"Safran. Mozza Safran is my full name."

"Hidden away, and yet you became an engineer?"

"A very limited engineer thanks to friends of my father who raised me after he was imprisoned for life. I served in an equally limited post, working in the debris field. So if your transfer was a trash picker, then I suppose I am a trash analyst."

"Well, you are very different from the Euthna I encountered while I've been here, although they were sweet and helpful to me."

"Truly?"

"Truly! They helped me escape."

"Mer Safran is seeking political asylum with us," the Fast said.

"If we get away, you're welcome to join us. Our Ib'r Republic is completely open to all sentient creatures."

"So I heard. But the invitation helps."

"Excellent," the Fast said, "Since I already assured her of the fact."

It was amazing, Holt thought. She was pretty and slender, just like the Transfer but unlike the Transfer he could recognize a mind at work.

"In a short while we'll be widely bypassing the orbit of planet Hieron," The Fast announced. "Would you care to enlighten Mer Safran and this Fast mind about this 'boyfriend'."

"His name is Andor Lazzor. He's Thane of Lazzor or some title like that and he's closely related to the Morbida System's main guy, whose name I forget. Andor is very cute, and sexy, and nice, and he's very protective of me."

"Admirable qualities in a human male. Now would you by any chance, Ser Hot, know the registration # of his vehicle?"

"No, I don't. Why?"

"I believe we are about to catch up to it. Mer Safran, do you recognize this vehicle's markings as possibly those of Andor Lazzor."

He flashed a hologram of the ship between them and she read the markings.

"They're Morbida. But I don't …"

"Yes, I'm hailing on a subfrequency so that I can be allowed in without being noticed," The Fast said. Then "And I'm inside their computerized system which is –you'll excuse me Mer Safran – quite primitive – and yes the ship does belong to The Grand Crantor of Lazzor. Does that title sound likely, Ser Holt? Perhaps a reference to Andor's parent?"

"Grand Crantor sounds right," Mozza agreed.

"If we continue at this speed, we'll catch up to them in less than an hour's time."

"Does this vessel have ship to ship connections?" Holt asked Mozza.

"This class of vessel and no doubt the Lazzor vessel can extrude lengthy wormlike-tunnels to travel ship to ship. But we must be stationary or at the exact same speed."

Some twenty minutes later, Holt asked Mozza how to message without being overheard by other vessels. She did some checking in the vessel's video user's guide and announced, "A distress signal would probably be your best frequency. Ship to ship."

The usual confusion occurred for a few minutes until the Fast assured the pilot of the Lazzorian vessel that only Thane Andor could receive the message.

Andor looked roused from sleep.

"Isn't he adorable?" Holt declared, and then, "Hey, sleepy-head. Guess who?"

Astonishment on that face, and then, "You didn't stay for the Council!"

"I got bored and left," Holt replied with a shrug.

"Where did you get that old Capalzar heap? In a junkyard?"

"They said it was a quote 'Lightly Formerly Utilized Vehicle,' unquote, but that's pretty much where we found it," the Fast replied.

"How far do you expect to get in it?" Andor asked, still amused.

"Not very far, we're taking over your ship!" The Fast answered.

"What? What do you mean by ..." Andor lurched suddenly, to one side.

Holt could hear panicked voices in Andor's control room.

"Ser Holt," the Fast said, "I've got complete control of the navigation system."

Andor reported: "*My* pilot says he's lost control of the vessel."

"Don't worry," Holt said "We've got it."

"You did that? How? And who's we?"

Some ten minutes later, the Lazzorian vessel pilot reported that their inter-ship transport coil had deployed.

"See you in a few minutes. We're boarding."

Some ten minutes later, Holt, the Fast and Mozza were on board the Lazzorian vessel and Holt and Andor were in a tight embrace. Intros were made and then Holt said to Andor's three crew men, "I'm sorry to say that you will have to trade places with us. The other vessel is solid and should get you to the Morbida system."

The pilot was a rigorous type and asked, "Dos this mean you are kidnapping the Thane? You do know that is punishable by slow death?"

"Seems like kidnapping the Thane is the only way I can get a boyfriend," Holt said. "So yes., I guess I am."

"Don't worry, Pilot Erlixx. I know this Holt." Andor said. "I'll be fine. Go to their ship."

"What shall we tell your father, and your liege?" Erlixx asked.

"Let my father, the Grand Crantor, know this is voluntary. Say that I'll see him soon,"

"I doubt it," the Fast subvocalized. Once the others were safely aboard, the connecting tube was retracted.

The Fast and Mozza left the cabin, headed to the engine sub-routine room, where they hoped between the two of them to could figure out how to get the vessel to go even faster and perhaps even do Fast Jumps of greater distance.

"Despite what you told them, I'm sorry to say you won't be seeing your father and ruler anytime soon. Because we're not going there." To Andor's complete surprise now. "I'm not accepting your ruler's offer," Holt went on, "What I'm doing is offering you a counter offer."

"And that is?"

"Come with me and be my love!"

Andor seemed amused more than anything. "Do I have a choice?"

"Not really."

"Then you should know that Second Fleet Admiral, Tanzen Raz, another rejected suitor, signaled to us, just before you boarded, that he was giving chase. He thought you were with me."

"Did he tell you what happened back there?" Holt asked.

"He said something about you taking everyone in the Imperium for fools. Also setting fire to the Convocation Hall." Andor couldn't stop smiling. "I see it's all true!"

Holt looked away and then asked, "Fast, did you hear that about half the Imperial Space Force being in hot pursuit?"

For an answer he heard Mozza say, "We've been aware of that, Ser Holt, yes. We're just about ready and we'll take it from here. You two had better strap down for some long Fast jumps. It might get bumpy!"

They moved into the recliners. Holt strapped Andor down, and kissed him. Then he moved to the other recliner and strapped himself in.

"We're ready Fast. Mozza? How about you two?"

"I just have one last question before we throw ourselves into the void between galaxies," Andor said. "Say I do agree to be your love and go with you ...?"

"Yes?" Holt asked

"Will it *always* be this exciting?"

"Count on it."

FELICE PICANO

Felice Picano is the author of more than thirty books of poetry, fiction, memoirs, nonfiction, and plays. His work has been translated into many languages and several of his titles have been national and international bestsellers. He is considered a founder of modern gay literature along with the other members of the Violet Quill. Picano also began and operated the SeaHorse Press and Gay Presses of New York for fifteen years. His first novel was a finalist for the PEN/Hemingway Award. Since then he's been nominated for and/or won dozens of literary awards.

A five-time Lambda Literary Award nominee, Picano's books include the best-selling novels *The Book of Lies*, *Like People in History*, and *Looking Glass Lives* as well as the literary memoirs *Men Who Loved Me* and *A House on the Ocean, A House on the Bay*. Along with Andrew Holleran, Robert Ferro, Edmund White, and George Whitmore, he founded the Violet Quill Club to promote and increase the visibility of gay author and their works. In 2009, the Lambda Literary Foundation awarded Picano its Lifetime Achievement/Pioneer Award. Originally from New York, the author now lives in Los Angeles.

About ReQueered Tales

In the heady days of the late 1960s, when young people in many western countries were in the streets protesting for a new, more inclusive world, some of us were in libraries, coffee shops, communes, retreats, bedrooms and dens plotting something even more startling: literature – highbrow and pulp – for an explicitly gay audience. Specifically, we were craving to see our gay lives – in the closet, in the open, in bars, in dire straits and in love – reflected in mystery stories, romance, paranormal and more. Hercule Poirot, that engaging effete Belgian creation of Agatha Christie might have been gay ... Sherlock Holmes, to all intents and purposes, was one woman shy of gay ... but where were the *genuine gay sleuths*, where the reader need not read between the lines?

Beginning with Victor J Banis's "Man from C.A.M.P." pulps in the mid-60s – riotous romps spoofing the craze for James Bond spies – readers were suddenly being offered George Baxt's Pharoah Love, a black gay New York City detective, and a real turning point in Joseph Hansen's gay California insurance investigator, Dave Brandstetter, whose world weary Raymond Chandleresque adventures sold strongly and have never been out of print.

Over the next three decades, gay storytelling grew strongly in niche and mainstream publishing ventures. Even with the huge public crisis – as AIDS descended on the gay community beginning in the early 1980s – gay fiction flourished. Stonewall Inn, Alyson Publications, and others nurtured authors and readers ... until mainstream success seemed to come to a halt. While Lambda Literary Foundation had started to recognize work in annual awards about 1990, mainstream publishers began to have cold feet. And then, with the rise of ebooks in the new millennium which enabled a new self-publishing industry ... here as both an avalanche of new talent coming to market and buryng of print authors who did not cross the divide.

The result?

Perhaps forty years of gay fiction – and notably gay and lesbian mystery, detective and suspense fiction – has been teetering on the brink of obscurity. Orphaned works, orphaned authors, many living and some having passed away – with no one to make the case for their creations to be returned to print (and e-print!). General fiction and non-fiction works embracing gay lives, widely celebrated upon original release, also languished as mainstream publishers shifted their focus.

Until now. That is the mission of *ReQueered Tales*: to keep in circulation this treasure trove of fantastic fiction. In an era of ebooks, everything of value ought to be accessible. For a new generation of readers, these mystery tales are full of insights into the gay world of the 1960s, '70s, '80s and '90s. For those of us who lived through the period, they are a delightful reminder of our youth and reflect some of our own struggles in growing up gay in those heady times.

We are honoured, here at *ReQueered Tales*, to be custodians shepherding back into circulation some of the best gay and lesbian fiction writing and hope to bring many volumes to the public, in modestly priced, accessible editions, worldwide, over the coming years.

So please join us on this adventure of discovery and rediscovery of the rich talents of writers of recent years as the PIs, cops and amateur sleuths battle forces of evil with fierceness, humor and sometimes a pinch of love.

The ReQueered Tales Team

Justene Adamec • Alexander Inglis • Matt Lubbers-Moore

Dryland's End
Felice Picano

City on a Star Trilogy, Book I - Five thousand years in the future, life itself is in jeopardy!

A rebellion of intelligent Cybernetic servants has left the Females of the galaxy virtually sterile, crippling the controlling political body – the Matriarchy. The race is on to find a solution, but will it be enough to save the Matriarchy as other galactic authorities attempt to dominate them using sabotage and all-out war? *Dryland's End* is Felice Picano's science fiction adventure for the new millennium. The novel touches on many of today's most controversial subjects, such as interracial relationships, gender conflicts, gender identity, and same-sex pairings-and views them with a lens toward the future.

"This book is further proof that Felice Picano can succeed beautifully in any genre of fiction. Here we have the colorful originality that is found in the greatest science fiction and fantasy writers, the wide-ranging imagination that creates not only fine writers, characterization, and gripping plot, but also fabricates entire worlds – worlds rich with warrior women, space travel, mysterious gods, political intrigue and rebellion, biological warfare, and sexualities both subtle and shifting. ... Like the best speculative fiction, [it] provides the lucky reader with both an escape into the extraordinary and a mirror for humanity's deepest issues and concerns." — Jeff Mann, Associate Professor of English, Virginia Tech

First published in 1995, this new edition of *Dryland's End* features a foreword by the author. The "City on a Star" trilogy continues with *The Betrothal at Usk* (Oct 2021) and *A Bard on Hercular* (Autumn 2022).

The Betrothal at Usk
Felice Picano

City on a Star Trilogy, Book II - With the end of the Galactic Matriarchy, Vir'ism has risen, centered on Hesperia, the City on a Star. But one leader, Mart Kell, is out of power, while another, the Great Father, Ay'r, is quietly retired.

On a small resort planet with a rainbow of rings, Ay'r Eise'nstein-Kell, a 16-year-old boy, air skates across the sands, dreaming of escape to the famed City on a Star. When the rulers of the galaxy-wide republic and their glamorous entourages arrive on Usk to celebrate a great betrothal, Ay'r finds himself thrust into their midst but even deeper into dynastic schemes and power manipulations he cannot understand. Except when they are revealed to be perilous to his freedom and to his life.

Abused and alone, he flees with few resources but knowledge into the unique dangers of The Great Salt Ocean of Usk. There, he will find all the adventure a boy could want. He'll also discover the plight of the oppressed worker-species, the pamps, who have long awaited their Messiah, and he will discover who he really is: could Ay'r be The One?

Meanwhile, Kri'nni, heiress to the defeated Bella=Arth. empire,escapes her long bondage and plots her return. Holt, the youngest son of the Great Father, a playboy known as "The Cadet," flees the media circus of his life for a mission into the heart of the galaxy in search of a new source of the Beryllium ore that makes galaxy-wide communication and travel possible. What else will he find to reinvigorate the new Ib'r society?

> "Set so far in the future that the exact location of the home planet of the Humes (humans) isn't remembered, this book examines relationships between the sexes, and between species from a new perspective and with more than a touch of levity. With its subjects of cloning and genetic manipulation, same sex marriages and other controversial issues, *Dryland's End* remains as pertinent today as when it was first published. In full-fledged sci-fi form, Picano has created entirely new civilizations, species, even new language forms for his society. A phenomenally well-written book." — *Virginia Gazette*

Dryland's End was first published in 1995 as a stand-alone novel. Now part of City on a Star Trilogy, *The Betrothal at Usk* and *A Bard on Hercular* are newly published for the first-time by ReQueered Tales.

Like People in History
Felice Picano

Solid, cautious Roger Sansarc and flamboyant, mercurial Alistair Dodge are second cousins who become lifelong friends when they first meet as nine-year-old boys in 1954. Their lives constantly intersect at crucial moments in their personal histories as each discovers his own unique – and uniquely gay – identity. Their complex, tumultuous, and madcap relationship endures against 40 years of history and their involvement with the handsome model, poet, and decorated Vietnam vet Matt Loguidice, whom they both love. Picano chronicles and celebrates gay life and subculture over the last half of the twentieth century: from the legendary 1969 gathering at Woodstock to the legendary parties at Fire Island Pines in the 1970s, from Malibu Beach in its palmiest surfer days to San Francisco during its gayest era, from the cities and jungles of South Vietnam during the war to Manhattan's Greenwich Village and Upper East Side during the 1990s AIDS war.

"It's the heroic and funny saga of the last three decades by someone who saw everything and forgot nothing." — Edmund White

"Harrowing and sad, and very funny, Like People in History manages to bridge the unnerving chasm between the queer present and the gay past." — Andrew Holleran

"A gay classic. Read it when I was in college and it helped shape my perception of myself as a gay man … It's a sprawling, propulsive epic that switches back and forth in time, taking the reader on a rollicking journey through gay America" — Christopher Rice

In a book that could have been written only by one who lived it and survived to tell, Picano weaves a powerful saga of four decades in the lives of two men and their lovers, relatives, friends, and enemies. Tragic, comic, sexy, and romantic, filled with varied and colorful characters, *Like People in History* is both extraordinarily moving and supremely entertaining.

Winner of the Ferro-Grumley Award for Best Novel, Gay Times Best Novel of the Year and Finalist for Lambda Literary Award Best Gay Fiction, this 25th Anniversary edition features a new foreword by Richard Burnett and an afterword by the author.

The Book of Lies
Felice Picano

Bright, ambitious, and handsome, Ross Ohrenst-edt is a high flier in the fashionable field of queer studies. He has just taken a prestigious university position in Los Angeles and has been appointed to oversee the collection of papers and works of a leading light of the gay literary salon known as the Purple Circle. Ross stumbles across a lost work by an unknown author and his quest to identify the mystery writer and achieve the glory of scholastic tenure unveils increasingly bizarre and unbalanced facts about a group of writers who in the 1970s and 1980s broke new ground in the creation of a gay literary sensibility. But the dark truth contained within *The Book of Lies* is even more startling.

> "Based on Picano's involvement with the Violet Quill Club (which included Edmund White and Andrew Holleran), this is an absorbing Henry James-style comedy of manners about how even when some writers find their way out of the closet, others still get left behind."
> — *The Mail on Sunday*

> "The *Book of Lies* is funny, dark, sexy, shocking, and yes, smart. Set in the near future ('decades after Stonewall'), the novel tells of a young scholar trying to make his academic bones on the literary bodies of the 'Purple Circle'. Picano skewers the pedagogically pretentious with ease and wit. A wonderful novel, with some of Picano's best writing."
> — *Bay Area Reporter*

With biting wit and a lush sense of place and character, Felice Picano's daring novel is at once a stylish mystery, a comical roman-à-clef, and a wicked send-up of the new Ivory Tower.

First published to acclaim in 1998, this new edition features a foreword by David Bergman (*The Violet Hour*).

Onyx
Felice Picano

Ray Henriques has success, love, friendship ... but lately it's not enough. Yet it's not just Ray who is on a quest for deeper meaning. For Jesse, Ray's lover of ten years, it is a quest accelerated by his imminent death from AIDS. And for young married father of two Mike Tedesco, it is a search for the heart of masculinity. The sexual exploration which begins when Ray and Mike meet awakens a restlessness in both men, which resoundingly alters their future paths. As Ray's life begins to draw him increasingly into the future, a future without Jesse, he attempts to tether himself to the here and now with frequent visits to a past where life's answers seemed simpler and more meaningful. But when Jesse's fundamentalist Christian mother rolls into town to take charge of her son's final weeks, he is yanked from his reverie to face an opponent unlike any he has ever known.

"A complex tableau of life and death." — Greg Herren, *Lambda Book Report*

"An incredibly rich and densely textured world ... It's a raw journey through death and dying, unsparing in his take on how survivors cope" — Roger Durbin, *Library Journal*

"You will be astonished by the intelligence, humor, and credibility of this masterfully executed tale, written by one of our best writers." — *Bay Area Reporter*

Marked by shifting points of view, humor, descriptive brilliance and unexpected revelation, *Onyx* is a multifaceted exploration of inner lives, motivation, love, and the sometimes hollow center beneath a polished surface.

First published to acclaim in 2001, this new edition features a foreword by the author.

Slashed to Ribbons in Defense of Love
Felice Picano

Felice Picano's first collection of gay short stories spans the period 1975-1982 as published by the pioneering Gay Presses of New York. Read again forty years later, they are a delicious time-capsule of gay life mostly before AIDS and set in iconic gay meccas such as New York and Fire Island. In "Spinning", we get inside the head of a DJ busy spinning for the customers, tricking in his mind and deftly conjuring up the disco subculture which has since faded away. In "The Interrupted Recital", we eavesdrop into the classical music world where ego clashes lead to disastrous outcomes.

There are marvelous character portraits as in "Teddy", about a handsome Vietnam vet back home for a quick furlough. Or the evocation of Christmas in multiple New York households in "Xmas in the Apple". Longer works such as "Hunter", set in a writer's colony, are pure horror fiction. The longest piece, the novella "And Baby Makes Three", spreads its wings recreating Fire Island of the 1970s and features Picano's trademark surprises and miscues which make the tale memorable long after the last page is turned.

First published to acclaim in 1982, this new edition features a foreword by Eric Andrews-Katz (*The Jesus Injection*).

The Blue Star
Robert Ferro

Two heroes, reflective Peter and Byronic Chase, indulge their youthful appetites in Florence. Over the next 20 years their paths diverge and reconverge. Chase marries into the Italian aristocracy and Peter pursues his passion for Lorenzo, a beautiful young Florentine. The past impinges on the present as the story of Chase's ancestor, Orvil Starkweather, is revealed -- the secrets of his life sounding a counterpoint to Chase's. New York City's Central Park and the imposing figure of designer Frederick Law Olmsted provide a mysterious connection to Chase's life. The story of the two men unfolds in Florence and New York exposing the unimagined and startling connection with the past, and taking them finally on a fateful cruise up the Nile aboard the luxury yacht.

"Incandescent angels of love ... an eclectic voyage. Authentic fiction... surprising, sad, funny, wise ... communicating gay experience knowingly and sensitively ... a treasure!" — *The Advocate*

"Enthralling ... euphoric imagination ... we can never forget the bliss we are allowed to share." — Richard Howard

Originally published in 1985, this new edition contains a foreword by Andrew Holleran (*Dancer from the Dance*).

And don't miss ...

The Family of Max Desir
Robert Ferro

It was a family dealing with old values, acceptance and death. Max Desir loved his Italian roots and he loved his American family. As he came of age, Max Desir found love in Italy. Now, at age 40, his American family is split: Max and Nick are accepted as a stable, long-term couple by mother and siblings, but his father John does not. When a needlepoint family tree is to be hung at Christmas, acceptance of family is re-examined. In this beautiful, haunting tale, told in a clear, impassioned narrative, Robert Ferro created a classic. His highly celebrated breakthrough novel is not to be missed.

"An honest, eloquent and entirely original novel ... at once realistic and mythological, intensely personal and public ... a triumph." — Edmund White.

Originally published in 1983, this new edition includes a foreword by fellow author and friend Felice Picano.

Life Drawing
Michael Grumley

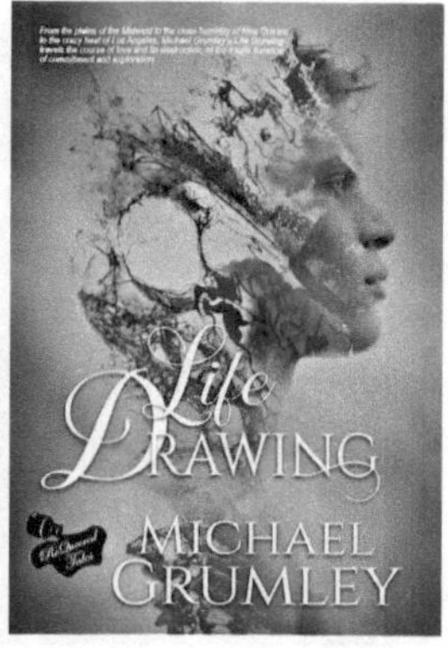

Born in Iowa to the sounds of Bob and Bing Crosby and the Dorsey brothers, Mickey grows up to the comforting images of his living room TV and the reassuring ruts of his parents' life. During the restless summer of his senior year in high school, drifting away from the girlfriend he could never quite love, Mickey spends a night with another boy, and his world will never be the same.

On a barge floating down the Mississippi, he falls in love with James, a black card player from New Orleans, and in time the two of them settle, bristling with sexual intensity, in the French Quarter – until a brief affair destroys James's trust and sends Mickey to the drugs and sordid life of Los Angeles.

> "A simple, classic, engaging, and beautifully written tale of a boy who ran away from home, a man who didn't make it in the movies, an artist who found himself earlier than most and did it all west of the Mississippi, in places which, while very American, few Americans have ever been." — Andrew Holleran

> "*Life Drawing* affirms the rich complexity of passion in the story of a small-town boy's difficult journey to manhood. Michael Grumley's crisp, direct language brings to life the demanding wonder of sexuality and the delicate tightrope of love between black men and white men." — Melvin Dixon

Originally published in 1991, it was Grumley's only novel, completed in the month's leading to his death from AIDS as he was cared for his lover Robert Ferro. This new edition contains the original foreword by Edmund White (*A Saint from Texas*) and afterword by George Stambolian (*Gay Men's Anthologies Men on Men*), close friends of the couple.

The Genius of Desire
Brian Bouldrey

Hopelessly drawn to the romantic notion of a double life, young Michael Bellman spends summers in Monsalvat, Michigan, coming of age in a loving tangle of highly eccentric relatives: Great Uncle Jimmy speaks to his dead wife during meals; Cousin Anne torments Michael beyond endurance; reckless Cousin Tommy secretly smokes cigars and can't wait to "kick butt in 'Nam" – and Michael watches every magical move he makes.

A few years and one driver's license later, as family alliances change and long-silent desires surface, Michael begins to understand his attraction to the double life because he's living one – at roadside rest stops, in library washrooms, and public parks. Coming out is the first step, coming to terms is the next ...

"A simply told story of a young boy growing into manhood and evolving into himself in the midst of the contradictions, deceptions, denial, ignorance, pretensions, confusions, prejudices, and all the other weaknesses that flesh is heir to ... In one way or another this is the same world we must all find our way through and/or out of."
— Hubert Selby, Jr. (*Last Exit to Brooklyn*)

A highly praised debut novel in 1993, this new edition includes a foreword by the author.

And don't miss ...

Love, the Magician: In April of 1997, Tristan Broder makes a pilgrimage of sorts from San Francisco to the prickly desert and scalped mountains around Tucson, Arizona, the place where he helped bury his partner Joe five years before. Guided by a comet that crossed the spring sky that year, he wanders toward renewal and resurrection, memory and mystery, deadly secrets and dark intentions.

There are plenty of people in the desert who still love Tristan as much as they did Joe. With open and glad hearts, they join Tristan to help him make a memorial to the whole-souled man he loved. Yet, despite the fact that they are all bound, like Tristan, by the memory and love for the saint who once lived among them, every one of them is hiding something.

Mountain Climbing in Sheridan Square
Stan Leventhal

A series of discrete episodes among friends provide snapshots of one gay man's life. There are parties, concerts, dinners with everyday life – and death – interwoven in the rich story-telling. An actress, a painter, a set designer, a writer – all sweating and surviving in Manhattan, all scoring their first successes. Part autobiography and part documentary, artfully written, it details the lives of these creative people. Young and professional, they know there is more to life than money. There is trust and the sort of love that trades in deeds of kindness.

> "Stan was a literary activist who always gave to, built and endorsed literature and writers. I can see still see Stan in his apartment window on Christopher Street, next door to the Stonewall Inn, overlooking Sheridan Square as he typed away." — Michele Karlsberg, LGBTQ publicist and friend

Stan Leventhal's debut novel was a Lambda Literary Awards Finalist in 1988. This new edition features a foreword by Christopher Bram (*Gods and Monsters*).

And don't miss ...

Skydiving on Christopher Street – Like bookends, *Skydiving* returns to the characters and bustle of New York a few years after *Mountain Climbing*. But now AIDS has settled in – the world is changed but still vibrant. The dialog is laced with a sharp humor and is right on the mark; the narrator and his friends spot on as we experience his joys, his pains, and his acceptance of who he is.

> "A tender, honest novel about that moment between diagnosis and the decision to grow. Messy boyfriends and dreamy crushes set against the back-drop of daily life make Levethal's characters vulnerable and familiar." — Sarah Schulman (*Let the Record Show*)

The Black Marble Pool – There's a dead body at the bottom of a pool in the backyard of a guest house in Key West. Who is he? And what caused his untimely demise? Maybe it's suicide. Or an accident. But more likely – murder! And who's responsible? One of the guests, the people who run the guest house or one of those mysterious women in town?

> "The pace is brisk: the plot keeps twisting, as no one is at all who they seem." — Keith John Glaeske, *Out In Print*

Winter Eyes
Lev Raphael

A coming-of-age novel set in New York and Michigan during the Vietnam War era, *Winter Eyes* shows how the past controls and divides the immigrant Borowski family, and isolates their American-born son Stefan. But when Stefan comes to learn the terrible secrets at the heart of his family, that knowledge transforms them all and points the way to a happy new future for him, despite his doubts about his sexual identity.

A haunting and remarkable novel, *Winter Eyes* is a tale of family secrets, silence, revelation – and the hope for healing and change. A spellbinding achievement from a talented author of American fiction.

"Loneliness, separation, desire and the struggle with gay identity are leitmotifs of Lev Raphael's novel. What distinguishes it is Raphael's handling of grand themes, and his ongoing exploration of worlds both Jewish and gay and how they intersect, daring himself and his readers to contemplate wholeness" — Jenifer Levin

"Raphael's *Winter Eyes* resembles a piano sonata, a piece he knows so well that his fingers breathed the music." — Los Angeles Times

Lev Raphael is a Lambda Literary Awards winner and multiple nominee for several books. This new 2022 edition contains a foreword by Brian Bouldrey (*The Genius of Desire*).

Murder and Mayhem
Matt Lubbers-Moore

An Annotated Bibliography of Gay and Queer Males in Mystery, 1909-2018.

Librarian and scholar Matt Lubbers-Moore collects and examines every mystery novel to include a gay or queer male in the English language starting with the 1909 Arthur Conan Doyle short story "The Man with the Watches," which is included in its entirety. Authors, titles, dates published, publishers, book series, short blurbs, and a description of how involved the gay or queer male character is with the mystery are all included for a full bibliographic background.

Murder and Mayhem will prove invaluable for mystery collectors, researchers, libraries, general readers, aficionados, bookstores, and devotees of LGBTQ studies. The bibliography is laid out in alphabetical order by author including the blurb and author notes, whether a hard boiled private eye, an amateur cozy, a suspenseful romance, or a police procedural. All subgenres within the mystery field are included: fantasy, science fiction, espionage, political intrigue, crime dramas, courtroom thrillers, and more with a definition guide of the subgenres for a better understanding of the genre as a whole.

A ReQueered Tales Original Publication.

The Male Homosexual in Literature: A Bibliography *and* The Male Homosexual in Literature: Supplement (2020)
Ian Young

Ian Young's bibliography has served as a basic guide to English-language works of fiction, drama, poetry and autobiography concerned with male homosexuality or having male homosexual characters. Entries include titles published through 1980. Works of primary importance (thosein which homosexuality is a major aspect or which are otherwise of particular relevance) are marked with an asterisk for the convenience of researchers and collectors. Works are identified by author, title, place of publication, publisher, and date. For easy reference, entries are numbered and a title index is provided at the end of the main text. Five highly acclaimed essays on gay literature by Ian Young, Graham Jackson and Dr. Rictor Norton, including essay on gay publishing, round out the listings. A title index of gay anthologies completes the work.

The present *Supplement* includes titles overlooked in the *Bibliography* Second Edition, plus works written before the 1981 cut-off date but published later, including works published for the first time in book form.

ℭℬ

**If you enjoyed this book, please
help spread the word by posting a short,
constructive review at your favorite
social media site or e-book retailer.**

We thank you, greatly, for your support.

And don't be shy! Contact us!

*For more information about current and future releases,
please contact us:*

E-mail: *requeeredtales@gmail.com*
Facebook (Like us!): www.facebook.com/ReQueeredTales/
Twitter: @ReQueered
Instagram: www.instagram.com/requeered
Web: www.ReQueeredTales.com
Blog: www.ReQueeredTales.com/blog
Mailing list (Subscribe for latest news): https://bit.ly/RQTJoin